BEHIND THE
SINGING MASKS

This book is edited and designed by the Editorial Committee of *Cultural China* series

Text: Wang Xiaoying
Translation: Yawtsong Lee
Cover image: Getty Images
Interior Designer: Xue Wenqing
Cover Designer: Wang Wei

Assistant Editor: Hou Weiting
Editor: Wu Yuezhou
Editorial Director: Zhang Yicong

Senior Consultants: Sun Yong, Wu Ying, Yang Xinci
Managing Director and Publisher: Wang Youbu

ISBN: 978-1-60220-247-4

Address any comments about *Behind the Singing Masks* to:

Better Link Press
99 Park Ave
New York, NY 10016
USA

or

Shanghai Press and Publishing Development Company
F 7 Donghu Road, Shanghai, China (200031)
Email: comments_betterlinkpress@hotmail.com

Printed in China by Shenzhen Donnelley Printing Co., Ltd.

1   3   5   7   9   10   8   6   4   2

BEHIND THE SINGING MASKS

By Wang Xiaoying

Better Link Press

Contents

An Explanatory Note

Of the many performance aesthetics unique to traditional Chinese theater, the use of masks represents an example that stands out.

The use of *jiamian*, or masks, in performances has its origin in religious sacrificial rites and the *nuo* dance to fend off evil spirits practiced in the Qin dynasty of far antiquity. The practice was preserved through the Han, Wei and the Southern and Northern dynasties and evolved in the Tang dynasty into a performance art form featuring music and dance and the wearing of masks. The facial makeup designs and variegated, colorful facial patterns used in later traditional Chinese opera genres to distinguish specific characters on stage were derived from and inspired by the drawings, painting and carving motifs on the ancient masks.

I have been fascinated by traditional Chinese theater from childhood. I envied the actors, who by donning different masks (in this case the face paint used in operatic facial makeup) had the good fortune to interpret to their heart's content the richly varying life experiences and stories of all manners of characters set in different times and places. What a thrill it must have been for them!

The small opera stage is a rich repository of the world's great wisdom.

As I attended more operatic performances, I began to wonder if the actors interpreting someone else's life stories behind a mask would undergo subtle changes in their own personalities. Would some mysterious link be established between their own life and the life story they were enacting in the opera? And when they removed the masks they wore on stage, what kind of face would they present to the real world? Would they wear some kind of mask even in their real life?

This is what motivated me to write this novel.

Personae Dramatis

Xie Yingge: famous actor playing the female role (*dan*) of Yueju opera, founder of the Xie School of Yueju opera art

Xie Jin'ge: Xie Yingge's younger half-sister by the same father, artist in a singing-only traditional opera (*qingchang*) troupe

Cai Lianfen: mother of Xie Yingge, actor playing the tragic female role of Yueju opera

Sister Ten: nanny waiting on Cai Lianfen and Xie Yingge

Wang Houcheng: husband of Xie Yingge; photo journalist

Qin Yulou: famous actor playing the young male role (*xiaosheng*) of Yueju opera, deputy general manager of the Provincial Yueju Opera Theater

Mi Jingyao: younger-generation actor playing the female role of Yueju opera

Feng Jianyue: younger-generation actor playing the young male role of Yueju opera

Yu Qing'e: younger-generation actor playing the female role of Yueju opera

Shi Xiaotong: younger-generation actor playing the female role of Yueju opera

Qian Xiaoxiao: younger-generation actor playing the male child role (*wawa sheng*) of Yueju opera

He Shuye: a rising-star director

Ma Hui: host of TV series *Operatic Kaleidoscope*

Party Secretary Zhang: party secretary of the performing arts productions company operated by the county tourism bureau

Lu Mingjiu: owner of a singing-only traditional opera troupe

Also appear: husband and in-laws of Yu Qing'e

Act I

The Imitation Eclipses the Original

Scene I Her Name Is Xie Yingge

This was the front parlor of a street-level apartment in an old building. Its French window with wooden lattice overlooked a rectangular yard entirely paved over with black tiles, with, standing in its southwest corner, a sweet osmanthus whose dense canopy shaded half of the garden. Next to the east wall of the yard, a ten-foot green-skinned bamboo pole stretched across the court with one end supported by an iron hook hanging from the eaves and the other end resting directly on top of the outer wall of the yard. Drying on the pole was an opera blouse with buttons on the front, high collar, embroidered hems and corner patterns and long water sleeves that spanned the length of the pole. The panels of the blouse fluttered and flapped in the early spring breeze, reminding one of an actor playing the female role of Yueju opera running gracefully and daintily in a circle on stage.

By the window sat an "Eight Immortals" table with peeling paint, with spread over it a white tablecloth with drawnwork pressed down with a glass top. The fringe of the tablecloth was erose and the glass top had an irregular crack in its lower right corner, which was mended with several strips of greasy tape that appeared at first glance to resemble a dead and dried centipede.

Wrapped in a beige woolen shawl, she was curled up in a rattan armchair with curved armrests lost in thought or perhaps nodding off. In the past two years this had increasingly become her normal state.

She was Xie Yingge.

Or was she?

Of course she was.

You mean the Xie Yingge of unsurpassed fame in the Yueju opera circles of the province?

There was a visible twitch in her left cheek but she choked up, unable to utter a word.

The bright orange evening sun crept over the ivied wall of the courtyard, penetrated the latticed sash of the French window and washed over the "Eight Immortals" table, spreading slowly across it like spilled orange juice. She sat up with alarm, pulled her left arm from under the shawl and tried to wipe the spill off the table with her sleeve. She was afraid that the orange juice might seep down through the crack in the glass top to reach the old newspaper clipping under the glass and dampen it. The newspaper bore the date of February 15, 1963 and had become yellowed and brittle with the passage of three decades; it couldn't stand the ravage of a single droplet of water.

She moved the sleeve of her dove gray woolen sweater across the table top and polished it to squeaky clean perfection. The old newspaper under the glass bathed in the orange light of the setting sun seemed to become more vivid with the splash of color.

This newspaper was to her more important than her life because it was the only surviving piece of documentation that proved she was indeed the famous actor in the female role Xie Yingge.

She heaved herself off her chair and brought her face closer to the table.

In the left column of the paper shouted a vertical headline in Imitation Song script with the font size of a nickel: "What a Handsome, Forlornly Beautiful Li Sanniang!" with the subtitle in a smaller font: "The Provincial Yueju opera troupe stages a traditional opera in a new production with a new cast, Xie Yingge plays the lead character to popular acclaim." The feature article took up two thirds of the page.

In the past thirty some years, she had read this article hundreds, thousands, tens of thousands of times, and had long since committed the entire article verbatim to memory; but at this moment she still voraciously and thirstily read this report from beginning to end before letting out her breath in a long exhalation.

The reflection of her face in the glass top still showed an ideal oval shape, with gracefully tapered "phoenix" eyes, a dainty nose and chiseled lips. How many years had it been that her apartment had been without a mirror, that she had had to content herself with examining her looks in this glass top, which sent back to her a blurry image that in a sense gave a face lift to her, correcting her drooping eye corners, dark eye pouches, a skewed philtrum and a face covered with fine, cobweb-like wrinkles?

In the lower right corner of the paper was a six-inch stage photo of her in the role of Li Sanniang in the *Legend of the White Rabbit*—that Li Sanniang that faithfully waited sixteen years in the mill shed, that Li Sanniang who defied death by biting through the umbilical cord after giving birth, that tragic, admirable, laudable, heroic Li Sanniang!

The photographer accurately captured the climactic moment of dramatic conflict, i.e. the instant of mutual recognition between Li Sanniang and her son from whom she had been separated since she gave birth to him by biting through the umbilical cord. In the photo, her brow was slightly knitted and tears gleamed in her eyes, which were filled with a complex emotional mix of surprise, joy, painful memory and sorrow. A pair of melancholy, charming dimples was vaguely visible on her cheeks.

She gingerly superimposed her blurry reflection on the stage photo and seemed to hear the beginning of a plaintive tune played on the main string instrument Chinese fiddle (*erhu*), accompanied by the tense, urgent, accelerating rhythm tat-tat-tat of the clappers that seemed bent on driving one's heart out of one's chest. She took a deep breath, walked on her knees, moving forward like straggling leaves rustling in the wind, crying: "I bit through the umbilical cord—my child—" In her heyday, this spoken line would earn her an eruption of bravos. She borrowed the "olive" vocal technique, crescendo followed by diminuendo, from Kunqu opera in her utterance of the two words "my child". "It was like the plaintive, heart-rending cry of a lone goose in flight, a silver arrow breaking through the clouds and shattering rocks to reach the bull's eye of the human heart ..." thus enthused the newspaper feature article.

With a "Da Guniang!" ("Senior Miss", what a servant calls the eldest daughter of the household) uttered in a thick Shaoxing accent, the wooden door was pushed open with a squeak to let in a woman whose hair was pulled back in a bun rarely seen nowadays, and who wore a dark blue blouse with shank buttons on the front and an apron made of rough napped blue cotton cloth. At first glance she had some resemblance to Sister A Qing in the revolutionary model opera *Shajiabang*, except that she was stockier in build than the character on stage and had silvered temples and a double chin, in other words, an elderly version of Sister A Qing.

At the sound of movement, she looked up from the glass top and immediately her face shriveled like a fading flower; a flinty glint peeked out from under her drooping eyelids and fell weightlessly like a dead leaf on the tray the woman was holding.

"Da Guniang, it's time to take your medicine!" The woman lifted a celadon bowl from the tray and brought it directly under her nose. The blackish brew filling half the bowl gave off a strong medicinal stench that instantly filled the entire room. Not quick enough to dodge the proffered beverage, she kept her lips tightly pressed together, causing her philtrum to go further askew.

The woman held the bowl perseveringly, with the rim of the bowl placed against the patient's lower lip, and said cajolingly: "Da Guniang, how can you expect to get well again if you refuse to take your medicine?" Then, turning around, she said, gesturing with her chin toward the French window: "Look at that opera costume left by Hao Ma (Mother Dear)! I, Shi Mei (Sister

Ten), hang it out under the sun once every year to kill the mold. I'm going to iron it later. I can't wait to see you in that costume to play Li Sanniang again!"

Those words acted like the "Open Sesame" that pried loose her lips. Sister Ten seized the opening to pour the medicinal brew into the patient's mouth. A trickle oozed out of the right corner of her mouth and ran down her chin into her neck. Sister Ten whipped out a handkerchief with a floral pattern from the pocket of her apron and wiped the overflow clean. Seeing that her face had screwed into a scowl and turned dark purple because of the bitterness of the medicine, she produced as if by magic a toffee, unwrapped it and stuffed it into her mouth. Then she said with a laugh: "That's a good girl! The prescription was written by a student of the great grandson of the famous founder of Lei Yun Shang Pharmacies. I read it closely and found it to contain musk, toad venom and ginseng, all of which aid blood circulation. It will limber up your limbs and enable you to return to the stage!" She put the bowl back onto the tray and was ready to return to the kitchen when she heard the patient behind her begin to hum an aria:

> In those sixteen years, the thousand-jin millstone
> be my witness,
> I have milled away many a morning and evening;
> In those sixteen years, the three-foot wide apron of
> the well be my witness,
> I have treaded upon it many a winter and spring;
> In those sixteen years, the tear-stained sweet
> osmanthus be my witness,
> I have shed many a bloodshot tear ...

Sister Ten felt hot, stinging tears stream down her cheeks, and quickly dabbed them off with the hem of her apron.

Of late Senior Miss had often been heard to hum this aria in which Li Sanniang berated her husband. It was the most important aria in the scene of the mill shed encounter of the *Legend of the White Rabbit*, the performance of which had catapulted Xie Yingge to overnight fame. After learning that her husband Liu Zhiyuan had married General Yue's daughter, she couldn't contain her grief anymore and started enumerating all the hardships she had endured during the sixteen years of waiting, cooped up in the mill shed, for his return. She lambasted her husband for his perfidy in marrying another woman to take her place, thus breaking his nuptial vows.

Sister Ten could empathize with the pain in Senior Miss's heart; she even felt the pain herself. She would often sigh in her private moments: Senior Miss has been ill for sixteen years! Although Li Sanniang waited all alone in the mill shed for ~~sixteen years, she at least was compensated in the end with the~~ good fortune of reuniting with the long separated son for whose birth she had had to bite through the umbilical cord. While Liu Zhiyuan had married the daughter of his general, he had at least recognized the error of his ways and had returned to the mill shed to take her home with him to share his fortunes and good life. In contrast, Senior Miss's illness has not seen any signs of improvement in sixteen years. "With resignation I watch the other's rise to prominence!" Sister Ten hummed this line of an aria without realizing she'd done so. After a lifetime of waiting on opera singers, Sister Ten, by the mere fact of daily immersion, had long become something of an "opera junkie/ encyclopedia".

The voice of Senior Miss had naturally lost the qualities of clarity, lightness, fluency and mellifluousness so characteristic of Xie Yingge in her former avatar. Since the onset of her illness sixteen years ago, Senior Miss's voice had broken and it struggled in her throat to get out but without success. She did not so much sing as murmur or hum; to any other listener the singing would sound like some disjointed, muffled, monotonous notes, but Sister Ten could sense that her rendition was without a single missed beat or note and bore comparison to the "melodious undulations of a spring earthworm and an autumn snake, and the tapering off to the murmuring of a spring" unique to Xie Yingge in her heyday.

Although Sister Ten never attended school and had picked up all the words she knew in theaters where Yueju opera was performed, she understood what those words praising Xie Yingge's singing meant. She had grown up in a village in the hills of Shengzhou and was familiar with the sight of earthworms weaving in and out of the soil in the field in early spring, turning the soil loose and fluffy; in late autumn she would see roving snakes slithering through the cogongrass field making a rustling sound and all day she heard the low murmur of the spring brook flowing past her home. When she thought about it more carefully, she realized that was exactly how Xie Yingge used to sing—with the unpredictability and protean nature of the spring earthworms and the autumn snakes and the depth and wistful sobbing of a mountain spring.

Sister Ten admired stage characters noted for their loyalty and devotion, like Li Sanniang. Sister Ten herself was such a character, never leaving Senior Miss unattended all these sixteen years, preparing medicinal brews for Senior Miss day in and day out. The totality of the dregs she discarded after the consumption of the medicine was enough to pile into a small mountain.

When she returned from the kitchen, she saw that Senior Miss's face had turned blood red as she strained her neck with effort. This was the cue that she was going to sing the last line of her "sixteen years" passage and she hurriedly stepped forward to take hold of her hand, to help her make the exertion.

Sister Ten had, since she was a child, heard first Mother Dear, then Xie Yingge, interpret Li Sanniang. She had heard Li Sanniang so many times that the melody and meters of that aria had been etched into her brain. In Mother Dear's rendering of Li Sanniang, this aria started out in adagio before going into singing without instrumental sound, with the lyric leading the melody and the meter, delivering the dozens of lines in one breath, hammering each sentence into the audience's heart. When Xie Yingge took the part of Li Sanniang, she redesigned the aria with the collaboration of the musicians.

She borrowed from Beijing opera the style of slow singing accompanied by a fast beat played by the percussion orchestra. The first four lines starting with "sixteen years" (*shi liu nian*) began with free-measure singing; at the *liu* of the fourth line, the singing abruptly went up an octave in spray-mouth fashion, soaring shrilly into the sky, to express the powerful indignation that was building up to a climax in Li Sanniang. This was followed by a long narrative part combining the three measures of slow tempo (*manban*, one strong beat followed by three weak beats), moderate tempo (*zhongban*, one strong beat followed by one weak beat) and quick tempo (*kuaiban*, one strong beat), with the tempo quickening and emotion erupting like a flood. In the last two lines the singing went into senza misura (*xiaoban*) evoking a fast flowing long river, then drew to a close by returning to slow tempo, drawing out the end in a despairing, wistful wail. The melody and meter of the aria varied dramatically with the changes in the emotions of the stage characters and were arranged according to the development of their thoughts to achieve a highly dramatic effect. One might say every word of the song of sadness and anger was a tear and a denunciation of wronged love!

This critical acclaim of the singing of Xie Yingge was of course not written by Sister Ten, who knew only if an operatic number pleased her ears or not and wouldn't have been capable of such a dissertation. The review was featured in the newspaper under the glass top of the "Eight Immortals" table. Whenever she had a chance Senior Miss would bend over the table and read out loud that piece in the paper again and again. After hearing it recited hundreds, thousands of times, Sister Ten almost knew it by heart.

With Sister Ten holding her hand in a tight grip, Senior Miss was finally able to produce that one-octave-higher note *liu*, admittedly in a dull, raspy voice evocative of the ripping of old fabric, but the note did soar …

> In those sixteen years, the bitter fish pond be my
>   witness,
> I have confronted many a crisis of life and death …

In the course of uttering the three words "life and death" Senior Miss fell back an octave to the previous register and her voice stumbled, causing a long fit of coughing. Sister Ten patted her on the back with her cat-leaf fan of a palm, saying: "Sing again after you've taken a rest. One of these days we'll ask Er Guniang ('Junior Miss', the second daughter of the household) to bring a musician so that you can exercise your voice with instrumental accompaniment. Singing a cappella ruins the voice." Then she hunched closer to her and said with a smile: "Why don't I wheel you out into the garden? There is a southeasterly breeze blowing that feels like a caress on your face, not at all chilly."

Since she fell ill sixteen years ago, Senior Miss's face had remained fixed in one expression—it was neither a smile nor a weepy grimace; you might call it pensive or indifferent. It was as if she were wearing a mask used in *nuo* opera, a local opera from Anhui. Only Sister Ten understood her; she knew Senior Miss was in a mood to go out the moment she saw that her gaze had shifted toward the latticed French window.

Sister Ten went into the hall to fetch a wheelchair. With her arms under Senior Miss's armpits, she helped, with great effort, her out of the rattan chair and settled her into the wheelchair. The effort brought out a sweat all over her. A few years ago this kind of exertion was effortless for her but nowadays she had been feeling inadequate. Her strength had been failing her. She was a few years older than Senior Miss. It crossed Sister Ten's mind that there would be nobody to take care of Senior Miss when she, Sister Ten, became too decrepit and old to stir about. But, Sister Ten being a born optimist, the worry soon blew away like a

breeze and she put it out of her mind. She was firm in the belief
that Senior Miss would get well under her care. To go into the
garden through the French window, there used to be a few steps
to negotiate; it was Sister Ten who took it upon herself to replace
the steps with a ramp and it was now much easier to wheel Senior
Miss in and out.

Once in the garden, Senior Miss yanked off the woolen
shawl with her left hand. Sister Ten tried to stop her from doing
it: "There is a breeze! You can't take it off!" With a lone hand,
Senior Miss put up a struggle with the much stouter Sister Ten,
pulling tightly at the shawl to prevent any move by Sister Ten to
wrap her in it again. Sister Ten did not insist, sensing that it was
airier, brighter and warmer in the garden than indoors.

Sister Ten wheeled Senior Miss in circles in the yard, carefully
dodging the cracks and pits in the damaged tiles so as not to
cause any bumpiness in the ride.

Stubborn tufts of tender green Mondo grass broke out of
the cracks between tiles to enliven and rejuvenate the dingy,
doddering yard. The low sun, bright as fire just before the plunge,
lit up the eastern half of the yard, making it an operatic stage
with curtains parting and gongs and drums beating a fast tempo
signaling the beginning of a performance.

Sister Ten's hands on the handles of the wheelchair felt a
strong jolt and she realized that Senior Miss was trying to get
to her feet and nearly tumbled out of her chair. Sister Ten's arm
shot out to grab Senior Miss's insubstantial shoulder. She felt
a tingling in her nose; she understood what Senior Miss was
thinking. Senior Miss cut her teeth on the techniques of Yueju
opera in the training program of the Yueju Opera Troupe since
the age of eleven. On off days she would go home and learn from
Mother Dear the ropes of running circles and pacing on stage,
leg-lifting, bending backwards and wielding water sleeves in this
courtyard in the first light of dawn until she was covered by a
thin film of perspiration. When day broke in full brightness and
the urban noise rose in the streets outside the high fence wall, the

two of them would face the sweet osmanthus and start exercising their voices. All that training took about two hours. After the death of Mother Dear, Senior Miss stuck to her morning training routine, through spring, summer, fall and winter. Even after she became a renowned opera actor, Senior Miss still got up every morning at first light to practice her stage gaits in the yard, put her voice through the paces and flourish her water sleeves. Much later she was made to wear the dunce hat of being a toxic seedling nurtured in the evil influence of capitalist literary theory and practice, as well as being a stalwart in propagating pernicious feudalist ideas, and was sent away to a stage props warehouse to take down and launder stage backdrops. After a hard day's work, no matter how tired she was, she would never deviate from her morning training in this yard at first light. Every brick, every tile and every blade of grass in this yard were familiar with the limber, graceful movements of Senior Miss's morning exercise, until that fateful day sixteen years before ...

Sister Ten whispered into her ear: "Senior Miss, sit tight! We are now going to run stage circles!" With that, she pushed the wheelchair a little harder and started to run in quick, short steps close to the fence wall. Clearly excited, Senior Miss was describing an arc in the air with her left hand—she was making a reverse "cloud hand" gesture!

When they passed the western and the southern wall to come to the eastern wall, Senior Miss suddenly withdrew her hand and belted out a dramatic "Stop—", shaking loose numerous wilted leaves on the sweet osmanthus.

Sister Ten read her mind and slowed down. It was at the exact moment when the wheelchair arrived at the opera costume hanging on the bamboo pole that she shouted "stop!" The long panels of the costume flapped in the breeze, and hovered, like a cyan cloud, over Senior Miss's face. Senior Miss lifted her chin slightly, closed her eyes and let the silky fabric fall gently on her cheeks.

The stage costume handed down from Mother Dear was

made from silk spun by a weaver surnamed Ma in their home town. It was a strong but flowing material. In his heyday, theater troupes from near and far flocked to him to order silk fabrics for their costumes.

It was in this cyan costume that Mother Dear played the role of Li Sanniang, except that her water sleeves were only two feet long at the time. When it was Xie Yingge's turn to play Li Sanniang, she donned this cyan costume also, but she had had the water sleeves extended to eight feet, because Xie Yingge had added a long sequence of dancing with the water sleeves to the scene of giving birth by the millstone to convey Li Sanniang's helplessness, her sense of frustration, anxiety, anger and sorrow at being abandoned by man, heaven and earth. Sister Ten still remembered it was she who accompanied Senior Miss to her home town to seek out the descendants of the weaver Ma and solicit their help. When they learned that it was a daughter of Cai Lianfen who needed to have a stage costume refitted, they agreed to sell them a bolt of white silk left to them by their grandfather.

Although Senior Miss's face remained expressionless, Sister Ten knew she had transported herself back to the stage amid the quickening tempo of cymbals and drums and the graceful notes of stringed instruments.

She was proved right. Senior Miss, her eyes closed, began to tap out a beat on her own knees and started singing in a low voice:

> Outside the window, the wind blows cold as ice,
> Indoors tears stream down my cheeks,
> Turning the millstone, I feel my head spinning,
> My feet weigh like lead and every step is an effort.
> Suddenly,
> A cold sweat breaks out and soaks me through,
> I feel an unbearable, acute pain in my belly …

In this "Giving Birth by the Millstone" scene of the *Legend of the White Rabbit*, the aria started out in a tune style, but switched to senza misura with free beats (*sanban*) and another tune style when it came to "in my belly". It was at his juncture that Senior Miss started to wriggle and struggle in her wheelchair.

Totally familiar with the *Legend of the White Rabbit* after attending so many performances of the play, Sister Ten remembered that at the close of this line, Li Sanniang was supposed to execute a leap and a maneuver of catching the sleeves, followed by a "cloud hand" gesture leading to a three hundred sixty degree turn of her body; then she would execute a high leap and throw out her long water sleeves and continue her spinning after landing back on the floor, the five-foot long water sleeves gyrating like little white dragons. Then with a slight flip she would fall on the floor in a heap like a coiled dark dragon, motionless and spent. This sequence of movements conveyed the unbearable pain in her belly. In the old days whenever Xie Yingge gave this performance, she would be rewarded by a round of deafening applause in the theater.

Senior Miss's struggle at this present moment appeared so pathetic and helpless. She was paralyzed in her right half and that made the efforts of her limbs on the left side appear even more futile. Sister Ten however was not going to dissuade her; she waited for her to calm down of her own accord.

After falling down on the floor, Li Sanniang still had two lines to sing in slow tempo; as Sister Ten waited for Senior Miss to hum those two lines, she heard someone pick up the tune and start singing:

> Alas I have no water, no scissors and nobody to help,
> I have no choice but to bite through the umbilical
> cord myself—

These two lines were sung strictly in the convention of the Yueju opera tune. The voice had lost some of its mellowness and crispness but was sweet and haunting nonetheless. At the sound Sister Ten and Senior Miss turned their heads in the direction of the source of the voice and there stood gracefully, before the latticed French window bathed in the flame of the low sun, a "Pedestal of Rouge Fragrance"; she was none other than the opera singer Xie Yingge, who had become the toast of the Yueju opera circles province-wide.

Arching her eyebrows and opening her eyes wide, Sister Ten said: "Oh, well, Er Guniang, I thought you said you were not eating supper at home tonight!"

Scene II   Mother Dear Cai Lianfen

Sister Ten's mother had been nanny to Mother Dear when the latter was still a Yueju opera actor, responsible for the care of her costumes and the paraphernalia of her trade. When Mother Dear made her stage appearance, she helped her apply face paints and did her hair, put her in her costumes and removed her makeup when she came off stage.

Mother Dear's name was Cai Lianfen and was a famous actor in the female role in a period when Yueju opera troupes consisting of female actors mushroomed. She was nicknamed the "queen of actors in the tragic female role".

Since a child, Sister Ten had tagged along when her mother worked backstage in the theaters. She would act as her mother's assistant, applying Paulownia extract to hairpieces to be worn by the actors in the female role, putting away the cosmetics cases and bejeweled floral-shaped tiaras and holding in her lap a pot of hot ginseng soup to keep it warm so that Mother Dear could drink it when she exited the stage in preparation for another scene. But most of the time she watched from the wings the young ladies and gentlemen act out their love and hate, joys and sorrows and separations and reunions on stage, and she would cry and laugh with them.

Sister Ten vaguely remembered being called "Ya Tou" (young girl) by others in her family when she was little. As soon as she was a little more sentient, she took to following her mother to the theater to watch Mother Dear perform in *The Tragic Romance of the Butterfly Lovers* and would melt in tears in the theater. From then on she became fascinated with Zhu Yingtai, one of the Butterfly lovers, and would sing in her childish voice, whenever the spirit moved her: "I have a little sister, Sister Number Nine, who is smart and admirable …" Others in the household, annoyed by the persistent noise, would taunt her: "Why don't you become the younger sister of Sister Number Nine?" and started calling her "Shi Mei" (Sister Ten). She liked being called Sister Ten and responded to it with alacrity. Soon Sister Ten eclipsed her given name.

Her mother had hoped Sister Ten would be initiated into the trade of Yueju opera. Sister Ten's father died in her early childhood; if Sister Ten could make it on the Yueju opera stage, her mother would have someone to take care of her in her old age. Mother Dear held Sister Ten's face between her hands and examined it lengthwise and sideways before saying with a smile: "Sister Ten can learn to sing as a comic civilian role (*wenchou*). She'd be just right in such a role." Sister Ten was not amused and said with a scowl: "I want to play Zhu Yingtai." Giving her a light tap with a hand formed into a shape of "orchid fingers", a common female theatrical hand gesture with middle finger and thumb touching, she said: "Don't you belittle the comic roles (*chou*). The theater had always depended on the comic roles for its survival. It has often been said that theater is impossible without its comic roles. When Emperor Ming of Tang performed in an opera, he had a white patch painted across his nose to hide his imperial identity; that was a comic civilian role too." When Sister Ten heard that she was going to play the same type of part as Emperor Ming of Tang, she immediately agreed to do it.

Sister Ten never got to sing as an actor in the clown role on stage. For one thing, she was tone deaf; she always sang off-key; and then, being a country girl used to a carefree life style, she couldn't take for long the strict, cruel discipline of apprenticeship in the troupe. After only a few days of doing front splits and 180-degree straddles with her legs, and handstands under the ruthless discipline of the master trainer, she was already in tears and refused to go on.

Although Sister Ten let down her own mother and Mother Dear and did not make a mark on the stage of Yueju opera, her life had been inextricably bound up with theater.

Sister Ten was barely fifteen when her mother died; she succeeded her mother as nanny to Mother Dear. She liked life and work around the stage and did her tasks with skill and efficiency. Mother Dear was very fond of her and treated her like her own daughter and she gladly called her Hao Ma. In 1952 the cultural section of the provincial government drew up plans for forming a state-run theatrical performance troupe and started a province-wide campaign to recruit old-time opera troupes of high quality and great popularity. Mother Dear's troupe was chosen. When Mother Dear brought her female troupe into the state-run theatrical performance troupe, she did not forget to put Sister Ten's name on the list of troupe members. From then on Sister Ten became a public employee drawing a salary, and when she retired, a pension. Sister Ten thought to herself: now mother can really rest in peace!

Sister Ten's official job title in the Yueju opera troupe was employee in the costumes section, in charge of the trunks containing the costumes and paraphernalia used by the troupe. Sister Ten was more than capable of handling the job. The top brass of the theater specifically told her that her main job was taking care of comrade Cai Lianfen in all her needs offstage to ensure that comrade Cai Lianfen had all the energy she needed to make a success of her performances. Sister Ten gave her word to the brass that she would proudly accomplish the task assigned to her. Mother Dear Cai Lianfen was the diva of the Yueju Opera Troupe of the province. Whenever the name of "Cai Lianfen" appeared on the billboards, the theater would hang out the red lantern announcing a packed house night after night. When the theater let out, there would gather at the back entrance large crowds of Cai Lianfen's fans. Some of them would offer gifts of nutritious dietary supplements, some asked for her autographs and others hoped to have a photo taken with the star. In the Yueju opera circles of the time it was predicted that: no actor could hope to surpass Cai Lianfen's interpretation of Li Sanniang decades hence! Li Sanniang was the heroine of the famous play the *Legend of the White Rabbit* and Cai Lianfen's portrayal of her earned her the proud nickname of "Li Sanniang in the Flesh".

Every time she watched Mother Dear perform in the *Legend of the White Rabbit*, Sister Ten made sure she had two handkerchiefs on her. Sometimes she'd still be crying and wiping off her tears in the theater wings, even after Mother Dear had already exited the stage. Fortunately for her the play had a happy ending, so Sister Ten got to smile through her tears in the finale. Mother Dear went back on stage repeatedly to make curtain calls, and Sister Ten clapped her hands behind the curtains until her palms smarted. After the last performance of the day Mother Dear always got invited to a late night nosh by someone. After her makeup was removed, Mother Dear would wait for Sister Ten to put away all the costumes, headdresses and makeup kits before taking her along to join the late-night snack in a teahouse or a restaurant.

In Sister Ten's memory, those days with Mother Dear, helping in the nuts and bolts of putting on the shows and watching the performances, crying and laughing, with not a care in the world, were the happiest in her life. Only, the happy days did not last.

It was not long before they were told by neighbors in their home town that in the course of the Struggle against the Three Evils, followed by the Struggle against the Five Evils, the former husband of Mother Dear had been found to have committed crimes of tax evasion and fraud, of cutting corners in materials and workmanship and bribing functionaries of the state. He was given a prison sentence and sent to a labor reform farm in the

Northwest of China. Mother Dear had been divorced from her husband for many years and had left his household with her daughters, giving up all property claims and severing all contacts with him. Therefore Mother Dear reacted to the neighbor's account with a shadow of a smile and gave no more thought to the matter.

It was toward the end of the year and all the performing arts groups of the province were busy rehearsing for their New Year festival shows. The Yueju opera troupe sponsored by the provincial government had signed a contract with the Yiyuan Theater located in the center of town to put on a series of shows from December 30 through January 15 of the lunar calendar. There would be a few traditional operatic selections performed by young actors and some short pieces written with the contemporary political environment in mind; the most watched-for number was the *Legend of the White Rabbit* with Cai Lianfen playing the lead part. The theater was plastered well in advance with colorful posters containing enlarged stage photos of Cai Lianfen and in only a few days seventy to eighty percent of the tickets had been sold.

In order not to let down her adoring audiences, Mother Dear spent an inordinate amount of time every day practicing with the musicians to achieve the best musical effect and to give a new flavor to an old play. Then word came from the stage manager that Cai Lianfen was not to continue rehearsing for the *Legend of the White Rabbit*. The reason given was that higher authorities had decreed that a sob story was not appropriate for a festive occasion like the New Year festival. Without giving it further thought, Mother Dear said: all right, I'll sing two "excerpted one-act plays" then. The "Telltale Tracks in the Snow" in the *Story of the Festival Pavilion* and the "Stepping on the Umbrella" in *Praying to the Moon* are both light-hearted and cheery, very much in tune with the mood of the New Year festival. But the stage manager hemmed and hawed, neither approving nor disapproving.

After brooding at home for two days without hearing anything from the theater about her proposal, Mother Dear started to feel uneasy. She must have sensed something was up but was still loath to believe it; she asked Sister Ten to accompany her to the Yiyuan Theater to get to the bottom of the matter.

Sister Ten recalled that it had snowed that day and the sky was overcast and the street was terribly slushy and muddy. The two of them trudged unsteadily through the slippery street, holding onto each other for support, to the theater. Mother Dear took one look and leaned limply into Sister Ten. The huge posters with Cai Lianfen's stage photo remained on the walls. Only, the names of the lead roles had been changed to those of some secondary and tertiary actors in the female role in the troupe. Sister Ten scanned the playbill twice without being able to find any mention of Mother Dear's proposed "Telltale Tracks in the Snow" or "Stepping on the Umbrella" Mother Dear fell ill soon after returning home. She was in a bad shape and running a persistent high fever. The doctor's diagnosis was a relapse of her tuberculosis.

A stream of visitors came to her bedside. In addition to groups of her fans and admirers, the musicians of the troupe, her co-stars and students all sincerely reassured her: "As long as the green mountain stands, there will be no lack of fuel wood," as the old saying goes. Just take good care of yourself and get well; the theater stage in the provincial capital city can't wait to have you, Cai Lianfen, back to make it shine again! Even the tertiary actor in the female role who had been chosen to play Li Sanniang in her stead came to visit and said worriedly: "Master Cai, why did you have to fall ill at this crucial moment? This was quite a short notice and no matter how hard I work at rehearsing I couldn't hope to fill your shoes. I panic at the thought of the audience demanding a refund of their tickets."

Thus was born the story that "due to the sudden illness of Cai Lianfen, the provincial government's Yueju Opera Troupe salvaged the show by substituting another actor for the lead part".

This altered version of the replacement of Cai Lianfen appeared even in the tabloid newspapers.

Sister Ten, who knew more than anyone else the whys and wherefores of the matter, was tempted to go straight to the top brass of the troupe to demand an explicit explanation. She knew that the moment Mother Dear was allowed to go on stage, all her illnesses would evaporate. But Mother Dear would not hear of Sister Ten going to the leadership of the troupe, for fear that it would have repercussions for Sister Ten's future. That was characteristic of Mother Dear; no matter how she suffered inside, she would maintain a calm, unperturbed exterior and put on a brave face. That explained why she was able to bring tears to the audience's eyes when she played tragic heroines on stage; her arias had been steeped in her inner suffering.

Using Mother Dear's illness as a pretext, the opera troupe never again allowed Mother Dear back on stage. Despite the combined care of doctors trained in western medicine and in Chinese traditional medicine, Mother Dear's health did not improve. By autumn that year, when the sweet osmanthus trees burst into bloom, Mother Dear was wilting and near death.

Before her death, Mother Dear left her eldest daughter in the care of Sister Ten.

Senior Miss was Mother Dear's only child. Mother Dear started her Yueju opera singing career in very harsh conditions; a total of eight or nine young girls, including her, stayed in a cramped cabin in a boat covered with a black awning, carrying the troupe's trunks of costumes and headdresses and other paraphernalia and putting in at various river ports, rain or shine, to set up their stage and put on a show. In order to maximize earnings, the owner of the troupe had the girls perform non-stop from morning till night; after the last show of the night they were sometimes required to perform in the private homes of some prominent local families. Mother Dear contracted her tuberculosis in that period. By that time Mother Dear had begun to cut a figure in the Yueju opera performance circuits and was often invited by other Yueju opera troupes as guest performer. No matter where she performed, the *Legend of the White Rabbit* that had brought her such accolades was a staple on the playbill. Once, she was invited by a prominent clan surnamed Xie, on the occasion of the fiftieth birthday of the lady of the house, to sing a few arias, for a handsome fee paid to the owner of the troupe, in celebration of the festive event. Mother Dear was already suffering from symptoms and signs of tuberculosis, including a low fever, night sweats and occasionally she would cough up blood. But she was helpless against the threats and cajoling of the troupe owner and went to the Xie residence to give a performance despite her illness.

The lady of the house, bored by the luxurious, easy life she had, developed a penchant for listening to tragic arias and she picked the aria "Bemoaning Fate through the Five Watches of the Night" in the scene of "Giving Birth by the Millstone" of the *Legend of the White Rabbit* that day.

Cai Lianfen struck a feminine pose in front of the audience in the reception hall of the residence and the moment the sad wail "Woe is me——" issued from her mouth, a round of bravos went up from the audience.

> The first *geng* (7–9 PM) has struck,
> I, Li Sanniang, have slaved away in the mill shed,
> I, who was treasured by my parents like a tender
> bloom,
> I am now treated like a slave girl by my evil brother
> and sister-in-law.

These four lines sung in an aria style without instrumental accompaniment by Cai Lianfen fell onto the audience's ears like so many pearls dropped into a silver salver and struck a deep chord in their hearts. When she dropped her voice from a high pitch to a low, weepy moan, as she pronounced the final words "a slave girl", tears leapt to Lady Xie's eyes. Wiping off her tears with a silk handkerchief, Lady Xie instructed a maid girl: "Cumshaw!" and the maid placed a string of coins in the copper plate held out by the owner of the troupe.

> The second *geng* (9–11 PM) has struck,
> I, Li Sanniang, have turned the millstone all night,
>   not daring to rest.
> This millstone is like my heartless brother and
>   sister-in-law,
> It is a crushing burden and breaking Sanniang into
>   pieces …

At the words "breaking Sanniang into pieces", she was supposed to go into a senza misura, but the already exhausted Cai Lianfen was unable to bring herself up into the high register required and flopped to the ground.

The owner of the troupe hastened to apologize to the Xie family and told them about Mother Dear's illness. Lady Xie, who had a compassionate heart, ordered her maid to give another gratuity to the troupe owner and instructed a male servant to take Miss Cai in a horse-drawn cart to see a traditional Chinese medicine man in the county town. At this juncture a handsome young man—the young master of the house—rose to his feet and said in a stentorian voice: "The horse cart is too slow. I'll drive Miss Cai in my car to the hospital!"

The young Master Xie later became Cai Lianfen's lover, her first and also her last.

To treat Cai Lianfen's tuberculosis, Master Xie spared no effort and expenses in taking care of her and even invited a renowned doctor from the provincial capital to attend to her medical needs. Master Xie stayed docilely by her bedside, extremely solicitous about her welfare, and showered affection on her, vowing his love. The young Cai Lianfen was powerless to resist such a charm offensive. Besides, daughters of poor families were driven by necessity to join theatrical troupes; if they had a choice they would have loved to be married into a socially and financially respectable family, be a good wife and a good mother and live happily ever after. By the time Cai Lianfen recovered three months later, she had become Master Xie's woman.

Whereas the Xie family were fans of Cai Lianfen's operatic singing, there was no way they were going to accept a lowly actor into their midst. Master Xie had to settle Cai Lianfen in a small house rented for the purpose and hired a capable maid to take care of her daily needs. This maid was none other than Sister Ten's mother. Despite pleas of other members of the troupe not to quit, Cai Lianfen resolutely withdrew from the world of the bejeweled headdresses and the sound of wind and string instruments of the Yueju opera stage to discreetly become a lover of Master Xie. She stayed patiently in the lonely house, waiting for Master Xie to overcome the objections of the elders in his family so that she could one day be accepted into the manor following all the proper rites and ceremonies and become the young mistress of the house with her head held high. This was Master Xie's solemn vow to her. The following year Cai Lianfen gave birth to a daughter, and Master Xie personally named his daughter Xie Yingge.

This was a typical story of a man betraying the love of a young woman that once held his interest, such an eternal theme on the theatrical stage!

Master Xie never did deliver on his promise. Not long after the birth of Yingge, the Xie family threw a big wedding for Master Xie; the bride was naturally some young lady from the boudoir of a wealthy family socially on a par with the Xie family. In celebration of this union, a festival was held at the "Ten-thousand-year" theatrical stage of the town, in which plays from the Southern traditional Chinese opera genre were performed for three days and nights. On the first day the play *Looking for the Husband* was performed, on the second day, *The Agarwood Fan* and on the third day, the piece de resistance *Three Meetings with the Imperial Sister*. All three were comedies chosen

for the festive occasion, and there was no occasion for people
to be reminded of the fate of the actor in the tragic female role
Cai Lianfen.

After learning of the wedding, Cai Lianfen, alone in her
little house, also sang three nights' worth of arias to the cold
moon—the first night she sang a selection from *The Story of the
Lute*, in which the heroine Zhao Zhennü cut and sold her hair in
order to bury her in-laws, who'd died of hunger, and personally
hauled the dirt needed to make the burial mound in the folds of
her skirt; the second night she sang a selection from *Lady Meng
Jiang*, in which Meng Jiangnü's bitter weeping for her departed
husband made a section of the Great Wall collapse; on the final
night she went into the courtyard wearing a black opera costume
and sang and danced a scene in which Yin Guiying denounced,
in front of the gods in the Sea God Temple, her husband Wang
Kui for abandoning her for another woman and pleaded for his
capture!

When she was finished singing, the ink of the night fell
away from the trees and the new dawn colored the courtyard.
Cai Lianfen picked up her daughter, who was still fast asleep,
and, taking swift, small steps over a bedewed dark tile path, she
resolutely left that little house that had once filled her with great
expectations of love, without once looking back.

After listening to three nights of tragic arias sung by Cai
Lianfen, Sister Ten's mother could no longer bear to be in the
employ of the Xie family and followed Cai Lianfen out of the
house, back to the theatrical troupe. She never left Cai Lianfen's
side again and helped the latter as her career took her through
small and large stages in towns and villages far and near, all the
way to the grand stage of the provincial capital.

When Mother Dear died, her daughter Xie Yingge was
twelve years of age and was learning the craft of Yueju opera in
the provincial Yueju opera school. It had not been Mother Dear's
wish to have her daughter follow in her footsteps, but Senior Miss
had grown up bombarded by arias sung in the *sigong, chidiao* and

xianxia tune styles[1], and no sooner was she able to speak than she began to mimic the singing the best she could—ling ga ling ga ling ling ga, and no sooner had she learned to walk than she began to walk in circles to the beat of the drum. Resignedly Mother Dear allowed her to enroll in the Yueju opera school.

At the time all of Sister Ten's kin tried to reason with her: both you and your mother have done all you could to take care of Cai Lianfen. You have been very good to her. Now that she's gone, Sister Ten, you are in your prime and draw a stable salary, it's time you find a suitable prospect and get married!

After helping Senior Miss take care of Mother Dear's funeral, Sister Ten had her first taste of insomnia. Tossing and turning, she was unable to fall asleep. She wanted to get married and have children of her own and live a normal life, but those eagerly expectant eyes of Mother Dear in the moments before her death were seared into her heart like burning coals. Try as she might, she was unable to erase them from her mind or from her heart!

After sleeping on it overnight, Sister Ten made up her mind. Her reply to the solicitous suggestions of her relatives was: "For someone like me, with no stunning looks, no education and no gift of gab, and awkward of hand to boot, what man would want to marry me? Besides, after seeing all the tears and weeping of men and women coming together and breaking up on stage, I've no illusions about marriage." Seeing that she had made up her mind and knowing how headstrong she was, her relatives decided to leave her alone.

Sister Ten never again left this small house bought by Mother Dear in the provincial capital, never again left Xie Yingge,

---

1   The *sigong* tune style is usually in F, the Yueju fiddle tuning for it is 6-3 (La-Mi), and it is characterized by simplicity, clarity and a vibrant rhythm. The *chidiao* tune style is usually in G, the Yueju fiddle tuning for it is 5-2 (Sol-Re), and it is characterized by a steady, even rhythm, suited for expressing complex emotions, grief, pensiveness and anxiety. The *xianxia* tune style is in D, the Yueju fiddle tuning for it is 1-5 (Do-Sol), suited for expressing indignant sorrow and agitated emotions, often used when the protagonist is in a state of inconsolable sorrow.

who was alone in the world. She stuck by her in weal and woe, when Xie Yingge was a shining star on the Yueju opera stage and when, as now, she became a half-paralyzed invalid who had lost the ability to make facial expressions. Sister Ten had been nanny, opera fan, sister and bosom friend to Xie Yingge rolled in one. People who knew how far they went back and how close they were said that good people like Sister Ten existed only in the world of theatrical fiction, such as the loyal majordomo Dou Gong in the *Legend of the White Rabbit*, the eunuch Chen Lin and the palace maid Kou Zhu of the *Fox Cat Substituted for the Crown Prince* and the retainers Cheng Ying and Gongsun Chujiu of the *Orphan of Zhao*.

In the beginning, Sister Ten called Xie Yingge "Miss" without any modifier. Since Master Xie's daughter by his lawful wife moved in with them in their little house sixteen years before, taking also the name "Xie Yingge", Sister Ten had taken to calling the original Xie Yingge "Senior Miss" and the one who came into that name later "Junior Miss".

Scene III Another Xie Yingge

While this Xie Yingge that Sister Ten addressed as "Junior Miss" was a woman of a certain age, she was well dressed and all dolled up. A flowing, deep red casual coat did a perfect job of hiding her slightly protruding midriff and her curls dyed a chestnut brown, by design or by accident, hid the excess fat of her cheeks. She gave a first impression of having preserved her youthful charm.

Sister Ten asked with a spite she could scarcely hide: "Hey, Er Guniang, didn't you say you were not coming home for supper?"

Without addressing Sister Ten, not deigning even a glance in her direction, she sauntered down the ramp, a faint smile hovering on her face, which bore a remarkable resemblance to Senior Miss's, saying: "Jieh (Elder sister)! The evening breeze in early spring has a nip in it; let's go back into the house." By this time she already arrived at the wheelchair; having wrapped a woolen shawl around her sister, she wheeled her toward the house. Senior Miss surprisingly allowed herself to be manipulated like a puppet in the hands of Junior Miss.

Sister Ten took a few quick steps and went ahead of them on the ramp, muttering: "You should have told me. Now I have to wash and cut the vegetables at such short notice ..."

Junior Miss said, as if she had just now remembered: "Oh—when did I ever say I was eating supper at home tonight? There is a reception later tonight given by the leadership of the Department of Culture of the provincial government in honor of the lead actors on the troupe that will tour Hong Kong. We have come home to change for the reception."

Sister Ten paused in her steps, wondering to herself: "We have come home to change? That means the other has come home with her too? Why hasn't he at least said hello to us?" As she opened the door, there Wang Houcheng was, settled comfortably in the rattan armchair with his legs crossed, flipping through the evening paper.

With anger eating at her insides, Sister Ten planted herself in front of him and reeled off: "Sir, listen closely now. Da Guniang had some porridge with ground pork and shreds of preserved egg for lunch. She forced down only half a steamed bun; she would eat it only with fermented bean curd sheets. It took much cajoling for her to eat a piece of marinated duck meat. She has just been given her morning medications. A way has to be found to make her take her afternoon medicines before she goes to bed."

Wang Houcheng lifted his face, his eyes magnified by his reading glasses; an indifferent but slightly startled expression gave his narrow, long face a look suggestive of the "demons with an ox head and with a horse's face" often featured in rural rituals to honor ancestors.

Sister Ten snorted, knowing Wang Houcheng was again playing deaf and dumb!

To be honest and fair, in the early days of Senior Miss's illness, Wang Houcheng was very affectionate with her. When he was working away from home, he always had her on his mind and phoned home to ask after her. Being a photo journalist that worked irregular, unpredictable hours, Wang Houcheng laid down a rule for Sister Ten: she was to report to him every detail of Senior Miss's daily life—what she ate, how long she slept, whether she went to the toilet regularly and any subtle changes in symptoms and signs. Sister Ten had faithfully and strictly followed this rule all these sixteen years. She would wait for the return of Wang Houcheng no matter how late he finished his day's work. In the first two years, Wang Houcheng listened attentively to Sister Ten's daily briefings, jotting down notes in a small notebook and coming up with suggestions for improving the care. At a certain point of time—exactly when could not be pinpointed—Wang Houcheng started to appear absent-minded at these briefings and he no long produced a notebook; he either yawned repeatedly or coughed when Sister Ten made her report, or pretended, as he did now, not to have heard anything.

How could Sister Ten not know? On a certain day of a certain month of a certain year, Senior Miss's husband started flirting with her younger sister, and as a result Wang Houcheng's interest in Senior Miss waned. This was no longer a secret in this little house; all four adults in the household were keenly aware of it. They merely did not wish to confront each other with the truth. So they each wore a mask appropriate to their respective role and did their best to maintain a façade of familial harmony that hid a greater secret under the roof of this little house.

Whereas Sister Ten had nothing but contempt for Wang Houcheng, she adopted a courteous manner toward him. No matter whom he slept with at night, it did not change the fact that he was Senior Miss's husband. Sister Ten knew from all the opera fare she had watched on stage that rare were the men who did not break a woman's heart. Those stage characters whose lack of a conscience was beyond redemption could be set aside; let's just take this man Liu Zhiyuan in the *Legend of the White Rabbit*, who had some conscience left: one moment he sat face to face with Li Sanniang "teary eyes to teary eyes, longing heart to longing heart" upon separation, the next moment he was flirting with Yue Xiuying, daughter of the commanding general. Most of Sister Ten's resentment was reserved for Junior Miss, who she believed was a rapacious wolf who repaid kindness with evil. "You, who live under Senior Miss's roof and take over her name, basking in reflected glory, have the nerve to usurp her husband too!" As she thought this, Sister Ten was sorely tempted to yank off Wang Houcheng's glasses and tell him to wipe off the gunk in his eyes and see Junior Miss as the temptress that she was and not be fooled by her. But Junior Miss had by this time pushed the wheelchair into the house; there was nothing Sister Ten could do except suppress her anger and turn around to go into the kitchen. She did not have the heart to cause any embarrassment to Senior Miss.

Rising to his feet from the rattan chair, Wang Houcheng took a few steps toward the wheelchair and slightly bent down to say: "Xiao Xie! How are you feeling today? Are you feeling better in the head?" He had continued to use the term of endearment by which he called her when they first fell in love. Lifting up her face, which wore a grimace of a mask that could easily be a smile or a scowl, Senior Miss had a moment of hesitation before launching into a verse:

> A long separation gives rise to a deep longing,
> A reunion brings surprise and joy,

Wang Houcheng shot a quick glance at Junior Miss and shrugged dismissively. Junior Miss however chose to chime in with Senior Miss:

> A thousand words in my chest cry out to be heard,

But they fail to find a voice—

At the close of the lyric, Junior Miss said with a giggle: "Jieh Fu (Brother-in-law)! Jieh was singing a segment in the scene of 'The Reunion in the Mill Shed' of the two protagonists after a long separation in the *Legend of the White Rabbit*. She was trying to cheer you up after your long, hard day's work."

Wang Houcheng gave an embarrassed laugh and wrapped his arms around his wife in an attempt to lift her out of the wheelchair and transfer her to the rattan chair. Senior Miss however struggled against him and hit him with her unparalyzed left hand. It was a fight worthy of the scene in the play *At the Crossroads* in which Sun Erniang and Wu Song had a blind fist fight in the dark. Sister Ten came upon the scene when she walked in with tea and said with a hint of reproach in her tone: "Sir, you are hurting her with the force you apply. If she prefers to sit in the wheelchair, just humor her. I'll transfer her later." With those words, she left the two cups of tea on the table and said, with an icy glance at Junior Miss: "I'm glad you have a dinner engagement. That saves me a lot of trouble. Have a sip of tea!"

Sister Ten's resentment was not without its reason. When Senior Miss first fell ill, it was Wang Houcheng who had this multi-function wheelchair made for her, after a period of frantic search. Sitting in the wheelchair, Senior Miss was able, with her left hand alone, to control its direction, move it forward or backward. As the stairs presented a problem for Senior Miss, her bed was moved from the front bedroom on the second floor to a room abutting the living room. When Junior Miss moved in with them, she was settled in the north room next to the second-floor landing of the stairs. One early morning several years ago, when it was not yet completely light, Wang Houcheng tiptoed out of Junior Miss's room and was on the point of returning to the front bedroom on the second floor when he suddenly saw Senior Miss, sitting in her wheelchair at the foot of the stairs, in the dim light of a bulb, her head tilted back and her eyes boring into him, a grimace on her face that was not quite a smile, but more like a phantom's mask. The sight set Wang Houcheng's hair on end and he wetted his pants. He hollered: "Shi Mei, Shi Mei—" The terrified cry jolted Sister Ten out of her army cot; she charged out of her room. She was astounded by Senior Miss's ability to get into her wheelchair without help. As she wheeled Senior Miss back to her room, she cursed to herself: "The hanky-panky that those two shameless people are up to!" Wrapped in his night robe, Wang Houcheng descended the stairs with a tap-tap sound and followed behind them, trying lamely to explain: "My bladder was full and I was emptying it in the bathroom when I heard movement downstairs, and I found her there … Shi Mei, you have to be more alert in your sleep! What if she should have a fall?" Following that incident, Wang Houcheng laid down another rule for Sister Ten to follow: for Senior Miss's safety, she was to spend as little time in her wheelchair as possible. Most importantly the wheelchair must be folded and stored in a closet in the evening!

Junior Miss was long used to the barbs and taunts of Sister Ten and dismissed them as just the low humming of some cicada in a shrub. Laying her ten slender fingers on Senior Miss's shoulders, she said with a bright smile: "Jieh, I have good news for you. The performance tour in Hong Kong of the provincial Yueju opera troupe is sponsored by a number of consortiums and they have made the *Legend of the White Rabbit* one of the mainstays of the tour. I've been told that there are many fans of Xie Yingge in Hong Kong!"

Predictably, that mask that was not quite a smile nor quite a scowl on Senior Miss's face, which was normally a sickly yellow, turned rosy. With some effort, she finally found her voice: "Who will play Liu Zhiyuan opposite you? Is it still Qin Yulou?" Senior Miss uttered the words slowly; speaking clearly required greater effort from her than singing the lyrics. She never volunteered to speak unless it was something important for her.

Junior Miss said with a smile: "How can they break up the star team of Xie Yingge and Qin Yulou? There have been suggestions that a younger actor should play my opposite because, they say, with makeup I look younger than a young miss. But I insisted on having Qin Yulou play my opposite. I've given some thought to it. In the first half of the *Legend of the White Rabbit*, my part Li Sanniang dominates the stage, because after the 'Parting at the Melon Patch', Liu Zhiyuan goes off stage. In the latter half, Liu Zhiyuan reappears, but in an old male role (*laosheng*), and Qin Yulou is entirely fit for that role. She has recently been promoted to the position of deputy general manager of the theater; it's only natural that she needs the exposure, am I right?"

Senior Miss was silent. Her face did not betray her thoughts. But Junior Miss, being her doppelganger, understood her inner conflict and added: "Jieh, you go back thirty years with her after all. I have pointed out to Qin Yulou that it is important that she lose some weight. Liu Zhiyuan, being an impoverished, famished young man from a modest home, couldn't very well be played by a portly Qin Yulou, right?" With those words, she leaned forward into Senior Miss's shoulders and laughed with great mirth.

Senior Miss waited quietly with that expression of hers bordering on a smile and a scowl; when Junior Miss was done with her mirth, Senior Miss picked up where she left off and said deliberately: "The *Legend of the White Rabbit* is a classic of the Xie School of Yueju opera art. Do it justice. When time allows, I'll parse some more the character of Li Sanniang for you. For example in the line just sung 'A thousand words in my chest cry out to be heard', the three words 'a thousand words' are fraught with emotional conflict and complexity and must be articulated with clarity ..."

Junior Miss couldn't wait to interrupt her: "Jieh, this singing segment has been changed by the director, who has decided to use backstage vocal accompaniment in the form of a multi-voice round, to emphasize the emotional complexity of the reunion of Li Sanniang and Liu Zhiyuan. The effect has been quite good."

Senior Miss choked on the words struggling to come off her chest and had a fit of coughing before asking glumly: "Who's the director of this play?"

Junior Miss said: "The theater has invited a director of stage plays who brims with brave new ideas for the express purpose of having him direct the *Legend of the White Rabbit*. The idea is to inject modern elements into a traditional play. The sets, the costumes are all to be redesigned. Jieh, I'll ask brother-in-law to take some stage photos to show you and to collect your views and suggestions." Then she suddenly remembered something and added excitedly: "The Theater has contacted the television network about making the *Legend of the White Rabbit* into a six-episode art film for TV upon our return from Hong Kong. Jieh, isn't that what you have always wished for?"

Senior Miss straightened her back, drew a breath and exhaled slowly through closed lips before saying: "If they are going to shoot an art film for TV, you must make sure the director add that dance with long water sleeves into the scene of Li Sanniang 'Giving Birth by the Millstone'. Otherwise the entire play would appear lifeless and incomplete."

The smile on Junior Miss's face remained brilliant but it was frozen into a rigid mask. Her elder sister mentioned the dance with long water sleeves clearly for the purpose of exposing her weakness. Since her makeover into the persona of Xie Yingge sixteen years ago, Junior Miss has been able to approach the accomplishment of the original Xie Yingge in stage presence, singing and acting when she performs in the *Legend of the White Rabbit*, but she has never mastered the skill of flourishing and flicking the water sleeves in the scene of "Giving Birth by the Millstone". Before coming to the Yueju opera stage, Junior Miss used to sing in *xiaotangming*, a local opera singing group for hire to spice up festivities in private homes at weddings, funereal events and other festivities. She could sing very well but she never had any formal training in acting, acrobatics and dancing. Whenever she came to the scene of "Giving Birth by the Millstone", and had finished singing the line "I feel an unbearable, acute pain in my belly", she would stumble toward the back of the millstone and in the meantime the backstage staff would create the sound effect of a baby crying to announce the birth. The veteran theater goers would invariably feel a letdown and comment afterwards: "Xie Yingge can't be young forever. She doesn't have the energy anymore to work her long water sleeves." Then they would go on to describe in glowing terms the incomparably exquisite dance with the long water sleeves that the Xie Yingge of yesteryear was capable of. Some theater critics even concluded with much regret: "The skillful water sleeves dance accomplished by Xie Yingge in the heyday of her enactment of the scene of 'Giving Birth by the Millstone' has become a swan song!"

But Junior Miss had been active in the Yueju opera circles for too long—a dozen years or so—not to be well versed in the art of dealing with situations and people and knew only too well the ways of the world. She certainly was keenly aware of how her elder sister felt at this moment. In the years since becoming half-paralyzed, she had withdrawn into obscurity and seclusion, cooped up in this dingy little house, much like the Li Sanniang making a home of the mill shed. And she had to look on from the sidelines as someone else took over her persona and parlayed it into a successful career on the Yueju opera stage, rising to prominence, winning awards and getting elected to the People's Consultative Conference at the provincial level. Anyone in her situation would have felt forlorn and depressed.

Junior Miss said in her mind to Senior Miss: "Jieh! I've been fair to you. But for my hard work all these years, would the name 'Xie Yingge' have enjoyed such renown? Most probably it would have sunk into obscurity, buried under the dust of time in some godforsaken corner." But she heaved an exaggerated sigh and said with an aggrieved face: "Jieh, think about it! I'm over fifty now, a regular bag of old bones and you expect me to perform that highly difficult maneuver of those long water sleeves? Oh, please, spare me that!"

Sister Ten overheard the dialogue between the sisters as she came in from the courtyard with the black opera costume. She interjected: "So Junior Miss is going to practice the long water sleeves dance! Well, well, well, I will take the liberty of loaning you this costume for that purpose. These sleeves are made with a silk fabric that is no longer available anywhere."

Junior Miss, who had a habit of ignoring Sister Ten, put on a smile and said to Senior Miss: "Jieh, don't worry! The director is using high-tech light effects to enhance the scene of Li Sanniang giving birth. The thunder-and-lightning effect is more powerful than Li Sanniang flourishing her long water sleeves alone on a bare stage. Brother-in-law will corroborate this; he has taken a set of photos showing the stage effects."

Wang Houcheng did not say anything but quickly took out a stack of photos and flipped through them before picking one out and placing it on Senior Miss's knees with an ingratiating smile on his face.

Senior Miss picked up the photo with two fingers of her left hand. The photo showed a huge stylized millstone center stage, with above it an indigo sky roiled by dark clouds and cleaved in two by a silvery bolt of lightning.

Junior Miss crowed close to her ear: "Jieh, what do you think of it? Imagine the powerful impact when accompanied by sound effects!"

Senior Miss made an indistinct gurgling sound in her throat, apparently trying to say something. Her fingers went slack and the photo flopped to the ground.

Sister Ten, who was looking through the stack of photos placed by Wang Houcheng on the tea table, cried of a sudden: "Oh ho! The Master took so many stage photos of Junior Miss! H'm! There is a resemblance there; only, Senior Miss had a slenderer face shape then. Junior Miss is more on the plump side nowadays. Well, she'll manage ..." Then she fell silent as she held a photo at varying distances to her eyes and studied it assiduously before nodding and saying: "The Master is an expert when it comes to taking head shots at this angle." Slapping down the photo on the "Eight Immortals" table and tapping on the glass top lying above the old newspaper, she commented: "Look! These two photos show Senior Miss and Junior Miss almost as two dead ringers. The only difference is, see, the charming dimple in the right cheek of Senior Miss, which is missing in Junior Miss, who just lacks that touch of je-ne-sais-quoi ..."

Senior Miss and Junior Miss had the same father but different mothers; both inherited the fine facial features of their father Master Xie. Senior Miss's dimple on one cheek came from her mother Cai Lianfen; Junior Miss was not that lucky on that score. This had become Junior Miss's pet peeve, and it was like Sister Ten to poke the sacred cow. Her polished manners notwithstanding, Junior Miss could hardly contain her peeve this time. Hardening her face, she said with a sneer: "Luckily Jieh no longer has a dimple now, so we are indistinguishable."

Sister Ten was agape and speechless, as if her mouth had been stuffed with sand and mud; Senior Miss on the other hand maintained a stony silence and a frozen posture, like a clay figurine just unearthed.

Sixteen years ago, Senior Miss suffered a cerebral infarction and was paralyzed on her right side; palsy on the right side of her face cost her the ability to make facial expressions.

Realizing the awkwardness of the situation, Wang Houcheng cut in with: "Er Mei (Younger sister), it's time. The car sent by the Department of Culture will be here any minute now. Go change and make up your face."

Junior Miss, who also sensed the brusqueness of her remark, took this as a cue to beat a retreat; she said with a smile: "I forget the time whenever I discuss opera acting with Jieh. Jieh, can you help pick a photo that I can use on the prospectus for the Hong

Kong tour?" With that remark, she executed a graceful volte-face and ascended the stairs.

Sister Ten vented all her pent-up anger at Wang Houcheng: "Master, the Department leadership is hosting a reception for the actors of the Yueju Opera Theater, not you; so you can at least stay home and have supper with Senior Miss. She always eats alone; that's why she can never get her appetite back. No amount of medicines will help if this goes on!"

Wang Houcheng replied sheepishly in halting sentences: "Their, their theater has recruited me to take stage shots … Er Mei said I was to take photos also in the rehearsals for use in future advertising. Therefore, therefore …"

With her back turned toward him, Senior Miss started to sing, in the manner of a spring silkworm spewing out thread through tiny holes in its jaws:

> Master Liu, you are going off to the army,
> With tears, I, Sanniang, see you off.
> With no wife to take care of you out there,
> Do keep yourself fed and clothed.
> Don't despair even if you don't get a commission,
> Sanniang will wait by the door for your return.
> In prosperity, don't forget your modest origins,
> And keep Shatuo Village in your heart.

Wang Houcheng collected the photos back into a neat stack. When the singing stopped, he said ingratiatingly: "Xiao Xie, I'll be back in no time. Er Guniang asked for your help in selecting a photo of her. Why don't you do that? She is such a poor judge."

Outside the courtyard fence a car sounded its horn. The car sent by the Department of Culture had arrived.

The sound of footsteps on the stairs preceded the voice of Junior Miss, who called through the door of the room: "Jieh Fu, Jieh Fu! The car is here. Let's go."

Wang Houcheng lightly pressed on his wife's insubstantial

shoulders, hesitated before hurrying out the door.

Sister Ten made a noodle soup with shredded pork and slices of young bamboo shoots for supper. She tasted it first and found it to be thick and delicious. She also made a sautéed dish of young, green, freshly harvested broad beans, which she thought would whet Senior Miss's appetite. But after forcing herself to eat two chopstickfuls of the noodles and picking up a few broad beans to chew—and spitting out the skin—Senior Miss couldn't be persuaded to eat any more of the food. Knowing she was preoccupied and there was no way she would touch it again, Sister Ten dumped the rest of the noodles into her own belly.

After supper Sister Ten washed Senior Miss's face and feet, picked her up and transferred her into the rattan chair, put the woolen shawl around her and settled her in. She crooned: "Da Guniang, *Operatic Kaleidoscope* is on. Let's watch TV first and you'll take your medicine later, all right?" She switched the television on with the remote.

Operatic Kaleidoscope was a daily must-watch TV series for Senior Miss; it was devoted to reporting on news in the world of Chinese traditional operas, the current activities of various performance troupes, performance schedules and anecdotes and tidbits about famous actors. As a lead actor enjoying top billing in the Yueju Opera Theater of the province, Junior Miss made frequent appearances on the program. Senior Miss closely tracked every move and movement of the Xie Yingge on the TV screen. Whenever the image of Xie Yingge appeared on screen, she would lean forward in her chair, bringing her face as close to it as she could. Watching it with her, Sister Ten never missed a chance to find fault with that other Xie Yingge, saying this or that was not right, that Yueju opera aficionados would surely see through her as a fake Xie Yingge. Senior Miss would chide her for being a chatterbox. The Xie Yingge in the person of Junior Miss has received awards at the national level and has been widely reported on in print and on TV. That means she has been publicly recognized as Xie Yingge. If what you said is heard outside this room, people would think there's something wrong with your head!

On the small screen, *Operatic Kaleidoscope* was reporting on the current performance activities and schedules of various major theaters and troupes in the province. In order to pick candidates to compete in the Young Actors of Beijing Opera Contest sponsored by China Central Television, the Beijing Opera Theater planned three special performances of single-act traditional opera selections, with a young cast; the Kunqu Opera Troupe was reviving *Palace of Eternal Youth* in a condensed, improved version in preparation for participating in a joint operatic performance of troupes from east China ... When the report went on to mention the imminent departure of the Yueju Opera Troupe for Hong Kong on a performance tour, the camera cut to a scene in which a reporter interviewed the deputy general manager of the Yueju Opera Theater.

The deputy general manager's name was Qin Yulou. She received the same formal training as Xie Yingge and often played her opposite; when Xie Yingge played Li Sanniang in her time, it was Qin Yulou who played Liu Zhiyuan. Just as this inseparable pair of actors in the male role (*sheng*) and the female role was shooting to fame, they collided with the "Cultural Revolution", the so-called Ten-Year Turmoil. Xie Yingge was run off stage on the charge of being a stalwart of the evil school of thought infesting the cultural and art world; Qin Yulou and many other actors of the Yueju Opera Troupe were dispersed among the groups dotting the landscape of the province dedicated to the performance of "model revolutionary operas", in which they played walk-on parts. By the time the troupe was reconstituted ten years later, Qin Yulou had gained considerable weight and her voice was not what it used to be. But she worked hard at her role, be it a lead or a minor part. After canvasing the views of the grassroots, the leadership of the theater decided to promote her to deputy general manager with shared responsibilities in personnel matters.

The lady journalist, who had handsome, fine features and possessed an aura peculiar to opera actors, looked with admiring eyes at Deputy General Manager Qin Yulou and asked: "The Yueju Opera Troupe is traveling to Hong Kong on the anniversary of the return of Hong Kong to the fold of the motherland. Is there any special significance in the choice of the play the *Legend of the White Rabbit?*"

With years of experience in administrative work, Deputy General Manager Qin Yulou spoke with authority and eloquence: "The choice of the *Legend of the White Rabbit* is based on artistic considerations. Our province was the cradle of southern drama in the time of the Song and the Yuan dynasties. Of the four classics *Jing, Liu, Bai, Sha* of southern drama, the *Legend of the White Rabbit* is the richest in romance and features the most unexpected twists of fate. We believe that the more local elements of tradition and culture inform a work of art, the greater the likelihood it will strike a chord with non-local audiences. This is the first consideration. Secondly, the *Legend of the White Rabbit* is a signature work of the renowned Yueju opera actor Xie Yingge. When it was first performed in the early 1960s, it immediately became popular and won wide acclaim. This present adapted version rests on the solid foundation of past successes. The third reason is that the *Legend of the White Rabbit* happens also to be the first choice of the sponsor in Hong Kong."

The lady journalist said with a smile: "Can Manager Qin elaborate on the four classics *Jing, Liu, Bai, Sha?*"

Qin Yulou nodded: "This is an acronym for the four most popular plays in southern drama. *Jing* is *The Romance of a Hairpin* (Jing Chai Ji). *Liu* is *Liu Zhiyuan's Legend of the White Rabbit*, now commonly shortened to the *Legend of the White Rabbit*. *Bai* is *The Moonlight Pavilion* (Bai Yue Ting) and *Sha* is *Story of the Slain Dog* (Sha Gou Ji). With the exception of *Story of the Slain Dog*, the other three are still being performed in various local operas."

The lady journalist said: "I thank Manager Qin for giving us a lesson in traditional Chinese operas. Compared to the version performed in the 1960s, what are the improvements and innovations in the revised *Legend of the White Rabbit* offered by the Yueju Opera Theater?"

Qin Yulou took the question in stride and answered suavely: "We set out to offer a finer, a designer product on this Hong Kong tour by adapting the original *Legend of a White Rabbit*. In order to adapt to the aesthetic taste of the contemporary audiences, especially the younger viewers, we've undertaken a complete makeover in the writing and directing of the play, choreography, music, costumes and lighting. There were even some radical changes. For example in the script followed in the 1960s, the reference to bigamy was problematic due to the political climate of the time. For that reason the part about Liu Zhiyuan's marriage to two women and his moving in with his second wife's family, the general's household, had been expunged from the script. In our revised version, we've restored the original script dating to the Song and Yuan periods. Having fallen on hard times, Liu Zhiyuan receives the affectionate care of the young mistress of General Yue's household and eventually marries into and moves in with her family. While this is understandable under the circumstances, it reflects his inner weakness and selfishness, in sharp contrast to the nobility and fidelity exhibited by his wife Li Sanniang in adversity. It is a deeper probe of human nature from a modern perspective."

The lady journalist said: "Manager Qin has put it so well! We look forward to seeing the play. I understand that you have also made some new arrangements in the cast."

Qin Yulou, exhibiting a generous spirit and a broad mind, said with a smile: "Older audiences must still remember that in the early 1960s it was I and Xie Yingge who played the lead roles in the *Legend of the White Rabbit*. In the first half of the play I was naturally in the young male role. In the latter half, Liu Zhiyuan appears as a middle-aged man, so I would don a beard and step into the old male role (*laosheng*). We are now in our fifties and we could probably, with elaborate makeup, get by in playing Liu Zhiyuan and Li Sanniang in the prime of their youth, but in order to achieve optimal artistic effect for the play, the directing team has decided that in the first half of the play Liu Zhiyuan and Li Sanniang will be played by two top-tier young actors of the troupe, while I and Xie Yingge will play these characters in the latter half."

On the small screen appeared a slide show of old stage shots of a performance of the *Legend of the White Rabbit* in the 1960s. Sister Ten excitedly shook Senior Miss's shoulders, exclaiming: "It's you, Senior Miss, it's you in the stage shots ..."

Senior Miss's face remained a mask of a fixed smile/scowl. Her real thoughts and feelings were indecipherable.

The handsome face of the lady journalist reappeared on the TV screen to announce with a bright smile: "Thank you for watching *Operatic Kaleidoscope*. In our next airing, we will interview the two young actors who will be playing for the first time Liu Zhiyuan and Li Sanniang in the Yueju opera play the *Legend of the White Rabbit* and hear them talk about their feelings and thoughts about it. See you next time!"

Still in an excited state, Sister Ten said: "There must be Yueju opera aficionados who could tell a difference in stage aura between the original Xie Yingge and the latter-day Xie Yingge. Come to think of it, we should ask the Master to find a way to get hold of those photos from the TV station and make copies of them for ourselves!"

With her eyes still glued to the screen now filled with scrolling sponsor advertisements, Senior Miss said slowly: "So it will not be my younger sister who plays Li Sanniang in the first half of the play. No wonder she doesn't want to practice the dance of the long water sleeves. Why didn't she tell us the real reason?"

Sister Ten said with a moue: "She would have been embarrassed to tell us the real reason. She must have been replaced by a younger actor for failing to perform satisfactorily."

After a silent spell during which Senior Miss sat like a stone statue, she muttered to herself: "Does it mean Xie Yingge is on the point of retiring from the stage?"

Sister Ten started, thinking to herself: "That pool of water in Senior Miss's heart and mind is too deep even for me to see to the bottom. Is it her wish that Junior Miss should continue to enjoy her fame and popularity? Or does she hope that Junior Miss will bow off the stage for good and restore the Xie Yingge name to its rightful owner?" After giving it some thought and judging by what was happening, Sister Ten figured that at that moment Senior Miss was more inclined to see Xie Yingge enjoy some more years of fame on the Yueju opera stage. Senior Miss's protective instinct toward the name of Xie Yingge easily trumped any resentment of Junior Miss. Having come to that conclusion, she said: "Da Guniang, you don't have to worry. How can Xie Yingge retire from the stage? The leadership of the Yueju Opera Theater wants her to make way for the younger actors, but her fans wouldn't allow it. It's obvious. Junior Miss keeps her part in the two important scenes in the latter half of the play—the reunion of mother and son by the well and the reunion of husband and wife in the mill shed. There, we'll go to bed after you drink up your afternoon medicine." With those words, she switched off the television.

Senior Miss balked: "I will not go to bed. Put me back in my wheelchair! I want to wait for their return by the door. I have to get to the bottom of this matter!"

Sister Ten was put in an awkward position: "Da Guniang, stay inside to wait then. You'll catch your death of cold with the draft in the hallway. The Master would give me a hard time if he found out. Let me listen for their return, and as soon as they're back I'll tell them to come into your room, all right?"

With an expression that couldn't decide between a smile and a scowl, Senior Miss turned her face toward the now darkened

TV screen and started softly singing again:

> A thousand words and ten thousand emotions!
> They can hardly fit in so short a letter.
> You promised to return in three years at the most,
> Yet countless three years have I waited in vain.
> Now Sanniang no longer has the looks of yore ...

Taking advantage of Senior Miss's absorption in her singing, Sister Ten went off into the kitchen to reheat the medicinal brew, into which she dissolved a pulverized Valium tablet. Blowing on the concoction with her puckered mouth to lower its temperature, she brought it before Senior Miss just as she finished singing a line. Holding her shoulder blade, Sister Ten deftly poured the medicine down her throat. This time she didn't put up too much of a resistance and after swallowing the brew, Senior Miss went right back to singing, except that before the end of the line her voice trailed off and her head dropped to her chest.

With much ado Sister Ten carried Senior Miss to her bed and settled her in before lying down in her own army cot in the same room.

Sister Ten had, for an unknown length of time, a smorgasbord of dream fragments before she was wakened by the front door being opened with a bang and then slammed shut. She figured those two had come home. She sat up in bed and threw a coat on. To avoid disturbing the sleep of Senior Miss, she tiptoed out of the door, which she opened quietly. The bulb overhanging the staircase threw a dim, murky light, the color of the cloudy water from rinsing rice, over the hallway. She found no one there. As she stared in astonishment, she was startled by the sound of something breaking on the floor coming from the bedroom on the second floor, followed by a stream of shrill recrimination: "Look! Take a look at these! You took such terrible photos of me! You made me look older than the actors playing the old female role (*laodan*). No wonder they wanted to replace me! Don't try to look contrite. You'd be like a cat feeling sorry for a mouse. You probably couldn't wait for me to bow off the stage just to avenge your wife …"

Not a peep came from Wang Houcheng.

Sister Ten wondered if she should go upstairs and stop the quarreling, but did not budge. Instead she listened for another moment before withdrawing to her room and easing back onto her cot.

Scene IV   Sisterly Affection

When she finished her studies in the school attached to the Provincial Yueju Opera Troupe at a tender age, Xie Yingge was given walk-on parts at the side of the famous actors. These actors were her mother Cai Lianfen's contemporaries and naturally gave her special treatment; they occasionally allowed her to play some important walk-on roles. Once the old actor playing Lady Li—Li Xiuying's mother—in the play *The Jade Hairpin* had an appendicitis attack and needed surgery; Xie Yingge was substituted for her at the recommendation of the actor playing Li Xiuying, playing mother to the latter who was twenty some years her senior. It was obvious that Xie Yingge was a natural for opera singing; she exhibited no stage fright at all.

The character Lady Li was older than an actor in the role of a virtuous lady (*qingyi*, usually a faithful wife, lover, or maiden in distress) but younger than an actor in the old female role; in traditional troupes the role was often given to compantion female (*tiedan*) actors. Xie Yingge specialized in playing the role of the virtuous lady with a subspecialty in the lead role of a beautiful young comic (*huashan*) in the training school. Modest by temperament, she talked little when rehearsing but made mental notes of everything. When playing Lady Li, she cut down on florid coloraturas and flourishes to give more depth and heft to the singing and added an element of the dignified bearing of an actor in the old female role to the character's stage gait in order to accentuate a sense of the character's rich life experience. In the scene of "The Bride Returns to Visit Her Parents", Xie Yingge's Lady Li and the famous actor's Li Xiuying equally excelled in the duet between mother and daughter, winning wide acclaim.

It had been Sister Ten's abiding belief that with Mother Dear watching over Senior Miss like a guardian angel and given Senior Miss's intelligence, her kind of looks and voice, she was destined to succeed and become a star.

Within two years, Xie Yingge made a name for herself in playing important supporting roles and a rare opportunity beckoned that would catapult her to fame.

In commemoration of the twentieth anniversary of Chairman Mao's "Talks at The Yan'an Forum on Literature and Art", a huge event was planned that year, in which opera troupes from across the province were invited to give performances. The Provincial Yueju Opera Troupe decided to participate with a revival of the classic of southern drama the *Legend of the White Rabbit* made famous by the "foremost actor in the tragic female role" Cai Lianfen in her heyday. For this purpose prominent personalities in the cultural circles of the province were invited to make drastic changes to the play script, cutting out details, such as the part about Liu Zhiyuan's bigamy, considered feudalistic and therefore not politically correct, so that the central message of the play would be a paean to the traditional virtues of mutual support in adversity, incorruptibility in poverty and conjugal fidelity. When the plan was made public, senior actors in the female role in the troupe couldn't contain their excitement in anticipation of being chosen for the event. They approached the leadership with vows of doing the troupe proud and demonstrated their determination by intensifying their daily training in singing, acting and dancing.

Xie Yingge was naturally eager to play Li Sanniang; she'd dearly love to remake and reinterpret this character defined and made famous by her mother on the Yueju opera stage. But she kept the wish buried deep inside, not daring to give away even a hint of it.

Xie Yingge had done a careful analysis and believed that if the script used in her mother's days had been kept, the role she probably would have got would be Yue Xiuying, daughter of General Yue, whom Liu Zhiyuan marries and with whom he moves into the general's household, a big supporting role often played by understudies. But in the script for the revived play, this story line was taken out and the character Yue Xiuying was no longer in the play. Therefore she could only hope for walk-on roles such as maid servants. In that period all the available rooms for training were booked solid every day and all the musicians had been drafted by actors to help with voice training. In contrast Xie Yingge seemed to "take it easy" and few saw any sign of her training for the coming event.

After many revisions the script was finalized and the directing team met behind closed doors to thrash out the cast. It produced two lists; the A list consisted naturally of famous and seasoned actors while the B list was made up entirely of young actors graduated from the training school. Xie Yingge was given the lead role of Li Sanniang in the B list! The leadership announced that before the commemorative event featuring performances of opera troupes from across the province, the Yueju Opera Theater would schedule a round of public performances of the *Legend of the White Rabbit* by actors from both lists. The audiences and professional opera experts would be the judge as to which list would be selected to perform at the commemorative event. Following the announcement the actors on both lists intensified their training and rehearsing. However, the way the director scheduled the rehearsals gave an advantage to the seasoned actors on the A list, who got to be the first to rehearse every day, while the younger actors on the B list sat in the audience's seats to watch and learn. This usually went on until three or four in the afternoon when the older actors called it a day and ceded the stage to the younger actors, who would have just enough time to do their stage walks and take their assigned places. There would be no actual rehearsal of the play for them; instead they had to figure it out for themselves individually after leaving the stage.

An ambition was quietly formed in Xie Yingge's mind to outperform the Li Sanniang of the A list so that she would be able to represent the troupe at the gala event. During the rehearsals she was modest, studious and discreet, never made a gratuitous remark, never asked the director any questions, but watched and listened quietly and made mental notes. When it was her group's turn to go up and do their stage walks and familiarize themselves with the precise movement and positioning of the actors, or blocking, called for by the script, she never took a misstep, nor did she take one step more than necessary, so much so that even Qin Yulou, the actor in the young male role, who played her opposite Liu Zhiyuan, never had an inkling of her secret ambition.

Only Sister Ten knew the fond wish of Senior Miss, for the real rehearsal began in earnest for the latter only after she came home from the rehearsal at the theater. She would don the *qingyi* costume of her mother and repeatedly practice and try to perfect the movements, the sung and spoken parts of the play in the tiled courtyard every night until the Milky Way sank low and the morning star faded before going to bed.

The day of the public contest finally came. The leadership of the troupe decided to let the B list actors perform in the matinee and the crucial evening performance was reserved for the veteran actors of the A list. The rationale for this decision was that in case the young actors botched the matinee, the older actors could save the day in the evening show. Most of the invited cultural luminaries, theorists, critics renowned in the province received tickets for the evening performance only. As far as the leadership was concerned, it was a foregone conclusion that the *Legend of the White Rabbit* of the A list would go on to the commemorative event while the *Legend of the White Rabbit* of the B list was merely an opportunity given to the younger actors to learn and improve.

But the outcome caught the theater leadership completely off balance. The matinee performance of the *Legend of the White Rabbit* by the young actors was a resounding success and received wild applause from the audience. Even after five curtain calls, the audience was still loath to leave and many opera buffs shouted out Xie Yingge's name; fresh-cut bouquets were thrown on stage. In comparison, the performance of the *Legend of the White Rabbit* by the seasoned actors in the evening show suffered from a less impressive stage presence and a poorer voice; their strict adherence to convention meant they lacked emotional impact and passion in climactic moments. Moreover, the professionals and experts invited to the evening performance, who were more restrained in their emotional response than the common opera fans, did not exactly contribute to an atmosphere of excitement and effervescence as happened in the matinee.

Just when the theater brass was planning a symposium of experts to "feel the pulse" of the performance of the *Legend of the White Rabbit* put on by the A list actors so as to identify possibilities of further refinement and improve its chances of success in the commemorative event, a long article appeared in the provincial newspaper about the lead actor Xie Yingge in the B list performance of the *Legend of the White Rabbit* with the banner heading: "What a Handsome, Forlornly Beautiful Li Sanniang!" and the subheading: "The Provincial Yueju Opera Troupe stages a traditional opera in a new production with a new cast, Xie Yingge plays the lead character to popular acclaim", followed in smaller print by "Finally someone to take over the mantle of the foremost actor in the tragic female role Cai Lianfen!" The feature article was accompanied by a large stage photo of Xie Yingge in the role of Li Sanniang, which accurately captured the aura emanating from Xie Yingge and recorded one of the most brilliant and beautiful stage moments of Xie Yingge. This spur-of-the-moment shot was taken by a young photo journalist working for the provincial paper by the name of Wang Houcheng. His photography, inspired by unique aesthetic ideas, brought out the understated and subtle beauty in Xie Yingge in its full measure and the capturing of the image of Li Sanniang made famous by Xie Yingge on the Yueju opera stage in turn catapulted him to fame as a foremost photo journalist. One thing led to another: in time Wang Houcheng became Xie Yingge's personal photographer, and later, her husband.

The feature article made a big splash and triggered a flood of rave reviews from newspapers big and small about Xie Yingge and the youthful version of the play the *Legend of the White Rabbit*. The brass of the theater was forced to reassess its plans and decided to send the B list actors to perform the *Legend of the White Rabbit* at the provincial commemorative event. Later developments would vindicate this decision that merely followed the natural law of generational change. The B list's performance of the *Legend of the White Rabbit* was to earn kudos at the provincial event and Xie Yingge would be thrust into the limelight overnight when she was awarded first prize in the best actor category.

When the B list actors received the surprise notification from the brass that they were to get ready to perform the *Legend of the White Rabbit* at the commemorative event, barely a fortnight was left for them to begin rehearsing in earnest. In that short time period Xie Yingge managed to add, in the scene of "Giving Birth by the Millstone", a whirling dance requiring the skillful maneuver of a pair of eight-foot-long water sleeves. It produced a stunning effect worthy of Du Fu's description of a dancer of antiquity: "a sea of spectators watched in blanched-face awe, heaven and earth shifted, following her motions." The dance earned her the media praise of "a rare actor in the tragic female role on the Yueju opera stage with superb singing, acting and martial skills".

The *Legend of the White Rabbit* catapulted Xie Yingge into the position of premier actor in the female role in the Provincial Yueju Opera Troupe and made her into a rising star in the various genres of traditional Chinese opera circles of the province. Recording companies scrambled to make LPs of the complete set of arias she sang in the *Legend of the White Rabbit*. Film studios also made plans for a film version of the opera.

In those years, rarely a month went by without news about Xie Yingge's stage appearances and stage photos of her, taken without exception by the photo journalist of the provincial newspaper Wang Houcheng, appearing in the papers. Sister Ten assiduously collected those newspapers and clipped every report and article about Senior Miss and preserved them in a carved rosewood chest in which Mother Dear used to keep her bejeweled headdresses, a chest given to Mother Dear by Master Xie when they fell in love with each other. With every clipping she put into the chest, Sister Ten would pray in her heart: "Hao Ma, your daughter has done you proud. Please watch over her from up there!"

In those years, Sister Ten felt she had rediscovered the simple pleasures she had enjoyed with Mother Dear, helping her apply and remove makeup, accompanying her to late night snacks; she thought Xie Yingge's successful acting career would endure. But the fortunes and misfortunes of life were unforeseeable. Even Sister Ten herself liked to say: when the moon waxes, it's soon going to wane. And the moon wanes more than it waxes.

Xie Yingge's good fortunes only lasted three years. Out of the blue an order came down from the top to ban a wide selection of traditional opera fare, including the *Legend of the White Rabbit* and to demand that all art performance troupes mount modern operas that would extol the heroic image of the workers, peasants and the army, in the spirit of Chairman Mao's "Yan'an Talks". It was a task particularly difficult for the Yueju Opera Troupe to fulfill, for it consisted of female actors only. They could competently play the cultured, dashing and handsome young scholars in traditional plays, but would look strangely feminine and sissy if they were to play men in modern operas, especially the workers, peasants and army men. But when it came to fulfilling a political task handed down by the party, all odds and obstacles had to be surmounted. The brass of the Provincial Yueju Opera

Troupe racked its brains without being able to create, in the short span of time, a new modern opera of its own. Finally they decided to adapt the revolutionary modern Beijing opera *Song of the Dragon River* for their use, with Xie Yingge as the natural choice to play the lead role of Jiang Shuiying. With a ready-made script, the play was quickly mounted. Without her water sleeves and her silk costumes, without an occasion to pose her fingers in an orchid form, having to walk with long strides on stage and to talk in militant fashion, Xie Yingge felt grievously out of her element. She felt awkward in every move of her hands or her feet or her body. She complained to Qin Yulou, her customary opposite number on stage, about the lack of femininity in this Jiang Shuiying character. Complaining aside, the play still had to be rehearsed and Xie Yingge toughed it out.

When ten days were left before the dress rehearsal for the Yueju opera version of the *Song of the Dragon River*, the theater invited, as was the custom, various personalities in leadership positions to give their illustrious views and valuable directives. The visiting luminaries surprised everybody by unleashing a torrent of scathing criticism: "That Xie Yingge has not a shred of the heroic fabric the workers, peasants and soldiers are made of! She was reported to have attacked the character Jiang Shuiying for lacking femininity. This was a serious slander of the revolutionary model operas!" In the aftermath of the visit, the group entrusted with the performance of the *Song of the Dragon River* was ordered dismantled and Xie Yingge was forced to wear the dunce cap of "being a toxic seedling nurtured in the evil influence of capitalist literary theory and practice, as well as being a stalwart in propagating pernicious feudalist ideas" and sent away to a stage props warehouse on the edge of town to be reformed through hard labor. An ominous cloud hung over the Yueju opera circles in the provincial capital, causing the art form to wilt and go into sharp decline.

Sister Ten felt Xie Yingge got a bum rap. She had no idea what was revisionist and what was feudalistic. All she knew was that Senior Miss's performances were popular; and what was wrong with that? Sister Ten was most traumatized by the noisy raids made by bands of Red Guards in the provincial capital to trash private homes in the name of "wiping out evil spirits in all shapes and forms". A dozen young students sporting half-foot-wide arm bands bearing the designation "Red Guard" invaded their little house and ransacked it. Those "Red Guards" fired by revolutionary zeal hacked to pieces with a kitchen cleaver the LPs containing the complete arias of the *Legend of the White Rabbit* and started a bonfire in the yard, into which they threw everything they considered feudalistic, capitalistic or revisionist—clothes, shoes, stage photos and more met a fiery end in the flames. What Sister Ten feared most happened: the Red Guards found the carved rosewood chest that used to belong to Mother Dear and threw it into the bonfire! When Sister Ten tried to salvage it, she was held back by Wang Houcheng, who whispered to her: "As long as the green mountain stands, there will be fuel wood!" They watched as the chest became charred and the thick stack of newspaper clippings inside slowly turned to ashes that floated into the air like black butterflies. As Sister Ten pounded her chest and stamped her feet in anger and frustration, Xie Yingge stood motionless and still like a statue enveloped in a black fog of spiraling smoke.

After accomplishing the great revolutionary act, the band of Red Guards left a round of denunciative big character posters on the fence walls before leaving the precarious little house, throwing out their chests and holding their heads high, shouting the slogan "Long Live Revolution!"

When the flimsy wooden door in the fence wall was slammed shut, the little house stood in the gathering twilight like a broken ship that had sunk to the bottom of a deep, murky lake. Only the embers of the bonfire still flickered like the eyes of a ghost. Xie Yingge, who had stood like a statue for hours, suddenly fell straight on her back, much like an actor performing a highly difficult stage act of "dead-body hard fall". On the stage, the "dead-body hard fall" act was normally executed by male actors only and required careful preparation, including holding the breath, stiffening the neck and landing on the back of one's shoulders to avoid head concussions. But Xie Yingge fell when she lost consciousness. Had it not been for Sister Ten's quick reaction in rushing over to buffer the fall with her own body, Xie Yingge would probably have landed on the back of her head with unthinkable consequences. Sister Ten's lunge to forestall the fall earned her massive bruises on her thighs and arms that took more than a month to heal.

With Wang Houcheng's help, Sister Ten moved Xie Yingge to the living room and placed her on a couch. She dabbed her face with a cold moistened towel and pinched her philtrum to help Xie Yingge regain consciousness. Sister Ten added condiments to the previous day's leftovers to make a rice stew, which the three ate with some marinated vegetables and fermented bean curd, just to make the hunger pangs go away. It took much cajoling from Wang Houcheng to persuade a reluctant Xie Yingge to eat half a bowl of it. After the meager meal, Xie Yingge, supported by Wang Houcheng, went upstairs to rest. Sister Ten rolled up her sleeves and started to clean up the mess in the house, all the while cursing the "damnable Red Guards!" When she went into the water closet with a mop to wash it down, she was startled by something black and white soaked in a wooden foot basin half filled with water. When she picked it up she realized it was Mother Dear's *qingyi* costume! She slapped her head and started to laugh. It turned out she had previously found yellowish sweat stains along the spine of the costume resulting from Senior Miss's daily practice in it and had soaked it in water with the idea of washing and starching it when she was less busy. And she had forgotten about the whole thing in the tumult of the Red Guards' raid. She had a good laugh; the arrogant Red Guards that threw their weight about and had their eyes wide open for things to smash had not discovered this "feudalistic, capitalistic and revisionist" classical opera costume! She ran up the stairs in great excitement to break the good news to Senior Miss, but Wang Houcheng shushed her with an index finger to his lips: "Don't wake her up! Let her have some rest." Then he added with a sigh: "What's the use of one costume when the rest is gone?"

Her enthusiasm unreciprocated, Sister Ten withdrew from the room, comforting herself with the thought: when Miss wakes up and sees the costume, she will feel a little better. After mopping the floor, she began putting into order the chest of drawers messed up by the Red Guards. Working from the top down, she pulled out each drawer, removed the old newspaper used to line the bottom, wiped off the dust with a dry rag and replaced the articles of clothing. When she came to the bottom drawer, she froze as if a spell had been cast on her, petrifying her—on the newspaper lining the bottom, a large stage photo of Xie Yingge's Li Sanniang stared back at her, in infinite pain and sorrow: "My child—I bit through the umbilical cord—" Then it dawned on Sister Ten: this was the feature article in the provincial newspaper about Xie Yingge's performance of the *Legend of the White Rabbit* with the heading "What a Handsome, Forlornly Beautiful Li Sanniang!" accompanied by a stage photo shot by Wang Houcheng. The latter had brought them a big stack of the day's papers. After Sister Ten cut out the article from one copy and gave out a few to neighbors close to the family, there were still many copies left. The next day when she was cleaning up the chest of drawers, Sister Ten had taken one copy from the stack to line the drawers. Repeatedly chanting "Amitabha", Sister Ten now gingerly picked the paper up off the bottom of the drawer. No longer able to contain her joy, Sister Ten ran upstairs and crashed the door to the front bedroom open.

Wang Houcheng was in the middle of talking tenderly to Xie Yingge held in his arms when he was abruptly interrupted by Sister Ten. He turned his head about and chided her with annoyance: "Shi Mei! What's the meaning of this? Have you gone out of your mind? Do you think she has not had enough excitement and shock for one day?"

Seeing Senior Miss wiping tears off her face with her head resting on the pillow, Sister Ten ignored the Master's questions and thrust the newspaper in front of her eyes and said, panting heavily and with a loud voice: "Miss, look, look! The Red Guards didn't burn everything! They missed this paper at the bottom of the chest of drawers!"

With her red, swollen eyes wide open, Xie Yingge was speechless for a good while. Sister Ten added: "Guniang, isn't there a line in your aria that goes: 'Don't mourn the fallen petals; the twigs will fill with pink buds next year?' It must be Hao Ma watching over you up there that this newspaper and that *qingyi* costume survived the ransacking by that band of adolescent bandits."

With that thin sheet of newsprint she held up in both hands, Xie Yingge took a long look at it before finally breaking her silence:

> I see nothing but darkness before my eyes; I'm
> afraid death is near,
> But I must be tough it out for the sake of Zhiyuan
> and my child …

She was singing one of Li Sanniang's lines from the *Legend of the White Rabbit*!

Xie Yingge did quietly tough it out for several years at the props factory—quietly in the literal sense, for she worked hard from morning till night with her lips tightly pressed shut, taking apart sets, washing props and mending things, never speaking a word. The most she did in the way of communicating with others was nodding or shaking her head. Workers at the factory who had been her fans tried to persuade her to sing for them during lunch breaks, but she invariably responded with a silent, wry smile. It was a charming smile; the dimple that quivered on her right cheek, its depth infinitely variable with the shifting of her emotions, resembled the petal of an orchid.

One day the model opera group of the provincial capital sent a few people to the props workshop to pick out some sets and Xie Yingge saw among them her old stage partner Qin Yulou; she quietly turned and walked away, pretending not to have seen her. She went into the temporary latrine outside the workshop, choosing to bear the fetid odor rather than face a past that had been ruthlessly shattered.

Qin Yulou followed her into the latrine and stopped her, saying: "Xiao Xie, there's something that I must explain to you. I did not snitch on you. It was because of your father and your mother's political problem that you had been in their crosshairs. They even put together a task force to deal with your case. The task force forced me to denounce you and manufactured a host of scary charges against you. I tried to defend you, saying to them that you were only complaining about the lack of femininity in Jiang Shuiying's gestures and movements on stage. I didn't think that was anything serious, but they immediately treated it as a cardinal sin, characterizing it as an issue of a black line, a pernicious school of thought in literature and art ..."

Mimicking a stage movement of "flicking the water sleeves toward the speaker", Xie Yingge interrupted her and started to move out of her way. Responding equally theatrically with a stage movement of "holding up the arms and flicking the sleeves outward", Qin Yulou cut off her evasive maneuver and said in a pleading voice: "Xiao Xie, I know you hold a grudge against me, but I too have a miserable time running errands for the provincial model opera group as an underling, bowing to the whims of others and being constantly reminded of my inferior position. In comparison I rather envy your carefree, insouciant life at the props factory ..."

Xie Yingge, jerking her head up, struck a theatrical "frozen pose", her eyes burning like two torches and the dimple in her right cheek deepening as if a piece of her cheek had been gouged out, and an icy smile crept into her face. Realizing their old friendship was beyond repair, Qin Yulou heaved a long sigh and left in shame and remorse.

In those years of patient and quiet suffering, Wang Houcheng felt the repercussions of Xie Yingge's fall into disgrace; how could the husband of a stalwart of an evil school of thought infesting the cultural and art world be allowed to continue working in the press, supposedly an advocate, a champion of the proletariat? As a result Wang Houcheng was sent down to an extra-system rural elementary school as a teacher and was allowed only a few days of leave every few months to return to his home in the provincial capital for a visit.

Word spread that the famous actor in the female role of Yueju opera Xie Yingge had lost her voice and could no longer sing. The sensational news originated in the props factory and soon roared through town.

When Sister Ten went out to get groceries or dump household waste, there would be acquaintances and strangers accosting her with solicitous inquiries about Xie Yingge: how could the crisp, golden voice of Xie Yingge be lost just like that, they wondered. Sister Ten would patiently explain to each and every one of them that it was a malicious rumor and that her Miss's voice was as good as ever. "Only, my Miss has decided to stop singing for the time being, because nowadays only the eight revolutionary model operas have the official seal of approval, and besides, every Dick and Tom knows how to sing them, so why bother!"

Sister Ten knew something that others didn't: Senior Miss had been patiently waiting and preparing for a chance to go back on stage. When she came home from a hard day's work at the props factory, Senior Miss was so exhausted she didn't even have the strength to lift a cup of water to her lips. But despite her fatigue, she would get up early in the morning and practice her craft in her yard, exercising her legs and doing the backward arch, walking stage circles and flicking water sleeves. When she practiced her singing, she would tell Sister Ten to close all the windows, even in the hottest days, and sang the octave scale at the top of her lungs to a big, empty wine barrel. In those years, only Sister Ten had the good fortune of listening to Senior Miss's singing of classical arias from the *Legend of the White Rabbit*. And she would pause every so often to ask Sister Ten for her opinion: was that change of tone and pitch a smooth transition? Did you like the way I ended that song? To Sister Ten's ears, Senior Miss's singing was more captivating than ever, and when she returned one day to the stage, she would create a sensation with her virtuosity and gain universal fame. That was why Sister Ten would always try to persuade Senior Miss to eat more, even though the food was crude and simple, so that she would have greater strength. How would she otherwise have the requisite strength to sing and act when the day came for her to return to the stage?

In those years of patient and quiet suffering, Sister Ten became the motivator and confidence booster behind Xie Yingge.

Seven or eight years rolled by and change seemed to be in the wind. First, Wang Houcheng was called back to the provincial newspaper to resume his work as a photo journalist. Half a year later, Xie Yingge was transferred from the props factory to the Provincial School of The Arts as a teacher in charge of basic posture training. At the time the Provincial School of The Arts had not resumed recruitment of students for other genres of opera except for two successive training classes for the study of model Beijing operas.

The Provincial School of the Arts was located in an idyllic rustic setting about two hundred kilometers from the provincial capital. It so happened that the rural community was Xie Yingge's home town.

Little did Xie Yingge know that there, in the home town she had left years before, she would meet for the first time her younger sister by her father's other woman. The two sisters would together play out a drama fit for legend.

The very first day Xie Yingge took up her post at the training program for revolutionary model operas, a curious thing happened. Her arrival in the classroom set off a buzz of whispered discussion and finger pointing and gesturing among the students, which made Xie Yingge nervous and induced a sense of embarrassment and inferiority in her, making her wonder if she had done something wrong or the students were scornful of her credentials as "a stalwart of the evil school of thought infesting the cultural and art world". After the class, she invited the class president to her office and respectfully and sincerely solicited comments on her teaching. The class president said: "Master Xie, you gave an exemplary lesson in posture training. No other teacher has taught such important basics to us since our enrollment in the School of the Arts."

Xie Yingge stared at him in bafflement: "In that case ... why did the class ...?"

The class president flashed a brilliant smile: "Master Xie, a while ago a woman singer from a singing-only traditional opera troupe was invited by the school to give a talk to us. Her surname is also Xie and she bears an uncanny resemblance to you. We were wondering if you were twin sisters."

Xie Yingge's heart gave an involuntary lurch and started beating wildly but she composed herself and asked with feigned casualness the class president for more details about the woman singer. It turned out the singer by the name of Xie was the most popular performer on the local opera singing group circuit within a hundred li of the town. She was credited with a good voice that never failed and was able to sing competently and convincingly any aria, any role type (young male, vivacious young female or *huadan*, old male, old female, you name it) in any tune style and any opera genre, such as Yueju opera, Shaoxing opera, and Yuyao opera. She was in high demand when entertainment was needed in private homes on festive or funereal occasions and she commanded the highest price among her peer singers in the area. With the launching of the "Cultural Revolution", the private, singing-only local opera troupes were outlawed as remnants of feudalist, capitalist and revisionist forces and the country was inundated with the eight officially sanctioned revolutionary model operas. This renowned traditional opera singer immediately aligned herself with the spirit of the times and switched to that particular brand of Beijing opera and soon she included in her repertory all the revolutionary model plays, including *The Legend of the Red Lantern*, *Shajiabang*, *Song of the Dragon River* and *On the Docks*. Her mastery of these model operas got her invited by the Provincial School of The Arts to give a talk about opera singing.

With some hesitation, Xie Yingge asked: "What—what's her name?"

The class president gave his head a few knocks before saying: "The name, I believe, is—Xie Jin'ge. She gave that name in her self-introduction at the start of her talk. It struck us as a nice-sounding name."

As if thunder-struck, Xie Yingge was petrified. The class president asked: "Master Xie, are you all right?" Xie Yingge quickly said with a smile: "I'm all right! Thank you!"

After work, Xie Yingge hurried—in the stage gait she had acquired from constant practice since childhood—back to the apartment she rented in town. With her hands and feet ice cold, she gripped Sister Ten's shoulders as she reeled off an account of the conversation about that traditional opera singer. As she listened, Sister Ten all of a sudden gave a slap on her thigh and said: "It must be her!"

"Who?" Xie Yingge asked with trepidation.

Sighing and shaking her head, Sister Ten said: "Who else? The second daughter of the Xie family, your own flesh-and-blood younger sister!"

It turned out the erstwhile prominent Xie family had fallen on hard times. Master Xie, i.e. Xie Yingge's father, reportedly died of illness in a reform-by-forced-labor farm, leaving behind him only a daughter by his second wife. The neighbors attributed the reversal of fortunes to what they believed must be some shady, unethical past practices of the Xie family in its rise to wealth and prominence. It was a divine act of retribution that had rendered them without a male heir.

For the first time Xie Yingge was brought to the knowledge of the existence of a woman who shared her blood. She couldn't wait to meet this younger sister who was said to resemble her. But before she acted on that impulse, the younger sister came to visit on the third night.

It was Sister Ten who opened the door to the visitor, at whose sight Sister Ten immediately called out: "Guniang, she's here!"

When Xie Yingge rushed to the door, with her hands pressed against her chest, Xie Jin'ge plopped down on her knees and cried teary-voiced: "Jieh—" and heaved in sobs.

Xie Yingge, her face also bathed in tears, hastened to help her up and walked her into the house.

Blood ties are a mysterious thing. Since a child Xie Yingge had hated his father for abandoning her mother and hated the Xie family, who denied her and her mother a place in their midst. She hated more than she hated anyone else that young lady from a wealthy family, who forced her mother out and usurped her place, and her progeny. But the very first time she saw Xie Jin'ge, all the resentment and bitterness in her heart vanished in an instant and gave way to a tender affection.

That evening the two sisters poured their hearts out to each other, bursting with things to tell each other. Xie Jin'ge told her elder sister that not long after her father was sentenced to forced labor in a reform farm in the faraway Northwest her mother succumbed to grief and bitterness and died. She was then not yet ten years old and survived by begging and scavenging in the streets. Later her luck turned as the charitable owner of a local opera singing troupe discovered her voice, sweet as a silver bell, and decided to take her under his wings and teach her to sing traditional arias, thereby giving her a livelihood.

This Xie Jin'ge, true to her fame, was articulate and witty. She had a way with words, and most of the time it was she who did the talking, in a vivacious, melodious, singsong tone, like cascading spring water washing over rocks of jade. As she spoke all her facial features danced in excited abandon—the picture of a heavily made-up stage beauty saying full of tender affection: "Jieh, I've known you are my sister for a long time. I wanted to come to you but I was too shy to do it because of your fame. When the record of your *Legend of the White Rabbit* came out, I immediately bought one. The singing was superb. I never tire of listening to it and eventually I learned all of it by heart."

Sister Ten clapped her hands enthusiastically and said cheerfully: "Er Guniang, so you still own LPs of the *Legend of the White Rabbit* by Senior Miss? That's wonderful. The ones we had were all smashed by those Red Guard bandits!"

The following evening Xie Jin'ge returned with a green canvas travel bag containing a phonograph and the complete set of records of the *Legend of the White Rabbit*. Even the normally reserved Xie Yingge couldn't contain the excitement and agitation in her heart and as she held the records in her hands, they trembled like leaves quivering in the wind.

They made sure the doors were securely locked and drew the curtains over all the windows. Adjusting the volume of the phonograph to the lowest possible setting, they sat around it and listened to the *Legend of the White Rabbit* from beginning to end. When she heard climactic passages of her singing, she couldn't hold back from getting up off her chair and enacting the scene.

> For sixteen years I've carried water in the day and turned the millstone at night,
> The well water is like my tears that spurt like a spring, though the well water is dwarfed by my tears.
> In the sixteen years, many a withered leaf has fallen from the sweet osmanthus,
> And I've added many a white hair to my head besides the years of misery.
> In the sixteen years my heart and these ten fingers of mine long for my dear child,

The longing has sustained me through adversity till
    this day.
Last night I dreamed of a white rabbit descended
    from the heavens,
Teary-eyed, it called me dear mother.
I recall having hung a jade rabbit against his chest
    at birth,
I wonder if he has changed into a white rabbit
To meet with me, his mother, in a dream ...

This was part of an aria sung in the scene of "The Reunion
at the Well" in the play *Legend of the White Rabbit*. Bearing herself
"like a frail willow", her slender fingers formed into an orchid,
she walked "like a cloud driven by the wind", "hugging the moon
and scattering stars behind her". Her impromptu acting elicited
cheers from Xie Jin'ge and Sister Ten. As the aria on the record
ended, Xie Jin'ge rushed toward Xie Yingge and gripped her
hands, eagerly imploring her: "Jieh, you must teach me how to
perform the *Legend of the White Rabbit*. You must!"

With the company of Xie Jin'ge, her flesh-and-blood younger
sister, Xie Yingge's life in her small home town was no longer
lonely. In that period, the opera singing troupe to which Xie
Jin'ge belonged could not yet openly solicit business, so the troupe
eked out a living by touring remote mountain villages to offer
clandestine performances. In her leisure time, Xie Jin'ge would
often bring fresh local groceries to her elder sister's apartment.
Together with Sister Ten, she would wash, cut, boil or fry the
food and prepare a hearty meal that they would share when Xie
Yingge came home from work. To outsiders, nothing could be
more ordinary than these visits between sisters, but little did
people know that when night fell, it was time for them to shine!
They would shut all the doors and windows, draw the curtains
together and begin listening to, singing and enacting the *Legend
of the White Rabbit*. In two years, Xie Jin'ge learned from her elder
sister the critical scenes of "Parting at the Melon Patch", "The

Reunion at the Well" and "The Reunion in the Mill Shed". Xie Yingge approved of her younger sister's performance, saying: "Er Mei, you can already perform these scenes on stage. Too bad you didn't have a chance to train from a young age and therefore have so far been unable to master the water sleeves technique in the scene of 'Giving Birth by the Millstone'. But it can't be rushed. You have to have the patience to keep practicing."

Xie Jin'ge on the other hand was already letting her imagination run wild. Hugging her elder sister, she said: "Jieh, if you ever go back to the Provincial Yueju Opera Troupe, please take me with you. Even if it means I'd only get to play walk-on parts such as a maid or man servant to your lead role, I would be perfectly content."

After a pensive, silent moment, Xie Yingge said with a sigh: "Who knows if I would ever return to the stage?"

The remark proved prophetic.

In the autumn of that year, in the wake of a political earthquake of great magnitude on a national scale, an immediate halt was called to the revolutionary model operas training program of the Provincial School of the Arts, and those trainees who had been recruited from opera troupes were sent back to their own troupes; those who had no prior work units had to pack up and go back to farming in their home towns.

Xie Yingge and Sister Ten had been packing in preparation for returning to the provincial capital, where they would wait for their work assignment orders, when the elderly president of the Provincial School of the Arts came to her and pleaded with her to stay and wait some more in her home town. Mr. Wei, the old president, had been an actor in a Shaoxing opera troupe. He disclosed to Xie Yingge the news that the School of the Arts would soon resume recruitment of new students in all genres of traditional local opera. It was his fond hope that he could retain teachers of the caliber of Xie Yingge, who had all the requisite professional skills, moral integrity, lineage and cachet. With great sincerity and frankness, President Wei said: "If you return to the stage in the provincial capital, the most you can hope to accomplish is the revival of one Li Sanniang. But if you stay to teach at the School of the Arts, you will be able to grow many more cultivars of Li Sanniang!" President Wei put in an application, in the school's name, to have a telephone installed in her apartment to facilitate communication with her family in the provincial capital.

It was a generous offer Xie Yingge did not have the heart to decline, so she held her horses. Truth be told, she was in no hurry to return to the provincial capital, firstly because she had not received any paper or oral message summoning her back to the Provincial Yueju Opera Troupe; she would just bring ridicule upon herself if she went there uninvited and ended up "cozying up to a cold ass with her hot cheeks", only to be spurned. Then also, the Provincial Yueju Opera Troupe had been, in these past years, composed mainly of second-rank and third-rank actors, who would not easily be persuaded to cede the stage to abler actors and who were mounting mostly modern model operas to suit the shifting political winds. With the awkwardness in playing Jiang Shuiying in the revolutionary model opera the *Song of the Dragon River* still fresh in her mind, Xie Yingge had no stomach for climbing on this bandwagon. It was Wang Houcheng who worried for her, saying that as long as you were tucked away in an obscure corner, nobody would be able to help you out even if they wanted to; why don't you just report to the troupe every day regardless of what people say or what happens? It's not as if they would run you out; maybe if there happens to be a part that's perfect for you, they would let you have it. But Xie Yingge was too proud and too much a stickler for her haughty principles to accept compromises. Unable to budge her will, Wang Houcheng could only continue the grueling back-and-forth commute between the provincial capital and the small town.

Xie Yingge, having made the commitment to the Provincial School of the Arts, spent her days eagerly waiting for the start of recruitment of students to the promised new programs so that she could show the ropes to the students, training their voice, having them walk stage circles, teaching them how to sing and dance. She wanted to rehearse and perform with the students so that they would be able to interpret on the stage, wearing their bejeweled headdresses, silk costumes, embroidered shoes and flicking their water sleeves, the lives of classic women with all their sorrows and joys, heartbreaks and reunions and bring out the goodness, faithfulness, courage and beauty of their heart with song. She aspired to that serene, relaxed and yet splendid life; that kind of life would truly give meaning to her individual life as a traditional opera actor! She had already begun making preparations for her budding teaching career by putting together a syllabus based on a retrospective of her acting career and a summing-up of her stage experiences. She even took an interest in the performances of private art groups in towns and villages nearby and scouted for artistic talent that could be persuaded to enroll when the Provincial School of the Arts started recruiting. Every few days she would call on President Wei to find out the dates of the launching of the new programs and recruitment schedules. President Wei would invariably counsel patience, saying the recruitment plans had been submitted to the leadership of the cultural department concerned and would be implemented the moment they were approved by the higher authorities.

Those were the years for righting wrongs and rising from the ashes across the nation; yet the approval of the recruitment plans was slow in coming and many seasons and years rolled by without anything happening.

In the meantime, the singing-only traditional opera troupe Xie Jin'ge worked for saw its business pick up and even thrive. She was coming less often to Xie Yingge to learn the art of performing the *Legend of the White Rabbit*. She gave the reason as being too busy but in fact she felt that the classic arias she had already learned from Xie Yingge were sufficient for her purpose. Every couple of months though Xie Jin'ge would visit her elder sister when she had some spare time, and she always brought presents for her. Xie Jin'ge often brought encouraging news, such as a certain troupe having called back its veteran actors, or a certain troupe starting to rehearse traditional one-act plays. She blamed her sister for being too unassertive and giving undue emphasis to playing by the book; she said by choosing to hunker down in this quiet town, her sister would grow musty. "Jieh, if I were you, I would return to the provincial capital and ask the leadership of the Yueju Opera Troupe to cast you in a play. The days of the ravages of the Gang of Four are over, so what are you afraid of?"

But Xie Yingge was no Xie Jin'ge. It was not in her reserved nature to follow the example of Xie Jin'ge in her dealings with the world; all she could do was patiently waiting. The feeling of being torn between hope and anxiety took a greater toll on her than the despair and hopelessness of the previous few years; she would often choke with an unaccountable anger and feel like a smoking bomb ready to explode. Whenever that happened she would put on her mother's *qingyi* costume and go through a vigorous routine of various maneuvers of the water sleeves (turning, throwing, shaking, lobbing), and poses such as "cloud hands", "back bends", "reclining fish" and "sparrow hawk pirouette" until her clothes were soaked through with sweat.

It was soon autumn and Xie Jin'ge paid her elder sister another visit, this time bringing with her not only bagfuls of presents but a middle-aged man, who had a pleasant enough appearance. He wore an indigo blue nankeen Chinese jacket over a white percale shirt with a popped collar and buttons down the front. His crew-cut hair had a touch of silver; he had a swarthy face, a bluish chin and a pair of beady eyes glinting like silver studs that he trained on people with a shadow of a sly smile on his face. Xie Jin'ge, with a bashful smile, introduced him. It turned out he was the owner of the singing-only traditional opera troupe she worked for. His name was Lu Mingjiu.

Xie Yingge, conventional and reserved though she was, possessed unsuspected wisdom and perspicacity under her prim veneer. She immediately detected an unusual relationship between this Lu Mingjiu and her younger sister. The realization annoyed her and she surmised that this Lu Mingjiu must be a dozen years older than Jin'ge. She decided to be discreet about it and kept the knowledge to herself.

Lu Mingjiu made the special trip with Xie Jin'ge to pay Xie Yingge a visit with the express purpose of inviting this actor in the female role, once the undisputed darling of the province's Yueju opera stage, to join their singing troupe. By forging this alliance, he calculated, his singing troupe would leave all competitors in the dust and would be able to corner the market of festive and funereal entertainment in the mountain villages in a hundred-mile radius.

Lu Mingjiu, true to his opera singer's training, was an eloquent speaker, "his breath a spring breeze, and his words burgeoning lotus flowers". Xie Jin'ge, already getting impatient and frustrated, interjected: "Jieh, what are you waiting for? The announcement of the recruitment of students for the Provincial School of the Arts has already been communicated to the various towns. Why is President Wei still keeping you in the dark?"

This remark from Xie Jin'ge had the effect of a cyclone that whipped up a tidal wave inside Xie Yingge. She kept her emotions in check until she saw the visitors off. Then she lost her restraint and rushed to the Provincial School of the Arts. She stormed into President Wei's office and asked, her eyes glaring: "President Wei, the recruitment plans have been approved, am I correct? Why have you kept me out of the recruitment team? Am I unqualified?" She had never employed such a harsh tone before, her every word hitting President Wei's desk like a rock.

President Wei put up a contrived smile, which was more disconcerting than a crying grimace, as he replied: "Master Xie, no one is more qualified than you to sit on the recruitment board. Our school is fortunate and privileged to have you on our faculty. But in the recruitment plans that came back to us, your name has unaccountably been struck out. It was my intention to travel to the provincial capital to find out the reason for that before giving you a definite answer ..."

Without waiting for President Wei to finish his sentence, Xie Yingge slowly wheeled about and walked out of the door. Despite President Wei's repeated calls after her, she never turned back, drawing, as it were, an emphatic point of exclamation with her back view.

Xie Yingge did not know how she made it back to her apartment. When Sister Ten opened the door for her, she gasped: "Guniang, are you ill? You look like the ghost of a woman who just hanged herself!"

Fixing her eyes on Sister Ten for a good while, Xie Yingge finally spat out the words: "Pack up our things! We are going back to the provincial capital!" After a pause, she added: "Telephone Lao Wang and tell him to pick us up early in the morning."

Sister Ten didn't know what Senior Miss was up to, but seeing the determined look on her face, she did not dare probe further but immediately called Wang Houcheng. Wang Houcheng, who was busy planning a journalistic interview, did not have the presence of mind to ask for a reason of the sudden decision, but answered enthusiastically: "That's wonderful! It's high time that she come back to the provincial capital. I have an engagement tomorrow morning, so I'll try to be there by noon time."

After she hung up, Sister Ten came back to tell Senior Miss about the phone conversation. She was surprised to find that Senior Miss had unprecedentedly missed her daily training and was reclining in her bed with her street clothes on. Sister Ten was going to get her out of her bed and tell her to eat supper before retiring for the day, when she saw that her eyes were closed and she was lying still, apparently asleep. Maybe she was too tired; Sister Ten decided not to disturb her and started packing up by herself.

When Sister Ten was done packing, she went to look in on Senior Miss and found her in the same state and same posture as before, like a dead fossil. Sister Ten thought with sadness to herself: Senior Miss has not had it easy these years; she has too much on her mind. It's all right if she skips a meal. The important thing is to get enough sleep and give her mind a chance to rest. After eating a quick meal of rice and leftovers boiled together in water, Sister Ten went to bed also. Sister Ten was never one to allow anything to occupy her mind, so the moment her head hit the pillow, she began snoring. It was just after ten.

"Drrring … drrring … drrring …" At long last Sister Ten was awakened by the fitful ringing of the phone and sat up with a start, half of her still in her dream. Then she saw Senior Miss sitting at the edge of her bed, looking into space, with a terrified and quizzical expression.

Sister Ten had by now completely emerged from her dream; she collected herself, patted her chest and cursed: "Damned ringing of the phone sounded like an air raid alarm! At this ungodly hour of the night!" She turned her head to look at the clock; it was a little past ten thirty. So she had slept only for half an hour. Sister Ten said with a smile to Senior Miss: "Maybe it's the Master calling about the time of his arrival tomorrow. I'll take the call." Stepping into her shoes, she trotted over to where the phone was and picked up the receiver and shouted into it: "Sir, it's very late in the night. Did you just get off work?"

"Is Xiao Xie … Xie Yingge at this number? I'd like to speak to Xie Yingge." The voice was husky but still recognizable as that of a female.

Thrusting the handset at Senior Miss, Sister Ten said: "It's for you. She sounds like that actor who used to play Liu Zhiyuan to your Li Sanniang."

Xie Yingge took the handset from Sister Ten with some hesitation and in puzzlement. Her "hello" triggered a torrent of words: "Xiao Xie, it's me, Yulou! Don't hang up! You must hear me through. The provincial government is planning an evening gala in celebration of the thirtieth anniversary of the founding of the People's Republic and the Yueju Opera Troupe is participating with a performance of the 'The Reunion in the Mill Shed' of the *Legend of the White Rabbit*, with the approval of the organizing committee of the event. The higher authorities have designated you and me as the lead actors of the performance. An official memo has been issued to transfer you back to the Troupe, and you will receive the transfer order in a few days. We have a little more than a month before the event. Try to come back as soon as you can. It's been ten years since we last performed the play, so there is some serious catching up to do …"

Xie Yingge whispered an "um" before putting down the handset.

Sister Ten couldn't wait to ask: "Was it that Qin Yulou who played Liu Zhiyuan to your Li Sanniang?"

With a slight lift of the corners of her mouth, a faint dimple appeared in Xie Yingge's right cheek.

Sister Ten's curiosity was piqued: "What was the call about? Did she call this late in the night to deplore once again the wrongs she did to you?"

The dimple on Xie Yingge's cheek deepened; she said pensively: "She asked me to return to the provincial capital to rehearse for a performance of the *Legend of the White Rabbit*."

Unable to contain her joy, Sister Ten jumped up and put her two palms together: "Is it true? Amitabha! The Buddha has blessed you!"

Without a word, Xie Yingge headed straight toward the door.

"Guniang! Where are you going?" Sister Ten asked after her.

"Give me that *qingyi* costume! I'm going to practice for a bit." As she said this, Xie Yingge turned her head, allowing Sister Ten a partial glimpse of a face lit up by emotion, her eyes gleaming and full of tenderness, her mouth red as if touched up by lipstick and a deep beguiling dimple that resembled a bedewed orchid that had just opened in bloom.

This was the last glimpse Sister Ten was to have of the breath-taking beauty of Senior Miss.

Xie Yingge stepped into the small courtyard in her mother's *qingyi* costume and began to dance. The eight-foot long water sleeves curled and spiraled in the air—"now the clouds hide the moon, the next moment the moon peeks through the clouds"—

leaving Sister Ten spellbound and breathless.

As Xie Yingge did two consecutive "sparrow hawk pirouettes", catching her water sleeves and throwing them out, she suddenly lunged forward and fell into a lifeless heap on the ground.

Thinking at first that Senior Miss did it in preparation for the next move "black dragon coiled around the pillar", which involved rolling on the ground, Sister Ten waited in excited anticipation. But the prostrate body remained inert after a long while. Sister Ten rushed forward and took Senior Miss into her arms. The latter's eyes were tightly shut and her face was a waxy yellow and something the color of soy sauce was oozing out of the corners of her mouth.

Act II

The Brew of Emotions before the Performance

Scene V The Rehearsal

Operatic Kaleidoscope was consistently a high-ratings series on the provincial TV station, produced by its culture and arts department. One reason for its popularity was the province had always been a center of traditional operas with a large audience of faithful opera fans. The second reason for its success was that the program's producer, director and host were serious about their work and produced a program with solid, richly varied contents that proved popular with the viewers.

A program of the Sunday *Operatic Kaleidoscope* series entitled "Pear Garden Glitterati" was normally devoted to interviews of famous actors of different opera genres, who were invited to the studio to talk about their rehearsals and performances and regale the viewers with interesting anecdotes. Opera fans were allowed to interact with them or to sing a few lines so that the invited actors could offer pointers and advice on the spot; or the opera fans and the actors would sing and act something together, to the enjoyment of all. The famous actors were eager to go on this show because it gave them an opportunity to have close contact and interchanges with their fans, and to broaden their mass appeal.

In the latest episode of "Pear Garden Glitterati", the production team trained its sights on a young actor in the female role of the Provincial Yueju Opera Theater by the name of Mi Jingyao, who was slated to play Li Sanniang in the first half of the reworked play the *Legend of the White Rabbit* to be performed on the troupe's Hong Kong tour.

The part of Li Sanniang had always been reserved exclusively for the famed Yueju opera actor Xie Yingge, not because the latter prohibited others from playing Li Sanniang but because no one else had ever played the role better than Xie Yingge; as a result few ever had an incentive to try that role. While Mi Jingyao had been Xie Yingge's star student, she had been given mainly minor roles around seasoned actors in the four or five years since she was recruited into the troupe following her graduation from the Yueju opera program of the Provincial School of the Arts. She had been told by her mentor that there was no getting round "eating rice with only preserved turnip to go with it" for a few years, meaning there was no other way than coming up through the ranks. Although she had some experience in performing traditional one-act plays and did very well in the recent provincial contest of young opera actors, she never played a lead part in a major opera like the *Legend of the White Rabbit*. How would she feel about sharing the role of Li Sanniang with her mentor Xie Yingge in the *Legend of the White Rabbit*? Was she stressed out? Excited? Or frightened? The producer believed that the program's focus on casting new actors for a new play would prove a big draw for the opera-loving public.

But when the producer of *Operatic Kaleidoscope* discussed their idea of the show with the leadership of the Provincial Yueju Opera Theater, the latter came up with a different proposal. The deputy general manager of the Yueju Opera Theater Qin Yulou was of the view that the most important difference between the new version of the *Legend of the White Rabbit* and the 1960s version was the restoration of the traditional story line of Liu Zhiyuan's marriage into the General's family, which was a deep probe into the hidden side of human nature and a critique of human weaknesses. The adding back of that element greatly increased Liu Zhiyuan's lines and stage time. Feng Jianyue, the young actor in the young male role, who was to play Liu Zhiyuan in the first half of the play, had excellent qualities as an actor and had distinguished herself by winning first prize in the province's young opera actors' contest.

Wouldn't it be nice if she could appear together with Mi Jingyao on the show? Also the Theater's decision to cast a younger pair of actors in the male (*sheng*) and female (*dan*) roles and an older pair to play Liu Zhiyuan and Li Sanniang in different stages of their lives was received with a generous spirit and a broad mind by the older actors. For example, Xie Yingge, who was in her prime and had perfected her stage craft, would have been perfectly capable of playing Li Sanniang through the entire play and the Hong Kong sponsor of the tour had specifically asked for Xie Yingge to play Li Sanniang, but in order to give the younger actors a chance to advance in their careers, she had voluntarily given her part to a younger actor for the first half of the play. She went even further by rehearsing with the younger actors, helping them perfect the details, in the hope that her students would give a better performance than she could. Shouldn't this selfless spirit be encouraged and given more publicity? Moreover, the Theater had invited a "rising-star" young director He Shuye to direct this play. Mr. He already made a name for himself directing stage plays; his joining forces with the production team of the *Legend of the White Rabbit* would inject modern aesthetic ideas into this classic of traditional opera, broadening its intellectual content. If he could also be invited on the show, an intellectual discussion would certainly ensue that would set off unexpected sparks of insight.

The production team of *Operatic Kaleidoscope* found the three-point proposal of Deputy Manager Qin convincing and decided to adopt it. Both pairs of actors playing Liu Zhiyuan and Li Sanniang and He Shuye, the director of the new *Legend of the White Rabbit*, would be invited on the next show of "Pear Garden Glitterati", with the topic of discussion changed to: how can a classic of traditional opera continue to preserve its appeal in a new era and in new circumstances.

It was a period of unprecedented activity in the rehearsal hall of the Provincial Yueju Opera Theater. From morning till night, the rehearsing of the new *Legend of the White Rabbit* was in full swing amid the tic-tac of the hardwood clappers and the reedy, nasal notes of the string instruments. According to the plans of the Theater, prior to the departure in fall for the Hong Kong tour, the troupe would present three previews of the new *Legend of the White Rabbit* at the new Art Garden Theater located in a bustling business district of the provincial capital with a view to gathering feedback that would help the troupe present its best face to the Hong Kong public, long estranged from the mainland.

Prominently displayed by the door of the rehearsal hall was the schedule of run-throughs for the day posted by the "rising-star" young director He Shuye: in the morning, "Marriage of Liu Zhiyuan into the Li Family by the Melon Patch", "Liu Zhiyuan Parts from His Wife and Goes off to the Army", "Liu Zhiyuan Taken in as Son-in-Law by His General" and "Giving Birth by the Millstone" from 8:30 to 11:30 AM; in the afternoon, "Reunion of Mother and Son in a Hunt", "Son Writes back to Father", "Sanniang Rebukes Her Husband" and "The Reunion in the Mill Shed" from 1:30 to 5:30 PM; in the evening, rehearsal of the play in totality, from 7 to 9:30 PM. Special reminder: all actors and staff must be present at the run-throughs! The exclamation mark was followed by the flourishing signature of the young Director He, which set off a sustained chatter and much jabbing and pointing of the fingers among a group of young girls gathered around the posted notice. Director He's slightly curled hair cascading to his neck, his avant-garde dress style and the stern, inscrutable look in his eyes sent tremors through the hearts of the girlish Yueju opera actors, who climbed over each other to be the first to arrive in the rehearsal room every day, training their voice and practicing their "mat skills", in hopes of coming to the notice of the young talented Director He.

The actor in the young male role Feng Jianyue, more than anyone, had a spring in her step and a gleam of delight in her eyes, just like the elated Liang Shanbo traveling to meet with Zhu Yingtai in the selection "Retracing the Eighteen-Li Journey" of *Butterfly Lovers*. On the day of Director He Shuye's arrival at the Yueju Opera Theater, the crew and cast of the *Legend of the White Rabbit* hosted a reception in his honor, at which Qin Yulou, the deputy general manager of the Theater, introduced the main actors to him. Feng Jianyue was to play Li Sanniang's son Yaoqilang, he whose umbilical cord was bitten off, as an actor in the male child role, an important supporting role. Deputy Manager of the Theater Qin Yulou steered her toward He Shuye and was going to announce her name when Feng Jianyue said with a loud laugh: "Hey—Ahye Ge (Brother Ah Ye) ! I didn't expect to see you here!" Then she gave his shoulder blade a punch with her fist, which prompted Qin Yulou to chide her: "Feng Jianyue, how can you ..." But He Shuye interrupted her with a hearty laugh and said, pointing a finger at Feng Jianyue: "Xiao Yue! This time you are under my direction. If you make any mischief, you have no idea how I'm going to make life difficult for you!" It turned out He Shuye and Feng Jianyue were neighbors from the same village and had played together in the hills and on riverbeds when they were little. He Shuye was five years Feng Jianyue's senior and had always humored her whims and had been protective of this girl he considered a little sister.

Director He Shuye repeatedly viewed the archived videos of the performances of the revived "White Rabbit" play by Xie Yingge and Qin Yulou in the mid-1980s, and studied several versions of the play, including a southern drama version, a Ming dynasty recension and a chantefable of the Jin dynasty, before forming his own ideas and plan for directing the play. In addition to making drastic additions and deletions in the script, he put younger actors in the roles of Li Sanniang and Liu Zhiyuan used to be given to Xie Yingge and Qin Yulou, now close to sixty, in the first half of the play. When the plan was made known, it made quite a splash in the Yueju Opera Theater, cheering some and alarming others.

Feng Jianyue took it for granted that Brother Ah Ye had made his bold decision to take the knife to the stage time of famed actor Xie Yingge and Deputy Manager of the Theater Qin Yulou in the face of tremendous pressure for the sole purpose of allowing herself to play the role of Liu Zhiyuan in his youth! Feng Jianyue buried Brother Ah Ye's clear manifestation of affection for her in the depth of her heart like a cherished treasure and vowed to herself that she would not squander this opportunity to give an outstanding performance as Liu Zhiyuan and prove to Brother Ah Ye that his trust in her had not been misplaced.

Before the start of the rehearsals, Director He Shuye gave the younger actors a few lessons in culture and talked about the historical context of the "White Rabbit" play, the evolution of the story and the personalities and traits of the characters. Feng Jianyue suddenly had a bold idea that got her all worked up. The *Legend of Liu Zhiyuan and the White Rabbit*, known in shorthand as the *Legend of the White Rabbit*, had as its prototype the rise of Liu Zhiyuan, the founding emperor of the Later Han dynasty in the era of the Five Dynasties, through years of poverty and obscurity; it was therefore only right that Liu Zhiyuan should be the number one lead part. It was only in later periods of history that growing sympathy for the misfortunes and suffering of Liu Zhiyuan's first wife Li Sanniang prompted a rewriting of the story with a new focus on Li Sanniang, making the latter the number one lead part. As a result the "White Rabbit" became a staple in the repertory of actors playing the virtuous lady role. Feng Jianyue's bold idea was that she would restore its original slant to the play through her distinctive, original interpretation of the character Liu Zhiyuan, which would make Liu Zhiyuan the number one lead part once again and the *Legend of the White Rabbit* a staple in the repertory of the male role-type.

Feng Jianyue decided to make a break with the clichés and conventions of the old version in the arias first. The new version of the play contained an added element of the romance between Liu Zhiyuan and young Lady Yue, which would entail a new libretto and arias her teacher had never sung before, giving her an opportunity to showcase her own distinctive singing style. She practiced singing every day with any young musician she could grab hold of in the Theater, trying out innovative ways of singing coloraturas and closing out a verse.

Qin Yulou was unfailingly the first to arrive in the rehearsal hall. In these rehearsals she wore two hats, one as the deputy general manager of the Theater in charge of operations, the other as player of Liu Zhiyuan in the second half of the play. As theater brass and lead actor, she must set a good example.

As the rehearsal room filled with actors and crew members going on the Hong Kong tour, only the diva Xie Yingge was still missing and was nowhere to be found. Director He kept looking at his watch and paced from one end of the hall to the other with his brow tightly knit.

Qin Yulou knew only too well the temper of Xie Yingge, who, she knew for a fact, deeply grudged being made to cede her part to a younger actor in the first half of the play. Qin Yulou couldn't very well say as much to Director He; she ended up explaining: "Director He, Xie Yingge has a paralyzed elder sister at home that needs care, so she may be a little late. There's not much stage time for Li Sanniang in the first half anyway, so we might as well start!"

Tsang—tay—chay—zah-dong! After this lead-in played by the percussion instrument section, followed by the introduction played on the main fiddle, the run-throughs began.

In "Marriage of Liu Zhiyuan into the Li Family by the Melon Patch", the opening act of the play, Liu Zhiyuan, whose family had fallen on hard times, hired himself out to Squire Li of Shatuo Village as horse wrangler and melon patch watchman. Squire Li, observing the portents of Liu's future greatness, took him in as son-in-law and the wedding of Liu Zhiyuan to his daughter Li Sanniang was immediately consummated.

This was a relatively simple act and its rehearsal went smoothly, entailing only a few pointers from Director He.

Next came "Liu Zhiyuan Parts from His Wife and Goes

off to the Army", in which the evil brother and sister-in-law subjected Liu Zhiyuan to unspeakable maltreatment after their father Squire Li died from illness. In sorrow Liu Zhiyuan parted from Li Sanniang and went off to the army. Husband and wife looked at each other teary-eyed and broken-hearted.

Liu Zhiyuan sings:

> The cruelty and bullying of your brother and sister-
>   in-law
> Leaves me no choice but to leave home and enlist
>   in the army.
> Sanniang!
> I worry so about you because you are three months
>   pregnant ...

Li Sanniang sings:

> Master Liu, go pursue you career,
> Don't worry about me.
> Sanniang is willing to bear all manner of hardship,
> And live for the day Master Liu comes home in
>   glory to take me away with him ...

All of a sudden Director He slammed the heel of one hand into the palm of the other and cried: "Stop!"

Feng Jianyue and Mi Jingyao exchanged blank looks, not knowing what they did wrong. They had performed this passage by following to a tee their teachers' example!

Glancing around the room, Director He said: "'Liu Zhiyuan Parts from His Wife and Goes off to the Army' is an important scene in which Liu Zhiyuan plays opposite Li Sanniang. They vow eternal love for each other and are pained by the parting, but their emotional makeups show subtle but clear differences. Unfortunately it is already three minutes and twenty-eight seconds past nine o'clock and the Li Sanniang of the latter half is still not here, so we'll not be able to continue the rehearsal of this part." After a pause for emphasis, Director He said, with another slam of the heel of one hand into the palm of the other: "All right, let's do this! We'll move the rehearsal of the next scene 'Liu Zhiyuan Taken in as Son-in-Law by His General' up. Mi Jingyao, go telephone your teacher and say we need her here in a hurry!"

Qin Yulou stepped forward and said eagerly: "I will call Xie Yingge." She figured there was no way Mi Jingyao would be able to budge Xie Yingge and would almost certainly get a chiding instead.

But Director He demurred: "Director Qin, Liu Zhiyuan is pivotal to the 'Taken in as Son-in-Law by His General' segment, we can't do without you here. Let Li Sanniang phone Li Sanniang."

Pouting and dragging her feet, Mi Jingyao went with great reluctance to the concierge's room to make the phone call to Master Xie. She had been praying that Master Xie would stay home and enjoy her rest in the first half of the day so that Mi Jingyao could go through her rehearsals without undue interference.

Mi Jingyao had a reason to feel greatly indebted to Xie Yingge. If she had not attracted the notice of Xie Yingge and got taken under her wings as her pupil several years ago upon her graduation from the Yueju opera program of the Provincial School of the Arts, she probably would not have been taken on by the Provincial Yueju Opera Theater and would have ended up in some small rural, village-hopping troupe that toured the countryside. Mi Jingyao freely admitted that Xie Yingge had been very supportive of her and never missed an opportunity to commend her to people. "Look, look! This is my student. Doesn't she remind you of me at a younger age?" had been a constant refrain in Xie Yingge's mouth. But of late, after she accepted the assignment to play Li Sanniang in the first half of the *Legend of the White Rabbit*, Mi Jingyao sensed a noticeable change in her teacher's attitude toward her. Nowadays she tended to pick on her faults more and often used unkind language such as "you are so contrived" or "you don't have a voice" that crushed her self-confidence. Whenever Xie Yingge sat in on a rehearsal, Mi Jingyao invariably made some mistake, such as forgetting her line or singing off key, which would occasion more criticism and rebukes from Xie Yingge.

Mi Jingyao was a born beauty, with an oval face, phoenix eyes, a high nose bridge, a pair of long legs and a slender waist. She moved with sinuous grace and when she struck a pose, she was the very picture of an actor in the maiden role (*guimen dan*), without having to sing or recite a line. Mi Jingyao was not without her weaknesses though. God gave her a beautiful face but not a good voice. She had a tinny, fragile voice that lacked range; when she hit the high notes especially, her voice would sound like a rubber band stretched precariously thin, making the listeners very nervous for her sake. Her first choice when she applied to the Provincial School of the Arts had been the film and TV program, but she was rejected due to her heavy eastern Zhejiang accent. By an accident of circumstances she ended up being admitted to the Yueju opera program, which was fine with her family, who were all loyal followers of Yueju opera. Her family were elated when she was taken under the wings of Xie Yingge, the actor in the female role dominating the Yueju opera scene, not long after she was taken on by the Provincial Yueju Opera Theater upon her graduation; they were sure they did not have to wait long to see Mi Jingyao's rise to fame on the Yueju opera stage.

In the original lineup for the Hong Kong tour, Mi Jingyao was to have played Li Xiuying in the act "Presenting the Phoenix Coronet" of the play *The Jade Hairpin*. This selection featured an ensemble cast of many characters, was humorous and boisterous and had a happy ending. Each and every character in it had an aria to sing; the most memorable of the arias was the popular "of the two of you, one is the flesh on the back of my hand and the other is the flesh on the palm side of my hand" which never failed to bring down the house in laughter and applause. The female character Li Xiuying also got to sing a few arias, all in traditional *sigong* tune style and at moderate speed with a flat intonation. It was a segment Mi Jingyao had already learned back in school and could sing masterfully and act effortlessly. But it would have been almost impossible for her to stand out among the many characters given equal stage time in this noisy, cheerful scene and attract the notice of the Hong Kong audiences and press. For this reason Mi Jingyao had had no illusions about benefiting from the Hong Kong tour; she would just be fulfilling a task assigned to her. Besides, she had recently cultivated some friends in the film and television circles, through whose intermediary a number of producers and directors of TV soap series had shown great interest in her. That presented a more alluring prospect.

Then out of the blue this handsome and talented Director He burst upon the scene!

Director He made bold, innovative changes to the traditional version of the "White Rabbit" and decided to cast two pairs of actors to play Liu Zhiyuan and Li Sanniang in two separate phases of their lives. Good fortune paid an unexpected visit to Mi Jingyao.

Sensing the approving and solicitous eyes of Director He, Mi Jingyao felt stirring once again inside her the desire to become a famous Yueju opera actor. She did an analysis in her head of where she stood in the Provincial Yueju Opera Theater and came to the conclusion that none of the younger generation of actors in the female role could compare favorably with her; her teacher Xie Yingge, admittedly still basking in old glory, was now past fifty and stouter and her voice had lost much of its former vibrancy and mellowness. The sharp-eyed Director He had gone against conventional wisdom and bluntly put forth the proposal to allow a younger actor to play Li Sanniang in her youth. Mi Jingyao decided to seize the opportunity to play the young Li Sanniang well on the strength of her remarkable physical appearance and aura, to make the young Li Sanniang come alive, to play her so well that Master Xie would never again dare to go back to playing the young Li Sanniang. This way she would eventually eclipse Master Xie and get to play Li Sanniang throughout the entire play.

Mi Jingyao had never been as ambitious as she was now since she stumbled into the world of Yueju opera. She naturally was not unaware of her own limitations, knowing that the greatest obstacle to her obtaining the part of young Li Sanniang was her singing, which would have to move the audience to tears by its vocal virtuosity and emotional projection to win over the opera fans. A careful study of the arias sung by the young Li Sanniang in the first half of the play showed that the scenes of "Liu Zhiyuan Parts from His Wife and Goes off to the Army" and "Giving Birth by the Millstone" were the most critical. In "Liu Zhiyuan Parts from His Wife and Goes off to the Army", the duet between Liu Zhiyuan and Li Sanniang vowing eternal love was dominated by the *chidiao* tune and moderate speed, which Mi Jingyao could handle with confidence. The difficulty for her lay in the lamentation part, when the *xianxia* tune went into the senza misura in "Giving Birth by the Millstone", just before parturition. Master Xie, who had a good voice, adapted a certain kind of Shaoxing opera tune to her advantage in singing this passage at a high, passionate pitch. Mi Jingyao, on the other hand, would sing with hesitation whenever she practiced this passage, and ended up singing off key. As the performance date approached, it was no longer possible to expand the range of her voice by hard training. Mi Jingyao decided to go to Master Zhu, who specialized in aria arrangements, for help.

Master Zhu, who was the composer for the older version of the "White Rabbit", had retired two years before. The Theater had now drafted the "old general" for the revised version of the "White Rabbit" and had retained him as the music director of the new version of the play. Mi Jingyao explained to Master Zhu her own view of the transition from the *xianxia* tune to a senza misura in that particular passage; she believed that there was no way Li Sanniang, in the midst of excruciating labor pains, could realistically have any strength left to sing at a senza misura. Wouldn't it correspond more to the despair and sadness felt by a helpless Li Sanniang if the music was changed to a *chidiao* tune at a slow tempo, with the music moving at a fast clip while the actor sang at a relaxed pace? Master Zhu nodded approvingly: "When your teacher performed the 'White Rabbit' in the 1960s, this passage was sung in a *chidiao* tune at a slow tempo. Coupled with a long sequence of dancing with the long water sleeves twirling in the air, the effect was stunning. In the 1980s when your teacher returned to the stage to perform the 'White Rabbit', she no longer had the strength to manipulate the water sleeves and it was decided to change the music to a *xianxia* tune at a senza misura in order to hype the atmosphere."

That very night Master Zhu wrote new scores based on those used in the 1960s edition of the "White Rabbit". The new music was languid, sad and wistful, perfect for Li Sanniang and perfect for Mi Jingyao. Mi Jingyao was immensely grateful to Master Zhu and went to show the new scores to Director He, who was after all no expert in this department and gave his nod simply because the few lines hummed by Mi Jingyao sounded pleasant to his ear. In the grand scheme of He Shuye's directing, this change in one small segment of the aria represented just a tiny, negligible instance of fine-tuning, dwarfed by his introduction into this classic of traditional opera powerful orchestral accompaniment and stage sets with a symbolically significant modern decorative art flavor.

Mi Jingyao had counted on singing the new tune style in the day's run-throughs and had hoped Master Xie would not attend the morning rehearsals, for she was certain that if Master Xie were to hear her singing the new tune style she would raise an objection. But now Director He had insisted on Xie Yingge's presence, against her hope. As she dialed her teacher's phone number, Mi Jingyao prayed in her heart that Xie Yingge would give all manner of excuses for not coming to the rehearsals; and she was seventy, eighty percent sure Xie Yingge would do so, as all famous actors were wont to do. But she was a little disappointed when someone answered the phone in a loud, thick eastern Zhejiang accent: "Who do you want to speak to? Which Xie Yingge? Master Xie? Er—Er Guniang left home quite a while ago. She said she had to attend the rehearsals for the 'White Rabbit'. You can try to find her at the Yueju Opera Theater."

A little discouraged, Mi Jingyao put down the phone; but then she wondered why Master Xie was not yet here if she had left home quite some time ago. The thought brightened her up: Master Xie must have expected Director He's call and had left home early to dodge that call; she was playing hide and seek with the director!

At a light brisk stage gait, Mi Jingyao returned to the rehearsal room and sang in stage speech style: "His Lordship Director He, Master Xie has gone missing! I have it from her servant that she left home very early this morning!"

With a light dig in the small of her back, Qin Yulou chided mildly: "Cut it out!" then turned a smiling face to Director He: "I know. Xie Yingge must have gone to the hospital to pick up the herbal medicine for her elder sister and you can never tell how long you have to wait in line in a hospital. Director He, I think we should continue the rehearsal."

Director He remained silent and expressionless. The grimness of his face accentuated the statuesque handsomeness of his features. In some corner of the room a soft sigh went up: "So like Ken Takakura!" and, as if blown by a spring breeze, a ripple of tittering went around the room. It was a time when the Japanese film *Across the River of Wrath* was showing to packed houses and the tough-guy image of its protagonist, played by Ken Takakura, made the latter into an idol among the girls.

Director He Shuye, barely over thirty years old, had risen to fame after successfully directing a number of experimental stage plays. Young Director He was one of those people who considered artistic creation as the prime mover of their lives. When he produced the experimental plays, he had had a few stars from the film and television industry join him, but he had not come across any celebrity as wayward as Xie Yingge. He was thinking at this moment that if he did not lay down the law now, there was no way he was going to make a success of this new edition of the "White Rabbit".

Qin Yulou silenced the girls' giggling with a look and led Director He out of the room before saying in a lowered voice: "Director, I'm so sorry. It's my fault that I didn't make it clear enough to Xie Yingge. I see that she is not yet accustomed to your style of work and I will talk to her. If neither of you would budge an inch and a standoff resulted, it would be demoralizing for the team. What do you think?"

Director He nodded thoughtfully, before vigorously throwing back the curly hair hanging over his forehead and eyes and loudly proclaiming: "The rehearsals will continue!"

Dah dah dah tay! The drum, the clappers and the small gong sounded together and the rehearsal went on.

The rehearsal of "Liu Zhiyuan Taken in as Son-in-Law by His General" had arrived at a point when Liu Zhiyuan and his general's daughter Yue Xiuying were singing to each other of their love. Shi Xiaotong, the young actor who played Miss Yue, went to the Provincial School of the Arts together with Feng Jianyue and Mi Jingyao. She had a good voice, crisp and sweet, but she didn't look good in costume. She was born with a concave facial profile and a high, prominent forehead as well as cheeks filled with baby fat. She looked quite pleasant when not in opera costume but once in costume and makeup she just didn't look right, although you couldn't pinpoint what detail was wrong no matter how you looked at her. Then there was the fact that she was a full ten centimeters shorter than Mi Jingyao. When they were admitted to the School of the Arts, those little girls were roughly of the same height. With the passage of time, when others grew taller like bamboo shoots in spring, she maintained her height; she graduated with the same height as when she entered the school. If she had chosen the male role type, she could have compensated for her shortness by wearing high-heeled boots, but her frail physical frame disqualified her for the young male role type.

It was a time when the Provincial Yueju Opera Troupe had been decimated in the ten years of the "Cultural Revolution". While a few first- and second-rank veteran actors were still around, after the dissolution of the troupe in that period, the third- and fourth-rank actors normally filling minor, walk-on parts either found jobs in other trades or went abroad and could never be called back into service. If the troupe needed to mount a lavish show, it couldn't even find all the extras to carry standards, beat gongs, hold umbrellas and deliver messages on stage. The Troupe decided to recruit a batch of recent girl graduates from the School of the Arts, who would play walk-on parts and minor roles to the more senior actors. They would continue to perfect their craft in the process and the Troupe would in due time discover the more talented ones to fill the void in the various role types.

Shi Xiaotong was among that batch. It didn't take long for the Troupe to discover her sweet voice and she was given assignments as background singer in many plays in addition to the usual walk-on parts.

For the rehearsal of the new recension of the "White Rabbit", Director He Shuye wrote four lines of opening remarks:

> A bloom has survived many a storm,
> Oh cruel have been the vagaries of fate.
> Liu Zhiyuan may be known in history,
> Li Sanniang lives on in popular song.

Director He directed Shi Xiaotong to sing this pithy prologue in a deep, melodious voice and in a thoughtful way so that when the curtains parted, it would immediately tug at the heartstrings of the audience.

Shi Xiaotong had been resigned to her fate. She could only blame it on her congenital deficiency. Once she had come to terms with it, she made sure she did her best with every song she sang as a background singer, and many of these songs became popular with the opera fans. Nobody had ever expected she would get a chance to perform on stage. The character of Yue Xiuying, expunged from the previous version of the "White Rabbit", was revived in the new recension. As Director He hoped to distance the image of this young lady of the general's household from that of Li Sanniang and as she had a few important arias to sing, the perspicacious Director He pointed with his golden finger and Shi Xiaotong was turned from Cinderella into a proud young mistress of the general's household!

Liu Zhiyuan goes off to the army and becomes a watchman at a border post. On a snowy day, he finds shelter from the cold under the eaves of a building. Yue Xiuying, General Yue's daughter happens to have her boudoir above where he stands. Young Lady Yue sees him shiver in the cold and feels compassion for him. His unusual aura strikes a chord in her heart and she throws her father's brocade battle dress down for him to keep warm. The two, one on the ground and the other at a higher level, speak of their mutual affection.

The alternate singing between Feng Jianyue and Shi Xiaotong was indeed impressive and a round of applause went up around the rehearsal room. The lines in Director He's face softened, who was visibly pleased. Someone whispered from the sidelines: "Ken Takakura has softened into Tang Guoqiang." The girls did their best to suppress their laughter.

There was not a word of praise from Director He, who on the contrary had some harsh words for Feng Jianyue: "When Liu Zhiyuan meets young Lady Yue, he sees, from the perspective of someone who has aspired to lift himself out of poverty and achieve great things, in her a good wind that will carry him to success. Therefore when young Lady Yue throws down the brocade dress as a token of affection, he should take the initiative and make a show of being solicitous and eager to please. You shouldn't turn him into a Zeng Rong of the play *Looking for the Husband*, who stays on his high horse and resists Yan Lanzhen's overtures of love."

Feng Jianyue had her own idea of how to play Liu Zhiyuan in this segment of the play and, emboldened by the fact that she and Brother Ah Ye were childhood playmates, defended herself: "Director, it is not so long ago that Liu Zhiyuan has vowed eternal love for Li Sanniang, and now I am supposed to flirt with young Lady Yue. Wouldn't that make me—Liu Zhiyuan—a heartless man no different from the likes of Chen Shimei and Wang Kui?"

He Shuye said, with a note of scorn in his voice: "When you analyze a character from that traditional moralistic point of view, you will not be able to probe deep into human nature. What differentiates the new recension from the previous version of the 'White Rabbit' is its more comprehensive interpretation of the character Liu Zhiyuan. Think carefully about it."

Feng Jianyue's further attempt to plead her case was stopped by Qin Yulou.

Qin Yulou was in private agreement with her student's view, but she could detect a hint of displeasure in Director He's expression and not wanting to antagonize the "rising-star" director in high demand brought on board by the Theater at a high price, she hastened to add: "In the rehearsal room, everyone listens to Director He. Artistic differences can be discussed after the rehearsals. Jianyue, you've finished your part of the rehearsal for now, so you can leave. Ah Yao, you're on."

It was Mi Jingyao's turn to play the important scene of "Giving Birth by the Millstone".

Mi Jingyao took a deep breath to calm herself and rooted for herself in her heart. Master Zhu had rearranged the aria to match her vocal capabilities, and she felt comfortable in the middle vocal range. She was not going to allow herself, under any circumstance, to be outdone by that Shi Xiaotong, who was normally given only walk-on parts and assigned to background singing!

While fortune smiles on Liu Zhiyuan, the happy second-time bridegroom who enjoys his first nuptial night with Yue Xiuying, the daughter of General Yue, his lawful wife Li Sanniang slaves away in the mill shed, in dire misery. The faithful Li Sanniang refuses to give in to the cavalier attempts by her brother and sister-in-law to force her to remarry into a wealthy family and prefers to continue "carrying three hundred buckets of water from the well during the day and turning the millstone all night till dawn". In a windy, snowy night Li Sanniang, alone in the mill shed, gives birth to a baby boy after biting through its umbilical cord!

Mi Jingyao gave a fine, intense performance, singing in the new *chidiao* tune at a senza misura with free beats characterized by fast instrumental music accompanying slow singing; the result was profoundly melancholy and hauntingly beautiful:

> Suddenly I am having unbearable, sharp pains in
>   my belly,
> Cold sweat drenches my body.
> All strength has drained out of me and I can barely
>   remain on my feet,
> Can it be that the baby, he, he, he is coming down—

This was accompanied by sound effects consisting of loud peals of thunder.

Qin Yulou breathed with relief and whispered to Director He: "Mi Jingyao's singing has improved a lot!"

Then Mi Jingyao sang the last two lines in senza misura with free beats:

> Alas I have no water, no scissors and nobody to help,
> I have no choice but to bite through the umbilical
>   cord myself—

This was the moment for sound effects to produce the crying of a baby, but a sharp rebuke was heard instead: "Stop—stop it now!"

All heads turned as one toward the source of the voice—at the back of the rehearsal room stood a tall, graceful figure in a stylish dress and of noble bearing!

The girls called out in confusion: "Master Xie!"

It was indeed Xie Yingge.

With all attention riveted on Li Sanniang and her baby son Yaoqilang, no one noticed when Xie Yingge had walked into the rehearsal room.

For a moment Director He was struck dumb by that brusque order barked by Xie Yingge. He had believed that he was the only one here who was entitled to shout out orders like that! Who could it be that sounded more imperious than he?

An overjoyed Qin Yulou, however, came toward her, saying: "Xiao Xie, you are finally here! When did you come in?"

Arching her finely painted eyebrows, Xie Yingge replied: "Hey, I've been sitting here watching the rehearsal for quite a while now!" With those words, she walked, her high heels clicking on the floor, to the center of the room, where she stared at Mi Jingyao and said, articulating each word: "Ah Yao, your singing was off again in this part! It should have been in the *xianxia* tune at the senza misura, why did you sing in the *chidiao* tune at the slow tempo?"

Mi Jingyao remained silent, biting her red lip with her fine teeth. She knew that if she opened her mouth to defend herself, she wouldn't be able to keep back her tears. In her eyes the teacher she had always respected, loved and felt indebted to had turned into an overbearing termagant at this moment!

Qin Yulou, who had no prior knowledge of the changes made to the music scores, turned to the main Chinese fiddle musician: "What happened? Did you misread the scores?"

The main Chinese fiddle musician held out the scores, so that they were right under her nose: "Manager Qin, I've played the music of the 'White Rabbit' for thirty years! How could I have misread the scores? These are new scores written by Master Zhu!"

Snapping the scores from his hand, Xie Yingge took a glance at them and said with a sneer: "What new scores? It's the same old tune, with a few additional instrumental arrangements, that's all. Who asked Master Zhu to change the music? Huh?"

Director He Shuye had by now understood why Xie Yingge was in such a towering rage. In deference to the fact that she was a pillar of the Theater and a renowned actor in the cultural circles of the provincial capital, Director He reined in his temper and said with elaborate civility: "Master Xie, due to the tight schedule we have not yet had time to consult with you about it. What happened was Mi Jingyao believed the senza misura was inappropriate for a supposedly exhausted Li Sanniang. So she consulted Master Zhu and it was decided to change the music for that segment to the *chidiao* tune and slow tempo. We were trying out for the first time this new aria in today's run-throughs. We are open to comments and suggestions."

Still fixing her stare on Mi Jingyao, Xie Yingge said: "Ah Yao, I know you. You have always worried that your voice would not go high enough, am I right? I have told you countless times that you must not shout; instead you should use proper breathing to lift your voice up. But you've resisted the hard work involved in training your voice. Hard training would have stretched your vocal range." Then she turned toward He Shuye and said with a restrained smile: "Director He, I seem to recall that when I rehearsed the scene of 'Giving Birth by the Millstone', you did not find the senza misura inappropriate. I believe that only the passionate, agitated senza misura is capable of doing full justice to the grief and indignation felt by Li Sanniang. In the *chidiao* tune and slow tempo, as sung by Ah Yao, the atmosphere clearly became flat ..."

All of a sudden, Mi Jingyao blurted out: "Master Xie, I was planning to add into that segment the long water sleeves sequence you were so famous for!" The moment the words were out of her mouth, even Mi Jingyao herself was shocked. She hadn't been aware that this idea had lurked in her subconscious for so long. When she studied Yueju opera in the Provincial School of the Arts, she'd already heard other teachers marvel at Xie Yingge's skill in maneuvering the long water sleeves. After her recruitment into the Provincial Yueju Opera Troupe, she eagerly asked Master Xie to teach her how to do the water sleeves sequence for that segment of the play, but Master Xie kept putting it off, saying it was not time yet, that the time was not ripe. In time she got the impression that Master Xie had no intention to teach her that sequence at all.

Xie Yingge, too, was startled by Mi Jingyao's sudden outburst. Li Sanniang's long water sleeves sequence in "Giving Birth by the Millstone" was precisely a chink in her armor! Xie Yingge couldn't believe that her hand-picked student Mi Jingyao, ever deferential to herself, would harbor such sinister designs to try to usurp her place on the strength of her ability to perform that sequence of dancing with the long water sleeves! She was suddenly so filled with indignation that her usually glib tongue was for once paralyzed.

Qin Yulou, on the other hand, got uncommonly excited and said, clapping her hands together: "Ah Yao, it's wonderful that you have the desire to tackle that. In the eyes of the public, Yueju opera nowadays is good at civil plays only and can't handle martial plays. You young people should have the courage to break out of that spell!" then she turned to Xie Yingge and said: "Xiao Xie! You've picked the right successor! If Ah Yao can master that water sleeve dance sequence, you will not have taken her under your wing in vain!"

Finally regaining the use of her tongue, Xie Yingge said with a strained smile: "I know Ah Yao aims high. I'm just worried she might be getting ahead of herself. In their years at the Theater, these girls have performed mostly civil plays and have probably forgotten what little basic martial and acrobatic training they had at the School of the Arts. Besides there are no video recordings of that water sleeve sequence I performed way back and I have no complete recollection of the details."

Qin Yulou was quick with an answer: "The Theater has in its archives stage photos of the performances in those years. I've seen at least a dozen taken from different angles of your graceful dance with the water sleeves. The sequence can be reconstructed on the basis of those photos. Ah Yao is still young, so she can surely pick up her old martial training after a few days of practice. I don't think there's a problem," then turning to He Shuye, she asked: "Director He, what do you think?"

Since agreeing to direct the "White Rabbit" for the Provincial Yueju Opera Theater, Director He Shuye had heard about Li Sanniang's water sleeve dance sequence in "Giving Birth by the Millstone". He had asked Xie Yingge if it was possible to replicate that feat of yesteryear on stage; he was not prepared for the reaction of Xie Yingge, who seemed dismissive of the water sleeve dance sequence everybody talked about in glowing terms. Rather, she thought that the "White Rabbit" was a civil play whose success was heavily dependent on singing prowess. In her opinion the gratuitous insertion of this water sleeve dance sequence in "Giving Birth by the Millstone" would appear awkward and unwarranted. Besides, thirty years had gone back since she last performed it, and she was no longer the same Xie Yingge of those years. She was no longer able even if she was willing to replicate the feat. Director He, never good at utilizing the stylized movements of traditional Chinese theater and deferential to the opinions of seasoned actors, decided to try another tack by looking for a solution in sound effects and stage sets.

After considering the question for a moment, Director He asked Mi Jingyao, looking her in the eye: "There is not much time left before the previews. Are you confident you can master it by then?"

The intense gaze of the director set Mi Jingyao's ears burning and her heart racing. She felt all the eyes zero in on her like so many arrows; she could hardly breathe. It was so much harder to exit than to enter the stage! The words "I can" were forcibly expelled from between her teeth and her tongue.

The walk-on actors started applauding, for no other reason than that they were so intrigued by Xie Yingge's water sleeve feat of almost mythical fame.

After a quick mental debate, Director He Shuye said: "Let's do this. We will have two contingency plans. Whether we add the water sleeve dance sequence or not depends on Mi Jingyao's progress in mastering it. To paraphrase a verse of antiquity, the egret, camouflaged by snow, becomes visible only when it launches into flight, and the parrot, hidden in the willow tree, gives itself away when it squawks." For once the very modernistic Director He waxed classical.

Mi Jingyao felt sweat pour down her spine.

Scene VI   Operatic Kaleidoscope

The crew of the "White Rabbit" had a rare day off, so that the director and principal actors of the play could go on the afternoon TV show "Pear Garden Glitterati" produced by *Operatic Kaleidoscope*.

As usual Deputy General Manager of the Theater Qin Yulou arrived very early at her office that morning. It occurred to her that the two young actors Feng and Mi would understandably be nervous before the camera given that this was the first time they attended a taping in a TV studio, and she thought she might as well take them ahead of time to the TV station to meet and get acquainted with the production team and the host so that there would be fewer hiccups during the taping. With that thought, she telephoned the host of "Pear Garden Glitterati" Ms. Ma Hui, who said she had thought the same thing, that the program was originally a special on Mi Jingyao alone; now that the older and the younger cast members were to appear on the show as a group, the script had been rewritten. She had yet to familiarize herself with the new script and therefore welcomed an opportunity to walk through it before the actual recording. It was agreed that the two sides would meet in a café near the TV station at 10:30 that morning. Ma Hui added: "I will call Director He and ask him to arrive on time."

Qin Yulou put down the phone and went to the dormitory of the Theater to get Feng Jianyue and Mi Jingyao, knowing that she would find the two still in bed because it was a rare half day of rest for them after rehearsing morning, afternoon and evening day in and day out.

The dormitory—a drab, crude, three-story building—was located in a dingy little alley adjacent to the Theater; it slept four to six to a room. On every floor there was a shared bathroom with toilet stalls and washstands. In the early 1980s when the Provincial Yueju Opera Theater was reinstated, it recruited several batches of young actors. To facilitate supervision, the Theater decreed that all unmarried staff and actors had to board at the dormitory and could go home only on national holidays and leave days. Feng Jianyue was Qin Yulou's last apprentice; she and Mi Jingyao had been recruited into the Troupe as a promising younger-generation actors in male and female roles combination to receive special attention and instruction, which included allowing the two of them to have a dorm room to themselves. Qin Yulou familiarly pushed open the door to her pupil's room and found Feng Jianyue in a practice outfit, stretching her muscles, with one leg supported on the bed frame and reciting histrionically, with script in hand: "Lady Yue, oh, Lady Yue! With my wife's vow of love still in my heart, how can we bare our hearts to each other in your boudoir?"

Qin Yulou said with a chuckle: "Jianyue, I don't think this line is in the script. Stop fooling around."

Seeing her teacher's unexpected entrance into the room, Feng Jianyue swung her leg off the bed frame and said with an unhappy face: "Master Qin, this part about Liu Zhiyuan being taken in as son-in-law by General Yue is really awkward for me. It is not so long ago that Liu Zhiyuan and Li Sanniang have vowed eternal love for each other and had a painful parting, and in the next moment he flirts with young Lady Yue. I just can't do it. My sense is that it is with great reluctance that Liu Zhiyuan marries young Lady Yue because he has fallen on hard times and has run out of options. But Director He doesn't agree with that view. He insists that I interpret Liu Zhiyuan as a heartless, fickle lowlife!"

Wagging a finger at her, Qin Yulou said: "You misunderstood Director He. My first reaction to his idea was similar to yours. In the 'White Rabbit' I and Xie Yingge performed for over thirty years, Liu Zhiyuan was a dedicated husband and a mensch. But after listening to Director He's explanation of the script, I began to see his point. The good and bad guys in the traditional plays of Yueju opera tend to be stereotyped. Director He intends to change all that; he wants to show human nature in its multiple dimensions and complexity and to elevate the aesthetic values in traditional plays. Your attention must have strayed when Director He gave those talks."

Feng Jianyue's ears burned. During those talks she was so caught up in the joy of the unexpected reunion with Brohter Ah Ye and so absorbed in being impressed by the masculine charm in every movement and gesture of the grown-up Ahye Ge that the message in Brother Ah Ye's class lecture never got through to her.

Watching and listening to her, Qin Yulou had some idea of her student's inner stirrings. She heaved a mental sigh: she is a girl after all. Since choosing the male role type, Feng Jianyue had taken to bobbing her hair, wearing slacks and even walking like a man, in long strides. Qin Yulou liked and approved of this favorite pupil of hers and hoped she could one day inherit her artistic mantle and build on her legacy. With that in mind, Qin Yulou had, of her own accord and gladly, ceded her part in the first half of the play to Feng Jianyue, giving her a chance to be introduced to the public. She said: "Jianyue, it looks like we need to sit down, you and I, some time to discuss this further. It is critical to have a general grasp of the character Liu Zhiyuan, and the way you portray the character in the first half will have an effect on my performance in the second half. I have confidence in you. Together we are going to create a Liu

Zhiyuan that stands out, adding a brand new artistic icon to the Yueju opera stage. Remember, however, that during the taping of the TV show this afternoon, we need to have the big picture in mind and try to be supportive of the thinking of the director. What do you say?"

Feng Jianyue nodded. It came as a surprise that her teacher happened to share her view, and she felt grateful for it: "Master Qin, don't worry. I won't cause Ahye Ge any embarrassment."

Glancing around the room out of the corner of her eyes, Qin Yulou asked: "Where is Mi Jingyao? I made an appointment with Ma Hui of the TV station. I'm going to take the two of you this morning to see her before the taping, a sort of warm-up so that you won't feel that nervous during the actual taping."

Feng Jianyue replied: "She must be in the practice room practicing her water sleeves dance sequence! Back when we were in school, Mi Jingyao barely scraped by in her 'mat skills'. With time running out, I'm sure she feels a lot of pressure. She has been getting up before dawn these days to bone up on her 'mat skills'."

Qin Yulou exhaled discreetly. She was all too aware of Mi Jingyao's weakness. When the Provincial Yueju Opera Theater went to the School of the Arts to recruit actors, it was Xie Yingge who discovered Mi Jingyao and took her under her tutelage. Qin Yulou reluctantly went along with the decision. To be fair, Mi Jingyao deserved high marks for her physical appearance and stage performance. She had a dozen one-act plays in her repertory in her years at the Theater and had quite a following among opera fans. But playing the lead in a traditional opera classic like the "White Rabbit" was a tough challenge for her. She said: "As long as she puts in the work, there is no reason she can't master the sequence. Go change and we will get her in the practice room."

Feng Jianyue said: "Why do I need to change? I'll go like this."

Qin Yulou chided: "No way. You look sloppy in this outfit. This is your first TV appearance and you will face an audience ten times, a hundred times, a thousand times larger than the audience in our theater. So you must pay attention to how you look."

Feng Jianyue took off her training outfit and changed into a white shirt and a pair of black oxford cloth slacks. Qin Yulou said, shaking her head: "No, no, no! Not black and white! You are not attending a funeral! Change into a skirt, preferably something in bright colors."

Feng Jianyue said in embarrassment: "Teacher, have you ever seen me in a skirt? I don't have one."

Qin Yulou searched her wardrobe and indeed found no skirt there. She then went through her suitcase and pulled out from its bottom a light olive green one-piece dress with a floral design. She draped the dress on Feng Jianyue and said: "It looks so pretty. Wear it!" Feng Jianyue said, shaking her head: "No, no! That dress is from years back. I've outgrown it because of my weight gain." Qin Yulou went through the suitcase again and finally found a blue print split skirt that didn't look too bad. She immediately had Feng Jianyue put it on. On the straight-backed, handsome Feng Jianyue, it had a quaint charm.

Teacher and pupil went to the practice to look for Mi Jingyao but found no sign of her there. Only Shi Xiaotong and another young actor Qian Xiaoxiao were busy practicing. Shi Xiaotong, wearing a makeshift pair of water sleeves, was doing a series of "sparrow hawk pirouettes", the sleeves whirling about her like a silver dragon flying through clouds and breathing mist. The chubby Qian Xiaoxiao was doing a sequence of front flips like a carp jumping through the air. Qin Yulou burst out: "Well done!"

At the sound, Shi Xiaotong and Qian Xiaoxiao stopped what they were doing and cried of one accord, panting: "Manager Qin!"

Qin Yulou asked: "Where is Mi Jingyao?"

Qian Xiaoxiao said, with a laugh she could hardly suppress: "My mother was tired, so she missed her practice today." This Qian Xiaoxiao had taken the place of Feng Jianyue in playing

Yaoqilang, the son of Li Sanniang, in the new version of the "White Rabbit". She was a walk-on martial actor, specializing in playing odd parts such as soldiers, bureaucrat's runners, man servants etc. The director picked her for the role of Yaoqilang because of her pleasant, chubby face well suited for a male child role part and because of her solid martial training. In the scene of "The Reunion at the Well", Yaoqilang had to perform very demanding jumps and somersaults as he pursued the rabbit in the hunt. Qian Xiaoxiao's personality was as cheery as her name Xiaoxiao, which meant "laugh laugh". She was happy playing walk-on parts and happy playing Yaoqilang. Since being assigned this part, she had taken to calling Mi Jingyao, who played Li Sanniang, "mother" both on stage and off.

Feeling the contagion of her happiness, Qin Yulou said with a smile, even though she felt frustrated: "If she's not here, where could she be?"

Qian Xiaoxiao cried with a shrug of her shoulders: "Oh daddy, would I have dared to ask mother where she was going? All I know is she went out dressed to the nines." Then casting a sidelong glance at Feng Jianyue, she said with a wink: "My daddy found me a stepmother. Maybe my mom is out finding a stepfather for me." Not only did Feng Jianyue and Mi Jingyao always play male and female roles as a pair and share a dorm room, they were also often seen in each other's company; co-workers jokingly called them a couple made for each other.

Suppressing a laugh, Qin Yulou gave the back of Qian Xiaoxiao's head a gentle slap and chided: "Are you confusing art and life? I need to find Mi Jingyao in a hurry."

Qian Xiaoxiao said, putting out her tongue: "I really don't know where she is."

Shi Xiaotong interjected: "Mi Jingyao said since we had a day off she'd made plans to meet with a friend."

Qin Yulou said with a slight frown: "She's really taking it easy." Glancing at her watch, she said resignedly: "Jianyue, we are not going to wait for her. Let's go." Then she said to Qian

Xiaoxiao with a chuckle: "When you see your mother, ask her to come immediately to the TV station and ask for Ma Hui. Don't forget!"

Shi Xiaotong in the meantime had started to whirl her water sleeves through the air. As if reminded of something, Qin Yulou turned around and asked casually: "Why is Xiaotong practicing the water sleeves also? Am I to understand that the young Lady Yue, daughter of the general, will dance a water sleeves sequence opposite Li Sanniang as well?"

Shi Xiaotong pulled in her water sleeves but could not immediately answer because of the panting. Qian Xiaoxiao answered for her: "My mom wants my stepmom to help her with the water sleeves dance sequence. Xiaotong was top of the class in martial skills at the School of the Arts."

By this time Shi Xiaotong had recovered her breath and said: "The martial coach comes only every few days, so I thought I would learn it first and then show Mi Jingyao how to do it."

Qin Yulou, mindful of the fact that since its reinstatement, the Yueju Opera Theater had in the past decade mostly staged civil plays, had contracted with a martial coach of the Provincial Beijing Opera Theater for the express purpose of helping with the rehearsal of Li Sanniang's water sleeves dance sequence and Yaoqilang's hunt scenes. The martial coach was simultaneously helping several theaters and troupes with their rehearsals and therefore was unable to attend the "White Rabbit" rehearsals every day. She said: "Very good, Xiaotong will help Mi Jingyao as much as possible. Time is pressing! But, Xiaotong, your Yue Xiuying is a newly added part, so you should not take it lightly."

Shi Xiaotong responded merely with a faint smile, like a deep lake whose surface was lightly wrinkled with only a few ripples even when undercurrents boiled underneath.

When Qin Yulou and her favorite pupil Feng Jianyue arrived at the café by the TV station, they saw, through the tinted brown glass, Mi Jingyao and the TV host Ma Hui sitting across from each other, sipping tea and chatting amicably. With a drawn-out exclamation of surprise "hey—", Qin Yulou pushed the door and entered the café. She jabbed a finger at Mi Jingyao, saying: "You beat us to it. We were looking everywhere for you back at the Theater!"

Arching her perfectly spaced eyebrows, Mi Jingyao said: "Ah Yue, I told you before I left that I had some business to attend to at a TV station. Did you forget to tell Manager Qin about it?"

Dumbfounded, Feng Jianyue stared at her painstakingly made up face and half asked herself: "Did, did you really tell me? How come I have no recollection of it at all?"

Mi Jingyao said, letting escape a chuckle: "Manager Qin, Ah Yue has turned into a regular Liu Zhiyuan! If I had said it as Li Sanniang, she would most certainly have remembered."

Feng Jianyue scratched her head in embarrassment, her silence letting the wrongful accusation stand. In her long partnership with Mi Jingyao, she had become accustomed to humoring her like a gentleman.

After greeting Ma Hui, Qin Yulou said: "Jingyao, how did you find out Ma Hui and I were going to meet here?"

Mi Jingyao said with a laugh: "I had an appointment with the producer of an entertainment TV channel. They were offering me a role in a sitcom. And it so happened that Ma Hui saw me and dragged me away from them."

Qin Yulou got into a tizzy and said: "Jingyao, you have a part with a lot of stage time in the new 'White Rabbit'. How can you juggle it with a sitcom role? You shouldn't get distracted."

Ma Hui said with a laugh: "That's why I wrested her away from them."

As a matter of fact Mi Jingyao already started playing a role in a sitcom on an entertainment channel a few years ago. When she got Li Sanniang's role in the "White Rabbit", she consulted the director of the sitcom for advice. The sitcom director was of the view that it was a win-win situation. If Mi Jingyao shot to fame in the Yueju opera circle, it would have a celebrity advertising effect on his sitcom. So he had asked the producer of *Operatic Kaleidoscope* to do a special interview of Mi Jingyao to be aired on the "Pear Garden Glitterati" program. Mi Jingyao had previously received from Ma Hui the outlines of the interview and had quietly prepared her answers and learned them by heart. Little did she expect the sudden change of plans, whereby "Pear Garden Glitterati" would do a group interview of the cast of the new "White Rabbit" instead of an exclusive interview of her.

Mi Jingyao was naturally upset. She wondered who the sneak was that worked behind the scenes to undermine her. Her first suspicion fell on her partner Feng Jianyue, for she knew that Feng Jianyue set great store by the part of Liu Zhiyuan and hoped to make a difference in her interpretation of the character. She would naturally hate to see Li Sanniang steal the thunder from Liu Zhiyuan. Besides, back at the School of the Arts the actor in the female role that regularly played opposite Feng Jianyue was not Mi Jingyao. When the Provincial Yueju Opera Theater came to the School of the Arts to recruit new blood, it was Mi Jingyao who was handpicked by Master Xie Yingge; Feng Jianyue acknowledged her as her ideal opposite only because this would help her get into the Yueju Opera Theater. But then it occurred to her that Feng Jianyue was not known to have any close friends at the TV station; would she really have the leverage to cause her grief? So her suspicion turned now to Director He Shuye. It was common knowledge at the Theater that Director He Shuye and Feng Jianyue had been childhood playmates; it would have been understandable if he had tried to help her career in any way he could. But from careful observation, Mi Jingyao found out that the feeling of camaraderie was one-sided, on Feng Jianyue's part; most of the time Director He treated all actors in the project even-handedly. Moreover, she vaguely sensed a special feeling for herself in Director He—the kind of attention a man usually reserved for a woman. She had to discount the possibility that Director He was secretly trying to undercut her. Then it struck her: there was a person who had the leverage to persuade the TV producer to change the plans for taping the segment on "Pear Garden Glitterati" and who had exhibited an abrupt change in her attitude toward her, becoming more critical and wary of her. She was thinking of her beloved teacher Xie Yingge! At this moment even saying this name sent a chill down her spine. Whoever makes you can break you too! It's so true! If Xie Yingge hadn't taken her as a pupil at a critical juncture, she probably wouldn't have been taken on board by the Provincial Yueju Opera Theater given her mediocre grades at the School of the Arts. But the teacher who was once so eager to help advance her young career had turned into an insuperable obstacle to her rise to stardom!

In the days since Mi Jingyao learned of the change in plans for the taping of her interview to be aired on "Pear Garden Glitterati", her obsession with the matter dampened her enthusiasm for singing and the water sleeves practice. On this rare day of leave, she arrived early at the TV station and sought out the producer of the entertainment channel that she knew and asked him to arrange a meeting with Ms. Ma Hui, the host of "Pear Garden Glitterati". Producing the outline of interview previously received from the TV station, she asked tactfully: "Ms. Ma, should I still base my answers on the questions listed on this sheet?" Well aware of where she was coming from, Ma Hui told her with equal tact: "The change in plans was made by the leadership with the big picture in mind, the implementation depends on each and every individual involved. You can answer the questions in the way you've prepared; only there has been a change in the order of the questions." Mi Jingyao quietly resolved to seize the opportunity, when it was her turn to speak, to show to advantage, in the limited time allotted to her, her shining qualities, so that she would leave a deep impression on the viewers. This valuable lesson was one of the rewards of spending time doing sitcoms for the entertainment channel.

It was during this conversation with Ma Hui that Qin Yulou and Feng Jianyue arrived.

Ma Hui, host of the "Pear Garden Glitterati" program of the *Operatic Kaleidoscope* series, had delicate features. Every time Qin Yulou saw her, she would observe: "Xiao Ma, you possess such assets! Why don't you join us at the Yueju Opera Theater? You would be a star no matter what role type you picked—virtuous lady, maiden, vivacious young female, even young male!" And Ma Hui would reply cheerfully: "That's a great idea, Manager Qin! Now you are formally my Shi Fu (master). Only, I hope Feng Jianyue won't hate me for stealing the thunder from her!" It was naturally said in jest, but the appellation stuck and Ma Hui would call her Shi Fu whenever she met Qin Yulou.

Ma Hui stood up and invited them to take a seat. Then she said with a smile: "Shi Fu, and Shi Jieh (fellow pupil with greater seniority)! What would you like? Juice, coffee or milk tea? Feel free to order whatever you like!"

Feng Jianyue said in embarrassment: "Master Ma, how can you call me Shi Jieh?"

Ma Hui replied: "I am Manager Qin's pupil too. Since you became her pupil before me, it's only right that I call you Shi Jieh." And all three laughed.

Qin Yulou ordered a kiwi juice and Feng Jianyue a milk tea with red beans. Ma Hui ordered in addition a fruit salad and cake.

Qin Yulou was thirsty from the anxiety of looking for Mi Jingyao and the stress of rushing to the meeting. Sipping off almost half a glass of her juice at one draught, she asked: "Ma Hui, you said Director He would be here on time. Where's he?"

Ma Hui said casually: "He probably won't make it today. He is in such demand. I've heard that he was needed in Shanghai to collaborate on a play being billed as a National Day special presentation. There's no need to wait for him."

Feng Jianyue was a little disappointed. During rehearsals, she was always seen in a sweat-soaked practice suit by Brother Ah Ye or reverently received instructions from him in her role of Liu Zhiyuan, a young scholar down on his luck. On this one day out of a thousand, when she was all dolled up in anticipation of displaying her youthful female charm to Brother Ah Ye, he failed to show up! Her spirits sank and she bent her head over her milk tea, sipping it mechanically.

After a hesitation, Mi Jingyao asked: "Manager Qin, why hasn't Master Xie come with you?"

Qin Yulou said: "Don't you know already your teacher's ways? She is a frequent guest on *Operatic Kaleidoscope*. She is never late for the actual taping of the program, am I right, Ma Hui?"

Ma Hui nodded: "I already express-mailed the interview outline to Master Xie yesterday." She produced copies of the outline and distributed one to each of them: "There was only a change of order. The listed questions are only for the purpose of drawing you out. The guests will be able to make impromptu remarks, add details and present different views. Controversy spices up the conversation and the order is not sacrosanct. Our program is aimed at presenting to the public the charisma and personalities of the older- and younger-generation actors; the format is quite free. Shi Fu, you are an old hand at this, right?"

Qin Yulou said: "Ma Hui, why don't you run through the main points for us? A trackless trolley still needs to be guided by traffic rules."

Ma Hui obliged: "Naturally the show is centered on the 'White Rabbit'. Guests will talk about their take on the characters in the play and how they are going to portray them. Xiao Feng and Xiao Mi can also talk about how they feel about playing lead parts for the first time ... oh—if the teachers have different takes on the characters from their pupils, they should feel free to express them."

Qin Yulou nodded and said with a laugh: "Ma Hui, you are trying to instigate a civil war between students and teachers!"

Feng Jianyue had by this time read through the outline, which listed only two questions for her. She already had an idea how to respond to them, so she felt reassured. Joining the conversation between Ma Hui and her teacher, she asked: "If my take on the character differs from that of the director, am I free to express it?"

Ma Hui clapped her hands together and said: "Of course you are! It will make the show more interesting!"

Mi Jingyao seemingly had it all figured out, appearing to look down at the outline in her hands and repeatedly rehearsing in her head what she was going to say on the show while her ears did not miss a word that was being said by the others. When she heard Feng Jianyue's question, she couldn't help thinking with a mental sneer: Feng Jianyue is too naïve. Just because you and Director He were childhood playmates, you think you can get away with anything. Don't you know that the person an actor can least afford to antagonize is the director? But she kept her own counsel, relishing the idea of seeing Feng Jianyue make a fool of herself.

Ma Hui took her time savoring the chrysanthemum Pu'er tea and broke the silence after twenty minutes: "You should have all finished reading the outline. What do you think of it? We can do a dry run and do some fine-tuning if we find problems. I will read off the questions listed in the outline and you can give abbreviated answers, just the gist will do."

The others duly complied and the rehearsal started, following the order of the listed questions, skipping those to do with Xie Yingge and He Shuye. It went smoothly, with some tips from Ma Hui concerning tone and phrasing and then they went through it a second time.

Soon it was approaching noon time; Ma Hui said, after phoning the studio: "The morning taping of *Travel World* was just completed and the crew is clearing out the studio. Why don't we grab a bite quickly and head there? There's the pre-taping makeup to consider."

Mi Jingyao and Feng Jianyue cried almost in unison: "My stomach is full with all that beverage, there's no room for food!" Ma Hui said: "You need some food. For a one-hour show, the taping session normally lasts three to four hours."

Spaghetti and sandwiches were ordered. Ma Hui said with a laugh: "Shi Fu, sorry for the meagerness of the fare today. When you come back from a triumphant tour, I'll throw a proper celebratory party for you."

Qin Yulou said: "It's you we should invite to a celebration in token of our thanks for a successful tour."

With Feng Jianyue and Mi Jingyao in tow, Qin Yulou followed Ma Hui through the security check at the entrance of the TV station building. As they made their way toward the studio, they ran into the invited guests who just got off the *Travel World* show in the hall outside the makeup room. Both parties halted in their steps due to the narrowness of the corridor.

Mi Jingyao was the first to cry out: "Yu Qing'e! You are here for a taping too?" and gripped the other's hand in a show of intimacy.

The girl appeared to be bashful, slightly shorter, thinner and swarthier than Mi Jingyao, with a small oval face and a well-proportioned body. While not dazzling in her beauty like Mi Jingyao, hers was a beauty more evocative of "crystal clear streams and lush hills", and "a gentle breeze caressing a moonlit landscape extending as far as the eye can see". Seeming not inclined to engage Mi Jingyao in further conversation, she made a curt affirmative "mm" and withdrew her hand from Mi Jingyao's grip.

Feng Jianyue called out sheepishly: "Qing'e …"

With a crack of her lips into a shadow of a smile, Yu Qing'e responded rigidly: "How are you, Feng Jianyue!" and moved her broody eyes away.

The muscles in Feng Jianyue's cheeks suddenly became taut, creating an expression that froze between a smile and a crying grimace. She wished she could disappear through the floor.

Qin Yulou also recognized Yu Qing'e, who had been one of the top performing students at the School of the Arts way back! In those days Yu Qing'e had caught the admiring eye of Xie

Yingge, who had several times impressed upon Qin Yulou her wish to take her under her wing as a pupil in the next recruitment campaign of the Provincial Yueju Opera Theater. But for some reason she no longer found favor with Xie Yingge, who chose instead Mi Jingyao as her pupil. After her graduation from the School of the Arts, Yu Qing'e returned to her home town, where she started working for an entertainment production company operated by the tourism bureau of the town. When Qin Yulou learned of this, she truly felt sorry for her.

Observing Yu Qing'e closely, Qin Yulou found her darker and prettier than when she was an adolescent. She still wore no makeup and still had that distant, unfocused look in her handsome eyes, in which an unsuspected eloquence and intelligence could be glimpsed. Qin Yulou was well aware that the main activities of this kind of entertainment production companies under local tourism bureaus consisted of performances of song and dance numbers with local color at sightseeing spots to promote tourism. With an involuntary sigh, she asked: "Yu Qing'e, are you still singing Yueju opera nowadays? You shouldn't let the skills you acquired as a teenager go to waste!"

Yu Qing'e's face was now a mask of a lady-in-waiting of antiquity, with lifeless eyes and a frozen shadow of a smile. It was enough to send a chill down one's spine.

A middle-aged lady next to her held out her right hand with an ingratiating smile: "Master Qin, my name is Zhang. I am the branch party secretary of the entertainment production company." Taking Qin Yulou's hand into hers, she added: "I have enjoyed watching Master Qin and Master Xie play opposite each other since I was a child. Master Xie's familial home is in our town and you have a large following in our town!"

Qin Yulou said out of politeness: "Oh, Party Secretary Zhang! It's a pleasure to meet you." Then she added with a smile: "Your company has a treasure in Yu Qing'e. She is an outstanding professional. You should put her talent and strengths to good use."

Party Secretary Zhang cast an affectionate, happy glance at her favorite performer and said: "Master Qin, you need not worry. Last year we launched a Yueju opera troupe in response to market demand, and Yu Qing'e was the natural choice to become its lead actor in the female role. While we cannot compare to the Provincial Yueju Opera Troupe, we do have our strengths. Our town is a tourist mecca, with the number of tourists increasing almost daily. We have collected folk legends associated with the many sightseeing spots and have created a series of shows and plays based on those tales. We put on the performances right at the tourist spots on a portable stage, one in the morning and one in the afternoon. They have proved very popular with the visitors. Frankly we are still experimenting and exploring, but the *Travel World* series of the TV station wanted us to share our experience with the viewing public. I wish we had more to share."

An idea flashed through Qin Yulou's mind. With the rise of a dizzying array of entertainment forms in recent years, Yueju opera, the most important traditional opera genre of the province, had seen its market share steadily erode. As deputy general manager in charge of business development at the Theater, she had racked her brain and lost sleep and appetite to find a way to stem the decline. Now, much to her surprise, a Yueju opera troupe of an entertainment company of a small town was able to blaze a unique path toward the genre's revival. She said: "Party Secretary Zhang, would you be amenable to the idea of having creative staff from the Provincial Yueju Opera Theater visit you to learn from your experience?"

Party Secretary Zhang, much flattered, said: "Master Qin, you put it so graciously! We certainly would love to have teachers of the Provincial Yueju Opera Theater come down to our company to give us your valuable opinions on our work!" then remembering something, she added: "Oh yes, we've recently written a playlet for Yu Qing'e with the title *Xishi Returns Home*. It is said that the Tiaoluo Creek that runs north south across our town was connected with the Yijian River by which Xishi escaped from the Kingdom of Wu a thousand years ago. The Guishi (Return of Xishi) Bridge in the north of the town is where Fan Li met the returning Xishi a millennium ago and sailed off with her on a small boat into a misty rain. A mock antique open-air opera stage erected by the town government next to Guishi Bridge is nearing completion. As soon as the stage is ready, *Xishi Returns Home* will be performed there. You experts and professionals at the Provincial Yueju Opera Theater are cordially and respectfully invited to attend and give your valuable opinions."

Glancing around at Mi Jingyao and Feng Jianyue, Qin Yulou found them unusually quiet. Her previous enthusiasm doused, Mi Jingyao appeared listless and couldn't wait to get out of there; Feng Jianyue in the meantime contemplated the toes of her shoes, much like a primary school pupil receiving a rebuke from a teacher. Turning her head back, Qin Yulou said with a smile: "Party Secretary Zhang, we expect to interact more with you and we will learn from each other's experiences."

At the door of the makeup room, Ma Hui the host called out to them: "Shi Fu, I'm sure you have a lot to talk about in the future. We have a tight schedule and the makeup artists have been waiting for you!"

The two groups started off in opposite directions.

Feng Jianyue fell back to the rear of her group by deliberately slowing down; when Yu Qing'e was abreast of her, she opened her mouth to say something, but Yu Qing'e, taking a fast, long stride past her, did not give her a chance to say it. They went past each other like two planets in different orbits, never meant to cross paths.

Scene VII The Tragic Romance of the Butterfly Lovers

Upon graduation from the School of the Arts, the students took jobs in different parts of China. After all these years, Feng Jianyue still dreaded facing Yu Qing'e. That aloof, distancing, despising, scornful look in Yu Qing'e's eyes had been indelibly seared into her mind.

They were so young then at the School of the Arts. Yu Qing'e and Feng Jianyue were considered by all the teachers as the best actors' combination in male and female roles, and Yu Qing'e was the top-performing student in the class of vivacious young female role of the Yueju opera program. She didn't normally stand out in a crowd, because she wore no makeup and dressed simply. But once she was in opera costume and planted her graceful self at center stage, she shone and radiated charm. She was also born with a crisp singing voice that sounded like "cascading spring water washing over rocks of jade", rising and falling effortlessly, orotund and melodious. She was favorably compared to the then famous actor in the female role Xie Yingge.

The recruiters came to the School of the Arts that year from the Provincial Yueju Opera Theater with the express purpose of picking the best students playing male and female roles to be groomed as the Theater's next generation of performers. Everyone at the school, from the brass to the students, was certain that Feng Jianyue and Yu Qing'e were unquestionably the top picks. But to everyone's wide-eyed and open-mouthed amazement, at Xie Yingge's suddenly arranged discipleship ceremony, the pupil she took under her wing turned out to be Mi Jingyao, uncommonly good-looking but mediocre in all else that mattered for her craft!

In that period all students in the Yueju opera program were in intensive rehearsal for their graduation performances, knowing the importance of these, given the fact that dozens of Yueju opera troupes and entertainment production companies from across the nation, especially from the Jiang'nan region, were converging on the school to recruit talents they needed.

Feng Jianyue and Yu Qing'e chose the scene of "Meeting on the Balcony" of the Yueju opera classic *Butterfly Lovers* as their graduation performance number. They knew that this was a popular act in a popular play that had been performed by many and therefore it would be a tough challenge to differentiate themselves and break out of the pack. But they were fearless; they intended to score a surprise win against the odds on the strength of their youth, their stage appearance in costume and their good voice. The complex changes of tunes and the wildly swinging passions involved in the alternate singing between Liang Shanbo and Zhu Yingtai in "Meeting on the Balcony" afforded them the chance to excel and shine. The two rehearsed day and night, repeatedly and thoughtfully going over every sung line and every move and motion to achieve the best effect.

One day at noontime Qin Yulou found Feng Jianyue in the student cafeteria of the School of the Arts and took her to a small partition in the faculty cafeteria on the second floor, where she ordered three or four dishes, saying she was rewarding her for the hard work she'd put into rehearsing these days. Feng Jianyue was so surprised by the unexpected honor that her speech became temporarily incoherent. At the time Qin Yulou was a top actor in the young male role at the Provincial Yueju Opera Theater and regularly played opposite the famous actor in female role Xie Yingge. She was also the artistic adviser of the recruiting team from the Provincial Yueju Opera Theater; there was no lack of people who tried to get into her good graces without any luck. Feng Jianyue had chosen the male role type when she was accepted by the School of the Arts and had always dreamed of the day she could be accepted by Qin Yulou as pupil to pursue the Qin school of Yueju opera art. And now the teacher she idolized was sitting across from her and even smilingly filled her glass with orange juice! Her breathing grew irregular with excitement and nervousness.

Qin Yulou first asked Feng Jianyue about her choice for the graduation performance and how her rehearsing was going. Feng Jianyue answered each question reverentially. Qin Yulou then mentioned her intention to find a disciple and groom her to be a successor to take over the mantle of the Qin school of Yueju opera art in the future and asked with a smile if Feng Jianyue was willing to be that pupil. Feng Jianyue uttered a string of enthusiastic yeses. Could her dear wish have been granted so easily, just like that? Could the gods have favored her with such unbelievable good fortune? She wondered if she was dreaming all this.

Then Qin Yulou broached the real subject of the meeting. Qin Yulou said, articulating each word as if reciting a line: "By now everyone must have learned that Mi Jingyao has been taken in as pupil-disciple by Xie Yingge. That means her recruitment by the Provincial Yueju Opera Theater is a foregone conclusion. What remains to be done is finding an actor in young male role to play opposite her." Qin Yulou paused significantly and looked Feng Jianyue in the eye: "I highly recommended you!"

Feng Jianyue still felt thirsty and tight-throated even after downing a glassful of orange juice. She managed, with some effort, to spit out: "Thank you, Master Qin!"

With a sigh and a resigned expression, Qin Yulou said: "Ah Yue! That means you can no longer do 'Meeting on the Balcony' with Yu Qing'e for the graduation performances. Mi Jingyao has chosen *Looking for the Husband* for her graduation performance, why don't you play Zeng Rong opposite her in that number?"

Feng Jianyue was dumbfounded, and remained speechless for a long while.

First of all she'd have a hard time explaining such an abrupt, major change to Yu Qing'e. In the four years in the School of the Arts, she and Yu Qing'e were not only a dream team on stage but were also as close as sisters in everyday life. Although several months older than Yu Qing'e, Feng Jianyue was by nature sloppy and inattentive to details and niceties and often it fell to the younger Yu Qing'e to take care of her in daily life. On the other hand Yu Qing'e had a reserved, introverted temperament and lacked social graces, and it was Feng Jianyue who, like a man, helped and protected her in social interaction. Their school mates often jokingly referred to them as a "loving couple", with Feng Jianyue being dubbed "Liang Shanbo" and Yu Qing'e "Zhu Yingtai"—the lovers in the classic *Butterfly Lovers*.

But at this moment the door of the Provincial Yueju Opera

Theater was thrown wide open for her and her idol Master Qin Yulou was eagerly awaiting her reply. Did she have the courage or the heart to say no to Qin Yulou or the Provincial Yueju Opera Theater?

Qin Yulou was keenly aware of her inner struggle. She poured her another glass of orange juice and said in a deliberate tone: "You don't need to discuss this with Yu Qing'e. The school administration will talk to her. Besides, the Provincial Yueju Opera Theater is looking to recruit not only the best actors in male and female roles, but also new blood in all role types, including supernumeraries. If Yu Qing'e is interested, she has other opportunities there too, and given her qualifications and abilities, she still has a chance to become an outstanding actor in the female role."

These words brought much relief to Feng Jianyue, who finally steeled her heart against any thought of contrition and said haltingly: "Master Qin, in two days the school will start dress rehearsals for the graduation performances, which means Mi Jingyao and I will have no time to rehearse …"

Qin Yulou patted the back of her hand: "Don't worry. You go ahead and do the dress rehearsal. You still have a few days before the performances. Besides, you've been practicing *Looking for the Husband* since you came to the school, so all you need is run through the script a few times with Mi Jingyao. Since the Theater has already made the decision to recruit you and Mi Jingyao, you can quit worrying about how your performance comes out." Raising her glass, Qin Yulou said, beaming at Feng Jianyue: "So the deal is done then!"

Feng Jianyue also raised her glass. She wondered why the half full glass weighed so much. Ka-cha! Why did it sound so jarring when they clinked their glasses together? Her prayer had been answered. When other school mates were fretting about their future after graduation, she could sit back and relax because her future was already assured. She should be happy and raise her glass in celebration; instead she felt like crying and a sadness and queasy feeling caused a lump in her throat.

All day Feng Jianyue was filled with anxiety and apprehension and the day felt like an eternity. She had to maintain her usual happy-go-lucky, nonchalant exterior to hide the interior cauldron boiling over with anxiety and apprehension. These days she was even more inseparable from Yu Qing'e than usual, following her everywhere, as if fearing Yu Qing'e would evaporate in the blink of an eye. This caused Yu Qing'e to taunt her: "Don't tell me you've become love-sick like Liang Shanbo!"

Finally the day of the dress rehearsals for the graduation performances was here, following much agonizing on the part of Feng Jianyue. Preparations were in full swing; students were practicing martial and acrobatic movements or in rehearsal to the accompaniment of the sound of clappers, drums and string instruments. Feng Jianyue wished that the matter raised by Qin Yulou the other day in a small banquet room of the faculty cafeteria would turn out to be a fairy tale and would not materialize.

"Meeting on the Balcony", the graduation performance prepared by Feng Jianyue and Yu Qing'e, was placed at the end of the evening's performance schedule as a piece de resistance. In the afternoon they watched performances by other school mates; toward evening the two of them went to a small noodle place outside the school for a beef vermicelli soup and some pan-fried pork and scallion mini buns, after which they entered the make-up room to paint their faces, do their hair and apply the collar liners. Just as they got ready to put on their costumes, a deputy director of the school's counseling and guidance office came rushing in and spirited Yu Qing'e away.

Feng Jianyue's heart sank like a rock tumbling down a precipice—what she feared most had happened! At that moment she had a visceral hatred for that deputy director of the counseling and guidance office as if she were the Councilor Zhu in the *Butterfly Lovers* who callously dashed all hopes of a happy marriage between Liang Shanbo and Zhu Yingtai! In no mood to put on her boots and costume, she sat like a figurine made of wood or clay, in shock, as Liang Shanbo would look, moments after he had just learned that Zhu Yingtai had been promised for marriage into a prominent family instead of to him. She tried to picture, her heart aching, what would happen when Yu Qing'e came back to the room. Would she reproach her, ignore her, throw a tantrum or refuse to go on stage? She was prepared for an unmitigated fiasco as far as the night's performance of "Meeting on the Balcony" was concerned!

"Cha Tay—dah dah dah dah ... Tay!" The clappers sounded, heralding the opening of the play selection preceding their performance. The backstage manager rushed in and prodded her: "Feng Jianyue, why are you still not in your costume! You will be on next! And where is Yu Qing'e? Where is she at this crucial moment?"

Feng Jianyue opened her mouth but no sound came out of it. All of a sudden someone behind her in the shadow said: "I am right here!"

When Feng Jianyue looked over her shoulder, a shiver ran through her: her Zhu Yingtai had returned, without being noticed, to the make-up room sometime and was already in full costume, standing there in all her grace!

"My good sister ..." Feng Jianyue called despondently in her gut; she did not have the courage to look at her face but shot a quick glance at her. She was more beautiful, lovely and charming than usual this evening. She couldn't see clearly her real expression hidden beneath the thick face paint, except for a flicker of her eyelashes that revealed two bright burning eyes, so bright that they struck terror in her heart.

They did not have time to talk. After they were all dressed up, the stage director led them to the wings to wait for their turn to enter the stage.

Usually when they played opposite each other in a play, they would exchange words of encouragement while waiting in the wings for their cue to enter the stage, but at this moment neither spoke. Yu Qing'e stood in front of the tab and Feng Jianyue stood behind it; the two, separated only by a curtain, seemed more like two complete strangers across a time warp.

The actors in the preceding performance made their curtain call amid applause and no sooner had the program announcer called out the title of the next number "Meeting on the Balcony" than the audience erupted in thunderous applause, without even waiting to hear the actors' names.

To the accompaniment of the sad, melodious voice of the background singer, a pensive Zhu Yingtai, played by Yu Qing'e, entered the stage at a deliberate pace.

> Meeting Liang Shanbo again after a long separation,
> I am happy but sad at the same time.
> I'm happy to see him again,
> But sad because I've been forced to marry another
>   man ...

Liang Shanbo was supposed to enter the stage in high spirits, but it was hard for Feng Jianyue to cheer up. Her smile was worse than a crying grimace.

> I see him in high spirits come to meet Sister Nine,
> And I have no choice but to ascend to the balcony
>   feigning gaiety ...

Repressing her sorrow and pain and burdened with a strong sense of guilt, Zhu Yingtai avowed haltingly: "By my father's orders, I have been promised for marriage to the Ma family—!"

Feng Jianyue read in Yu Qing'e's lines a sharp rebuke intended for her: you betrayed my trust; you allow personal gain to obscure your sense of fairness and you sell out a friend to advance your career! She sang, wincing from shame: "Yingtai, how are you—in Changting you acted as your own matchmaker, saying you had in your family a little Sister Nine whose hand I could ask for in marriage. Now that Sister Nine turned out to be none other than yourself, I can't understand why you have been betrothed to Ma Wencai?" This was a fitting rebuke from Yu Qing'e to her!

Zhu Yingtai, who had no control over her own fate, said consolingly, against her own heart: "Brother Liang, you'll find another good woman to marry ..." Without waiting for her to finish her sentence, Liang Shanbo categorically rejected her disingenuous advice: "I will not love another woman, even if she were a fairy lady from the ninth heaven!"

Feng Jianyue wished she had rejected as categorically as Liang Shanbo the offer made by Master Qin the other day. Then she wouldn't have had to endure the reproach of her conscience, the pain and the shame that had tormented her these days. But she had to admit to herself that if the same thing happened again, she still would not have the courage to refuse Master Qin!

"Thinking of You" is the most touching, the most classic aria in "Meeting on the Balcony". Disregarding the feudalist taboos against public displays of intimacy between man and woman, Liang Shanbo and Zhu Yingtai hugged each other and looked lovingly into each other's teary eyes as they poured out their hearts—

> My good sister, thinking of you, I lose my head, my sleep and appetite.
> Brother Liang, thinking of you I find food and drink tasteless.
> ...
> My good sister, I've been thinking of you, every day into the late night.
> Brother Liang, I've been thinking of you, every night until the rooster crows.
> ...

As Liang Shanbo held Zhu Yingtai's hands in a tight grip, Feng Jianyue felt her heart give a lurch against her ribcage: Yu

Qing'e's hands were as cold as two chunks of ice! Feng Jianyue was now more afraid than before to look her in the eye, in the certain knowledge that those eyes must be ten times, a hundred, nay, a thousand times colder than her hands. She was reduced to fixing her eyes on the pearls and jade-studded headdress on her head. The glitter and glare of the dangling strands of crystal beads in the intense spotlights trained on the stage gave her a splitting headache. When she barely managed to finish singing the last verse, her voice had been strained and cracked to pieces:

I've been thinking of you, thinking of you...

With final resolve, Zhu Yingtai pushed Brother Liang away:

We are destined not to be man and wife in this life—

This line sung by Yu Qing'e, orotund and melancholy, enough to "soar into the sky and halt the moving clouds", shot through Feng Jianyue's heart like an arrow. Next Liang Shanbo was supposed to sing: "I'm taking leave of my good sister now ... I can't very well die on your family's grounds!" But Feng Jianyue suddenly lost her voice and couldn't utter a word. Yu Qing'e, with a flick of her water sleeve, reached out and steadied her and sang, with even greater passion and haunting tenderness: "Brother Liang, let little sister walk with you a way—" There was a quality, a color of sound that rendered her voice strikingly beautiful and opulent!

The curtains closed slowly amid sustained thunderous applause.

The stage manager waiting for them by the tabs said enthusiastically: "Good, very good! This performance of 'Meeting on the Balcony' was simply wonderful, particularly Yu Qing'e's Zhu Yingtai. You exceeded yourself in that portrayal!"

Feng Jianyue, on the other hand, felt this was her worst ever performance of "Meeting on the Balcony" since she began studying Yueju opera.

Shortly thereafter the list of students recruited by the Provincial Yueju Opera Theater was posted by the school. As top students to be groomed for important roles, Mi Jingyao and Feng Jianyue topped the list and the name of Yu Qing'e also figured among numerous students recruited as supernumeraries and walk-ons.

Yu Qing'e refused, however, to report for work at the Provincial Yueju Opera Theater but instead returned to her home town, carrying with her the school report card, which certified that she scored highest in academic and professional achievement.

Scene VIII   Long Sleeves Are Good for Dancing

Yu Qing'e invariably got out of bed every day at the first crow of the cock of some household of the little town, a habit from her School of the Arts days, when she would usually be the first to arrive in the practice room to do her morning training, doing leg stretching and backbends. After her graduation she came to work for this entertainment productions company, spending the first few years performing songs and dances, with precious few opportunities to perform Yueju opera. That did not stop her from continuing to practice martial and acrobatic skills and training her opera-singing voice. In the Yueju opera troupe recently created by the entertainment productions company, Yu Qing'e immediately established her first billing status in her vivacious young female role type, given her solid basic training and her strength in singing, reciting, acting and martial skills.

Yu Qing'e did not turn on the light for fear of waking her husband. In the dark blue natural light, she pulled on her sport shirt, put a backpack on her back and, carrying her shoes in her hands, walked barefoot like a cat out of the door, which she pulled lightly closed with an inevitable creak.

Yu Qing'e was married barely a year before. Her husband, whose family name was Zhao, was a long-time neighbor who lived right across the lane. Yu Qing'e had gradually grown distant from this childhood playmate when she went away to study at the School of the Arts, where she was a boarder and where the regimented life did not allow her to go home for frequent visits. After returning to town upon her graduation, she immediately caught the amorous eyes of many young men, who were struck by her demure prettiness and elegant charm.

The well-off Zhao family had two daughters, followed by a much younger son, who just graduated that year from the university in the provincial capital and got an enviable job in a town-owned company in the foreign trade business. He lost no time in a full-court press courtship of Yu Qing'e. Since their parents were long familiar with each other's background, they looked with an approving eye on this relationship. Yu Qing'e, who had been in low spirits because of the frustration with the unsatisfactory job placement she was given upon graduation, craved the comfort and nourishment of love. The two young people hit it off and soon were discussing marriage. Yu Qing'e laid down only one condition before she went with young Mr. Zhao to obtain their marriage certificate: in order to fulfill her dream of stardom on the Yueju opera stage, she would not have a baby before age 30. The husband was understanding and readily agreed to the demand. Her in-laws were not so thrilled by the idea but they were unable to change their son's mind.

A young couple like them—both good-looking and well-educated—stood out in an ancient town like theirs. At the wedding, the bride sang a selection from the scene of the "Reunion of Husband and Wife" in the Yueju opera play the *Legend of the White Rabbit*, in which Li Sanniang poured out to her husband her suffering and longing for him during the sixteen years of his absence. Both the singing and the acting were so outstanding and had such a powerful emotional impact that she brought down the whole house in thunderous applause.

The top brass of the productions company—chairman of the board, president and party secretary—were invited guests at the wedding of Yu Qing'e. They were elated when they heard Yu Qing'e's Li Sanniang, direct from the lineage of the Xie Yingge school of Yueju opera. It was at that moment that they woke up to the fact that what they had picked from the leftovers of the School of the Arts placements was a rare gem! If they continued to assign Yu Qing'e to perform the usual chorus and group dance routines, they would be "shooting a sparrow with a luminous pearl", or throwing away a precious talent. The very next day the powers that be at the company met to discuss the matter and decided to create a Yueju opera performance troupe, with a strategic plan to make Yu Qing'e into a shining star, a gilt-embossed calling card of the productions company.

Yu Qing'e put on her shoes outside the door—a pair of black, round-toed cloth shoes with a strap and rubber soles that her mother-in-law had specially made for her, fitting her feet perfectly. They felt lighter and gave more of a spring than sneakers when she practiced basic martial skills and walked stage circle in them.

The Zhao family had a spacious home with two buildings, a front and a rear courtyard, in which Yu Qing'e could perfectly well practice singing and martial training. But she was loath to disturb other people in the household and always chose to go to the sand banks of the Tiaoluo Creek at first crack of dawn to train her voice and do leg kicks, backbends, butterfly kicks and run stage circles. The sand banks hugged a small hill covered with mulberry trees, among which birds were already warbling and insects in the grass were chirping. The dark blue, gently rippled river flowed with a murmur. Upstream the Guishi Bridge, with its silhouette appearing like a paper cut in the morning fog, embodied an ancient legend. Above it a few remaining stars melted, like crushed ice, into the lightening sky.

According to old folks, the Tiaoluo Creek had flowed for at

least two thousand years. In the Kingdom of Yue of antiquity, it was once a wide, mighty river and it was on the Tiaoluo River that a small boat carried Fan Li and Xishi downriver into the great lakes and out to sea. With the passage of time and changes of dynasties, high banks sank to become valleys and deep gorges heaved to form hills, and the Tiaoluo River dwindled to this slow-flowing, meandering stream that was no longer navigable and that could be forded in low water season with one's trousers folded to mid-calf.

After a round of martial workout, Yu Qing'e found herself in a fine perspiration, all loosened up, refreshed and in high spirits. She took out from her backpack a pair of simple water sleeves; these eight-foot long water sleeves made of a light fabric was hand-made by her with needle and thread. She had decided to add a significant sequence of long-sleeve dancing in the new version of the play *Xishi Returns Home* she'd been rehearsing so as to more vividly and intensely express the despair and sadness and heartbreaking and mortifying pain in the involuntary departure from her homeland. She had often heard high praise for the long water-sleeves dance sequence performed by Xie Yingge in the scene of "Giving Birth by the Millstone" in the "White Rabbit". Under the influence of such oft-expressed sentiment of awed wonder by opera goers, she started to have dreams in which she played Li Sanniang herself and danced, manipulating the long water sleeves, which coiled and floated weightlessly and gracefully about her like white clouds, and the next moment she would soar into the sky, light as a swallow, with the sough of the wind in her ears …

Yu Qing'e was already a fan of Xie Yingge when she was a child. Born too late to have had an opportunity to watch Xie Yingge perform the full-length "White Rabbit" on stage, she nonetheless heard in her swaddling clothes her mother hum snippets of Li Sanniang's arias in the Xie style and was often lulled to sleep by these fragments of Xie-School singing.

In her mother's youth, Xie Yingge was at the zenith of her career; she performed the "White Rabbit" in theaters for months-long runs, to packed houses. Her mother became a diehard fan of Xie Yingge; she collected many stage shots, playbills of Xie Yingge's performances, newspaper articles about and interviews of Xie Yingge, as well as two records containing the full-length performance of the "White Rabbit" by her. As a result of being steeped in the artistic influence of Xie Yingge since a child, it was only natural and only a matter of time that Yu Qing'e developed an admiration for Xie Yingge and an urge to emulate her.

And at the age of nine, Yu Qing'e met, in unforeseen circumstances, Xie Yingge in the flesh!

Back when Yu Qing'e was in third grade, she returned home from school one day to find her mother busy at the stove. Being the good daughter that she was, Qing'e put down her satchel and went to help her mother, who was cooking while humming Li Sanniang's aria: "... I love the red plum blossom that retains its beauty in wind and frost; I admire the cedar branch that stands erect against the bitter cold ..." Swish, swish, swish—she was flourishing the spatula like a short lance carried by actors on stage. Young Qing'e said with alarm: "Mom—what are you doing? The vegetables are going to fly out of the wok!"

The spatula came to rest and her mother said with a smile: "Qing'e, we will have an early supper today. I and a number of aunties in our neighborhood are going to watch a performance by students of Xie Yingge tonight at the Provincial School of the Arts."

A few years back the Provincial School of the Arts had been converted into a "Revolutionary Model Beijing Opera Training Program", and had moved from the provincial capital to an ancient town in the outer suburbs, only a short dozen kilometers from their village. The latest news was that the Provincial School of the Arts had been reinstated and a number of famous actors, the renowned actor playing the female role of Yueju opera Xie Yingge being one of them, were invited to teach at the school. The night's event was a public performance by the students to showcase what they had learned and achieved, but word spread that after the performance the teachers would appear together with the students on stage at the curtain call. This elated the fans of Xie Yingge of nearby towns and villages, who spread the word. They were flocking to the School of the Arts, ostensibly to watch the performance, but in fact they had an ulterior motive: they fully intended to seize this opportunity to make offerings of farm products from home to Xie Yingge in a show of support for the actor, who had suffered so much in the "Cultural Revolution".

Her interest piqued by her mother's account, young Qing'e tugged at her mother's sleeve and clamored to be taken along to see Li Sanniang in person. Her mother said with a laugh: "Well, only if you eat a proper supper this evening!" Not to miss the rare opportunity to accompany her mother to a show featuring Xie Yingge's live appearance, young Qing'e quickly tucked in two bowls of rice, sent down with eggs scrambled with Chinese toon.

That night the students of the School of the Arts performed selections of revolutionary model operas. Yu Qing'e drifted off to sleep in her mother's lap and dreamed of being hustled onto the stage to perform Li Sanniang. She often listened to Xie Yingge's record and sang along. She was most familiar with the long passage in which Li Sanniang sang "In those sixteen years, the thousand-jin millstone be my witness". She was singing this passage with gusto in her dream when her mother shook her awake. She found that the theater had erupted into a cyclone-like round of applause and there was a standing ovation. Her mother picked her up and stood her on the seat: "Look! Look! Xie Yingge has come out on stage to acknowledge the applause and standing ovation! Did you see? Did you?"

On the stage the students, still in their makeup and costumes, marshaled five or six mentors to front stage and presented bouquets to them. The mentors greeted the audience in turn in front of the mike. Xie Yingge did not speak but only took a deep bow. Young Qing'e immediately recognized her! She was too familiar with her arias and she was convinced that a superb voice like that could have issued from the throat of none other than that pretty lady! With her hair bobbed about her ears and wearing a drab, old blouse, but no makeup or any jewelry, she radiated a natural, unadorned beauty.

The curtains finally closed for the night. Some of the fans of Xie Yingge, loath to leave after only a brief glance at their idol, declared that they knew the location of the apartment rented by her in the ancient town, and they decided to wait at the entrance of the alley leading to her temporary home for Xie Yingge's return. They were determined to present the farm products they had brought from their respective homes to Xie Yingge in person.

In a little over one hour Xie Yingge appeared. She was modest and easy-going, and gave herself none of the airs of a star, but invited her fans into her courtyard for a rest and a sip of hot tea. It was toward the middle of the lunar month when the moon was at its roundest and the courtyard was awash in moonlight, and the flowering shrubs cast dense shadows on the tiled patio. As the fans piled their gifts onto the stone table in the little courtyard, Xie Yingge thanked each of them in turn and insisted on paying for them. But the fans would have none of that: "Master Xie, just give us tickets to your next performance! When are you going to play Li Sanniang again?" Leaving the question unanswered, Xie Yingge shifted so that her face was in the shadows of the flowering shrubs. The woman next to Xie Yingge, who answered to the name "Shi Mei", said with a laugh: "Soon, soon enough! The Provincial Yueju Opera Troupe will resume its performances in very short order. And the first play to be rehearsed is sure to be the 'White Rabbit'."

At this moment, Yu Qing'e's mother, with a courage she didn't know she possessed, shoved her daughter in front of Xie Yingge: "Master Xie, my daughter is also a fan of yours. She can sing your 'White Rabbit' from beginning to end!"

Young Qing'e's heart started racing and as Xie Yingge held her hand she could feel a cool, smooth sensation course through her body.

Xie Yingge pulled young Qing'e closer and carefully examined her face by the moonlight before saying in a soft tone: "H'm, with this oval face, you'll look very good as an actor in the young female role (*xiaodan*). My little girl, can you sing a few lines for me?"

The aunties around her started clapping their hands and her mother nudged her with a finger jabbing at her spine, urging her on: "Sing! You can't stop singing while at home. Don't tell me you've suddenly turned mute."

Young Qing'e felt as if she were returning to her dream.

> In those sixteen years, the thousand-jin millstone
>   be my witness,
> I have milled away many a morning and evening;
> In those sixteen years, the three-foot wide apron of
>   the well be my witness,
> I've treaded upon it may a winter and spring ...

Young Qing'e finished singing the four "sixteen years" stanzas without a hitch and even effortlessly sang the last verse at an octave higher without going off key, without a single false note. Amid the bravos of the aunties around her, Xie Yingge nodded approvingly: "The little girl does have a gift. Do you want to sing Yueju opera on stage when you grow up?"

Her mother hastened to answer on Qing'e's behalf: "She does, she does! She has always wanted to study under you. Master Xie, would you consider taking her as your pupil?"

A smile lit her face as Xie Yingge replied: "The School of the Arts will soon create a Yueju Opera program. When she graduates elementary school, she can apply to the School of the Arts." That was as good as agreeing to take young Qing'e as her pupil!

The adults, speaking all at once, tried to make young Qing'e get on her knees right then and there to acknowledge Master Xie's kindness, but were dissuaded by Xie Yingge. During the "Cultural Revolution", the practice of an actor taking in a private pupil was criticized and denounced as a vestige of feudalism.

Young Qing'e fixed her eyes on Xie Yingge in fascination. She found that delicate, gentle face to be an exact match with what she had imagined Li Sanniang to look like—as Xie Yingge chatted with her fans in a soft voice, a dimple the shape of an orchid petal would appear every so often—when she moved her lips or arched her eyebrows—in her right cheek in varying depth and intensity, "pregnant with dew and rain and shrouded in mist", adding a heart-stopping, breath-taking charm to her physiognomy.

This orchid-shaped dimple was seared into young Qing'e's memory and would play a pivotal role in changing her fate at a critical juncture in her life. But I am getting ahead of myself.

Steeped since a child in the sight and sound of Xie Yingge's exquisite art, Yu Qing'e developed an almost irrational demand for perfection in artistic creation. *Xishi Returns Home* was to be the first salvo in her effort after her graduation from the School of the Arts to make a name on the Yueju opera stage and she set a goal of a perfect performance for herself. To accomplish it, it was crucial that she master Xie Yingge's legendary water sleeves dance.

Putting on the eight-foot water sleeves, Yu Qing'e took a deep breath, did a "sleeve catch" and then a "sleeve throw". When she did a "sparrow hawk pirouette" ... the two long sleeves got tangled together and she fell limply on the ground. Gritting her teeth, Yu Qing'e leapt up again, threw out her sleeves, and did a roll ... when a sleeve coiled around her body, causing her, now entangled in synthetic silk, to fall on the floor of the sand bank.

Yu Qing'e was tired, both physically and emotionally. She stretched out her limbs and lay face up on the fine sand and gravel, which, though warmed by the early morning sun, remained slightly wet. At this moment her mind was as pale and empty as the morning sky. The ever-flowing Tiaoluo Creek murmured and sobbed at her ears, telling ancient stories of sad partings and joyful reunions that wearied her; she tiredly closed her eyes.

Yu Qing'e invested much hard work and careful thought in choreographing this water sleeves sequence herself, as the Yueju opera troupe only recently created under the entertainment productions company had not yet had time to hire a technical director. Yu Qing'e, a high achiever in both singing and martial skills when she studied Yueju opera in the School of the Arts, gritted her teeth and took on the task of designing the sequence herself. All she had to go on was her mother's collection of Xie Yingge's stage photos, among which figured two taken of her in the scene of "Giving Birth by the Millstone". In one, Li Sanniang's two long sleeves formed a closed loop after a "sparrow hawk pirouette", surrounding her like a ring circling Saturn; in the other, Li Sanniang was shown bending backward, with her arms spread apart and the long sleeves ballooning into two magnolia blooms. Yu Qing'e repeatedly studied the two moves to find the tricks involved; she also paid visits to old Yueju opera fans who had watched Xie Yingge's past performances of the "White Rabbit" and entreated them to describe in unsparing detail the long-sleeves maneuvers of Li Sanniang in the scene of "Giving Birth by the Millstone". The result was a sequence of movements involving the manipulation of the long water sleeves in which Xishi sang and danced as she took leave of her homeland.

But when she started to practice each of these movements in earnest, she discovered that the sleeves would not obey her commands as they did in her dream. The two eight-foot water sleeves were elusive like two sly water snakes and would often do the exact opposite of what she intended them to do. She was taught a series of water sleeves tricks in the School of the Arts, but those water sleeves were only two or three feet long. After starting work at the entertainment productions company, she had occasion to take part in performances of the red silk ribbon dance. While the ribbon was ten feet long, a bamboo baton was attached to one end of it, with which the dancer could better flourish and control the red silk ribbon. Her two water sleeves, longer than regular water sleeves, and wider than the ribbon in the red silk ribbon dance, could hardly be expected to "soar like a dragon and fly like a phoenix" no matter how she waved and agitated her unaided arms.

Xie Yingge did it in her time. Why couldn't I?

At the thought, despair and sadness built up inside Yu Qing'e and weighed on her like a millstone, suffocating her. Does it really mean I won't be able to master Xie Yingge's long sleeves feat? Will my aspiration to be a celebrated actor in the female role like Xie Yingge on the Yueju opera stage remain an unattainable dream?

She had secretly nursed that aspiration for too long. Now that her aspiration, like the seed of a tree, had barely broken through the ground and sprouted leaves, it was smashed down by a sudden gust of wind and driving rain, buried yet again and almost turned into a fossil.

Yu Qing'e couldn't cherish more this platform built for her by the productions company. She knew that if she wasn't able to seize this rare opportunity, she'd forfeit the right to blame heaven or earth or anybody but herself!

Yu Qing'e! Are you really going to concede defeat to these two sleeves? With an inner roar, she twisted around and threw out her leg in a "black dragon coiled around the pillar", which involved rolling on the ground, then straightening her back she drew herself up to her full height and crossed her arms before flinging out fiercely the two long sleeves.

"Xiao Yu—"

At the sound of her name being called from a distance, Yu Qing'e dropped her arms and turned toward the source of the voice. The Tiaoluo Creek, bathed in the early morning sunlight, rippled and glittered like a million golden flowers. Someone was walking toward her on the trail by the brook, the face falling in the shade because of back lighting. Yu Qing'e was able to recognize her by her long strides and brisk gait and answered with some hesitation: "Party Secretary Zhang, you have something to tell me?"

Party Secretary Zhang of the productions company came up to her and said with a broad grin: "No wonder everyone says you are the earliest riser in our town. How long have you been practicing? You are swimming in sweat. Take a rest!"

Yu Qing'e was seized by a sudden apprehension. The beaming face and gentle tone of Party Secretary Zhang reminded her of that deputy director of counseling and guidance of the School of the Arts who came up to her many years back. She was already made up and costumed waiting to go on stage to give her graduation performance, when the deputy director got hold of her, also smiling and gentle-mannered and soft-toned, to break the cruel, heart-breaking news to her: her name, originally on the list of graduates recruited to the Provincial Yueju Opera Theater, had been replaced by someone else's name!

With drooping eyelids and eyes fixed on her shoes wetted by morning dew, she mumbled in a thin voice: "What could be so important that Party Secretary Zhang would come for me this early in the morning?" and braced apprehensively for the answer.

Patting her on the shoulder, Party Secretary Zhang said: "Good news, that's what!"

Yu Qing'e cast a doubtful glance at Party Secretary Zhang and found a relaxed, unaffected smile on her face, not the mask that the deputy director of counseling and guidance of the School of the Arts put on to break the awful news to her years back.

And indeed it was good news that Party Secretary Zhang had brought her. The productions company had been notified by the Department of Culture of the provincial government that there would be a contest featuring the younger generation of Yueju opera actors performing new plays co-sponsored by the six provinces of eastern China and Shanghai and the productions company had already entered her *Xishi Returns*

Home in the contest.

Yu Qing'e, in undisguised excitement, put her palms together and asked: "Really? Thank you, Party Secretary Zhang! I am grateful to the leadership for all it has done for me …" But her initial ebullience was quickly dampened by worry and she sighed heavily before she could finish her sentence.

Party Secretary Zhang said in puzzlement: "You are too young to be sighing like that! Are you confident you can win a big prize for us in the contest?"

Yu Qing'e said, slowly shaking her head: "I am not worried about singing, acting and reciting, but that water sleeves dance sequence, I have not yet been able to master it no matter how hard I've tried … Without this sequence, my contest entry would not have anything to differentiate it from others …"

Party Secretary Zhang gave a full-throated laugh: "You've only just started! And already you are talking about giving up? I, for one, have full confidence in you! Of course hard work alone is not enough. Smart work is important too. Don't you agree?" With those last words, she produced a small manila envelope from her pocket and handed it to her.

The envelope felt light-weight and slim in Yu Qing'e's hand. She asked in bafflement: "Party Secretary Zhang, what important tips are contained in this envelope?"

Party Secretary Zhang said with a meaningful glance at her: "Open it and see for yourself!"

Yu Qing'e looked at the envelope: it showed on its front in a vertical column the words "For the personal attention of Deputy General Manager Qin Yulou". Her heart started racing. She found the envelope was not yet sealed and quickly removed the sheet of paper, her shaking hand causing the paper to make a crinkling sound—it turned out to be a reference letter stamped with the red-ink official seal of the productions company: "We hereby commend Yu Qing'e of the Yueju opera troupe of our productions company to the Provincial Yueju Opera Theater for the purpose of learning from your valuable experiences!"

Her puzzlement still unresolved, Yu Qing'e looked quizzically at Party Secretary Zhang with her eyes wide open, like two giant question marks. It was then that Party Secretary Zhang enlightened her: "This is the standard way a reference letter is written. You take it with you to see Deputy General Manager Qin in the provincial capital. I've come to an agreement with her over the phone; she will take you to visit Xie Yingge. You can take advantage of the occasion to ask Master Xie to give you a few crucial tips on how to perform the water sleeves dance. She might even personally demonstrate a few moves to you."

As if waking up from a dream, Yu Qing'e rushed up to Party Secretary Zhang and put her arms around her neck, jumping with joy, laughing and crying at the same time and unable to produce the words "Thank you" because of the lump in her throat.

Very early the following morning, Yu Qing'e boarded the first bus to the provincial capital. After traveling a distance along the Tiaoluo Creek overhung by the morning mist, the bus started the climb into the lush green mountains. The vista opened up following a long series of hairpin turns and the bus entered the inter-province freeway, passing by "mist-shrouded willow trees and colorful painted bridges, and wind curtains and green draperies in houses of varying shapes and heights", and fava bean flowers blanketing the landscape like a carpet of snow.

The fine weather and pleasant views along the way should have buoyed Yu Qing'e's spirit and bolstered her confidence, but with the increasing density and height of the buildings by the road and the decreasing distance to the provincial capital, a vague sense of unease crept through her body.

An insignificant incident in the distant past that she had kept to herself all these years and that had faded out of her own memory with the passage of time now broke through a breach in her memory after the long bumpy bus ride. It sprung like a jack-in-the-box to the fore of her consciousness.

After her graduation from elementary school, Yu Qing'e sailed through the qualifying examination of the Yueju Opera Program of the School of the Arts. Once admitted, she chose the female role type as her major and devoted herself to studying the Xie Yingge school of Yueju opera art. At first she thought she would be able to meet once again that congenial and accessible Xie Yingge with her right cheek imprinted with an orchid-shaped dimple, but she was told by the teachers at the School of the Arts that Xie Yingge had been transferred back to the Provincial Yueju Opera Theater and that it was out of the question that a celebrity like her would consent to be a mere teacher at the School of the Arts. In her four years of Yueju opera studies, Yu Qing'e never had a chance to be personally mentored by Xie Yingge, but she had never wavered from looking upon Xie Yingge as her role model. It was the consensus among the faculty that Yu Qing'e's imitation of Xie Yingge's arias was so good that one could hardly tell the difference.

In the year of her graduation, when actors in all role types from Yueju opera troupes far and near descended on the School of the Arts to recruit students, Yu Qing'e nursed a fond hope: maybe Xie Yingge would also come to the School of the Arts to recruit. Would she still remember that in a moonlit night many years ago a little girl had sung an aria of Li Sanniang imitating her style in her courtyard dappled with shadows of flowering shrubs and had won her approval and praise?

And Xie Yingge did come to the school. The faculty of the Yueju Opera Program arranged performances by student actors in the female role for her viewing; one of the short segments was Yu Qing'e's "Giving Birth by the Millstone" of the "White Rabbit", which was one of her strong suits. In the School of the Arts, "Giving Birth by the Millstone" had been incorporated into the syllabus as a teaching example but its emphasis was on singing and did not include the water sleeves dance sequence invented by Xie Yingge. Yu Qing'e had been singing this aria segment ever since a child and had internalized its every line and verse and every tune. Her performance went well and when she left the stage, her mentors all gave her the thumbs-up sign.

Every time Yu Qing'e performed "Giving Birth by the Millstone", she stepped right into the role. The moment she opened her mouth to sing, she became Li Sanniang. She was so engaged that she normally wouldn't see the audience and only got a glimpse of neat rows of dark silhouettes at the time of bowing off the stage, without being able to pick out Xie Yingge from the crowd. She hurried to the makeup room and had just got out of her costume when her mentor stormed into the room with a cheery face and dragged Yu Qing'e with her, saying: "You'll remove your makeup later. We must hurry now. Master Xie specifically asked to have a talk with you. Yu Qing'e, you must not let this opportunity slip through your fingers. If Xie Yingge agrees to take you in as her pupil, your recruitment into the Provincial Yueju Opera Theater will be a done deal."

Her mentor led her into a small conference room normally reserved for receiving honored guests of the school. The school president and the director of counseling and guidance were all there and the sofas bristled with people. The mentor led her to a central, privileged seating location in the room and said with a smile to a middle-aged lady: "Master Xie, you have an eye for talent! Yu Qing'e here is known among the students as Xie Yingge the Second."

Yu Qing'e finally got to see the Xie Yingge she had missed and admired for so long. Her idol sat on the sofa, erect as ever, elegantly but not flamboyantly dressed; her face was delicately made up and was so radiant that an observer would have a hard time telling her real age. While a winning smile played on her face, her penetrating eyes glowed with fire and fervor. Without the shadow of a doubt she stood out above the crowd sitting around the small conference room. As if spellbound, Yu Qing'e hungrily scrutinized her face: it was the same face, the same well-proportioned and well-coordinated features, but ... no matter how she tried she couldn't match it to the Xie Yingge in her memory. Could it be simply explained by a weight gain? Or a few wrinkles more at the corners of her eyes and her mouth?

The way she stared at the guest was indeed a little rude and the mentor gave her a surreptitious pinch. She snapped out of her reverie and said in a reverential tone: "Master Xie!"

"Come, come here and sit by me, sit down." Xie Yingge greeted her effusively and slid laterally on the sofa to make room for Yu Qing'e. Holding her hand affectionately in her own, she asked question after question about what year she came to the School of the Arts, what other Xie-School plays she had learned, and her favorite among those, and much more. Yu Qing'e gave her answer to each and every question, but distractedly. The closer she got to Xie Yingge, the stronger her perception of a difference between the Xie Yingge before her and the Xie Yingge in her memory. The way she carried on a conversation was different; the feel of her palm was different, and what else was different? There had to be a crucial difference; Yu Qing'e sensed it but couldn't for the moment put her finger on it.

Seeing the two hitting it off, the president of the School of the Arts decided to strike while the iron was hot: "Master Xie, for when do you intend to schedule the ceremony to take her as your pupil? Our school will take care of all the preparations."

Xie Yingge, apparently in a good mood, said: "What do you think would be a good time? I need to take into consideration the school's calendar." With those words, she took hold of Yu Qing'e's arm and told the photographer to take a picture of the two of them together. The photographer aimed the camera and shouted: "Ready, let's have a smile!"

In that split second, Yu Qing'e unaccountably turned her head around to glance at Xie Yingge and had a reaction as if her eyes had been stabbed by a needle—she finally discovered the greatest difference between the two versions of Xie Yingge: the Xie Yingge at her side did not have the orchid-shaped dimple in her right cheek!

Later that day the school president hosted a banquet in honor of Xie Yingge and asked Yu Qing'e to be present. Yu Qing'e was in no gastronomic mood before the delicacies on the table, obsessed as she was with the charming orchid-shaped dimple she saw in Xie Yingge's cheek years ago, the image of which was stubbornly superimposed on her mind at the moment and niggled at her, causing confusion and anxiety. Finally she had a private moment with Xie Yingge when she was asked to show her where the bathroom was. No longer able to suppress her curiosity she asked, in a hushed voice: "Master Xie, what happened to the dimple on your cheek? It's gone, I've noticed."

Xie Yingge did a double take before giving a burst of laughter, followed by an expression of regret: "I am getting on in years and my face has plumped up considerably!" then added quickly: "How did you know I had a dimple when I was younger?"

Biting her lip, Yu Qing'e said bashfully: "Master, have you forgotten? When I was a child, my mother once took me to your home and it was then that you encouraged me to apply to the Yueju Opera Program of the School of the Arts."

Slapping herself on her forehead, Xie Yingge said: "Oho—I am so terribly forgetful!"

In a couple of months, a shocking, jaw-dropping reversal caught everyone by surprise. A solemn ceremony of disciple initiation was presided over by Xie Yingge, the celebrated actor in the female role on the Yueju opera stage, at the School of the Arts. Yu Qing'e, everyone's favorite candidate, lost out to Mi Jingyao, who had been a mediocre performer in all areas but was now favored by fortune to become Xie Yingge's private pupil and had an easy time being inducted into the Provincial Yueju Opera Theater.

Yu Qing'e had a huge pride despite her modest small-town origins. While many people around her thought she got a raw deal and urged her to seek reconsideration, or at the very least, an explanation from Xie Yingge, Yu Qing'e merely gritted her teeth and kept her silence, unmoved by all the advice and suggestions. Her delicate face, like a fresh washed mirror, was smooth and clean, undisturbed by the merest trace of emotion. She kept up her practice routine and rehearsal schedule. She ate and slept regularly. Nobody imagined the ruins left behind by a hurricane that her inner landscape really was! Soon after her return to her home town upon graduation, she collapsed and fell ill.

Several versions circulated among the faculty and students of the School of the Arts about how Xie Yingge came to her disciple-taking decision. The most bruited about version revolved around Mi Jingyao's skills in areas unrelated to Yueju opera art. Mi Jingyao had made a name for herself in the School of the Arts. While giving a mediocre performance in her major field, she had superb, uncommon looks and charm and had appeared in commercials and several soap operas on television. Her deft social skills earned her great popularity. It was widely rumored that she knew many luminaries in the arts, who all highly recommended her to the Provincial Yueju Opera Theater. Once the leadership of the Provincial Yueju Opera Theater made its decision, Xie Yingge had no choice but to go along.

Yu Qing'e envied Mi Jingyao and inevitably felt jealous and bitter about it, but deep down she knew Xie Yingge's sudden change of heart had nothing whatsoever to do with Mi Jingyao. It had to be that rude question of hers at the banquet on that fateful day that had led to the disastrous result. In other words, it was the orchid-shaped dimple that had ruined her career prospects. Yu Qing'e did not disclose to anyone this surmise of hers, for she was completely baffled still: why is this Xie Yingge so touchy at the mention of the orchid-shaped dimple? Did the dimple in her cheek really disappear as she aged? The most important question was: Is the present Xie Yingge the same Xie Yingge of her memory? These questions shrouded in deep mystery still intrigued her as she resolutely left the School of the Arts and returned to the small town that had raised her.

The bus finally entered the city limits of the congested provincial capital bristling with high-rise buildings, and after another hour in stop-and-go traffic through traffic lights on busy streets, arrived at the bus terminal.

Yu Qing'e was the last passenger to step off the bus. It was after repeated urgings from the driver and the ticket collector that she finally, with great reluctance, left her seat.

Now that she was in the provincial capital with a reference letter prepared specially for her by the well-meaning Party Secretary Zhang, her courage failed her and she hesitated to step out of the bus terminal. With trepidation she asked herself how she was going to confront that face made cold and aloof by the disappearance of the dimple? Would she still nurse an old grudge against her for a youthful rudeness in her less mature years? More importantly: would she be willing to coach her in performing the long sleeves dance sequence?

With a resolute stamping of her foot, Yu Qing'e strode out of the bus terminal. Now that she was already here, she might as well give it a try!

To burnish the unique cultural credentials of the province, the provincial government had in recent years invested heavily in the revamping of the administrative wing and the Yueyin Theater wing of the Provincial Yueju Opera Theater. The administrative wing was a six-story building of mixed Western and Chinese architectural styles, comprising a dozen rehearsal and practice rooms of varying sizes that could accommodate the simultaneous rehearsing of four or five plays and playlets. Abutting the administrative wing was the Yueyin Theater, which featured a faux-classical gable and hip roof with flying eaves and upturned corners. The wood carvings on its beams and pillars and the murals all depicted characters from traditional Chinese opera, vividly modeled on famous actors who had interpreted them. The theater consisted of two levels. The upper level accommodated two small stages and the lower level was a grand theater with a capacity for a thousand spectators. The main entrance of the theater was flanked by two massive columns, their circumference about two arm's lengths, carved with a pair of antithetical couplets in sober, solid Yan style calligraphy. The first couplet was, in paraphrase, "The sandalwood clappers sounded, the scudding clouds stopped, and a new chapter between heaven and earth regales your eyes" and the second couplet "The musical notes float up in wind and moonlight, and a melodious verse from past and present feasts your ears".

Standing rooted before the grandiose building of the Provincial Yueju Opera Theater for a good, long moment and making a mental comparison between it and the stopgap, simple rehearsal rooms of the Yueju opera troupe of her small town productions company, she couldn't help but feel the unfairness of it all and a deep, inconsolable regret.

The man in the door guard's cubicle kept sticking his head out to eye her, probably thinking she was another Yueju opera fan waylaying her idol. Finally he decided to step out of his booth and intervene: "Young lady, please don't stand there and gawk like that. None of the stars have come in today, so you'll be wasting your time ..."

Her face flushing furiously, Yu Qing'e quickly produced the reference letter and showed it to the guard. After taking a look at the letter, the guard said with a smile: "So, young lady, you are a Yueju opera actor too! No wonder you look like a character out of a play. You wait a second. I'll call Manager Qin for you."

After dialing the number twice without getting through, the security guard said: "Since no one is taking calls in the office, they must be in the rehearsal room. It's been hectic these days because the public performance of the 'White Rabbit' is only a few days away." Just then some girls in practice suits walked by and the guard hailed them: "Will you please go to the rehearsal hall and tell Manager Qin that a comrade from a brother troupe is paying her a visit."

In a short while a middle-aged woman, slightly on the plump side, hurried out, also in a practice suit. Recognizing her from a brief encounter at the TV station, Yu Qing'e went in quick steps toward her and said in a reverential tone: "Manager Qin, Party Secretary Zhang of my company told me to see you ..."

With a smile Qin Yulou looked her up and down and said: "I know, I know! Party Secretary Zhang explained everything to me." After a short pause, she took a closer look at her and asked: "You must be Yu Qing'e, am I right?"

With a pressing together of her lips, Yu Qing'e acknowledged the question. After a brief word with the guard, Qin Yulou led Yu Qing'e upstairs. All the way Yu Qing'e could feel Qin Yulou repeatedly looking over her shoulder to examine her, with an intensity, she thought, that was enough to harden the skin of her face. She wondered with unease and trepidation: did I somehow offend her?

Qin Yulou had intended to take Yu Qing'e to her office but as they came to the elevator, she had a sudden idea and paused in her steps. She said tentatively: "Xiao Yu, why don't I take you to the rehearsal room? The cast and crew of the new version of the 'White Rabbit' are in the final fine-tuning stages of rehearsing separately the first and second half of the play. It so happens that the director and the technical coach are at this moment helping the young actors in the first half of the play to refine their performance. Feng Jianyue and Mi Jingyao were your school mates, I understand. Mi Jingyao is performing a long sleeves dance sequence in 'Giving Birth by the Millstone' also, why don't you watch her do it and maybe come away with some useful ideas? I will take you to see Xie Yingge in the afternoon, what do you think?"

Yu Qing'e took a step back in a fluster, blurting out a string of no's. In all the years after graduation from the School of the Arts, she had had almost no contact with any of her former school mates, least of all with Feng Jianyue and Mi Jingyao, whom she had the least desire to see. But for that dream of hers in which she performed to perfection a long sleeves dance sequence, she'd never have set foot in the Provincial Yueju Opera Theater!

Qin Yulou had been in the Yueju opera circles for decades and seen the vicissitudes of the trade; besides it was she who oversaw the recruitment of graduates of the School of the Arts the year it all happened, so she was aware of the tangled circumstances involved and therefore quite understood how Yu Qing'e felt at the moment. With a whispered sigh, she placed her hands on Yu Qing'e's soft, seemingly boneless shoulders and said gravely: "Xiao Yu, let bygones be bygones. Refusing to forget only wears you down. Let me give you a heads-up. The long sleeves sequence Mi Jingyao is rehearsing today was choreographed by a technical coach from the Beijing Opera Theater. You don't want to miss out on this chance to watch the performance and perhaps learn something from it." After a pause, she went on: "In order to attract a larger young audience, our theater would always invite some Yueju opera fans to the final rehearsals in which all the different parts were put together and performed from start to finish. The rehearsal hall is nearly full today, so if you enter by the back door, you would not attract much notice."

Yu Qing'e was now filled with gratitude for the consideration and understanding of Qin Yulou, who had thought of every detail in her behalf. Besides, she was certainly eager to see how Mi Jingyao managed the long sleeves sequence. As suggested by Qin Yulou, Yu Qing'e slipped into the rehearsal hall through the back door and let herself into a vacant seat close to the wall. She took the extra precaution of hunching her shoulders and watching through the gaps between the heads of people sitting in rows ahead of her.

On the rehearsal floor, the long-haired "rising-star" director was directing Mi Jingyao to repeat the scene in which Li Sanniang bit through the umbilical cord after giving birth to her baby son, and Mi Jingyao sang: "… a cold sweat drenches my body, All strength has drained out of me and I can barely remain on my feet …" At the close of the verse, Mi Jingyao backed up in quick steps and flicked her long sleeves in an exaggerated "cloud hand" movement, sending them out in coils; then she executed a quick advance, opening her arms to give a more restrained flick to the sleeves. When she almost reached the edge of the stage, she spun at a fast clip toward the back, causing the two long sleeves to form a circle around her body. This occasioned a round of applause from the opera fans. Amid the applause, Mi Jingyao executed a "reclining fish" movement to assume a prostrate posture and the long sleeves, like flakes of snow or autumn leaves, floated down to the ground; this was followed by the last two sentences uttered by an exhausted, enfeebled Li Sanniang in slow tempo: "... Alas I have no water, no scissors and nobody to help, I have no choice but to bite through the umbilical cord myself ..."

It was with bated breath and undivided attention that Yu Qing'e watched this performance by Mi Jingyao to the end. Notwithstanding the enthusiastic applause of the opera fans, a stone seemed to have been lifted from her heart. She thought to herself: so much for a dance sequence choreographed with the help of a Beijing opera martial coach! She did see the long water sleeves fly all over the stage, but except for the footwork, no demanding, intricate body movements were attempted. Yu Qing'e had no doubt whatsoever that she could easily master a water-sleeves sequence like that, and would certainly do it better than Mi Jingyao! She was a little disappointed; it seemed that Beijing opera martial coach did not get the knack of that long water sleeve dance made famous by Xie Yingge years ago.

On the stage Mi Jingyao was catching her breath and fanning herself with folded water sleeves; with a demure smile she nodded acknowledgment of the applause and cheers.

The martial coach went onto the stage and said with a hearty laugh: "Not bad, not bad! Li Sanniang did well; all the movements flowed smoothly. A few days more of intensive practice will ensure a flawless performance."

Obviously in a buoyant mood, Mi Jingyao did a coquettish curtsy: "All thanks to you, coach. Your valuable help made it possible!" Then she walked up to the director and said, not without some complacency: "Director He, give me some more pointers. Tell me where I can make improvements."

With his eyebrows deeply furrowed, and thrusting ten fingers into his long hair and combing it back with a jerk, he said: "The water sleeve dance was well done, but ... somehow I have a feeling that this dance sequence didn't exactly go with the despairing, helpless, painful and tormented mood of Li Sanniang. Let's put it this way, when a fairy maiden scatters flowers, when she joyously showers the earth with hundreds of flowers, this long sleeves dance sequence will serve equally well, am I right?"

Mi Jingyao's face fell; she bit her lip and fixed her eyes on the martial coach.

The martial coach said: "Director He, when we design the movements, we need to take into consideration the performer's capability and martial training. Besides, the 'White Rabbit' is a civil play in the first place and overly elaborate martial moves would seem out of place."

After some consideration, Director He said: "All right. There's no time to change the choreography anyway. Li Sanniang, what was on your mind when you did the water sleeve dance? The important thought is not whether the dance movements look good or not; remember it's a moment when Li Sanniang is in the throes of excruciating labor pains and is alone and helpless! Try to let your feeling move the water sleeves, personalize the water sleeves, invest sorrow and anger in the water sleeves, and don't worry about flaws in the dance movements. Perfection isn't always or necessarily beauty. You will have succeeded if you can move the emotions of the audience."

These words of the director did much to enlighten Yu Qing'e. She seemed to realize now the chief cause of her failure so far to master the water sleeve movements. It occurred to her that when choreographing her own water sleeve dance, she must not seek simple emulation of Xie Yingge to the exclusion of other considerations. The sequence should be informed by Xishi's feelings and emotions—longing, regret to leave and heroic readiness to sacrifice her life for the homeland.

On the rehearsal stage, Mi Jingyao was instructed by the director to do the water sleeve sequence once more. With the long sleeves trailing on the floor and her mouth pouting, Mi Jingyao walked reluctantly to the center of the stage and started singing, in an anemic voice: "A cold sweat drenches my body, All strength has drained out of me and I can barely remain on my feet …"

Director He thundered from the sidelines: "Li Sanniang, open up your voice! Remember, feel the emotions!"

This happened when Mi Jingyao was in the middle of retreating in quick steps and doing an exaggerated "cloud hand" to send the long sleeves out in curls. Startled by the sudden loud voice, she missed the rhythm and stepped on her sleeves and fell sideways on the floor with a thud. The music ground to a halt and there was a rush toward the fallen figure. Qin Yulou was the first to reach her and help her back on her feet. She asked Mi Jingyao: "Are you okay? Where does it hurt?"

Mi Jingyao, her face twisting with pain, said: "Down there. I sprained my ankle …"

The rehearsal had to be interrupted. After apologizing to the opera fans on behalf of the theater, Qin Yulou quickly arranged transportation to take Mi Jingyao to the hospital. With the Hong Kong tour of the new version of the "White Rabbit" fast approaching, the first priority was to restore health to Mi Jingyao's foot.

The opera fans lingered behind, loath to leave, and discussed in groups. Yu Qing'e remained in her seat, in a daze, not sure what to do or where to go. Should she stay put and wait for Qin Yulou to come back for her? Or should she leave and come back on another day?

She was brought out of her reverie when a juvenile actor, her eyes squinting in a smile, ran up to her: "You must be big sister Yu Qing'e. Director Qin suggested that you grab a bite in the cafeteria first and wait there for her." She pressed a few meal coupons into her hand before bounding away.

Yu Qing'e had no wish to eat in the cafeteria of the Yueju Opera Theater for fear of running into some old school mate from the School of the Arts, with whom she would have to exchange civilities and pleasantries. She wanted to avoid the eventuality at all cost. Then she remembered having noticed, as she came in, a few restaurants and noodle eateries across the street from the

Yueju Opera Theater. She'd much prefer to go to one of those to have a quick, simple meal and wait in the doorman's booth for the return of Qin Yulou. It would be simpler and she would have a quiet moment to herself.

With her head inclined and eyes kept straight ahead, Yu Qing'e walked out of the Yueju Opera Theater and was relieved that she did not run into any acquaintance. Attracted by the interesting name of an eatery called "Grandma's Homemade Noodles" and enticed by the menu posted at the side of its entrance featuring a rich variety of dishes at reasonable prices, she pushed past the self-closing door.

The minute she set foot in the store, she stopped short, as if her feet were immobilized in quicksand. She had spotted her old school mates from their School of the Arts days Shi Xiaotong and Qian Xiaoxiao sitting in the back of the restaurant.

The small storefront had space only for a dozen tables. Yu Qing'e was going to beat a hasty retreat when the hostess already came forward to greet her: "Welcome to our restaurant! How many of you are there?" Desperately trying to avoid attracting the notice of the two school mates, Yi Qing'e hastily found an unoccupied table and sat down with her back turned toward them. Without much thought she ordered a bowl of noodles with shrimps and shredded eel.

Shi Xiaotong and Qian Xiaoxiao, totally oblivious to the comings and goings of the restaurant, were huddled together in rapt discussion of what just transpired in the rehearsal hall.

Shi Xiaotong said in a resentful tone: "You heard her. She really sucked up to the martial coach! The coach's valuable help! Has she forgotten who it was who had helped with her daily morning water sleeves practice?"

Qian Xiaoxiao said with a sneer: "That was all that she had to show for it after all the practice? When she did the exaggerated 'cloud hand' move, I was so apprehensive for her, and she tripped! She has such an intelligent face, but she just can't coordinate her movements and gestures!"

Not without a shade of schadenfreude, Shi Xiaotong said: "The conventional wisdom says injury to bone and ligaments takes a hundred days to heal. It appears the Hong Kong tour of the 'White Rabbit' will be scrubbed."

Qian Xiaoxiao thought otherwise: "That's out of the question. The contract has been signed. Worse comes to worst, Master Xie will play Li Sanniang through the entire play." Then she slapped the table, struck by a sudden idea: "That's it! I'm going to suggest to Manager Qin that you play Li Sanniang in her stead. Your singing and martial skills are better than hers!"

Shi Xiaotong gave her head a knock with her chopsticks: "What nonsense! If this became known, it would appear as if I were trying to steal her part. I don't covet that part!"

Yu Qing'e slurped down the entire bowl of noodles in hurried mouthfuls, giving herself no time to find out the taste of Grandma's Homemade Noodles. She paid the check and darted out of the store without looking back; the self-closing door slammed shut after her. Glancing over her shoulder after regaining her breath, she saw, through the glass front plastered with ads, the silhouettes of Shi Xiaotong and Qian Xiaoxiao, as if in a play viewed from a great distance—a story of their youthful innocence and ignorance.

Scene IX   The *Qingyi* Costume

The paintbrush of spring always came a few days late to the Xie residence to color its little courtyard. When outside in their alley "plants and flowers vied in myriad colors" already, the shrubberies and vines along the base of the Xie family's fence wall were only starting to turn green a patch at a time until little by little the entire wall was painted green in soft rains and gentle breezes.

Sister Ten woke up to a fine, sunny day, ideal for airing the *qingyi* costume in the sun. She quickly got out a bamboo pole, wiped it off to a glistening jade green; she then strung it through the two long sleeves before hoisting it up. The normally quiet, forlorn courtyard was enlivened by the flapping of the costume in the breeze. As the weather got warmer, Senior Miss preferred on a clear day to be out in the yard, sitting in front of the *qingyi* costume, allowing the costume flapped by the breeze to stroke her face and her hair.

A couple of months before, when watching the TV series *Operatic Kaleidoscope*, Senior Miss saw the interview of the cast and crew of the Yueju Opera Theater's new production of the "White Rabbit" conducted by a young, pretty host. She watched and listened with her face very close to the TV screen as if she had every intention to inject herself into the box if she could. When Mi Jingyao, who played Li Sanniang in the first half of the play, revealed that she was going to rehearse and perform the long sleeve dance sequence created years ago by Master Xie Yingge for the benefit of all the fans of the Xie School of Yueju opera art, Senior Miss, as if galvanized, tried to get up from her wheelchair!

Since then, Senior Miss had been hounding Junior Miss with questions like: How is Mi Jingyao's long sleeve dance sequence progressing? Is she able to bring aloft the water sleeves with the "sparrow hawk pirouette" move? Is she able to execute faultlessly the move combining a backbend with the twirling of the sleeves? In the last move, the "black dragon coiled around the pillar", does she get herself entangled in her sleeves?

She finally succeeded in irritating Junior Miss, who objected: "Jieh, you live in the past. Are you still clinging to the idea that your dance sequence is a big deal? They say they are reviving your long sleeve dance sequence but the fact is they hired a martial technical director to choreograph the movements from scratch. So stop your useless worries!" Then she added with some vehemence: "This Mi Jingyao has her own calculations and ulterior motives. You think she really intends to promote the Xie School of Yueju opera art? Think again! She is intent on vying with me for the limelight through the play. Since she knows she can't sing as well or act as well as I do, she hit on the idea of beating me with the water sleeve dance. Too bad her martial skill is weak. Jieh, she can't hold a candle to you!"

Silent like a deep lake for a moment, Senior Miss finally spoke, in a measured tone: "You personally picked her as your pupil despite my recommendation of Yu Qing'e. You found fault with Yu Qing'e, raising one objection after another. You were determined to reject her."

With a shrug of her shoulders and a contrite twitch of her mouth, Junior Miss said with a smile: "Jieh, after all these years you still hold it against me? It was those teachers at the School of the Arts who sang the praises of Mi Jingyao; what could I have done? I was no farsighted strategist like Zhuge Liang and I was no Monkey King able to burrow into people's mind!"

The proverb has it that the onlookers see most of the game and Sister Ten saw everything with a cold eye. Soon after the airing of that episode in the *Operatic Kaleidoscope* series, Junior Miss's enthusiasm for the "White Rabbit" rehearsals plummeted; she would often beg off the rehearsals on the excuse of not feeling well. Senior Miss would feel compelled to chide her: "This play is a showcase for the Xie School of Yueju opera. You must not bungle it as a result of your muddling through!" Junior Miss would retort that her worries were misplaced: "Jieh! Since you taught me this play, I must have sung it, what, for twenty some years. If I over practice, my singing will sound too slick, and the director thinks so too. He is now focusing on the detailed rehearsing of the two young actors of the first half of the play. My presence in the rehearsal room would only make them feel self-conscious and inhibited in their performance."

It did not escape the observant eye of Sister Ten that when Junior Miss absented herself from a rehearsal on the pretext of illness, she did not stay in either. She was after all a celebrity, with many social obligations and activities.

After hanging out the *qingyi* costume to dry, Sister Ten did Senior Miss's toiletries, helped her into the wheelchair and pushed her into the courtyard to take some fresh air. Afterwards

Sister Ten began preparing breakfast for the household. The pearl barley and millet porridge, a staple in Senior Miss's daily regimen, had been placed in a pot earlier to braise. One of pearl barley's claimed benefits was the alleviation of water retention and swelling; from long confinement in a wheelchair, Senior Miss was susceptible to swelling in her legs. A pot of fresh soybean milk was made especially for Junior Miss in the automatic soybean milk maker. According to Junior Miss's diet theory, soybean milk helped preserve and prolong women's youth. Sister Ten made the daily pot for her although deep down she pooh-poohed the idea: despite drinking her daily portion of soybean milk, Junior Miss hadn't prevented more wrinkles from lining her face or her waistline from bulging!

When Sister Ten worked in the house she would hum, like a mantra: "I have a little sister we call Sister Nine, she's smart and adored by all ..." She sliced the pickled cucumbers, peeled the preserved eggs, made the jellyfish salad, fried the peanuts and voila the four dishes to go with the porridge were ready! Then she went out and bought some thousand-layer cake, a kind of flaky pastry and scorch-fried ravioli. When everything was neatly arranged on the table, she went to the yard to bring Senior Miss in and shouted upstairs at the foot of the staircase: "Er Guniang—Sir—breakfast is ready!"

It was always Wang Houcheng who came down first. He would come around to his wheelchair-bound wife, look at her complexion and routinely ask: "Did you sleep well? Are you feeling well? Is your blood pressure in the normal range?" before picking up, as he settled into his chair, a newspaper from the tea table to read.

Junior Miss took her time in coming downstairs after the breakfast call. She needed to make up her face and change into her day dress. After her fiftieth birthday, Junior Miss absolutely refused to show her face without makeup.

Knowing her dawdling ways, Sister Ten began feeding Senior Miss her daily pearl barley and millet porridge, without troubling to wait for Junior Miss. Wang Houcheng would appear absorbed by what he was reading, but Sister Ten knew he was waiting for Junior Miss to join him at the table.

After ten minutes, or was it twenty? Junior Miss finally made her appearance downstairs, her high heels clicking, like the sandalwood clappers on stage, and her effusive perfume preceding her as she walked into the room.

At the start of the "White Rabbit" rehearsals, Junior Miss made a solemn announcement of her weight loss plan to the other members of the household and asked Sister Ten to act as a vigilant watchdog over its implementation. In the first half of the "White Rabbit", Li Sanniang is still a married woman in the prime of her youth, and in order to portray a pretty young woman with a graceful figure, she vowed to shrink her girth down to 25 inches. Following the announcement by the director of his decision to cast younger actors for the first half, however, the weight loss plan of the now infuriated Junior Miss existed in name only.

Junior Miss poured herself a full glass of soybean milk and picked up two pieces of flaky pastry with her chopsticks and placed them onto her plate. Then after a slight pause in the air of her chopsticks, she picked up two pot stickers, at which point Wang Houcheng said: "Er Mei, you are exceeding your portion!"

Junior Miss shot him a baleful glance: "Do you expect me to have the energy to sing Li Sanniang on a half-empty stomach? Besides, by the time I go on stage in the second half, Li Sanniang is already an ageing woman, and I would be perfect for the role with my plumpness."

Wang Houcheng said: "How can Li Sanniang be plump after all the hard work and harsh life she's been through? In all stages of her life, she should appear thin and frail. You might get away with it on stage but the plumpness will show in the stage photos. If you have even a slight hint of excess flesh on your face, it would look really bad in the photo …"

Throwing her chopsticks down on the table, Junior Miss said: "So you find me bad-looking in photos! No wonder you've been hovering about Mi Jingyao and Feng Jianyue of late. Jieh, there's no dearth of pretty young things in the Yueju Opera Theater. Make sure you pray a lot to Buddha!"

Wang Houcheng was livid. After taking a quick glance at his wife, who was sitting motionless and unperturbed facing the yard, he chided: "Er Mei, you are becoming more and more unreasonable. You know more than anyone that the leadership of the Theater pays me to take photographs of the entire cast and crew of the 'White Rabbit' project. I can't very well take only your pictures!"

Junior Miss retorted: "With my mediocre qualities and looks, I dare not entertain any illusion of attracting the notice of as great a photographer as you, Mr. Wang! On the other hand there's no lack of other photographers who'd love to take pictures of me. You are not the only one who has the right to choose!"

Wang Houcheng laughed, but the laugh sounded more like crying. He was at a point where he had no one to confide his hurt to, couldn't vent his bitterness and was powerless to change what he now regretted he'd done. His reputation, which he had taken a life time to build up, was in ruins because of this woman that was increasingly eluding his control.

It was at this moment that Senior Miss, who had been sitting stock still, suddenly started to sing:

> For sixteen years I've carried water in the day and
> turned the millstone at night,
> The well water is like my tears that spurt like a
> spring, though the well water is dwarfed by my
> tears ...

Although Senior Miss's singing voice, now much like a piece of old, faded, napped brocade riddled with holes, was no longer pleasing to the ear, the forlornness and melancholy conveyed by her unsteady, labored humming caused discomfiture, alarm and ultimately shamed silence in the two persons who were closest to her yet who had both betrayed her. The only sound in the entire house was the hoarse, monotonous, off-key singing of Senior Miss that hovered and reverberated through the convoluted spaces of the house.

Junior Miss, who couldn't stand it anymore, uttered a shrill "Jieh—" striking a jarring note like a fiddle whose string snapped during play. Putting her hands on the shoulders of Senior Miss, she said with a strained smile: "Jieh, I know the importance of the 'White Rabbit' to you. It is the signature work of Xie Yingge. It represents the zenith of the Xie School of Yueju opera art. Don't worry. I am also Xie Yingge after all. Would I pull the rug from under myself? No matter how young and pretty the Li Sanniang in the first half of the play may be, the Li Sanniang played by our Xie Yingge will remain second to none!"

In a voice as raspy and hoarse as before but in a calmer tone, Senior Miss said: "Shi Mei, listen closely. Take out that wild ginseng root from the pantry, and cut it into small pieces. Steam one piece a day. Oh, don't forget to add two slices of Astragalus propinquus into the preparation. It will help replenish Er Mei's energy."

Junior Miss said with a pout: "Jieh, I can read between the lines. You mean you are replenishing the energy of your Li Sanniang!" and giggled with mirth. She stole a glance at Senior Miss, who still wore an expression that couldn't decide between a smile and a crying grimace, but whose formerly rigid back had slacked. Relieved, Junior Miss raised her wrist to look at her watch before bending to speak close to Senior Miss's ear: "Jieh, get as much rest as you can these days to store up your energy. When the public performance of the 'White Rabbit' starts, ask Shi Mei to wheel you to the theater to watch your Li Sanniang, okay?"

Senior Miss took one glance at her. Junior Miss tried to hide her shock—despite the seriousness of her elder sister's illness, that one glance revealed the intensity of her inner longing. She averted her eyes and said with a laugh: "Jieh, I'm already late. I got to go."

When he heard Junior Miss announce her departure, Wang Houcheng, who had sat there brooding all this while, blurted: "There will be a stagger-through rehearsal with Feng Jianyue and Mi Jingyao today. Are you going to the rehearsal room too?"

Junior Miss retorted annoyedly: "Do you think the rehearsal room is the only place I can go to? I have a meeting of the board of the Dramatists Association of the province today!" and left, her heels clicking on the floor.

Wang Houcheng couldn't decide whether to catch up with her. After a brief moment of fluster, he turned to say to his wife: "Xiao Xie, I got to go too. I am going to the rehearsal room of the theater. Qin Yulou wants me to take more stage photos of the young actors." After a pause, he continued: "Just ignore Er Mei's ranting!"

As soon as Wang Houcheng was out the door, Sister Ten made a spitting gesture at the floor.

This Wang Houcheng was once a man of easy manners and generous spirit, talented and debonair; he couldn't be more considerate and loving toward Senior Miss. Who'd have thought that he'd turn into a completely different person once he came under the power of Junior Miss: now he was petty and vulgar and spoke on sufferance, wary and self-effacing "like a child bride". When she turned her head to look at Senior Miss again, she found Senior Miss bathed in the early morning sunlight slanting into the room, which created a halo that filtered out the details of her body, leaving only drab, broad-stroked contours. She saw a bone-chilling solitude and bitterness that only she, Sister Ten, could understand.

Sister Ten suppressed her own antipathy toward Wang Houcheng. She mustn't reopen Senior Miss's old wounds. Sister Ten knew that the wounds to Senior Miss's heart had never healed and her heart had been bleeding all these sixteen years. But Senior Miss bore it stoically. You couldn't help admiring this stoic fortitude: when she saw her husband and her own younger sister engaged in an illicit affair right under her nose, she was able to maintain her serenity and a discreet silence, occasionally finding solace in humming a few verses of Li Sanniang. Li Sanniang was Senior Miss's talisman, her raison d'être, her reason for tolerating what others could not.

Sister Ten sighed deeply to herself as she cleared away the plates, bowls and chopsticks. When she returned from the kitchen, she found Senior Miss had already wheeled herself to the French window and leaned forward to press her forehead against the glass sash. Through the glass the teal blue costume could be seen fluttering in the breeze, adding a vivid accent to the yard now fully greened by spring.

Sister Ten said with a laugh: "Da Guniang, you couldn't wait, could you? All right, let's go out in the yard and enjoy springtime together with Li Sanniang! 'Tis a clear day, the sun shines bright red and the earth has thawed; leaving my ornate boudoir, I crossed the well-appointed parlor into the garden for a stroll...'" Mangling verses sung by Li Sanniang on a spring outing, Sister Ten pushed open the French window to a heart-stirring view of a sheer curtain of willows and floating gossamer. Sister Ten pushed Senior Miss in her wheelchair to circle the yard once along the fence walls before parking it before the *qingyi* costume. Sister Ten knew that Senior Miss would often keep company with the *qingyi* costume for hours at a time and that would free her to finish her kitchen chores. And as if on cue, Senior Miss buried her face deep into the folds of the costume. At this moment she must have morphed into Li Sanniang, turning the millstone, or perhaps reuniting with Yaoqilang, her long lost baby now grown up, who was out on a hunt?

Sister Ten left Senior Miss to go back to the kitchen to wash the dishes and clean up the stove top and the counters, with the sink faucet running. Although getting on in years, Sister Ten still had good ears. She detected a bell ringing "drrrring—drrrring", punctuating the rushing sound of the tap water. She quickly shut off the faucet and the persistent "drrrring—drrrring" became the dominant sound. Finally Sister Ten realized it was the phone ringing and she raced to take the call.

It was Deputy General Manager Qin Yulou of the Provincial Yueju Opera Theater, who inquired first when Senior Miss would wake up from her afternoon nap. Sister Ten replied: she never really goes to sleep during the nap. She'd nod off for a brief while, maybe for ten minutes or half an hour, and could wake up at any moment. Qin Yulou next asked Sister Ten to pass on to Senior Miss that about two or three in the afternoon she was bringing a staunch follower of the Xie School of Yueju opera art to see Senior Miss. She then added for emphasis: "It's someone Da Guniang knows. Her name is Yu Qing'e."

Putting the phone down, Sister Ten wondered to herself: was Qin Yulou thinking right today? It has long been agreed that any visiting follower of the Xie School would without exception be brought before Junior Miss, who was the currently recognized Xie Yingge.

Despite her misgivings, she faithfully conveyed Qin Yulou's message to Senior Miss, with the thought that as soon as Senior Miss said she didn't wish to receive visitors, she'd immediately call Qin Yulou back to cancel the visit.

With her cheek rubbing against the folds of the *qingyi* costume and her eyes slightly closed, it was hard to know if she was listening to Sister Ten. But when the words "her name is Yu Qing'e" rolled off Sister Ten's tongue, the eyelids of Senior Miss snapped open and her eyeballs seemed to fly out of their sockets, leaving a pair of gaping holes in their place.

After Mi Jingyao sprained her ankle during the afternoon rehearsal in a maneuver involving "spinning" which is similar to chaînés, "cloud hands" and "sleeve flicks", Qin Yulou accompanied her to the orthopedics department of the Provincial People's Hospital. The doctor examined her and made the felicitous diagnosis that no major concerns were found and ordered ice compresses, followed by the application, in a few hours, of an ointment to aid blood circulation and alleviate bruising, and a few days of bed rest. Qin Yulou was relieved. With the public performance of the "White Rabbit" fast approaching, it would be hard to find a replacement for Mi Jingyao on such short notice, if she were to be prevented from going on stage on account of her foot injury.

It was past noon when Qin Yulou returned to the Theater; she headed straight to the staff mess hall but could no longer find Yu Qing'e after looking around a few times. She figured that Yu Qing'e must have finished her lunch. Where could she have gone to wait for her? She decided to attend to her hunger pangs first. Carrying a bowl of fish flavor pork noodles, she found a vacant chair and sat down in it. When she looked up, she was surprised to see Wang Houcheng drinking beer across the table, with two dishes and a bottle of draft beer in front of him.

Qin Yulou said with a smile: "Lao Wang, why are you drinking by yourself? Where's Xiao Xie?"

With the prominence of his cheeks and the tip of his nose flushed with drink, Wang Houcheng said with a shake of his head: "She had no rehearsal this morning, so she went to a meeting of the Dramatists Association board."

Qin Yulou smiled to herself, thinking: "This Xie Yingge! Couldn't even tell a plausible lie when she gets in the bragging mood! And only Wang Houcheng is gullible enough to believe her. It would occur to anyone with an average IQ that I am a deputy chairman of the board of the Dramatists Association. Could anyone imagine a meeting of the board without its deputy chairman?" The fact was shortly after Qin Yulou arrived for work that morning, she received a call from this Xie Yingge, saying that her co-workers in the singing-only traditional opera troupe in the old days had come to the provincial capital for sightseeing and she needed to take them around as their local host. And she asked to be excused from the day's rehearsals. According to the rules originally set by Director He for the entire cast and crew, whenever the cast of either the first or the second half of the play was rehearsing, the cast for the other half must be present, because it took the two casts working together to build a coherent picture.

But Director He couldn't make the rule stick when it came to Xie Yingge. Xie Yingge was after all a celebrity in the cultural circles of the province and wore many hats in various organizations. Even the imperious Director He was powerless over her. Qin Yulou did not disabuse Wang Houcheng of his naive belief but merely offered the advice: "Lao Wang, cut down on the beer. If you go home reeking of alcohol, she would be upset."

Wang Houcheng naturally knew which "she" Qin Yulou was referring to. He said after some consideration: "There will be no rehearsal the rest of the afternoon, so I plan to take the stage photos I've shot so far to the photo studio and have them developed and printed. I need to sort through them and maybe take some more for scenes that are not well covered."

Qin Yulou nodded, then bringing her face closer, she asked in a hushed voice: "How has she been these days?"

Wang Houcheng's eyelids opened and immediately drooped. He murmured: "Same as usual. She has been like this for so many years now. Not getting any worse and not getting any better either."

Qin Yulou said with a sigh: "I know; she has never come to terms with ..." She stopped short and took a glance at Wang Houcheng. She wasn't sure which "she" had pride of place in his heart. After an interval, she said in a cheerier tone: "This afternoon I'm going to take a young actor from a small town Yueju opera troupe to pay her a visit. She is a follower of the Xie School. I've been meaning to visit her myself but haven't been able to free myself from the hectic schedule of late."

Wang Houcheng stared at Qin Yulou in astonishment: "What happened? Did this Xie Yingge refuse to see this young actor?"

Qin Yulou was prepared for this; she said: "The young actor came with a reference letter and expressed a wish to learn the Xie style long sleeve dance. You know that this Xie Yingge has never done the long sleeve dance; so the other Xie Yingge is our only hope."

Wang Houcheng said hesitantly: "But won't this Xie Yingge resent it if she finds out? Besides, she ... how is she going to teach the young actor? She can't even stay on her feet."

"Tay—" a small gong was struck in Qin Yulou's mind: it appeared that Wang Houcheng was more concerned about this Xie Yingge! With a shadow of a smile, she said: "Lao Wang, don't worry! When the board of the Dramatists Association meets, which is infrequently, it takes up a whole day. As long as you don't tell her, this Xie Yingge is not going to find out. I've been told this young actor has solid martial training, so there's no need for Master Xie to demonstrate the moves herself. All she needs to do is give a few pointers at critical points."

That silenced any further questions from Wang Houcheng, who said: "I'll go with you then. I can tidy up the place for your visit."

Qin Yulou said with a smile: "Do whatever you've planned to do. There's Sister Ten who can tidy up the place. I wouldn't dream of troubling you with such chores."

Their conversation was interrupted when a doorman hurried toward them: "Manager Qin, the girl who came to see you this morning is now waiting in the doorman's booth for you."

Qin Yulou said: "Good, very good, I'll be right over." And tilting her head back, she downed the rest of the soup.

For sixteen years, Qin Yulou had kept a shocking secret for the two Xie sisters and she was the only one, outside of the Xie household, who was in on the secret.

Sixteen years before, the Provincial Yueju Opera Theater, which had been forced to disband during the "Cultural Revolution", was reinstated. The first major assignment they received from the Department of Culture was the production under a tight schedule of a short Yueju opera play reflecting the highest quality and standards in the province to be performed in a gala event planned for the Spring Festival. After careful consideration and a full discussion, the new leadership of the

Theater chose Qin Yulou and Xie Yingge to perform the scene of "Reunion of Husband and Wife" in the "White Rabbit". First of all, Qin Yulou and Xie Yingge had always worked together as a dream team and they were familiar with each other's acting style; secondly, they performed the "White Rabbit" to packed houses in the early 1960's and had acquired a solid following; thirdly, a hiatus lasting a decade due to the Upheaval notwithstanding, Qin Yulou ended up during that period playing walk-on roles in a troupe that performed model revolutionary operas and Xie Yingge was also fortunate enough to be transferred at a later stage to the School of the Arts as a teacher. Their Yueju opera skills therefore did not go to total waste. The fact that they were now past forty meant they had matured intellectually and in their acting skills; it was the ideal time in these opera actors' life to produce great works.

In that period, the many troupes performing model revolutionary operas were disbanded one after another, and Qin Yulou had only just been transferred back to the Yueju Opera Theater. When she was notified of the leadership's decision, she leaped with excitement and got all fired up with passion. What actor would not relish the opportunity to return to the stage to show her talent and charm to the world? And there was another reason: in the early stages of the "Cultural Revolution", due to a careless slip of the tongue on the part of Qin Yulou, Xie Yingge was wrongfully condemned. The incident drove a wedge between the two good friends, creating a rift and turning them into strangers to each other. Laden with a guilty feeling toward Xie Yingge, Qin Yulou had been looking for an opportunity to mend fences. Now the opportunity finally presented itself. That same night, Qin Yulou went to the post office, waited in line to make a phone call to Xie Yingge, who was teaching in the School of the Arts of a small town on the remote edges of the city, to break the good news to her and urge her to return as soon as possible to the provincial capital to start rehearsing.

Ten days later, Qin Yulou met Xie Yingge, who'd reported

for work at the Provincial Yueju Opera Theater. At first sight she could hardly believe her own eyes—in her memory Xie Yingge shone with charm and beauty on stage but was a quiet, bashful and modest person in her private life; she disliked publicity, eschewed expensive, flashy dresses and was frugal with words. But the Xie Yingge in front of her wore her hair short, curled and going off in all directions as if frazzled in an explosion; she sported a pair of tight-fitting, leg-hugging flare bottom slacks and a rose red blouse with a fine floral pattern and drawn in at the waist and featuring ruffle-like trims on the collar and cuffs, setting off a face that looked like a blooming flower.

Qin Yulou stood in a daze before her, mortified by the sharp contrast to her own plumpness and drab dress. After years of estrangement, she was holding herself back, not knowing what to say, when this Xie Yingge already lunged at her and grabbed hold of her arms, laughing and jumping: "Qin Dajieh (Big Sister Qin)! Now we can rehearse together once again!"

Qin Yulou responded, tentatively, to her ebullience; she was baffled: Xie Yingge had never called her Dajieh. A few months younger, she had always affectionately called her Yulou. After their estrangement, she would rudely call her by her full name on the rare occasions when they ran into each other. Qin Yulou couldn't wrap her head around it! Didn't the proverb say leopards do not change their spots? What were the circumstances that had so radically changed the personality of Xie Yingge?

Qin Yulou's suspicion grew in the intensive rehearsals that followed. This Xie Yingge's voice was surprisingly louder and crisper than when she was younger and in the high registers it threatened to shatter the eardrums. But the smooth undulating inflections, the melodious and poignant quality of her singing, so much prized in arias sung by Xie Yingge in the past, were no longer there. What further fueled her suspicion was the inexplicable unfamiliarity of this Xie Yingge with the blocking arrangement in the scene of the "Reunion of Husband and Wife" in the "White Rabbit". At the height of their popularity, the two of them had performed that scene of the "White Rabbit" close to a hundred times and they could get the blocking right, moving to the right spots at the right moments, even blindfolded. Could the harsh treatment she'd been subjected to in those ten years have caused amnesia in Xie Yingge? Moreover, while in costume and makeup she looked not much different than before, she had so far failed to convey Li Sanniang's visceral pain and bitterness. Actors who played opposite each other on stage should be mutually stimulating and complementary to each other, but when Qin Yulou played opposite this Xie Yingge, she consistently failed to step into the role. If she could not correctly convey Li Sanniang's emotions and feelings, how could I be expected to convey to what degree Liu Zhiyuan was ashamed, touched or contrite? The day came when finally Qin Yulou could no longer hold her curiosity back. This Xie Yingge managed to sing the plaintive "sixteen years" aria as a light-hearted folk song! Qin Yulou cut her off and asked: "Xiao Xie! When you sang this aria in years back, you used to make the listeners feel so racked with grief that their hearts seemed torn to pieces, a far cry from how you sing it now. Are you really Xie Yingge?"

This Xie Yingge stared at her for a confused instant before flashing a smile: "Qin Dajieh, I haven't sung for over ten years. I really need to brush up. But don't worry, I'll get in more practice and with your guidance and help I will get back to where I was before."

This further confounded Qin Yulou, who found this Xie Yingge's modesty a little overdone. Why would she use words like "get in more practice" or "your guidance", words that the former Xie Yingge would not be caught dead using? She and Xie Yingge had occasions to disagree when they rehearsed in the past. Xie Yingge didn't easily change her views on questions of art, unless she could be persuaded otherwise after thorough discussion and analysis. If your argument won over hers, she would say let me think about it. And by the next rehearsal, you'd find that she had quietly incorporated your idea into her performance. Qin Yulou missed that candid, uncompromising Xie Yingge and was put off by this over-solicitous, compliant smooth operator of a Xie Yingge.

Obsessed with the baffling phenomenon of a changed personality residing in a look-alike Xie Yingge, Qin Yulou tossed and turned all night. After a night of fitful sleep, she woke up a bit late and when she arrived at the rehearsal room, that Xie Yingge was already sitting there, waiting, but out of her practice suit and dressed to the nines.

Qin Yulou was irritated: didn't you say you wanted to get in more practice? What are you doing sitting there like a VIP guest? And she couldn't help raising her voice: "Hey, Xiao Xie! Why are you not in your practice suit yet? We have a full schedule today …"

Xie Yingge rose to her feet with a winning smile: "Qin Dajieh, I will practice hard. But can we take the morning off today? I'd like to take you to see someone."

A fireball of anger rose in Qin Yulou: "We don't have much time left for rehearsing. Xiao Xie, if we don't pass muster at review time, our entry could still be withdrawn and replaced!"

This Xie Yingge said with a hearty laugh: "Qin Dajieh, I know, and I will do my best to practice, but this person wants very, very much to see you!"

"Who is this person?" Qin Yulou blurted out. A basketful of questions tumbled out, like a squad of somersault walk-ons waiting in the wings flipping their way onto the stage at the sound of the percussion instruments.

Recovering herself from her fit of laughter, this Xie Yingge said with a serious mien: "Qin Dajieh, she is what you'd consider a veteran of Yueju opera. When she heard about the new production of the 'White Rabbit', she insisted on seeing the two of us. I already agreed to the request. What about you?"

As if struck by a beam from a spotlight on stage, Qin Yulou felt her entire body illuminated; she said with an excited shudder: "Yes, let's go see her!"

It turned out this Xie Yingge was taking Qin Yulou to the inter-city bus terminal. Qin Yulou did not ask why, expecting a sensational, shocking twist at the end of the drama, and watching with a cold eye to find out what more was up her sleeve.

After traveling for over an hour, the long-haul bus arrived in an ancient-looking small town. This Xie Yingge signaled Qin Yulou to get off the bus. A look at the place name of the bus depot gave Qin Yulou a start: this was the ancient town where the Provincial School of the Arts was located and where Xie Yingge made her home a few years before. In that instant it dawned on Qin Yulou who it was that this Xie Yingge was taking her to see. The mystery that had haunted and troubled her for days would finally be unraveled; Qin Yulou's heart had a sudden lurch and started to beat like a single-headed high-pitched drum, signaling the actors to enter the stage with a quickening tempo.

This Xie Yingge led Qin Yulou through meandering streets and alleys to arrive before a run-down, out-of-the-way house. Hanging by the wooden door whose black paint had peeled in numerous places was a weather-beaten wooden plank declaring the building to be a Convalescence Hospital. Qin Yulou's heart sank with a thud—like a beater landing on a cracked gong.

Qin Yulou finally met the Xie Yingge from the past, the bona fide Xie Yingge, the Xie Yingge who had been in her dreams all these years!

The sick ward was not spacious, a bare room occupied by six beds. This Xie Yingge led her straight to the bed by the window. A middle-aged woman of generous proportions shot up from her chair at the foot of the bed and called out: "Master Qin ..." and started sobbing with a hand covering her mouth.

The window was opened a crack but covered with a drab cloth curtain, which dimmed the room, making it appear to be in the twilight hours instead of the noon time they were in.

Qin Yulou bent over the bed only to see, under an equally drab bed sheet, an emaciated body, with only the face showing—a face that was an exact copy of that of this Xie Yingge, who stood at her side, but with a completely different complexion and expression—the face outside the bed sheet was sallow and wore an expression that could be a smile or a crying grimace, as if molded in plaster!

But Qin Yulou could immediately sense that aura of unconcern and cool serenity seen in the Xie Yingge of yesteryear. An in-born aura could not be copied, nor could it be destroyed! She called in a soft voice: "Xiao Xie ..." and her voice broke.

Sister Ten pulled up a chair and invited Qin Yulou to sit down. Sticking a hand under the bed sheet, Qin Yulou carefully laced the five fingers of Xie Yingge's hand into her own; she had the sense of having a handful of jagged jade fragments pressed into and hurting her palm.

"What ... what happened to her?" Qin Yulou asked, her teeth chattering.

Sister Ten said through her sobbing: "Master Qin, you called the other night, right? Da Guniang was so excited she practiced the long sleeve dance until late in the night and fell. The doctor said she had a cerebral hemorrhage. Fortunately she received timely medical attention. She lived but one side of her is now paralyzed ... How is Da Guniang going to live the rest of her life? She lives for the performance of Yueju opera!"

It was then that Qin Yulou felt a transient stirring of the jade fragments-like fingers of Xie Yingge under the bed sheet. When she hovered closer to her, the eyelids on that mask of a face slowly opened, revealing a pair of eyes that twinkled like two dim, faraway stars. Qin Yulou immediately called out: "Xiao Xie! Xiao Xie! This is Yulou! This is Liu Zhiyuan!"

Xie Yingge's eyelids flipped open, and a light flickered in her eyes; another flip of the eyelids was followed by another flicker of light in her eyes.

Sister Ten edged closer to say: "Master Qin, Da Guniang is trying to say something to you!" then brought one ear close to the patient's lips.

Qin Yulou heard what sounded like the gurgling of a deep

well, after which Sister Ten straightened up and said in a whisper: "Master Qin, Da Guniang wished that you would treat her—she is the younger sister of Da Guniang—as Xie Yingge!" She bent down a second time to listen and straightened up to say: "Da Guniang said her sister can sing the entire play of the 'White Rabbit'. Master Qin, your Liu Zhiyuan will now have your Li Sanniang." She stooped to listen a third time and this time the gurgling sound seemed to have an urgency in it. Sister Ten hastened to put out a hand to stroke her forehead: "Guniang, I know, I know what you mean …" When she drew herself up, she said through her sobs, as tears streaked her plump face: "Master Qin, Da Guniang entreats you to treat her as the real Xie Yingge; she hopes that the 'White Rabbit' performed by the two of you would endure on the stage; she hopes that Xie Yingge will make a comeback on the Yueju opera stage and be restored to her former glory …" Unable to finish her sentence, she threw herself on the patient and burst into a lusty cry.

Qin Yulou drew in a long breath as she tightened her grip on the skeletal fingers; she bent down too, her eyes holding those that reminded her of stars in a cold night, and softly but clearly declared: "Xiao Xie, don't worry, get well first. For now your younger sister will play Li Sanniang posing as you. I will not divulge the secret. When you recover your health, you and I will pick up where we left off as the couple Liu Zhiyuan and Li Sanniang. I will wait for you!"

Qin Yulou couldn't have been more wrong! In sixteen years there was not the slightest sign of improvement in Xie Yingge's disability; with one side paralyzed, she struggled through her days confined in her wheelchair. Her younger sister, on the other hand, popularized the name "Xie Yingge" again by performing on the Yueju opera stage as Xie Yingge, and had since been popularly recognized as the famous actor in female role of Yueju opera Xie Yingge. No one would now suspect that this Xie Yingge was not that Xie Yingge from the past.

It was after careful consideration that Qin Yulou had decided to break the vow of secrecy and take Yu Qing'e to pay a call on the Xie Yingge from the past. She knew that that Xie Yingge had a high opinion of Yu Qing'e. When she went to the School of the Arts years ago to recruit for the Provincial Yueju Opera Theater, it was that Xie Yingge who told her to make sure Yu Qing'e was recruited. She also knew that this Xie Yingge had a particular distaste for Yu Qing'e and that Yu Qing'e was kept out of the Provincial Yueju Opera Theater because of the obstruction of this Xie Yingge; thus a prized Glossy Ganoderma plant was swamped by a sea of thistles and thorns.

Qin Yulou had long felt contrition toward Yu Qing'e. Some years ago it was through the agency of Qin Yulou that this Xie Yingge succeeded in breaking up the dream team of Yu Qing'e and Feng Jianyue. It was a time when this Xie Yingge was at the zenith of her fame. Not only the Provincial Yueju Opera Theater needed her, but also Qin Yulou herself, who needed her to play her opposite on stage. She therefore went against her own conscience and acted as the Devil's henchman in helping her to substitute Mi Jingyao for Yu Qing'e.

Qin Yulou never found out why this Xie Yingge disliked Yu Qing'e so much. Her guess was that given the youth and professional potential of Yu Qing'e, this Xie Yingge might very well have felt threatened, thinking that Yu Qing'e would quickly shoot to stardom and steal the limelight from her.

While others did not realize it, Qin Yulou immediately detected a huge difference between this Xie Yingge and that Xie Yingge in performance style and character. But this Xie Yingge had going for her an outstanding appearance in costume and a clear and limber voice, which earned her sustained applause the moment she appeared on stage. Soon the name "Xie Yingge" soared like an eagle as she rocketed to prominence. It should be said that in the beginning it was the name "Xie Yingge" that created this Xie Yingge, but in turn this Xie Yingge, by her talent and her hard work, propelled the name "Xie Yingge" into greater prominence and added to its glory.

What worried Qin Yulou was: since her rise to stardom, this Xie Yingge had morphed from a humble, compliant rookie into an arrogant, spoiled diva who would lord it over and browbeat actors who played in the same scenes as she. No one dared contradict her, much less offer any suggestions or comments. But this Xie Yingge was past fifty and her figure was inexorably getting stouter and wrinkles proliferated in her face. More ominous was the roughening and drying up of her voice, which often strained in the upper register, thereby giving away its vulnerability. Since taking on administrative responsibilities, Qin Yulou appeared in fewer performances than before, but she still managed to keep up her daily *taichi* and *qigong* practice in order to strengthen breathing and ensure smooth vocal delivery. In contrast, this Xie Yingge couldn't be bothered to worry about or plan for the future, and was as wilful and capricious as ever.

What concerned Qin Yulou was not this Xie Yingge's artistic slide; after all it was a law of nature that "flowers eventually fade and the full moon will wane". The greater worry for Qin Yulou was how much longer the cachet of the "Xie Yingge" brand could last. If the "Xie Yingge" brand were to be forgotten and sink into obscurity along with the decline of this Xie Yingge as a stage artist, it would be an injustice to that Xie Yingge who'd been cooped up in her little house confined to her wheelchair for sixteen years. Qin Yulou had found a trust-worthy, promising heir to her own school of Yueju opera art in Feng Jianyue, who was unassailable in stage appearance, singing, acting and martial training, and more importantly, in her devotion to the art and style of her master. But who could be an heir to the art of "Xie Yingge"? Clearly Mi Jingyao was not a qualified candidate, given that she set her sights higher than a mere Yueju opera stage. A month ago, when Qin Yulou ran into Yu Qing'e for the first time after many years in the studio of the Provincial TV Station, she was struck by an epiphany and blurted out: "Yu Qing'e, are you still singing Yueju opera nowadays? You shouldn't let the skills you acquired as a teenager go to waste!" A few days ago she received a phone call from Party Secretary Zhang of the productions company of the small town, who said that the new production of a romance play *Xishi Returns Home*, with Yu Qing'e in the lead role, would soon be shown to the public and there was a long sleeve dance sequence to be performed by Yu Qing'e in the play. Would it be possible, she asked, for Xie Yingge to give her some coaching? Qin Yulou agreed without hesitation. In fact it was in that instant that she was struck by the idea of taking Yu Qing'e to pay a call on the original Xie Yingge.

About two o'clock in the afternoon, Qin Yulou, with Yu Qing'e at her side, arrived at the door of the Xie residence. The blazing sun, filtered through the clouds that crowded the sky, felt soft and mellow. The fence walls of the courtyard were covered by vines of unknown names, sprinkled with white and yellow wild flowers, which attracted two butterflies that flitted among them. Qin Yulou knew that this double wooden door was not locked in day time and would open with a light push. But she decided to stick to etiquette and knocked on the door.

"Just a minute!" The response was followed by the sound of vigorous, bouncy footsteps and the door was opened wide.

Sister Ten said with a broad smile: "Master Qin! I'm glad to see you. She is waiting for you." She looked Yu Qing'e up and down before saying with a smile: "The young lady looks familiar. Have I seen you in a painting?"

The voice and the face of Sister Ten stirred up something buried deep in Yu Qing'e's memory. In the sunny afternoon, she felt as if transported to a courtyard bathed in moonlight and paved with swaying shadows of flowering shrubs.

"Xiao Xie!" Qin Yulou called out as she broke into a brisk walk, "Why are you out here?"

It turned out Sister Ten had wheeled Senior Miss into the courtyard and parked her in front of the fluttering *qingyi* costume. She had also set down a small, foldable square table and two square stools; on the square table sat a teapot and a number of cups, plus two platters filled with a variety of candies, eagerly waiting to serve the honored guests.

Sister Ten said, as she poured the tea: "When Da Guniang heard that Master Qin was visiting, she wouldn't have her regular nap and instructed me to get everything ready well ahead of your arrival."

Qin Yulou grabbed Yu Qing'e and dragged her to where Senior Miss was seated and said in a meaningful voice: "Xiao Xie! Look who I've brought to you!"

Senior Miss slowly turned her head and looked up in the direction of Yu Qing'e, who found, with a start, that this face wearing a fixed expression frozen between a smile and a crying grimace struck her as familiar. Had she seen it in a dream? She asked in a whisper: "Manager Qin, she—who is she?"

Putting a hand on Yu Qing'e's shoulder, Qin Yulou explained in a muted voice: "Xie Yingge is too busy. This is Xie Yingge's elder sister. She used to be an excellent Yueju opera actor. It was from her that Xie Yingge learned the 'White Rabbit'!"

"Oh—" Yu Qing'e let out a long breath, then added: "How should I address her then?"

Qin Yulou said with a smile: "You should naturally call her Master Xie to show proper respect!"

Yu Qing'e made a ninety degree bow and said reverentially: "How are you, Master Xie?"

In a sign of recognition, Senior Miss suddenly lifted her left hand and held it out to her. As Yu Qing'e hesitated in her confusion, Qin Yulou gave her a shove and she stumbled forward, caught the hand stretched out by Senior Miss—and immediately felt a cool, smooth sensation course through her body. Her memory came back in a tidal rush, sweeping her under. In that small courtyard bathed in bright moonlight and paved with swaying shadows of flowering shrubs in the distant past, she held her hand just as she did now and listened to her sing those verses "In those sixteen years, the thousand-jin millstone be my witness" and asked her "Do you want to sing Yueju opera on stage when you grow up?" Although that orchid-shaped dimple was no longer detectable in this mask-like face, Yu Qing'e had no doubt whatsoever that this was the Xie Yingge she'd been longing to see all these years!

"Master Xie, here I am—" it was a call fraught with affection, coming from the depth of her heart. Qin Yulou quickly wiped off the tears that welled out of her eyes and, picking up her cup, drank off the fragrant tea in one draught. She had been burdened by a deep sense of guilt for having hurt these two women and today she finally acquitted herself of this old debt.

Patting Yu Qing'e on her back, Qin Yulou said with a smile: "Xiao Yu, don't squander this opportunity to learn from Master Xie! Don't be shy to ask questions, all right?" then bending toward Senior Miss, "Xiao Xie, the director is coaching my pupil Feng Jianyue in rehearsal, so I've got to be there. I'm leaving Qing'e in your hands. Please give her unvarnished, critical advice; as Confucius says, the gem cannot be polished without friction. I'm going to leave you to your work now. I'll visit again as soon as I'm free."

Sister Ten saw Qin Yulou out while Senior Miss already started Yu Qing'e singing.

Yu Qing'e was going to sing the verses of the new play *Xishi Returns Home*, but when she opened her mouth to sing, what issued forth was the old tune sung by Li Sanniang upon her reunion with her husband Liu Zhiyuan:

> In those sixteen years, the thousand-jin millstone
> be my witness,
> I have milled away many a morning and evening;
> In those sixteen years, the three-foot wide apron of
> the well be my witness,
> I've treaded upon it may a winter and spring;
> In those sixteen years, the tear-stained sweet
> osmanthus be my witness,
> I have shed many a bloodshot tear;

In those sixteen years, the bitter fish pond be my
  witness,
I've confronted many a crisis of life and death …

Now she was solidly back to that small courtyard bathed in
bright moonlight and paved with swaying shadows of flowering
shrubs of many years ago, and in front of her idol and to that
beautiful face imprinted with an orchid-shaped dimple, she was
pouring out all the anguish, troubles, disappointments, bitterness
and yearning she had been put through all these years. Her
feelings of being wronged, pent up for so many years, were now
being released in a cathartic burst of free-flowing tears as fits of
sobbing interrupted almost every line of the aria she was singing.
When she came to the last "sixteen years" verse, where the pitch
went up an octave, she was overcome by sobs and could not finish
the sentence. She shot a panicked glance at her teacher Master
Xie, whose mask of a face remained unchanged, but who lifted
her left arm to press a handkerchief into her hand. Yu Qing'e
quickly covered her face with it; she could smell a faint whiff of
herbal medicine.

Then she heard her teacher Master Xie say, slowly and
deliberately, pausing at each word: "Good. You sing well. You've
got good spray-mouth projection and good diction, breathing
and phrasing but some of the flourishes in my opinion should
be avoided. Imagine what goes through Li Sanniang's mind in
the circumstance. Singing with less ornament would be more apt
to move the audience in this instance. What's most important
for you is to learn to control your emotions. Rein in your tears,
invest them into the verses instead, so that 'every note contains
a tear and blood pulses through every word'. That's the proper
way to move the audience to tears. Just now you sobbed so that
you couldn't hold your notes. If this happens on stage, you risk
singing out of beat and off key."

"Wham—" Yu Qing'e, as if waked up by a crash of cymbals,
suddenly saw the light. She wiped the tears off her face and said

with eyes shining: "Master Xie, I understand now. Can I sing this part over again?"

The expression on the mask-like face of her teacher Master Xie remained unchanged, but Yu Qing'e could sense the tender affection and encouragement in her eyes. After taking a sip of tea to lubricate her throat, Yu Qing'e began singing.

She sang the "sixteen years" verses three times. After she finished the last repetition, her teacher Master Xie started vigorously hitting the armrest with the left hand, which still had sensation in it. Clueless about what it meant, Yu Qing'e looked at her teacher in a fluster. Then Sister Ten started giggling: "Da Guniang is applauding you!" With a twitch of her mouth, Yu Qing'e bowed her head in modesty.

Master Xie told Sister Ten to pour tea and unwrap a candy for Yu Qing'e; this had the effect of further discomfiting her. Sister Ten said, tendering the candy to Yu Qing'e's mouth: "Girl! I have not seen our Da Guniang in such a good mood in over ten years. When Master Qin comes to visit, the most she is offered is a cup of tea. So I hope you'll visit often."

Yu Qing'e understood for the first time that Master Xie could no longer communicate her feelings through facial expressions, and one could tell her moods and emotions, such as joy, anger or sadness, only by the subtle details of her gestures.

After about a quarter of an hour, Master Xie asked Yu Qing'e to do the long sleeve dance. Yu Qing'e took out from her bag the home-sewn, lengthened water sleeves and put them on, not without some hesitation: "Master Xie, I am not so good at it yet. Please bear with me." She then did a series of "sparrow hawk pirouettes", only during the first of which her long sleeves were deployed out to form a circle but then they got tangled. Shaking her head, Yu Qing'e tried again but equally failed to sustain the sleeves in a circle. She gave up and looked at her teacher for help.

Master Xie surprised her by propelling herself toward her, turning a wheel with her left hand; Yu Qing'e hastened to meet her half way. Master Xie picked up her long sleeves and felt them with her face before saying, in stage speech: "Shi Mei, take down that *qingyi* costume of mine and put it on Qing'e—"

Sister Ten slipped the costume off the bamboo pole and handed it to Yu Qing'e, who quickly took two steps back, "No, no! I have no right to wear my teacher's costume!"

It pained Sister Ten to see the costume on anyone other than Senior Miss, but she knew that Senior Miss had her own reason for doing this and couldn't be talked out of it. So she said: "Since it's your teacher's wish, feel free to wear it!"

Reluctantly Yu Qing'e took off her own homemade water sleeves and put on Master Xie's *qingyi* costume. Once in the costume, she tried the various sleeve maneuvers, such as shaking, flipping, throwing, and found immediately she was able to manipulate the sleeves with ease and freedom. Tracing circles in the air with her left hand, Master Xie signaled her to start dancing. After a series of "sparrow hawk pirouettes", she began the dance, manipulating the long water sleeves, which coiled and floated weightlessly and gracefully about her like white clouds, and the next moment she would soar into the sky, light as a swallow, with the sough of the wind in her ears ...

As if waking from a dream, Yu Qing'e stopped and gave a cry of delighted surprise: "Master! I did it, didn't I? Just as in my dream!"

Hitting the armrest of her chair with her left hand again, Master Xie said: "You demonstrate solid martial training. It's the poor quality of the material of your long sleeves that prevented you from fully deploying them and caused them to get tangled."

Sister Ten added: "The fabric of Da Guniang's costume was woven by the best weavers of our home town with top quality silk. Silk of this quality is hard to come by nowadays."

Master Xie told Yu Qing'e to pull up a stool to sit by her and asked: "Is that series of 'sparrow hawk pirouettes' part of *Xishi Returns Home?*" Yu Qing'e was astonished to find that her teacher, despite being home-bound, knew about her rehearsal of *Xishi*

Returns Home. Overcome with emotion, she didn't know what to say and only nodded in reply.

After an interval of silence, Master Xie said all of a sudden: "Shi Mei, it's such a coincidence that my mother played Xishi also. The script she performed was *Washing Silk* adapted from the version of Liang Yuchen."

Wiping off tears that began to form, Sister Ten said: "Hao Ma's was a civil play, without the use of long sleeves. Her singing was so soft and sweet—"

Feeling fate must have a hand in their crossing paths, Yu Qing'e said: "Master Xie, was your mother also a Yueju opera actor?"

Sister Ten said with a loud voice: "Have you heard of the name Cai Lianfen? Nobody performs tragic Yueju opera plays as well as she did!"

Seemingly paying no attention to their exchange, Master Xie followed the thread of her thinking and said: "I did a series of 'sparrow hawk pirouettes' in the scene of 'Giving Birth by the Millstone' in the 'White Rabbit' …"

Yu Qing'e said eagerly: "Master Xie, I choreographed my long sleeve dance sequence on the basis of stage photos of your performance in the scene of 'Giving Birth by the Millstone'."

She could be asking a question or talking to herself when Master Xie said: "Can the 'sparrow hawk pirouette' done by Xishi be the same as the 'sparrow hawk pirouette' done by Li Sanniang?"

Not knowing what to say in reply, Yu Qing'e said timidly: "Master Xie, I only saw photos of you doing it, so I had no success when I tried to imitate …"

Master Xie interrupted her by slapping her knee with her left hand: "Of course they can't be the same. When Xishi takes leave of her homeland, there is the sadness of parting, mixed with a heroic willingness to sacrifice herself for her country. When Li Sanniang gives birth in the mill shed, she feels helplessness, physical pain and bitterness. Her heart is broken. Their feelings are different and therefore they do the 'sparrow hawk pirouette' and manipulate the water sleeves in distinct ways. The sequence of movements may be the same, but the emotions of the performers of those movements are not. The same sequence of movements will take on different meanings as a result. You must know that the long sleeves have their own emotions, joy, anger, sadness, what have you …" Master Xie went into a fit of coughing, as if she were going to spit her heart out.

Alarmed by the sudden access of coughing, Yu Qing'e rushed over and stroked her back. Sister Ten brought a cup of tea to Senior Miss's lips and said with disapproval: "Da Guniang, you haven't talked so much in one sitting in all these years! You probably said more words today than all the words you said in the past ten years added together. What's the hurry? You have all the time in the world and Miss Yu will visit often, right?" and she sought Yu Qing'e's corroboration with significant winks.

With a lump in her throat, Yu Qing'e was afraid to open her mouth lest she burst out crying and merely nodded vigorously.

A late afternoon haze rose in the deep wood,
As the low sun climbed down the little pavilion.

Treading the fragments of light and shade playing on the ground and mossed paths, Yu Qing'e left the Xie residence. In order to catch the last bus home, she had taken regretful leave of her teacher. At their parting, Master Xie offered no word of advice or encouragement, but only told Sister Ten to fold the *qingyi* costume neatly and put it into Yu Qing'e's backpack. The backpack felt heavy on Yu Qing'e's shoulders; her mood, like a stage shortly before the opening of a major show, was fraught with the quiet before the orchestra struck up, the eager wait for the characters to burst onto the scene.

Sister Ten was seeing Yu Qing'e to the door in the fence wall and was going to open it when it was pushed open from the outside. Sister Ten cried with a big smile: "Er Guniang, you are home early today!"

Appearing preoccupied, Junior Miss said "uh-huh" distractedly and strode past her, only to run into Yu Qing'e, who naturally recognized her and was in a fluster, not knowing whether she should acknowledge her or not when Sister Ten gave her a shove and she was out of the garden door.

After closing the door Sister Ten turned around to find Junior Miss fixing her suspicious eyes on her: "Who was that? Why did we have a stranger in the house?"

Sister Ten said with a smile: "Er Guniang, she's a distant niece of mine from my home town. After losing touch with me for many years, she finally found me. Now I will have one more relative with whom I can visit."

Junior Miss was not fully convinced: "But I seem to have seen this distant niece of yours somewhere."

Act III

For Whom the Peach and Plum Trees Bloom

Scene X   I Am a Girl

The rehearsals were for the past few days in the final dash for the fast approaching public performance, prior to its Hong Kong tour, of the new version of the romance play the "White Rabbit", a major new production of the Provincial Yueju Opera Theater. These rehearsals were interrupted as a result of the hospitalization of Mi Jingyao, who was playing the role of young Li Sanniang, to treat a sprained ankle. The Theater brass was in anguish, but Director He was not worried, for now he was freed to concentrate on the reworking of Liu Zhiyuan's role.

In the view of the "rising-star" director He Shuye, what differentiated the new production of the romance play "White Rabbit" from its previous versions was the redesign and repositioning of the character Liu Zhiyuan; it incorporated a humanitarian concern and an analysis of the complexities and mystery of human nature from the perspective of modern consciousness. Traditionally the characters in the legends and romance plays of traditional Chinese opera have tended to be stereotypes; they are either all black or all white and there is no shade of gray between good and evil. Director He hoped, through his reinterpretation, to create on the Yueju opera stage a brand new, multi-dimensional and complex artistic image capable of setting people thinking about the meaning of life. He believed this to be the only path to the renewal of traditional Chinese operas.

Director He took out a copy of *Historical Records of the Five Dynasties* from the library and instructed Feng Jianyue and Qin

Yulou, who were playing Liu Zhiyuan in the first and second half of the play respectively, to read the relevant chapters in it so as to form a rough idea of the historical context in which Liu Zhiyuan lived and acted. He took pains to emphasize to the two portrayers of Liu Zhiyuan: the Liu Zhiyuan you re-create on stage is not your ordinary young scholar fallen on hard times, featured in traditional romance plays starring talented young men and beautiful heroines. He is a man of great purpose and ambition in unsettled times. Director He painstakingly explained the psychological context of the character Liu Zhiyuan to them and asked them each to submit a report on the psychological basis of Liu Zhiyuan's behavior in different periods. This kind of rigorous and in-depth rehearsing was new not only to Feng Jianyue but also to Qin Yulou, a seasoned actor who had four decades of Yueju opera performance under her belt. The pair, master and pupil, took it very seriously and plunged into work, rehearsing the role of Liu Zhiyuan during the day and reading at night to get a better feel and measure of Liu Zhiyuan. Even when they slept they dreamed of becoming Liu Zhiyuan, that founding emperor of the Later Han dynasty in the era of the Five Dynasties a millennium ago.

To better work on the character Liu Zhiyuan, Qin Yulou had of late decided to make her office her home to obviate the need of rising early in the morning to catch the bus. On this day she went first thing in the morning to an eatery across the street from the Yueju Opera Theater and took out some salted soybean milk and Shanghai pork dumplings made with glutinous rice and waited for Feng Jianyue. After breakfast, they would go to the rehearsal room, where they would repeatedly rehearse the changes suggested by the director the previous day and would be able to relax only after they felt mastery was achieved.

But the wait proved long. When Feng Jianyue still did not show up and the piping hot soybean milk was already cold, Qin Yulou began to worry. Her favorite pupil must have overslept as a result of fatigue from days of non-stop rehearsing. Feng Jianyue had always been a careless, worry-free girl who fell asleep the moment her head hit the pillow. Now that Mi Jingyao was hospitalized and she had the dorm room to herself, who knew but that she might sleep until tomorrow morning, since no one else was there to disturb her! The thought prompted Qin Yulou to act; she put the soybean milk and the pork dumplings in a plastic bag and took it with her to look for Feng Jianyue in the actors' dormitory.

Qin Yulou found Feng Jianyue's door was left ajar and she thought to herself: this girl is too careless by far! Leaving her door open when she sleeps! She quietly pushed the door open only to find Feng Jianyue standing in front of the mirror examining herself. She said with annoyance: "Ah Yue! Do you realize what time it is? Director He could already be in the rehearsal room by now. Why are you still dawdling here?"

Feng Jianyue was happy to see Qin Yulou: "Master Qin, I'm glad you've come! Tell me what you think. Does this skirt look good on me?"

Qin Yulou noticed only then that Feng Jianyue had for the first time put on that light olive green one-piece dress with a floral design that had been kept at the bottom of her suitcase all this time. It was a little tight at the shoulders and the waist; the tight-fitting dress showed off her curvaceous figure and she looked sexy and charming in it. Qin Yulou said in astonishment: "Ah Yue! Are you attending some important event today? Have you asked Director He for leave?"

Feng Jianyue said bashfully: "I'm not attending any event. I was getting ready to go to the rehearsal room."

Qin Yulou sensed that a lot of things must have escaped her notice because she had been possessed by the ghost of Liu Zhiyuan in the recent period. Resuming her role as the deputy general manager of the Provincial Yueju Opera Theater, she took a good look at her favorite pupil. She saw a Feng Jianyue with eyes bright and clear as autumn waters, white teeth and red lips, obviously wearing light make-up. In the one-piece dress, she looked elegant and beautiful, a changed person from the nonchalant tomboy that she normally was. Qin Yulou's eyes were dazzled by the sight but her heart did a flip-flop: this girl is being serious! That started her worrying; she'd heard about Director He Shuye's being a ladies' man who had regularly dated more women than could be counted on the fingers of one's hand. It was also said that his latest girlfriend was Ma Hui, the host of the TV series *Operatic Kaleidoscope*. Feng Jianyue, on the other hand, was an ingénue who had never before been romantically involved. If she were to be misled into unrealistic sentiments and get hurt in the process, it would get in the way of her understanding and mastery of the character Liu Zhiyuan and in turn affect the flawless execution of the entire play.

Qin Yulou thought about it for a moment and decided not to let on that she was on to her little secret. She wanted to spare her the embarrassment for fear of creating difficulties for the rehearsal. Feigning ignorance, she said in a chiding tone: "The one-piece dress is unsuitable for the rehearsal room. Take it off! Show off your beauty some other time. Change into your practice suit now. If we are late for the rehearsal, Director He will be cross with us. Director He doesn't look too bad when he is not angry, but he looks really hideous when he loses his temper and pulls a long face!"

Feng Jianyue smothered a smile at hearing this and found no choice but to get out of her dress and don the less glamorous practice suit that had the dull, uniform look of all practice suits. After drinking a few mouthfuls of soybean milk, the two headed to the rehearsal room.

They entered the rehearsal room almost at the same time as Director He Shuye. Shi Xiaotong, who had the part of Yue Xiuying, General Yue's daughter, was wielding a lance and Qian Xiaoxiao, who played Yaoqilang, was performing a series of back flips, flying through the air like a dragon, winning a hearty cheer from Director He. Stealing a glance at Brother Ah Ye, Feng Jianyue saw the shadow of a smile flicker across his rugged face, like a shaft of sunlight projected into a deep gorge. Averting her face, she thought, putting out her tongue: lucky I was not late!

With economy of words, Director He gave clear, complete

instructions on the day's rehearsing tasks: "Feng Jianyue and Shi Xiaotong stay here to continue their rehearsal of the scene 'Liu Zhiyuan Taken in as Son-in-Law by His General' and Director Qin, you and Qian Xiaoxiao go to the practice room next door and carefully go over the scene 'Son Writes back to Father' again, okay? I'd like to remind you all that these two scenes are the crux of the new production of the 'White Rabbit', the turning points in the fate of the characters. If these two scenes fail to come alive, the entire play would fall flat. You will rehearse your lines for your respective scenes until eleven o'clock before coming back here to rehearse the two scenes back to back to see if the psychological context of Liu Zhiyuan transitions smoothly. Go!"

Feng Jianyue had been following Brother Ah Ye out of the corner of her eye and when she saw that he was staying, her heart was flooded with sweet joy. Picking up the gong used by Liu Zhiyuan to announce the time as a night watchman, she gave it a cheerful whack: "Wham!" surprising herself with the force of the impact. The sound of the gong reverberated in the rehearsal room "wham—wham—wham!" Taking a fright she quickly put a hand over the gong to smother the sound.

As expected, Brother Ah Ye spoke up: "Feng Jianyue, you are now Liu Zhiyuan. He has come to the barracks filled with a towering ambition to accomplish great things and advance his career only to find he has been assigned as a night watchman. Try to imagine how he feels! Furthermore in a freezing night with a heavy snowfall, can he realistically have produced a loud sound like that with his gong?"

Feng Jianyue bit her lip, unable to smother a burgeoning smile. To her ears, even the chiding of Brother Ah Ye was fraught with care and intimacy. Struggling to quiet the joyous beating of her heart, she gave the gong two gentle taps, "wham—wham—", and started to sing: "The second *geng* (9–11 PM) has struck, I, Liu Zhiyuan, have endured much suffering in the army. My many skills and talents go unrecognized and I've been relegated to the lowly job of a night watchman ..."

Interrupting her with a raised hand, Director He glared at Feng Jianyue and said in a gruff tone: "Liu Zhiyuan, I did not detect any frustration or bitterness in your aria! The two taps on the gong were too light. Try making it sound grave and hoarse. Do you understand? Now do it over!"

Feng Jianyue, realizing her mind had strayed, refocused herself, "wham—wham—"; this time they sounded like a sigh.

At this moment Yue Xiuying entered, in army garb, wielding a red-tassel spear on a patrol on horseback.

In an earlier version of the southern romance play the *Legend of Liu Zhiyuan and the White Rabbit*, Yue Xiuying, the daughter of Generalissimo Yue was a girl who never ventured out of her boudoir. One day when she opened a window of her second-floor apartment, she caught sight of Liu Zhiyuan on his night watch round in a blizzard. In an access of compassion, she threw down a coat to help him ward off the cold. In the new version of the "White Rabbit" being produced by the Provincial Yueju Opera Theater, Director He made Yue Xiuying into a dashing woman warrior who chanced to meet Liu Zhiyuan the watchman on one of her mounted patrols through the barracks. Director He believed that this change would create richer, more intriguing drama between Liu Zhiyuan and Yue Xiuying; moreover, magnifying the differences between Li Sanniang and Yue Xiuying in status and personality traits would create more room for rationalizing Liu Zhiyuan's betrayal of his wife: Liu's taking Yue Xiuying as second wife had an emotional motive in addition to that of changing his destiny through the marriage.

Yue Xiuying's horse narrowly misses stepping on something covered by snow. When she dismounts to take a look, she finds the night watchman buried under snow, who has fainted from hunger and the cold. The compassionate woman officer has him carried into a tent by her aide.

Liu Zhiyuan wakes up to find himself lying in young Lady Yue's tent; in delighted surprise, he quickly gets up and bows before her in gratitude. Impressed by his civil manners and uncommon bearing, young Lady Yue, driven by curiosity, wants to know more about him. Liu Zhiyuan gives an account of his trials and tribulations, but omits, intentionally or otherwise, the fact that he's married to Li Sanniang of Shatuo village. He seizes the opportunity to make known his decision to give up his scholarly pursuits to go into the army and accomplish great military feats so that he can make a name for himself in history even if it means giving his life on the battlefield. This has the effect of instantly endearing himself to young Lady Yue and the two talk by the fire until dawn.

This scene was a psychological duel between a young man and a young woman, who, each with his/her own calculus, tried to sound out the other, before opening their heart to each other and committing themselves to a lifelong relationship. As the rehearsal progressed, Shi Xiaotong's Yue Xiuying soon received the approval of the director. The psychological context of Yue Xiuying was relatively simple and straightforward, comprising on the one hand the reserve and demureness of a well-bred young lady, and, on the other, the strong will and headstrong impulsiveness of a woman general. Director He praised Shi Xiaotong for finding the right balance between tenderness and toughness in her singing, while reserving criticism for Feng Jianyue, who, in his opinion, did not enter her part and failed to give full expression to Liu Zhiyuan's sentimental journey fraught with inner conflict.

Shi Xiaotong chimed in: "Ah Yue, I've noticed these days that you sound so girlish it's difficult for me to fall in love with you."

Shooting a baleful glance at her, Feng Jianyue said with a snort: "Without my make-up, how can you fall in love with me?" Subconsciously, Feng Jianyue was increasingly disinclined to play a male role, particularly in Brother Ah Ye's presence, when she would, without realizing it, allow her female charms to shine through.

Catching her out, Director He said: "Feng Jianyue, that's where you are so wrong! Even without make-up, you should be able to show Liu Zhiyuan's manliness, his fortitude and perseverance, otherwise, even in make-up and costume, you would not come through as a real man and Yue Xiuying could not possibly fall in love with you. You must keep in mind that you are now no longer Feng Jianyue the woman, but Liu Zhiyuan the man!"

She gave Brother Ah Ye an annoyed look and wanted to shout to him: "Brother Ah Ye! Take a good look! I am a woman!" But of course she wouldn't shout it, because she had to continue to play that male character Liu Zhiyuan under Brother Ah Ye's direction. In Brother Ah Ye's presence, she had to hide her female charms and tenderness and transform herself into a man!

The rehearsal lasted into noontime; by then Qin Yulou and Qian Xiaoxiao had returned to the rehearsal room and were waiting for Director He to review the results of their rehearsal. But Director He was working Feng Jianyue hard, painstakingly discussing every phrase, every line and every verse with her and having her do over repeatedly. At long last, Liu Zhiyuan's soul repossessed her; now with a stylized movement of her hands and feet, she strode forth with her head held high and with a judicious, urbane bearing, she started to sing: "Young Lady Yue!" with so much affection and tenderness that Shi Xiaotong was moved to take a circular stage walk, with two peacock feathers in her hands and in "cloud walk", or "shuffling steps" to come face to face with Feng Jianyue before executing a "reclining fish" and a "back bend", and calling out: "Liu—Lang—"

Qin Yulou was the first to applaud and cheer her favorite pupil: "Bravo!"

Director He was finally able to smile with satisfaction and also clapped his hands. The cell phone in his pant pocket gave a sudden, strong vibration—being a trend-setter, Director He was one of the early possessors of a black Nokia. Clutching his cell phone, Director He mumbled a few indistinct words before announcing: "That will be all for this morning. Manager Qin, I am needed at the TV station. We will meet here at three this afternoon and do a run-through. What do you think?"

That pretty host Ma Hui of the TV station immediately came to Qin Yulou's mind and she merely said with a smile: "We defer to Director He's decision."

He Shuye appeared to be in a rush as he shouldered his backpack and headed out the door. In a moment of impulse, Feng Jianyue followed him, saying: "Ahye Ge, you don't have a rehearsal waiting for you, so why the rush? I have something to say to you."

Glancing at his watch, He Shuye said: "Xiao Yue, I have an engagement at noon. We'll speak after I come back this afternoon."

Feng Jianyue said bashfully: "My mother heard that you are directing our play. She wanted to express her thanks and prepared a lot of stuff for you. It's in my dorm ..."

He Shuye said with a smile: "Auntie really takes good care of me! Don't you take any of it for yourself! Bring it to me this afternoon at rehearsal."

Feng Jianyue fell silent, but, loath to let him go yet, she stared at him.

He Shuye said in a lowered voice: "Xiao Yue! I was mean to you at rehearsal. Don't tell Auntie about it! I only wanted you to play the Liu Zhiyuan part well ... Remember this: when you successfully play the role of Liu Zhiyuan, the 'White Rabbit' will be a success, and you will have succeeded as a consequence!"

Feng Jianyue could now feel the considerateness and care shown by Brother Ah Ye, but was afraid to utter a word for fear that she would not be able to contain her tears and merely nodded vigorously.

Some distance away, Qian Xiaoxiao said with a chuckle: "Manager Qin, did you see how coquettish Feng Jianyue acted? Is she dating Director He?"

With a knock on the back of Qian Xiaoxiao's head, Qin Yulou said: "Don't be a gossip! Stop seeing drama where there is none. They are just old neighbors. Being childhood playmates doesn't mean a thing because they have lived separate lives for so many years now."

With a snort, Shi Xiaotong said: "So that's why. I was wondering why Feng Jianyue had taken to dolling herself up recently!"

Although He Shuye was of the avant-garde, trendy set, he was serious about art and his work. He had announced that the afternoon rehearsal would begin at three and at two fifty-eight sharp he punctually stepped into the rehearsal room. By that time, Qin Yulou, with Feng Jianyue, Shi Xiaotong and Qian Xiaoxiao had done a run-through without him; they were quite pleased with their performance and expected praise from the director.

Director He was in high spirits and his normally grim, pensive face now appeared softened and friendly, and even a little child-like. He brought good news: the *Operatic Kaleidoscope* TV series had agreed to make an art film of the new version of the "White Rabbit". "Of course," Director He paused for emphasis: "It would depend on the outcome of our public performances. Therefore, let's all work hard for it!" and he bowed with his hands clasped before him.

This galvanized those in the rehearsal room. Qian Xiaoxiao leapt in the air and did a forward "plunging move"; Shi Xiaotong, whose reaction was not as exaggerated, couldn't help giving her spear two twirls.

Qin Yulou said with a smile: "Director He, you must have persuaded the TV station with your unparalleled eloquence. You have the gratitude of the Yueju Opera Theater!"

Director He said, resuming a serious mien: "If our play has no real merit, then no amount of eloquent lobbying would have persuaded them. I have said all along that the success of the play turns on these two scenes!"

Feng Jianyue, oblivious to the occasion and the atmosphere in the room in her obsession with delivering her mother's gift into Brother Ah Ye's hands, thrust a bulging plastic bag of home town products at Director He and said coyly: "Brother Ah Ye, my mother says these are good for your health, and if you don't know how to prepare them, I am to help you."

A little embarrassed, Director He muttered "Thanks!" and shoved the bag to a corner; then, clapping his hands, he called out: "We need to make good use of our time. We'll try to get in two run-throughs. Manager Qin, you and Qian Xiaoxiao will do the 'Son Writes back to Father' scene first. This is a crucial scene, which shows the emotional change in Liu Zhiyuan when he finds out his wife Li Sanniang is still alive."

Qin Yulou leaned toward the back of Feng Jianyue's head and said in a low voice: "Ah Yue, get hold of yourself, don't let your mind wander! Now enters Liu Zhiyuan!" and she walked briskly to the center of the room. In the "Son Writes back to Father" scene, set sixteen years later, a middle-aged, bearded Liu Zhiyuan made his first tableau appearance, which was also Qin Yulou's first tableau appearance in the entire play. Qin Yulou therefore gave it her best. Liu Zhiyuan, a general, adjusted his helmet and armor, ran a hand across his beard before singing:

> With unending war and strife,
> I hardly get off my steed.
> As a man determined to defend his country,
> I gladly shed my blood on the battlefield.
> Alas I'll never reunite with Sanniang, who is dead,
> But my son, oh joy, has grown up in these sixteen
>   years.
> I'm lucky to have a virtuous wife in the
>   generalissimo's daughter,
> To soothe my pain in the trials and tribulations of
>   my life.
> Years of warring hastened my ageing,
> In no time my dark hair has acquired silver streaks.

Next entered Yaoqilang, who carried a letter written by Li Sanniang in blood. When Liu Zhiyuan was told for the first time that Li Sanniang was still alive, and Yaoqilang also found out that the piteous woman by the well was his mother, emotion swelled in their chest and blew with the strength of a hurricane. Qian Xiaoxiao's Yaoqilang enters and sings:

> Carrying a letter written in blood, I urge my horse
>   on,

I wish I could reach the capital in one bound—

Amid a quickening beat of the gong, Qian Xiaoxiao, with a white-tassel horse whip in hand, signifying she's riding a white horse, walks in an "army scout" gait, does two "jumps with twist kicks" and stands still on one leg in a tableau-like freeze frame before starting to sing:

> At the well I chance upon an indigent woman drawing water,
> She has the same name and surname of my deceased mother.
> I am in shock and racked by doubt …

"Excellent! Xiaoxiao's singing has made great strides." The rehearsal was suddenly interrupted by a loud voice and when those in the room turned their eyes toward its source, they saw a full-figured, well-dressed woman standing in all her elegance at the door, her dark eyeshadow setting off her eyes that glittered like two diamonds. Putting out her tongue while turning her eyes back to Qin Yulou, she said in a whisper: "Father, it is Mother who's come here to settle scores with you!"

At the sight of this Xie Yingge, the faintest shadow of an involuntary frown creased Qin Yulou's brow as she wondered with unease what new tricks Xie Yingge was up to. Despite her misgivings, she greeted her with a smile: "Xiao Xie, Director He is conducting a remedial class for Liu Zhiyuan today. You, Li Sanniang, feel you have to see for yourself?"

Despite his arrogance born of an exalted opinion of himself, Director He Shuye showed due deference to celebrities like Xie Yingge, who was after all the star of the play. So he too went up to her: "Master Xie, it's wonderful that you've taken the time to come down here. Take a look, with Li Sanniang's eyes, to see if the young and the older Liu Zhiyuan fit your idea of Liu Zhiyuan."

Shi Xiaotong, good pupil that she was, had already brought

a chair for Xie Yingge, who sat down in it as if it were the most natural thing in the world. Qian Xiaoxiao was quick to bring her a bottle of mineral water.

Xie Yingge said with a smile: "Director He, I'm sorry for interrupting your schedule. I won't be long. Qin Dajieh, I'm glad you are here. I'm worried. It's only two days before the play opens and Mi Jingyao has not yet fully recovered from her ankle sprain. I was at the hospital to see her. The leadership needs to think about what to do if she is unable to go onstage by the time of the performances. The tickets are sold out, so there has to be a contingency plan."

At this mention of the problem of Mi Jingyao's ankle sprain, Qin Yulou, who was quite unhappy about Xie Yingge's unexpected arrival that interrupted their rehearsal, found it, upon reflection, to be an issue that could not be lightly dismissed. She turned to look at Director He.

Cool as a cucumber, as if he had it all figured out and had everything under control, Director He said: "Master Xie, not to worry. Mi Jingyao will not miss the opening performance. I talked to the doctor in charge of her care only yesterday and the doctor said her ankle has healed and she is medically cleared to perform onstage. I asked her about it and she told me she will not miss the final run-through."

Sharply arching her eyebrows painted like two distant hills, Xie Yingge said: "Not possible, not possible at all! I was just at the hospital and when she accompanied me to the elevator, she was still limping!"

Qin Yulou got the feeling that she had come prepared, that she had formed a plan. She asked: "Xiao Xie, in case Mi Jingyao really couldn't make it to the stage, what do you think we should do?"

With a twinkle in her diamond-like eyes, Xie Yingge said: "I've given it some thought. Since time is so pressing, I would have to play Li Sanniang through the entire play in that eventuality."

Qin Yulou breathed an "Oh!" that sounded like a soft sigh. Now she knew what Xie Yingge wanted; she should have known long before this. Qin Yulou was in a quandary; if she disagreed with the plan, did she have a better plan? Nobody except this Xie Yingge had the ability to master the part of Li Sanniang of the first part of the play in two days' time! But she was uncomfortable with the idea of going along with Xie Yingge's proposal, for that would give the impression that the two of them were conspiring to muscle the younger actors out of the "White Rabbit". In uncertainty, she turned her eyes toward Director He.

Upon the briefest reflection, Director He said: "Master Xie, it was heroic of you to come to our rescue. But there's only one problem: your Li Sanniang and Feng Jianyue's Liu Zhiyuan would be a difficult, unlikely match as far as appearance is concerned. You can't deny the age gap, can you?"

It appeared Xie Yingge had been prepared for this question and had a ready answer. She shot back: "That's easy to solve. Just substitute Qin Dajieh for Feng Jianyue. The two of us used to perform as a team through the entire play of the 'White Rabbit', after all." With those words, she fixed her glowing eyes on Qin Yulou.

This tactic was what Qin Yulou had most feared; she quickly averted her eyes: "Xiao Xie, with my kind of figure, I don't think I can tackle the part of the young Liu Zhiyuan."

Xie Yingge gave her a glare: "Why can't you? This is an emergency, Qin Dajieh! You can't sit on your hands!"

Director He said: "The problem is 'Liu Zhiyuan Taken in as Son-in-Law by His General' is not in the old version of the 'White Rabbit' and it is quite a long and important scene. I doubt that you can tackle it in two days' time."

Unable to contain her excitement, Xie Yingge shuffled to where Qin Yulou was sitting and said in a lowered tone: "Qin Dajieh, you must have watched Feng Jianyue rehearse this part many times and must have known it by heart by now. Tell him that!"

Qin Yulou vigorously shook her head but there seemed to be something stuck in her throat that made her unable to utter a word. Deep down in her heart she certainly wished she could play Liu Zhiyuan from beginning to end; it would be a nice coda to her acting career. But at the taping of the interview for the *Operatic Kaleidoscope* TV series she had publicly announced to the viewers that for the next two years the Provincial Yueju Opera Theater has set a strategic goal of training a new generation of Yueju opera stars and that she would devote much of her energy to teaching these promising young actors.

As the standoff between Qin Yulou and Xie Yingge continued, an unlikely person joined the fray. Shi Xiaotong rushed up to Director He and said: "Director He, if Mi Jingyao should be unable to recover in time, let me take her place and play Li Sanniang in the first half. I can do it. I've committed every verse and every line of hers to memory. And it was I who taught her the long sleeve dance after I learned it first."

Shi Xiaotong was endowed with a good voice. She articulated every word and every phrase of those sentences with such force that everyone in the rehearsal room heard her clearly. Everyone was caught by surprise. Who would have thought that this Shi Xiaotong who had been a background singer all these years would harbor such secret ambitions?

Qian Xiaoxiao was the first to react. Tittering, she pointed first at Shi Xiaotong, then at Xie Yingge: "No, no! Xiaotong! If you play Li Sanniang in the first half, the audience would wonder why Li Sanniang at an older age is prettier than when she was young." She was going to continue when she suddenly fell silent—she saw Shi Xiaotong's fire-breathing eyes glaring at her.

It was Director He who intervened, saying tactfully: "Shi Xiaotong, you are a hard worker. Everyone can see that. But if you played Li Sanniang, who would play Yue Xiuying in your place? Yue Xiuying is an all-new part. I don't believe anyone else can tackle it in the two days left."

Shi Xiaotong was unfazed: "Director He, think about it. In the first half, Li Sanniang and Yue Xiuying never appear onstage at the same time. There is a long aria sung by Liu Zhiyuan, the night watchman, in a snowy night between the scene of 'Liu Zhiyuan Parts from His Wife and Goes off to the Army' and the scene 'Liu Zhiyuan Taken in as Son-in-Law by His General'. I'll have plenty of time to quickly change roles and costumes in that long interval."

Shi Xiaotong succeeded in astonishing the others a second time. This background singer with no stunning looks and little name recognition had the audacity to covet the two female roles of both Li Sanniang and Yue Xiuying in the new production of the "White Rabbit"! Wasn't she trying to bite off more than she could chew?

What worried Qin Yulou most was Shi Xiaotong might have succeeded in stepping on Xie Yingge's toes. No actor of the Provincial Yueju Opera Theater had yet dared to make an open attempt to grab a role from Xie Yingge. As the Theater's deputy general manager, she was ready to jump in to appease one and to comfort the other should Xie Yingge react in fury and start taking Shi Xiaotong to task. But surprisingly Xie Yingge did not utter a word, but merely looked Shi Xiaotong up and down with incredulous eyes. Qin Yulou said a mental "Amitabha!" She thought to herself: our diva-bodhisattva is in a rare charitable mood today!

It so happened that the arrogant Xie Yingge who intensely disliked losing suddenly felt an affinity to the Shi Xiaotong who was not afraid to think the unthinkable. She had never given a thought to the background singer when she was performing on stage. In the new production of the "White Rabbit", her Li Sanniang and Shi Xiaotong's Yue Xiuying would be on stage at the same time only after the final act of happy reunions when they would step forward to acknowledge the audience's applause. Truth be told, Xie Yingge had not taken a real look at Shi Xiaotong since the beginning of the rehearsals, and if she met Shi Xiaotong in the street, without her makeup and costume, she would probably not even recognize her. But at this moment Xie Yingge was fascinated by the impudence and bravado of fearless Shi Xiaotong and was examining her with interest.

Director He however felt a tinge of displeasure under the

gaze of Shi Xiaotong's eyes glittering with tears and bright with eager expectation. With her plain looks, Shi Xiaotong was already minimally acceptable as Yue Xiuying and yet, never content with what she had, coveted now the part of Li Sanniang to boot! With a mental sneer, Director He said deadpan: "Let's not be too quick to make changes to the cast. Everything turns on the progress of Mi Jingyao's recovery. Why don't we do this? After today's rehearsal I will go to the hospital to find out how Mi Jingyao is doing before we decide on the next step."

Xie Yingge said, rising slowly from her chair: "Director He, you should go visit her in the hospital. There's no reason to put the entire project at risk for the sake of one person!"

Leaving the subject, Director He said in a cold voice, clapping his hands: "Let's continue the rehearsal. Whatever change there might be, the most important thing is for each to play her role well."

After seeing off Xie Yingge, Qin Yulou quickly returned to her role as Liu Zhiyuan. Director He said: "Qian Xiaoxiao, you redo your part in the first half."

Qian Xiaoxiao hurriedly looked everywhere for her horse whip and finally found that Shi Xiaotong was sitting on it. As she shoved her off her seat and retrieved the whip, Qian Xiaoxiao grumbled: "Have you still not snapped out of your dream?"

The performance by Qin Yulou and Qian Xiaoxiao of the "Son Writes back to Father" scene was relatively free of hiccups and got a passing mark from Director He, who suggested some minor improvements. Now came the turn of Feng Jianyue and Shi Xiaotong to rehearse the scene "Liu Zhiyuan Taken in as Son-in-Law by His General", but the two's performance was lackadaisical and in singing and acting fell short of the level achieved in the morning rehearsal. In any other, normal day, Director He would never have let them off the hook, but in his anxiety to find out Mi Jingyao's status at the hospital, he decided to get off their case, merely telling them to work on it some more when they went home.

Director He picked up his backpack and went out of the rehearsal room; in his haste, he left behind, in a corner of the room, the bag of local products Feng Jianyue's mother insisted on giving him. Staring at the bulging plastic bag, Feng Jianyue felt, in her heart, the same despair and pain felt by Liu Zhiyuan as he announced the watches of the night in a freezing snowstorm.

Qin Yulou felt some guilt toward her favorite pupil, who had a lost look in her eyes. Imagining that Feng Jianyue's sour mood must have resulted from Xie Yingge's proposal for Qin Yulou to take the place of Feng Jianyue as Liu Zhiyuan in the first half, she said, patting her back: "Jianyue, ignore that silly idea of Master Xie's. It's never going to fly. Casting younger actors for the 'White Rabbit' has been decided by the leadership of the Theater. It can't be changed arbitrarily. Besides, look at my figure! How can I possibly play the young Liu Zhiyuan?"

Feng Jianyue hastened to reassure her: "Master Qin, it's not like that, not that …" Then what was it? Feng Jianyue couldn't reveal the real reason. When she realized from Brother Ah Ye's own words that he seemed to have paid frequent visits to Mi Jingyao at the hospital, her suspicion had already been aroused and her suspicion was further stoked when she heard the last few words of Master Xie: "There's no reason to put the entire project at risk for the sake of one person!" The "one person" referred to by Master Xie was clearly Mi Jingyao. Could Brother Ah Ye's enthusiasm for directing the "White Rabbit" of the Yueju Opera Theater have been for the sake of Mi Jingyao? When in his haste to visit Mi Jingyao at the hospital Brother Ah Ye had left behind the bag of local products from her home town so affectionately presented to him by her, she finally came to the conclusion that Brother Ah Ye cared more about Mi Jingyao than about her. That was what drove her to distraction!

Qin Yulou didn't know what to make of Feng Jianyue's reaction. She didn't seem to have heard what she had just said. Her eyes wandered, looking unfocusedly into space; her face was white as a sheet, like the mask of Cao Cao on the opera stage, with a distracted, listless, depressed look. Qin Yulou got really worried and said, gripping her shoulders: "Jianyue, what's the matter with you? Are you tired? Are you feeling unwell?"

Feng Jianyue had a sudden idea. Forcing a rueful smile that bespoke her hurt, she said: "Master Qin, I am all right. I will defer to the director's decision. I would like to visit Mi Jingyao. I haven't yet done that since she sprained her ankle. We can rehearse our lines a bit there." Freeing herself of Qin Yulou's hands, she ran to the corner where the bag of local products sat, picked it up, waved goodbye to Qin Yulou and ran out the door at a trot.

Only when she saw Feng Jianyue pick up the bag bulging with local products did Qin Yulou wake up to the real reason for the girl's unsettled emotions and she was relieved. What woman has not, in her youth, been through the torment of love, shed tears for it and felt romantic passions seething in her breast? It's as well that she is going through that stage; it might even help her in the creation of the artistic image of Liu Zhiyuan.

Feng Jianyue resolved to pay a visit to Mi Jingyao in the hospital—she was by temperament frank and straight as an arrow, and yet she had lately been hiding and tucking her feelings, become vague and evasive, all for the sake of sounding out the intentions of Brother Ah Ye. All that disguising and circumlocution was asphyxiating her. She hadn't expected falling in love to be such a bumpy ride. Now she was determined to go to the hospital and, in the presence of Brother Ah Ye and Mi Jingyao, pour out all the suspicions and doubts that were eating her insides and hear the verdict straight from the lips of Brother Ah Ye. If it turned out Brother Ah Ye really fancied Mi Jingyao, very well, then I would generously wish them happiness and leave with a smile on my face, and head straight to the new restaurant offering Western food opposite the Yueju Opera Theater and have myself a feast!

Now, when Director He rushed to Mi Jingyao's sick room, she was nowhere to be seen, so he inquired with the two other patients sharing the room.

The two patients happened to be Yueju opera fans and one of them was a diehard fan of Xie Yingge. Since learning that Mi Jingyao was the favored pupil of Xie Yingge, they had taken great care of Mi Jingyao. With He Shuye visiting every couple of days since Mi Jingyao's admission to the hospital, the two roommates had acquired the impression that He Shuye was Mi Jingyao's boyfriend and found in the young couple a perfect match. At the sight of He Shuye, one of the roommates said, with a smile: "Director He, Jingyao's foot injury has healed and the doctor has already cleared her for discharge for tomorrow. So you needn't worry." The other roommate said: "Director He, Jingyao already promised us two tickets to the public performance of the new production of the 'White Rabbit'. We hope you will honor her kind offer."

He Shuye nodded before asking: "Where is Mi Jingyao? Where have you hidden her?"

That tickled no end the two opera fans, one of whom observed: "Director He must miss her very much after a separation of one day from our Jingyao." The other said, pointing in the direction of the window: "These past two days Jingyao have been going to the little garden down there in the late afternoon to exercise her voice and run stage circles. I'll go fetch her for you."

He Shuye was quick to stop her: "There's no need. Don't bother. I'll go myself." That said, he left the room.

He Shuye felt Mi Jingyao's spraining her ankle in rehearsal was partly his fault. If he had not been so demanding in asking her to repeat the long sleeve dance so many times, the accident could probably have been avoided. His greater worry was whether Mi Jingyao could recover in time for the public performance scheduled for two days later, and whether the new production of the "White Rabbit" would produce the desired impact. It was that worry that had prompted him to go every two or three days to the hospital to inquire with the doctor about the progress of Mi Jingyao's recovery. A few days ago he was assured by the doctor that Mi Jingyao's foot injury presented no major problems and therefore she could perform on stage. But why then did Xie Yingge insist on saying Mi Jingyao was still walking with a limp? Now He Shuye's worries had been laid to rest; the two roommates couldn't be wrong, could they?

He Shuye arrived in the little garden in the back of the ward building. At this hour the twilight already rose slowly from the grass, the pearly afterglow hovered among the trees at mid-height; shrubs, rocks, flowers, vines, in a patchwork of light and shade, were either in quiet obscurity or caught fire with the sunset, creating an illusion of a stage with spotlights trained on it. On the stage Mi Jingyao was lightly singing a section of the "Giving Birth by the Millstone" scene just before labors: "A cold sweat drenches my body. All strength has drained out of me and I can barely remain on my feet, alas I have no water, no scissors and nobody to help ..." then turning and turning, she flung out her arms and began a swirling dance.

Without announcing himself, He Shuye stood behind an old pagoda tree with a massive trunk to watch her practice in silence. By He Shuye's standards, Mi Jingyao's singing and acting remained flawed, but he made the decision not to judge her too harshly or ask too much of her. He was touched by her persistence in practicing even when she was under treatment. Besides, in his artistic conception of the new production of the "White Rabbit", Li Sanniang did not occupy pride of place. When Mi Jingyao rested from her dancing and slowly hummed the last verse: "I have no choice but to bite through the umbilical cord myself ..." He Shuye applauded her.

Mi Jingyao was closing out the aria when she heard hands clapping. She turned her head and saw He Shuye: "Director, you are sneaky, coming quietly up here to spy on me!" With that, she came toward him along the pebble-paved path.

He Shuye said, smiling: "I did not have the heart to interrupt you, seeing that you were so rapt in your performance. By the way, Xie Yingge came to the rehearsal room this afternoon and told us you still could not walk normally and were not ready for the public performance. What's the situation?"

Mi Jingyao said: "She couldn't have said that. When Master Xie came to see me, I told her that I will be discharged tomorrow and will be ready for the run-through."

With a mental sneer He Shuye said, after taking a few steps: "We'll just ignore what she said. Mi Jingyao, it's great to have you back after your recovery!" and made to shake her hand. In order to extend her right hand, Mi Jingyao turned sideways but tripped on a bump in the pebbly path and stumbled. Quick-eyed and fast reacting, He Shuye shot out an arm to stop her fall and she stumbled right into his arms.

This scene was enacted at the very moment of the appearance of Feng Jianyue, who had just arrived at the little garden in great haste. She saw it all. The image of their embrace burned her eyes like a searing iron. She drew in a sharp breath and shut her eyes with a shudder.

Feng Jianyue and He Shuye had narrowly missed each other, with one taking the up elevator and the other the down elevator. When she walked into Mi Jingyao's sick room, she was told casually by the two roommates: "Jingyao and her boyfriend went for a stroll in the little garden down there." She had been anxious and apprehensive, and now she had seen what she feared most! Although she had come prepared for the worst, at that instant she couldn't help feeling her heart was being shot to pieces in a hail of bullets.

With a hand supporting Mi Jingyao, He Shuye said as they walked on: "Li Sanniang, oh, Li Sanniang, you must not fall again, otherwise your Liu Zhiyuan would surely challenge me to a duel."

Mi Jingyao said with a giggle: "Director He, everyone calls you behind your back the Chinese god Erlang Shen incapable of human emotions. Who would have thought you were capable of humor!"

As they left the pebbled path talking and laughing, they were surprised by the sight of Feng Jianyue, who was hovering like a wraith at the end of the path. They cried in astonishment: "Hey—why are you here?"

With a forlorn smile, Feng Jianyue said: "I'm here to see you, Mi Jingyao. I am glad you've fully recovered. Tomorrow

I'll be able again to vow eternal love to you." In her own ears, these words had the sound of an actor singing in a cavernous hall without the aid of sound equipment, so far away and so insubstantial.

He Shuye found there was an odd air about Feng Jianyue, who was moving about as if she were but an eviscerated shell. A little alarmed, he asked in a softened tone: "Xiao Yue, is there something the matter with you? Do you have a cold?"

Feng Jianyue had a sense that centuries separated her from Brother Ah Ye, whose facial features became indistinct because of the great distance. She quickly raised the bag of local products: "Ahye Ge, you forgot the stuff my mother wanted you to have …" Her tone was that of Liang Shanbo singing in the *xianxia* tune in *The Tragic Romance of the Butterfly Lovers* moments before his death.

He Shuye developed a sudden stutter as he took the bag of local products from her hand: "No—no—no, I, I did not forget. I thought since I was going back to the rehearsal room tomorrow anyway …"

Without waiting for Brother Ah Ye to finish his sentence, Feng Jianyue turned on her heel and stalked away, her form melting into the dark masses of trees and plants.

Mi Jingyao roused him out of his reverie with a prod: "Director He, my Liu Zhiyuan was being jealous on account of you!"

With a start He Shuye said: "What?"

Mi Jingyao said with an amused chuckle: "That Feng Jianyue! I am the cause of her jealousy. You will have to ask for her forgiveness!"

Scene XI Xishi Returns Home

When the cast and crew of the new production of the "White Rabbit" of the Yueju Opera Theater went into the final run-through, the Yueju opera troupe of the productions company run by the tourism bureau of the ancient town launched on the mock antique stage newly built on the bank of the Tiaoluo Creek the new production of the romance play *Xishi Returns Home*. The show was a resounding success. Yu Qing'e, who played Xishi in the Yueju opera play, became overnight a Yueju opera star basking in new found fame and enthusiastic praise among Yueju opera fans of the towns and villages near and far. Before she regretfully took leave of her homeland, for the greater good of which Xishi had selflessly decided to sacrifice herself, she performed a long, sorrowful, heart-rending water sleeve dance, which, many older fans said, rivaled the long sleeve dance sequence performed thirty years before by the famous actor in the female role Xie Yingge in the "White Rabbit". As a result of the good notices *Xishi Returns Home* received and the spread of its fame by word of mouth, tourists flocking to the old town grew four-fold in a month. The economic as well the cultural benefits that accrued galvanized the leadership of the productions company. Party Secretary Zhang showed her increased appreciation by writing a memo to the town's tourism bureau requesting a salary raise for Yu Qing'e in recognition of her contribution, and a memo to the town's Department of Culture to apply for the title of national grade II actor for Yu Qing'e, something unheard of for an out-of-the-way little ancient town.

Now that Yu Qing'e was a local celebrity of the ancient town, she'd often be recognized in the streets of the town. People would point at her and say: "Xishi, that's Xishi over there." Yueju opera fans would come up to her asking for an autograph or press a little gift into her hand, such as scarves, hair ornaments, handbags. Yu Qing'e however did not get complacent for all the acclaim and adulation. Measured against her vaulting ambition to scale the highest, and nothing but the highest, heights, the little renown she enjoyed now was but a molehill compared to a mountain—nothing worth mentioning.

Yu Qing'e followed closely the happenings in the traditional Chinese opera circles of the provincial capital despite her geographic remoteness in an ancient town. She subscribed to the provincial gazette, the "Culture and Entertainment News" section of which she read through every evening after work, no matter how tired she was, before she could go to bed with peace of mind. Since the success of *Xishi Returns Home* in the small town, she paid ever more attention to the traditional Chinese opera events in the provincial capital, privately hoping to see mentions of her performance of *Xishi Returns Home* in the newspapers there. But after searching through a week's worth of the "Culture and Entertainment News" section, she found no mention at all of the new production of the romance play performed on the mock antique stage of the old town. It was some time later that she chanced upon a news item in the "Local Highlights" section of the provincial gazette of about a thousand words that reported on the success of the new production of the Yueju opera romance play *Xishi Returns Home* launched by the tourism bureau of the old town as a novel way of drawing tourists by promoting local folk culture, but without mentioning the names of the actors. Yu Qing'e breathed a long sigh, with the sober thought that she was a hard, long way from achieving the status comparable to that of the famous Yueju opera actor in female role Xie Yingge. Her only hope now was that in the contest of new plays starring young Yueju opera actors from the six provinces of east China and the city of Shanghai to be held toward the end of the year, her "Xishi" would outshine the others and win the top prize.

Since the successful opening of *Xishi Returns Home*, and the spread of its fame, a visit to the mock antique stage to watch the show became a staple of organized tours to the old town. As a consequence, on the antique stage by the Guishi Bridge straddling the Tiaoluo Creek, a nightly story was enacted about Xishi sacrificing herself for the greater good of her country the Kingdom of Yue to the sound of clappers, drums, reeds and strings. For over a month now Yu Qing'e had been playing beautiful Xishi every day with gusto, slipping into her part and giving her best, moving the audience to tears. The gales of applause greeting her at the end of the play threatened to blow out the pavilion roof with a caisson ceiling, flying eaves and animal figures on its ridges.

The audience dispersed only after the fifth curtain call. Yu Qing'e walked, totally exhausted, into her dressing room and slumped into her chair, without the energy even to remove her makeup and change out of her costume. She still felt the generosity of spirit, sorrow, bitterness and heartbreak of Xishi, who sacrificed her youth, her love, her virginity and her reputation for the sake of her country; on stage she had kept back her tears but now they flowed freely, smudging her eyeliner and rouge.

It was then that the door opened and the stage manager put his head in and said: "Yu Qing'e, your husband is here to pick you up." Yu Qing'e quickly pulled out a few paper napkins and wiped off her tears together with the face paint.

Her husband was a considerate man; with Yu Qing'e performing every evening, he would always come around to the backstage to take her home, as long as he wasn't sent on a business trip out of town. Seeing that Yu Qing'e had not yet removed her makeup and costume, he said: "Qing'e, drink the Astragalus propinquus and ginseng tonic first to restore your energy." With that he removed a small purple clay pot from an insulated container. Taking the pot into her hands, Yu Qing'e felt the warmth of the soup flow straight to her heart. As she opened the lid to drink from the pot, she suddenly felt a surge of acid reflux from her stomach. She quickly moved the pot aside, saying: "Can I drink it later? I can't make it go down just now."

Her husband proceeded to remove her jade ornaments and headgear. Yu Qing'e took off the orange-red sheer cape embroidered with phoenixes, worn over the *qingyi* costume, a gift from Master Xie, her teacher. The productions company had spent a considerable sum on an all-new wardrobe, but for the sake of the long sleeve dance sequence Yu Qing'e had insisted on wearing this *qingyi* costume on stage. Her superstitious dependence on the *qingyi* costume bordered on idol worship; without it she would feel unable to do the long sleeve dance well.

She carefully hung the *qingyi* costume on the rack before covering it with an old practice suit. She was not taking it home with her since she needed it for the next day's performance.

Her husband had come on a Bluebird motorcycle; on their way home, Yu Qing'e had her arms wrapped around her husband's waist and laid her head softly against his back. Her husband said over his shoulder: "Don't fall asleep. You could catch a cold in the strong wind if you did." Then he added: "Mother made wonton with ground pork and chopped greens for filling for you. She said you must be exhausted from singing all evening and the hot soup would make you feel better."

With a soft "mm" Yu Qing'e pressed her brimming eyes into her husband's jacket.

Since *Xishi Returns Home* became a big hit, there had been a subtle change in Yu Qing'e's status of underappreciated daughter-in-law in the Zhao household.

Early on in their marriage, Yu Qing'e had a "gentlemen's agreement" with her husband: no child before she was thirty so that she could devote herself to her career as a performing artist. The mother-in-law obviously found the agreement unacceptable. The Zhao family had only one son; if the daughter-in-law refused to have a child, the Zhao family would be left with no heir! Despite the son's repeated explanations and promises that when the daughter-in-law reached thirty, mother would get a big, chubby grandson, the mother-in-law harbored a niggling resentment and would from time to time make snide remarks intended for the ears of the daughter-in-law. "What? Have a child at thirty? You would be past child-bearing age! What if it turns out you can't have a child anymore at that age? What if you give birth to one with a birth defect? You must have heard about the play *Peacock Flying towards Southeast* when you attended the School of the Arts. Why does the mother of Jiao Zhongqing force her son to divorce Liu Lanzhi, a virtuous, beautiful and capable wife? It is because she has failed to produce a son three years into their marriage!" Yu Qing'e had a retiring and serene temperament and she quietly put up with the mother-in-law's constant nagging and carping as long as she had the support of her husband.

Most people of a certain age in this small town were Yueju opera fans and could hum a few verses or arias of Yueju opera classics. Yu Qing'e's mother-in-law was no exception; she always carried a transistor radio with her and tuned in to stations that broadcast sections of Yueju opera arias at all hours. After *Xishi Returns Home* starring Yu Qing'e took the town by storm, her mother-in-law often ran into long-time neighbors who congratulated her: Auntie Zhao, you must have earned a lot of credit in your previous incarnation to be rewarded so handsomely with a daughter-in-law as beautiful as Xishi; Auntie Zhao, you are so lucky to have Yu Qing'e sing Yueju opera arias at home every day to entertain you! Your ears are so lucky! Listening to opera promotes longevity; Auntie Zhao, your daughter-in-law is destined to be a big star in the future, so you better not allow her to be pried away … Now that Yu Qing'e had brought such respectability to the Zhao family, the mother-in-law mellowed toward her, becoming solicitous and affectionate. Every evening she insisted on going into the kitchen to prepare night snacks for her daughter-in-law; when her daughter-in-law came home from her performance, she would watch with a smile and make sure she finished the snack.

Before the big wontons with pork and vegetable filling boiled in soup seasoned with algae and shrimp shell specially made by her mother-in-law for her, Yu Qing'e had little appetite; instead, she had a queasy feeling in her stomach, as if it were stuffed with straw. But with the face of her mother-in-law, who was grinning like the Laughing Buddha, right next to her, waiting eagerly for her to slurp up the nourishment, she forced herself to spoon a wonton into her mouth and swallow it without much chewing for fear of involuntarily spitting it up. Her mother-in-law eagerly asked: "Was it tasty? Was it too salty or too bland?" Yu Qing'e nodded; unable to tell whether the wonton she forced down was salty or bland, she answered: "It was just right." This allowed her mother-in-law to claim credit: "I had to pick the tender tips off each sprig of this shepherd's-purse and I used lean pork ham for the filling because I knew Qing'e disliked fatty meat. It took me the whole afternoon to grind it—"

It was at that moment that her husband walked in after parking his motorcycle; he said loudly: "It smells so nice! Mom, is there any left for me? As a matter of fact I'm feeling a little hungry."

The mother-in-law said chidingly: "There's nothing left for you! Haven't you been talking about losing weight?"

Yu Qing'e quickly pushed her bowl toward her husband: "I've eaten quite a few and I'm full. You can have the rest." The fact was she only ate the one, which was churning, indigestible, in her stomach.

Her husband hoisted the bowl to his mouth and gobbled one wonton after another with great gusto. While cheered by the respect and affection between the young couple, the mother-in-law kept the chiding tone in her voice: "Watch out! If you grow too fat, Qing'e might divorce you!"

It was midnight when they finally went to bed. The moment her husband's head hit the pillow, he began snoring. Yu Qing'e was sore all over, as if she had just been lashed with a whip. No matter how she tossed and turned, she couldn't find a position of comfort. Giving up any thought of falling asleep, she switched on the bed lamp and started leafing through the day's provincial gazette. She read reports about traditional Chinese opera events in the "Culture and Entertainment News" section again, this time item by item from top to bottom. There was a report, taking up one third of the page, on the success of the public performances of the new version of the "White Rabbit" produced by the Provincial Yueju Opera Theater. Tickets to the three performances were hard to come by and were scalped for three times the original price. The reporter quoted critics as saying the public unanimously hailed the artistic image of Liu Zhiyuan, the hero of the play, finding in him a brand new character in traditional Chinese opera classics, one that combined noble and base instincts, could be warm-blooded and cold-blooded at the same time; alternately principled and chameleonic; ambitious yet unscrupulous. The appearance of such a complex character in the new production of the White Rabbit took the play a giant step up the esthetic scale in comparison with the older versions of the "White Rabbit". The critics reserved, for the two veteran artists Xie Yingge and Qin Yulou, only a few bland remarks such as "could still muster the old skills and old charms" but offered high praise for the young actor Feng Jianyue's portrayal of Liu Zhiyuan in the first half of the play, citing her good stage presence, singing and, more importantly, her accurate grasp and interpretation of the psychological context of this complex character. Her masterful, on-target portrayal of Liu Zhiyuan created an unforgettable character on the Yueju opera stage. A number of critical comments and suggestions were offered by the critics with regard to the portrayal of young Li Sanniang by Mi Jingyao, which they characterized as lacking in conviction and passion; her singing was described as flat. The overall effect was to make Li Sanniang, the heroine and main character of the play, pale in comparison with Liu Zhiyuan. Some critics faulted her performance of the water sleeve dance sequence in the "Giving Birth by the Millstone" scene for its levity, which hardly befitted the mood of Li Sanniang in her dire circumstances. They believed the play could do without it.

Yu Qing'e carefully read the article twice. The Mi Jingyao she knew, she thought, must find it difficult to stomach the criticisms reported in the article and would sulk and maybe decide to walk away from the play in a fit of pique. Yu Qing'e wondered if she herself would be able to take such withering criticism of her performance. Yu Qing'e told herself: if I could get so many critics to see my performance in *Xishi Returns Home*, I'd gladly face their criticism, even if they did so by pointing their fingers at me. At least they would have given their attention to my performance and noticed my existence. But it was inconceivable that critics of their caliber and fame would deign to pay any notice to the performance of an obscure play by an obscure actor of an obscure troupe in an obscure small town. From this perspective, Mi

Jingyao was much luckier than herself.

Yu Qing'e grew increasingly sensitive to what she perceived as a substantive change in a certain part of her body! That feeling of nausea came upon her with greater frequency. Normally she would not be tired from singing all day, but lately she had been feeling hollowed out after the performance of the three-quarters-of-an-hour play *Xishi Returns Home* and sweat soaked through two layers of her costume. She refused to believe this was what she thought it was. How could it be? She had an agreement with her husband not to have a child before she was thirty and they had been carefully calculating the days to make sure that they performed the conjugal act only during safe periods when ovulation was least likely to occur.

Facts could not be wished away. The natural processes and changes in her body were constant reminders that what she least wished to happen had happened. Remembering that a distant cousin a few years her senior was an obstetrician-gynecologist in a town clinic, she bought some gifts and, without telling anyone, went alone to see this cousin.

The cousin was happy to see her, particularly because she was now a star on the Yueju opera stage; she proudly presented her to her colleagues: "This is my younger cousin, you know, the Yu Qing'e who plays Xishi!"

With forced cheerfulness, Yu Qing'e followed her cousin through the various offices. After a round of this her legs became sore and weak and she became short of breath; she quickly found a chair and lowered herself into it. After taking a good, long look at her, her cousin asked: "Qing'e, you are pregnant, right?"

Yu Qing'e said with a start: "How can you tell?"

Her cousin laughed: "Don't forget I am an obs-gyn! Look at those dark circles around your eyes and the complexion of your face! Nothing could be more obvious."

Chills went through Yu Qing'e, who sat motionless, her eyes filling with tears.

Her cousin pulled her up from the chair: "You must be here for that. Let's run a blood test and look at your urine. I promise, my eyes are more accurate than the instruments," then added: "But this is good news, why the sad face?"

When the blood work report came back, it confirmed her cousin's prediction. With the report in her hand, Yu Qing'e was rendered speechless and she didn't know what to think or feel anymore. Her cousin tried to comfort her: "Qing'e, don't worry. Every woman goes through this. Leave the rest to me. You are now one month pregnant, be sure to have plenty of rest. As for the play, well, it would be best if you stopped performing ..."

"Impossible!" Yu Qing'e cried: "Tickets have been sold out to tour groups from all over until the Mid-autumn Festival!"

Reading her mind, her cousin changed her tone: "Of course, as long as the bulge is undetectable and before the fetus is three months old, you can perform on stage if you want to, except that you'll have to be extra careful and also closely watch your nutrition."

How could her cousin understand the inner struggle in Yu Qing'e? Yu Qing'e was not prepared to bare her soul to her older cousin and thinking of the evening performance she took her leave. As her cousin saw her out, she repeatedly stressed: "Come in for a checkup in a month's time!"

That evening, physically inadequate and mentally tormented, Yu Qing'e felt she did not perform at her best, singing with less than full voice and dancing with reduced energy. She was worried she might be booed, but to her surprise the audience rewarded her performance with thundering applause and sustained cheering. After the show was over, an excited Party Secretary Zhang came backstage to tell her: "Xiao Yu, your performance was excellent tonight! You gave full expression to Xishi's bitterness and sorrow at parting from the man and the country she loved. This should be how you perform in the future too. With less effort in singing and acting, you make the performance more poignant. I'm now full of confidence in your chances of success at the new plays contest scheduled for the end of the year!"

Yu Qing'e was nonplussed. The thought of Party Secretary Zhang's pinning excessive hopes on herself and of changes in her body, which would balloon into a barrel at year's end, saddened her and rendered her at a loss to respond to Party Secretary Zhang. Luckily she had not yet removed her makeup and the painted mask covered up her emotions; Party Secretary Zhang, not detecting anything out of the ordinary and attributing her silence to her usual reticence and reserve, offered more words of encouragement and left.

Her husband came as usual on a motorcycle to take her home. Normally they would take the highway, but with the banks of the Tiaoluo Creek deserted at this late hour, her husband decided to take a shortcut along the pedestrian path running parallel to the brook. On this path paved with pebbles of different colors the motorcycle ride was very bumpy and Yu Qing'e had a feeling her guts were on the verge of spilling out of her body. Unable to hold it in any longer, she laid her head against the broad back of her husband and began crying.

At first her husband thought his wife had not yet emerged from her Xishi mode and was continuing to sing for her own enjoyment. It was only when he felt a chill on his back as Yu Qing'e's tears soaked through his jacket and his undershirt that he sensed there was something wrong. He applied the brakes and asked, turning his head around: "What's the matter, Qing'e? Why are you feeling so wretched? Unlike Fan Li in your play, I'm not sending you to the Kingdom of Wu as a spy!"

This sent Yu Qing'e into a new fit of crying; she began to weep unrestrainedly now. Her husband, in a fluster, jumped off his bike and took her into his arms, saying soothingly: "What's the matter? What's the matter? Did someone give you a hard time? Who had the nerve …"

Raining blows on her husband's chest and shoulders with her hands clenched into fists, she chided through her sobs: "It's you! You're giving me a hard time. It's you who make life miserable for me!"

Her husband, mystified by the blows, cried, shaking her by the shoulders: "Wake up! Qing'e! What are you saying? I couldn't love you and adore you enough. How could I possibly want to make life miserable for you! What on earth do you mean? Explain yourself!"

Flinging herself into her husband's arms, she said with bitterness: "I'm pregnant. What am I to do? Tell me, what am I supposed to do?"

The full significance of her words did not instantly sink in. Then it dawned on him. Her husband went wild with joy and, picking her up, started to whirl her around. Yu Qing'e cried with fright and alarm: "Watch out! You'll fall!"

Finally he put her down and said, clasping her tightly to him: "Isn't that wonderful! We'll be parents now!"

Pushing him away Yu Qing'e said with vehemence: "What's so wonderful about it? We have an agreement not to have a child before I'm thirty! Now you've broken your promise. You did not stick to our agreement!"

Her husband cried foul, feeling himself wronged: "I did not break my promise. I have always been very careful. Didn't we always make sure you were in your safe period?"

Yu Qing'e, also puzzled by how it happened, muttered: "I can't think of a rational explanation. I made doubly sure of my calculations …"

Clutching her to him, her husband said in a tender tone: "Qing'e, I did promise you we'd not have a child before you were thirty, and we did take precautions, am I right? But the child couldn't wait. Why? Because the gods think it's time we have a child. This child is a godsend, so we must cherish it, don't you agree?"

Her tears flowing freely, Yu Qing'e said between sobs: "But, but what about my Xishi?"

Her husband said smiling: "You little fool! You've made a name for yourself by playing Xishi, and everybody now thinks Xishi is you and you are Xishi. So there's no danger of anyone trying to steal the part from you. They couldn't even if they tried, because your fans wouldn't allow it. In a year's time you will go back to playing your Xishi, after you give birth!" While comforting her with these soothing words, he helped her back on the motorcycle. On the rest of the way home her husband rode his bike as if he were taking a plane through the clouds.

When they got home, Yu Qing'e, not wanting her tear-stained face to be seen by her mother-in-law, went directly to her room. With not enough time to wash her face, she pulled out a few moistened napkins to wipe off her face and then applied some moisturizing cream. The face in the mirror, despite the slightly puffy eyelids, was peachy pink, with bright starry eyes, clean, handsome features. She was getting ready to leave her room when the door was thrown open, letting in her mother-in-law accompanied by her husband. Chuckling with joy and happily ignoring the tears streaking her cheeks and the snot dripping from her nose, her mother-in-law grabbed Yu Qing'e's hands and, looking her up and down, left and right, mumbled: "Qing'e! You are pregnant! Qing'e! The entire Zhao clan, going back eight generations, is indebted to you for this! Qing'e! From now on you have to take extra care of your physical well-being …"

With a shrug, Qing'e's husband signaled to her that he was powerless to restrain his mother. Taking his mother's arm and dragging her toward the door, he said: "Mom, that's enough. Now you've seen. It's very late and Qing'e needs to go to bed early!" It was this last sentence that persuaded the mother-in-law to leave, but not before turning her head around to give her son one last instruction: "Go out and buy breakfast yourself tomorrow morning. Don't make Qing'e get up early in the morning to serve you breakfast, you hear?"

News of Yu Qing'e's pregnancy, "running like a rabbit and flying like a bird", quickly spread through the entire Zhao clan. The next day at noon time, came unsummoned two elder sisters of the husband, aunts and uncles on the mother's side and aunts and uncles on the father's side. Nutritional supplements in packages of varying sizes they brought as gifts covered every inch of the "Eight Immortals" table. Words of congratulations poured in buckets. Surrounded by all the solicitous attention, Yu Qing'e felt like the Li Sanniang forced into slave labor in the mill shed by her evil brother and sister-in-law, drained of all strength and drenched in sweat.

Yu Qing'e grappled with her inner conflict all night, but not having the heart to throw cold water on her husband's enthusiasm, she did not have the courage to broach the matter when her husband got ready to leave for work early in the morning. Now that her husband was not present, she made up her mind and mustered her courage to make her wish known to all the kin present. With a loud cough to clear her throat, she said to her mother-in-law: "Mom, I think this baby's conception is poorly timed. Party Secretary Zhang of my company says the Xishi play has been booked solid until the Mid-autumn Festival. A contract is a contract and cannot be easily annulled. Moreover, Party Secretary Zhang has already entered me in the contest of new Yueju opera plays starring young actors from the six provinces of east China and the city of Shanghai to be held toward year's end. The leadership pins high hopes on me!"

After getting it off her chest, she braced herself for her mother-in-law's rebukes and attempts by the many aunts and uncles to contradict her. But she found to her surprise that a hush came over the big living room after she finished what she had to say. The aunts and uncles exchanged looks and finally their eyes rested on the mother-in-law, who in turn swiveled about to look at the father-in-law, who had been leafing through the newspaper all this time, as if he were oblivious of what was going on around him.

The reaction was understandable. After all the daughter-in-law had become a famous Yueju opera star in town!

The father-in-law put aside his paper, took off his reading glasses and then lifted his cup and took a deep draft of his tea. The father-in-law was not normally in the habit of poking his nose into the running of the household and left it to the mother-in-law. Before his retirement, the father-in-law was the president of a town-operated company engaged in foreign trade, a local big shot not without some reputation and status. The father-in-law set down his cup and said in a measured tone: "Qing'e, I know Party Secretary Zhang. Her husband was a secretary in my office. Let's do this. I'll make a phone call to her and tell her your situation. I don't expect any major problems. I've seen my share of contracts and as far as I know none contains any provision prohibiting childbirth!"

That set off a collective laugh as the aunts and uncles chimed in: "Yes, that's right! A woman giving birth to a child is a law of nature!"

Yu Qing'e naturally would not argue with her father-in-law but harbored the secret hope that Party Secretary Zhang would be able to persuade her father-in-law to change his mind and to agree with her abortion decision.

That night Yu Qing'e went as usual to the mock antique stage to perform her Xishi and as usual won thunderous applause and loud cheering. After the curtain call she stepped down from the stage, expecting Party Secretary Zhang; she sat at her dressing table and started to slowly remove makeup in front of the mirror, her heart beating like a drum as she waited. As expected, Party Secretary Zhang's beaming face appeared in the mirror, and Yu Qing'e bolted up from her chair and called out: "Party Secretary Zhang—" then she saw her husband standing behind Party Secretary Zhang, looking at her with a silly grin. An ominous feeling descended on her like a thick fog, and she slumped back into her chair.

Party Secretary Zhang pulled up a chair to sit down beside her and looking at her in the mirror said smiling: "Xiao Yu, are you physically able to do a few more performances? Think you can manage?"

Opening her mouth to say "I can", she choked up and tears started streaming down her face. Stroking her back, Party Secretary Zhang said in a soft, gentle tone: "Don't cry, don't cry!

This was not your fault. Your father-in-law told me everything over the phone. You must be worried about our company incurring losses due to the breach of contract. Rest assured; our team already discussed the matter this afternoon. Our company is rush-producing a grand musical *Four Beauties*, which consists of four sections: 'Beauty Enough to Make Fish Sink to the Bottom', 'Beauty Enough to Stop Wild Geese in Flight', 'Beauty Enough to Drive the Moon behind Clouds' and 'Beauty Enough to Shame the Flowers into Closing'. The 'Beauty Enough to Make Fish Sink to the Bottom' section tells the story of Xishi also, so if you can perform until the end of this month, its panel of the quadriptych will be a natural extension of your Xishi play. What do you think?"

Yu Qing'e was deeply disappointed by Party Secretary Zhang's total ignorance of her feelings. Her husband repeatedly thanked Party Secretary Zhang on her behalf: "Thank you! She's grateful for the leadership's thoughtfulness!" But Yu Qing'e, slumped over the dressing table, was now weeping harder and with an utter abandonment.

Her husband was thrown into a fluster by her crying; Party Secretary Zhang helped her back into an upright sitting position, pulled out a few napkins and handed them to her: "Xiao Yu, I know you hate to miss out on the year-end contest. It's not a big deal. You are still young and will have many such opportunities in the future, next year, year after that; you'll have plenty of opportunities to win prizes. Stop crying now, otherwise you'll give birth to a baby that cries all the time."

Party Secretary Zhang left only after she finally got Yu Qing'e to stop sobbing. In great deference, the husband saw Party Secretary Zhang to the entrance of the Theater. He returned to the dressing room to find Yu Qing'e still sitting there with a wooden expression. Putting on a smile, he helped her take off her costume, change her shoes and tidy up the dressing table. Then he said gingerly: "Qing'e, can we go home now?"

Yu Qing'e slowly rose to her feet, her joints creaking as if rusted. Her husband reached out to support her but the hand was slapped away by her. She shot him a baleful glance and said bitterly: "Now you got what you wished for!"

Those words reassured the husband; his wife had finally given in! He became doubly gentle with her and more affectionate, so that Yu Qing'e found it hard to raise a stink.

Yu Qing'e resigned herself to her fate. She was like a floundering insect stuck in a spider's web; the more she struggled to be free the tighter the web closed in on her. Resignedly she thought, maybe her husband was right: they had taken all necessary precautions in their conjugal life and carefully calculated her safe periods, and yet the baby came unbidden! Maybe it was all written in their karma! So Yu Qing'e gritted her teeth and erased from her mind all her dreams of stardom on the Yueju opera stage and said to herself: all right, I'll give my best to the last few performances of my Xishi. After that I will focus my mind on the birth of my child!

Qing'e's mother-in-law was constantly urging her to have a proper pregnancy examination at a better equipped hospital at the county seat. Her father-in-law, through his connections, actually made an appointment for her with the director of obstetrics and gynecology of the county People's Hospital. Since her husband had to work and couldn't free himself to take her there, her mother-in-law volunteered to accompany Qing'e to the appointment in the county seat. Yu Qing'e said: "Mom, the county seat is only a few bus stops from here. You don't think I am too incompetent to manage that! Dad already made the appointment with the doctor, so I can go by myself." Seeing that Yu Qing'e meant what she said, her mother-in-law did not insist. She put some dried bamboo shoots, tea, dried dates and ginkgo nuts in a plastic bag and told Yu Qing'e to take them to the chief obstetrician-gynecologist as a gift. Finally she sent her off with earnest urgings to be careful on the way.

Yu Qing'e had no trouble finding the chief obstetrician-gynecologist at the county People's Hospital. It turned out the obstetrician was a silver-haired male doctor. He ran blood works on Yu Qing'e and did an ultrasound examination and concluded the embryo was developing normally. The chief obstetrician-gynecologist said the embryo was only one month old and had not fully developed. He gave her an appointment in two months' time; by then the fetal heart could be heard and its sex known. The chief obstetrician-gynecologist added for emphasis: "Regulations absolutely do not allow us to identify the sex of the fetus for pregnant women." What was left unsaid was of course not lost on Yu Qing'e, who immediately placed the plastic bag filled by her mother-in-law near the chief obstetrician's feet. Without asking what the bag was for, the obstetrician-gynecologist wrote her some prescriptions for vitamins, folic acid and other trace element supplements.

Yu Qing'e was waiting on line at the hospital pharmacy when she suddenly heard her name called and felt an arm placed on her shoulder. She turned her head around and saw it was her old school mate Qian Xiaoxiao!

Yu Qing'e said in astonishment: "Xiaoxiao, what brought you here?"

Qian Xiaoxiao laughed and turned the question back to her: "Yu Qing'e, what brought *you* here?"

Yu Qing'e had known from her School of the Arts days that this Qian Xiaoxiao was a klutzy loudmouth, so she naturally could not reveal her pregnancy to her. She retorted: "I am unwell so I am here to see a doctor. This is the best hospital in the county, you know. Why did you come all the way from the provincial capital to see a doctor here? You must have better hospitals there."

Qian Xiaoxiao looked at her with a mysterious air and said teasingly: "Do I look like I am sick? If I were sick I certainly wouldn't come here to see a country doctor!"

With much on her mind, Yu Qing'e was uninterested in her gossip and asked, just for something to say: "Then you are here to visit relatives? Aren't you performing in the 'White Rabbit'?"

With eyes nearly out of their sockets, Qian Xiaoxiao said: "You didn't know? Yu Qing'e, you must be from another planet!"

Her curiosity piqued, Yu Qing'e asked: "What happened?

Don't tell me there was a change of dynasties!"

Qian Xiaoxiao shook her head: "Not quite but close! Mi Jingyao wrote a memo asking to be excused from the cast of the new production of the 'White Rabbit'. She got herself a role, third or fourth support actress, in the provincial TV station's serial drama *When Will the Spring Flowers Fade and the Autumn Moon Wane*. It's no wonder she no longer wants to play Li Sanniang; she worked so hard and in the end she was slammed down hard by the critics. It was disastrous for the new production of the 'White Rabbit'. The plan was for a number of public performances before the Hong Kong tour, but now the tour itself is in question."

Yu Qing'e was aghast: what a shocking change! It's like Rip Van Winkle waking up from his sleep to find a completely different world! After a pause she asked: "So you have come to the country for a change of scenery?"

Again, with an air of mystery, Qian Xiaoxiao moved closer to say: "Yu Qing'e, can you swear you'll not tell anyone what I'm going to divulge to you?"

Yu Qing'e said: "Mi Jingyao's withdrawal from the role of Li Sanniang will become known at least to the entire Provincial Yueju Opera Theater, so how do you expect to keep it a secret from others?"

Qian Xiaoxiao said: "I'm not talking about Mi Jingyao. There's more shocking news!"

Yu Qing'e tried to guess: "Are you saying Feng Jianyue ..."

"Feng Jianyue is now all the rage in the provincial capital and might soon overtake her master in popularity!" then moving a step closer to her, Qian Xiaoxiao said, keeping her voice low: "It's Shi Xiaotong! She wanted to play Mi Jingyao's Li Sanniang, but the director found her plain looks unfit for the stage, so she has come here to have a facelift!"

Nearly shocked out of her shoes, Yu Qing'e looked left and right: "Shi Xiaotong? Where is she?"

Pointing at the plaque inscribed with the words "ENT Clinic" at the entrance of a long annex, Qian Xiaoxiao said:

"She already went in there. A nose lift is a half-day outpatient procedure. Double eyelids will take longer. So we have booked a room in a little inn nearby."

Still baffled, Yu Qing'e said with a shadow on her brow: "Don't you have cosmetic surgery in the bigger hospitals in the provincial capital? These procedures have only just started in our little county town; can you really trust the doctor's skills and equipment here?"

Qian Xiaoxiao said: "Shi Xiaotong wants to keep this a secret. She hasn't even told her family. She merely said she and I would be going on a sightseeing tour during the slack. Some friend referred her to this clinic, so I guess it should be OK."

They were interrupted by a nurse who emerged from the ENT Clinic and called in a loud voice: "Who's family of Shi Xiaotong?"

Qian Xiaoxiao responded with alacrity: "Here, here!" then turning her head around, repeated her plea: "You must keep the secret!" before walking briskly into the ENT Clinic.

Yu Qing'e also turned around quickly and headed out of the hospital, worried by the prospect of running into Shi Xiaotong when she came out of surgery. What could she say to her? She and they now seemed to live on two different planets.

That night after coming home from the performance, Yu Qing'e went straight for the newspaper. She had neglected the papers these days because of her preoccupation with the unexpected pregnancy. There was indeed a mention in the paper of Mi Jingyao's decision to withdraw from the new production of the "White Rabbit". Her reply to the interviewing journalist was: "I want to strike out on my own path in the pursuit of art and try different media of the performing arts. Our Yueju opera has developed and grown by assimilating elements of stage drama and Kunqu opera, among others. I believe that when I return to the Yueju opera stage after acquiring skills and experience in TV serial drama, I will have attained a higher artistic plain."

In the following day's paper there was this news item:

"… Riding to the rescue, the famous Yueju opera actor in the female role Xie Yingge has bravely stepped into the breach to play the part of Li Sanniang through the entirety of the new production of the 'White Rabbit'. In the first half of the play, Xie Yingge will play, for the first time, opposite the able young actor in the young male role Feng Jianyue as Li Sanniang and Liu Zhiyuan respectively in the two scenes 'Marriage of Liu Zhiyuan into the Li Family by the Melon Patch' and 'Liu Zhiyuan Parts from His Wife and Goes off to the Army'. Many have expressed doubt about the suitability of their playing husband and wife on the stage given an age gap of more than thirty years. Xie Yingge is of the view that one of the wonders that traditional Chinese opera is capable of working is its ability to rejuvenate through the use of makeup. She has expressed the confidence that on the strength of her acting and singing she will work in perfect sync with Feng Jianyue to give a seamless rendition of this poignant, timeless love story."

Remembering Qian Xiaoxiao's account of Shi Xiaotong going to the length of getting a facelift in order to get the part of Li Sanniang and reflecting on her own circumstances, Yu Qing'e couldn't help feeling empathy and pity for her.

The end of the month was approaching and this would be Yu Qing'e's last performance of her Xishi. In late afternoon Yu Qing'e saw on her way to the dressing room set pieces for the "Beauty Enough to Make Fish Sink to the Bottom" section of the musical *Four Beauties* already moved into the corridor. The moment her performance of *Xishi Returns Home* drew to a close, the props crew would start disassembling the old set and loading in the new set.

At this moment Yu Qing'e's mood coincided with the grief and forlornness of Xishi bidding her last farewell to her lover and her beloved country. As she made up her face for the performance, she took special pains in painting around her eyes. Under her brush the two eyebrows now looked like silhouettes of distant hills blotted under drifting mists of rain; for eye shadow she used dark gray in place of brownish red so that her eyes seemed to glitter with tears; for the lips she applied ruby red instead of vermilion, with, at the corners of the mouth, a touch of silver white that seemed to drip with hurt. Party Secretary Zhang came this evening to the backstage to root for her. When she saw her makeup, she stared for a moment before saying with a sigh: "Xiao Yu, all you need to do is thrust yourself to the center of the stage, silent and still, and the audience will be moved to tears by this heartbroken look on your face alone!"

Yu Qing'e merely smiled forlornly.

> The silk rinsing in the stream connects me to my
>   love Fan Li,
> I may be in far corners of the world, but my only
>   thought is for the old country ...

Yu Qing'e found her voice unusually smooth and fluid that evening; the moment she opened her mouth to sing, her voice, crisp and clear, projected far beyond the heads of the spectators, who exploded in applause. Spinning on her feet and flinging out the long sleeves, she arrived at center stage, pulled in the sleeves and stood still just as the beam of a spotlight picked her out. The exquisite, well synchronized "frozen pose" set off a tidal wave of cheering and applause.

As her eyes panned across the audience, Yu Qing'e suddenly froze—sitting in the middle of the third row was Deputy General Manager Qin Yulou of the Provincial Yueju Opera Theater! Her heart started beating wildly and she immediately commanded herself to calm down. Yes, when Qin Yulou took her to visit Xie Yingge, she did say she would watch her perform Xishi if she had the time. Yu Qing'e had thought she was being polite and gracious. Would a famous Yueju opera actor, and a leader of the Provincial Yueju Opera Theater to boot, really come to a rural town to watch the performance of a beginning young actor? But Qin Yulou kept her promise and really came! She was deeply moved and yet profoundly sad at the same time: Manager Qin, you wouldn't know that this will be Yu Qing'e's last performance.

Pulling herself together, Yu Qing'e doubly focused her mind on her portrayal of Xishi. In this last performance of hers, she melted into the role, erasing any boundary between herself and her character. The performance was punctuated by applause from beginning to end.

At the curtain call, Yu Qing'e took a deep bow in the direction of Qin Yulou—Manager Qin, thanks for coming to see my performance, thanks also for taking me to Master Xie, whose coaching enabled me to manipulate with ease the eight-foot water sleeves in this performance!

The curtains finally drew slowly together. Yu Qing'e, suddenly feeling limp and weak in her limbs, plunked herself down on the stage floor. She dearly wished she could sit like that forever and not have to leave. The stage manager and the props crew crowded up, ready to carry her down the stage. She sprang to her feet and said with a rueful smile: "I'm all right. I merely wanted to sit for a minute on the stage."

Back in her dressing room, Yu Qing'e gazed fixedly at the Xishi in the mirror. It was indeed a Xishi of great beauty! And Xishi was at her most beautiful in her sad, angst-filled moments, hence the survival to this day of the story of the "Dongshi who mimicked the frown of Xishi with disastrous effect". Look at this Xishi in the mirror! Her tired, grief-stricken face, still streaked with tears, could easily be what was described by these phrases in *The Story of the Western Wing*: "A treeful of cherries dripping with rain and red as blood, a rare flower with red and purple petals flaunting its beauty." Even Yu Qing'e herself was mesmerized by the resplendent beauty of this Xishi. But it was precisely Xishi's beauty that prompted the King of Yue to send her to the Kingdom of Wu as a spy! Yu Qing'e reached out to pass her palm across the mirror, smudging the image. She slumped into her arms on the dressing table and felt a strong urge to bid a last farewell to her stage by crying with abandonment.

She felt a hand gently stroking her nape. "Xiao Yu, you must be bone tired. You gave an excellent performance tonight ... Guess who came to see your performance?"

The voice, like a balmy night breeze, tickled her ears. As Yu Qing'e slowly lifted her face, she saw, through her tear-blurred eyes, first the kindly smiling face of Party Secretary Zhang, then Qin Yulou, next to Party Secretary Zhang, slight bent over her, gazing with concern at her.

Yu Qing'e scrambled to her feet, nearly knocking over the chair in the process, and called out bashfully: "Party Secretary Zhang, Manager Qin, please have a seat! I'm sorry ...".

"Sit down, sit down." Party Secretary Zhang said with a smile and pulled up two stools, "Manager Qin, Director He, have a seat. You should have told me you were coming to see the performance. I am sorry I saw you only at the end of the show. You must forgive me!"

Yu Qing'e discovered only then a fashionably dressed young man standing next to Qin Yulou. The memory came back to her: she had already witnessed his imperious manner in the rehearsal room of the Provincial Yueju Opera Theater last time she was there; he was He Shuye, the director of the new production of the "White Rabbit"! Although he had not spoken a word, his keen, scanning eyes already made several passes over her. This had the effect of accentuating Yu Qing'e's nervousness, so much so that her normally awkward tongue tripped more than usual over the words: "I wasn't in top form ... Manager Qin, Director He, I'm quite ashamed ... I'm eager to hear your criticisms ..."

After everyone was seated, Qin Yulou said with a smile: "Yu Qing'e, don't be so modest! We have long heard that the Xishi of antiquity has come back to life by the Tiaoluo Creek. The major tour operators in the provincial capital have been using Xishi in their ads to draw more business!"

The smile blossoming on Party Secretary Zhang's face threatened to make her eyes disappear. "You are too kind! This was after all only the first production of the Yueju opera troupe of our company. Manager Qin, and Director He, do give us frank opinions about the performance! We plan to further refine and revise it. The 45-minute playlet will be expanded into a 2-hour plus multi-act play in the second round of performances."

Qin Yulou said: "Actually a good, short, one-act playlet is quite suited to a tourist destination. Of course the number of performances can be increased. What do you think, Director He? We'd appreciate any constructive criticism you might offer."

After a brief reflection Director He said: "This playlet is indeed very good. With the evolution of the plot closely following the development of Xishi's psychological context, it has great artistic appeal. If there was any shortcoming, well, the actor could have done with a little more restraint in expressing the emotions of the character. Some innermost feelings need not be exposed in their entirety and could be left to the imagination of the viewers."

Vigorously nodding, Party Secretary Zhang said: "Xiao Yu doesn't normally talk much, but on stage she is very engaged and may sometimes overdo it a bit. Xiao Yu, did you hear what Director He said?"

As Yu Qing'e's mouth twitched in the shadow of a smile, a surge of acid rushed up to her throat; she swallowed it back with some effort.

Then Director He changed the subject: "Your long sleeve dance sequence was perfectly executed. Where did you get the technical director to choreograph it for you?"

Yu Qing'e hesitated before saying, with a glance in the direction of Qin Yulou: "It was done under the guidance of my master Xie Yingge ... we had first done an imitation based on stage photos of Master Xie doing it years ago, then we asked Master Xie to coach me ..."

With an "Oh" of sudden understanding, Director He said, glancing over at Qin Yulou: "I really don't get Xie Yingge! She was adamantly against having Mi Jingyao performing the long sleeve dance sequence in the new production of the 'White Rabbit', and here she has helped choreograph the long sleeve dance in someone else's play!"

With a glance at Yu Qing'e, Qin Yulou said with a smile: "Xiao Xie made her decision based on the merit of each individual. Mi Jingyao's skills are undeniably inferior to Yu Qing'e's."

Director He had a pensive moment before asking Yu Qing'e: "According to Manager Qin, you learned to play Li Sanniang from Xie Yingge when you were a child. Do you still remember how to do it?"

Yu Qing'e said bashfully: "I did it for sport when I was a child. I learned to play the 'Giving Birth by the Millstone' scene in the 'White Rabbit' when I attended the School of the Arts."

Director He and Qin Yulou exchanged a quick look.

The stage manager came in at this moment and whispered something to Party Secretary Zhang, who then said: "Manager Qin, Director He, why don't we go have a night snack?" Qin Yulou was quick to excuse herself: "Not this time, it's already quite late and we should be going back. Our driver must be getting impatient. He has to drive upwards of two hours on the return trip."

Party Secretary Zhang insisted on playing host: "Why don't you have some night snack and stay in our town overnight and leave tomorrow morning? We are honored to be your host. A table has been booked at the restaurant. It is a small rustic establishment, nothing to compare with the big restaurants in the provincial capital, but it does offer unique flavors."

But Qin Yulou and He Shuye were firm about not having any snack, so Party Secretary Zhang had the stage manager rustle up some local products as gifts for them and escorted them to the parking lot herself.

Since she still had her makeup on, Yu Qing'e could accompany them only to the entrance of the theater. No sooner had the visitors left than her husband emerged from a neighboring door. "What kind of Yueju opera fans were they? Didn't they have any consideration for your need to rest, talking for such a long time?" He had apparently arrived a while before, and finding visitors in the dressing room, had waited nearby.

Yu Qing'e gave him a sharp glance: "Didn't you see they were accompanied by Party Secretary Zhang? They are important people from the Provincial Yueju Opera Theater to see my play."

A red flag went up in her husband's mind: "The Provincial Yueju Opera Theater? Why would they come to our town to watch the performance?"

Yu Qing'e snapped: "How would I know why? Why did all those people come to see the play? Do you want a why from each of them?"

Her husband was quick with a smile: "No need, no need. Let me help you remove your makeup. Mom must be wondering why we're not home yet. Thank heavens it's over finally. You won't have to work so hard anymore starting tomorrow."

Yu Qing'e's hands were in the middle of removing the beaded ornaments on her head when she heard these words; there was a momentary pause before she proceeded to savagely yank off all the floral-design decorations, jade hairpins and dangling strands of crystal beads and fling them on the table.

That night her husband appeared in unusually high spirits. Even in bed he was still rhapsodizing to her about his vision of happy harmony in the Zhao household after the birth of their child. In no mood to chat, Yu Qing'e pleaded fatigue and huddled herself in bed in feigned sleep.

Very early the following morning Yu Qing'e got out of bed as usual, ready to go to the sandbanks along the river for her morning practice but was pulled back by her husband. "Silly you! From this day on you have no more performances to go to, and no more need to practice. You might harm our son in your practice!" As if jolted out of a happy dream, Yu Qing'e had a dazed moment before flopping back into bed in resignation.

After breakfast, with her husband off to work, Yu Qing'e found that once she had no performances to go to, no need to practice and no lines to memorize, she had nothing else to occupy herself. In boredom she placed a bamboo chair next to the door and sat motionless in it to contemplate vacuously a thicket of bamboo in a corner of the courtyard swaying like so many claws in the wind, leaving a carpet of fallen bamboo leaves on the ground. Now she found something to do; she sprang to her feet and got hold of a bamboo broom, with which she started sweeping the courtyard. As she herded the leaves into a big pile, the swishing sound alerted the mother-in-law in the kitchen, who hurried out to pry the bamboo broomstick from her and called out: "Old man, come out to stretch your limbs a bit. Sweeping the yard will help your circulation! Have you forgotten the doctor's advice? Doing a bit of household chores is good for your health?" Then, pressing Yu Qing'e to go inside, she kept reminding her: "Qing'e, we don't need you to do any house work. For you the first priority is to take good care of your body so that our little grandson will have an easy time coming into this world, understand?"

Yu Qing'e pleaded: "Mom, I'm so bored. Let me help you with preparing the vegetables."

The mother-in-law said: "Oh-yo! It's just a small bunch of vegetable. I don't need any help from you. It's one two three and the picking is done. If you are really bored, just watch TV or listen to some music. It'll be good for fetal education, I've heard."

Reluctantly Yu Qing'e went back to her room, then, remembering that it was her husband who had stuffed her clothing the previous night into her backpack in their haste to leave, she emptied the contents of it onto the bed and piece by piece returned the items to their respective places of storage. She came last to the *qingyi* costume. Lifting it with both hands she buried her face in its folds which gave off a scent of fragrant powder mixed with a faint smell of medicinal herbs. She drew a long breath to inhale the smell and her mind went back to the scene months before in the little yard of the Xie household in the provincial capital. It already felt like a life time away!

A few days of this indolent existence were enough to drive Yu Qing'e to distraction, causing her to lose sleep for nights on end and seek relief in sleeping pills. She wished she could be asleep and dreaming twenty-four hours a day; in her dreams at least she had her stage, the orchestra, her Xishi and her Li Sanniang. Sleep was far preferable to wakefulness!

One afternoon, having taken a valium tablet before her nap, Yu Qing'e sank into a deep sleep and was enjoying a long dream from which she was loath to emerge when she was wakened by her mother-in-law: "Qing'e, Qing'e, a phone call for you! I said you were taking a nap but the caller said it was urgent. Could it be from the county hospital?"

Dizzy and groggy from the lingering effect of the tranquilizer, Yu Qing'e picked up the receiver, staggering a little; her mother-in-law quickly pulled up a chair for her.

"Hello—is this Yu Qing'e?" the voice sounded far off but was clear and pleasant on the ear.

Yu Qing'e woke up with a jolt: "Manager Qin, I didn't expect it would be you calling. How did you find my phone number?" Her hand gripping the receiver started to tremble.

Qin Yulou said: "I got the number from Party Secretary Zhang of your company. I was going to talk to you about a matter, but after hearing Party Secretary Zhang's description of your present circumstance, I'm afraid what I intended to say has been somewhat overtaken by events."

Thinking the call was most probably about organizing a group of young actors of the Provincial Yueju Opera Theater to attend a performance of *Xishi Returns Home*, she said: "Manager Qin, it's all right, I'm listening."

After a brief reflection, Qin Yulou said: "Yu Qing'e, you probably have heard that Mi Jingyao has withdrawn from the new production of the 'White Rabbit' to join the cast of a TV serial drama."

Yu Qing'e said: "M'mm, it was in the papers. I understand Master Xie Yingge has thrown herself in the breach and agreed to play Li Sanniang through the entire play."

Qin Yulou said: "Yes. It was the original plan. But after she tried out the part in costume, it was obvious that Xie Yingge no longer looked the way she did in her younger days, and the age gap stood out even more when she played opposite Feng Jianyue. The upcoming Hong Kong tour is the first in thirty years for the Provincial Yueju Opera Theater. In order to achieve the best possible effect and an optimal balance between the respective strengths of older and younger actors, the director still hopes for a suitable young actor to succeed Mi Jingyao in the role …"

Yu Qing'e seemed to sense where the conversation was leading, but refrained from any rash surmise and merely said in a low voice: "I heard that Shi Xiaotong was keen on playing Li Sanniang …"

She was interrupted by Qin Yulou. "That's out of the question. She is already playing Yue Xiuying in the play."

Quickly trying to tame a heart that nearly jumped out of her chest, Yu Qing'e waited with held breath.

Qin Yulou suddenly raised her voice: "Without discussing it with you first, I recommended you to Director He. Due to the pressure of time we came unannounced to your performance. You gave an excellent performance that night and Director He already made the decision to cast you in that role on our drive home. The brass of the Theater called a joint meeting of the creative and production teams to discuss the matter and unanimously approved Director He's proposal …"

Yu Qing'e's heart stopped beating and her blood froze.

"Yu Qing'e, are you listening?" The silence prompted Qin Yulou to ask.

"I am listening!" The loudness of her reply surprised Yu Qing'e herself.

Qin Yulou's voice coming across the telephone wire was full of sincerity and hope: "… Qing'e, you must know that it wasn't easy for me to get the role for you. There was strong opposition … Anyway now the leadership of the Theater has made the decision to second you to the provincial capital first and leave the personnel question until after the completion of the Hong Kong tour. This is an opportunity that comes along only rarely! I heard about your condition from Party Secretary Zhang and know what your family thinks about the matter. Party Secretary Zhang has said that your productions company will not make any difficulties for you; the key is making up your mind and being able to put your case across to your family. But you must let me know before next Monday because there's only one month left for rehearsal!"

Yu Qing'e didn't know how she had put the receiver down. Her mother-in-law rushed up to ask: "Qing'e, whose call was that? It was a long call!"

When Yu Qing'e lifted up her face, it was covered with tears. Her mother-in-law was sent into a panic: "What's the matter? Is there a problem with the baby?"

Yu Qing'e smiled through the tears that kept welling up in her eyes. "Mom, the Provincial Yueju Opera Theater is seconding me to play Li Sanniang for the Hong Kong tour!"

Her mother-in-law was taken aback. "What? Didn't you say you were done with performances? What are you going to do about the baby?"

Yu Qing'e didn't seem to have heard her mother-in-law. She did a "butterfly kick"—flinging out her arms, kicking her legs, getting airborne, her body spinning horizontally in a circle, and out she flew into the yard. She followed with a "sparrow hawk pirouette". All this so worried the mother-in-law that she cried in distress: "Watch out! Think of the baby!"

With her elation crying out for a further outlet, Yu Qing'e ran into her room and put on the *qingyi* costume. Singing Li Sanniang's "Giving Birth by the Millstone": "Cold sweat drenches my body. All strength has drained out of me and I can barely remain on my feet," she sashayed into the yard, did a "cloud hand", a "cloud walk" dancing like a "dragon flying and a phoenix dancing" in the clouds.

Her mother-in-law stamped her feet in frustration: "She's out of her mind! She's gone crazy!" She went inside and said to the father-in-law: "Someone called Yu Qing'e on the phone and all of a sudden she wasn't herself anymore. She's gone off her rockers. You stay here and watch her while I go fetch our son! It's getting dark and he should be home from work now!"

When the mother-in-law rushed out the door Yu Qing'e was still singing her "Giving Birth by the Millstone": "Alas I have no water, no scissors and nobody to help, I have no choice but to bite through the umbilical cord myself ... my son—"

The door opened with a crash and her husband stalked up to her and yelled at her: "Qing'e, don't you think you've caused enough trouble already?" It turned out he had already turned into the alley leading home when he ran into his mother, who lost no time in telling him: your wife went crazy after receiving a phone call, go and straighten her out!

At the sight of her husband, Yu Qing'e stopped and rushing forward wrapped her arms around his massive frame: "Lao Gong (my man), Manager Qin of the Provincial Yueju Opera Theater just called to say that they were transferring me to the provincial capital to play the character Li Sanniang! I've been praying for this day! Lao Gong! I count on your support. You will support me, won't you? We had an agreement not to have a child before I reach the age of thirty after all ..."

Her husband savagely pried loose her arms and roared: "I don't support you! Now take off that gown and go back to your room!"

Yu Qing'e stared with astonishment at her husband's face, now distorted by anger and transformed into a stranger's face. Was this the generous, gentle and considerate husband she had known? With pleading in her eyes, she said beseechingly: "Lao Gong! You know I've had this dream! You have said you'd support me in that. If I pass up this opportunity, I will never be able to get into the Provincial Yueju Opera Theater!"

The mother-in-law sneered. "Oh, so you wanted to go to the provincial capital to seek a higher perch! You have used the Zhao family as but a stepping stone for your advancement! You won't stop even if it means killing our grandson! What a heartless woman!"

Completely ignoring her mother-in-law, not deigning even a glance out of the corner of her eye, Yu Qing'e kept her eyes fixed on her husband.

Her husband, his face fiery red with agitation, said after a moment in a low but emphatic voice: "No way, you can't go to the provincial capital. This child is mine and you have no right to dispose of him!" then added in a slightly softened tone: "Qing'e, so what if you can't get into the Provincial Yueju Opera Theater? Let's forget about Yueju opera! You worked your head off and in the end you got paid a few ten-yuan notes. Be a good girl and stay home to carry the baby to term. My salary is big enough to support you and the child!"

Yu Qing'e fell silent, her lips pressed tight into a jagged lip line. She told herself: it's useless begging them. The Zhao family will not understand me! I need to see Party Secretary Zhang. She has clearly stated that the company is not going to get in her way but that the job of persuading her family falls squarely on her own shoulders. Should she go to her own family for support and help? That won't work either. Her own parents set great store by this marriage of hers and would only take the side of the Zhao family and try to talk her out of it. She came to the realization that her salvation could come only from herself!

The night was dark, as dark as a dried-up well. With all sleep gone, Yu Qing'e stared wide-eyed into the pitch-dark night; some critter, a cat or a rat, skittered along an overhead beam. She had not taken her tranquilizer that night; she had enough of dreaming, it was time to face up to reality. She had made up her mind!

Placing her hands gently on her belly, she spoke with boundless sadness to the yet unformed baby—baby, you must understand, don't you, the quandary your mother is in. Mother started learning Yueju opera since a child and has always dreamed of becoming one day a famous actor in the female role performing to packed houses on the Yueju opera stage just like Xie Yingge. If I don't go to the Provincial Yueju Opera Theater when I have the opportunity, and if I stay behind in this small town to perform indifferent plays on festive occasions on the small stage here, mother will never realize that dream of hers. Dear child, forgive mother. It's not that mother doesn't love you. It's just that you've chosen the wrong time to come. Mother is going to send you back to heaven and when mother's dream becomes reality, mother will meet you there. Agreed? Be sure to wait for mother! Tears soaked through the pillow cover.

When the first glimmer of dawn, the color of egg white, peeped in through the crack of the window curtains, Yu Qing'e got out of bed noiselessly amid the loud snoring of her husband. With only a few hundred yuan in her inside pocket, and stuffing only that *qingyi* costume into her backpack, she noiselessly sailed out of the house with the minced steps she had practiced for the stage since she was a child. Crossing the yard, she pushed open the gate in the wall and floated out. When the gate closed with a squeak, she shuddered but never turned back. She knew she would never be allowed back into this home.

In the yard of some house in the small town a rooster gave two long crows; the remnant moon paled and was inexorably swallowed by the breaking light of dawn.

Yu Qing'e went, with unshaken resolve, to her cousin's town clinic and had an abortion, following which she slept for three days at her cousin's home. First thing on the Monday morning she got on the bus to the provincial capital and never looked back, just as Xishi boarded the official boat sent by the Kingdom of Wu for her, never looking back.

Scene XII Finding True Love

As autumn wore on, the vines and creepers trailing on the garden wall of the Xie residence began to wilt and thin out. The fragrance of autumn blossoms of the sweet osmanthus floated above the courtyard. The tassels of small, silvery white flowers on that sweet osmanthus in the southwest corner of the garden were in full bloom against a background of dark green, mature leaves, like so many twinkling stars in a night sky.

On the surface life went on in much the same way it always had in the Xie household, quiet and secluded as an ancient lake. Even the sweet osmanthus, its branches weighed down by the thousands, tens of thousands of clusters of burgeoning flower buds, was a sight so taken for granted by the members of the household that it no longer sent a thrill through their heart. The quiet was only occasionally broken by Sister Ten who'd remark casually as she swept the courtyard: "Da Guniang, when are you getting back that *qingyi* costume of yours? I need to air it in the sun. Without it the yard does feel more spacious but also emptier."

But a storm was brewing at the bottom of the ancient lake, the ominous storm clouds gathering, lying in wait, and threatening at any moment to sweep away this little abode and shatter its calm.

One day after lunch Junior Miss came tap-tap down the stairs, and bending at the waist, put her head around the door of the living room: "Jieh, I'm going out now. I won't be back for supper."

Senior Miss, who had been contemplating the sweet osmanthus in her chair near the French door, turned her face forever frozen in a rictus to gaze at her and said with a drawl: "Aren't you feeling unwell? Why do you want to go out in your condition?"

Junior Miss gave a snort. "You mark my word. There will be more people dropping in to inquire after my health. I'm sick of those formulaic words of comfort and want to get away from it all. I am going to spend some time at a teahouse run by a friend."

Emerging from the kitchen, where she'd just finished cleaning up, Sister Ten put on a smile as she said: "Er Guniang, are you going out? You look fabulous!" and saw Junior Miss all the way to the street door.

Back in the house, Sister Ten said with a sardonic tilt of a corner of her mouth: "She doesn't look the least bit ill! The way she dyed her hair as black as the bottom of a wok and painted her lips as red as a pepper, she looks more like an ogress!"

Senior Miss said in a low, quiet voice: "She suffers from emotional trauma."

Tapping her head with a fist Sister Ten said: "Da Guniang, did you smell? The perfume she wears makes me dizzy. I can't take it. I have to clear my head a bit by the sweet osmanthus. Da Guniang, why don't I wheel you outside to get some fresh air? You'll find the shade under the osmanthus quite refreshing."

Senior Miss's silence signaled consent and Sister Ten pushed open the French door. In that instant the fragrance from the sweet osmanthus rushed through the opening to fill the entire room.

In the meantime the Hong Kong tour of the new production of the "White Rabbit" rolled out by the Provincial Yueju Opera Theater proved a great success, which grabbed the headlines in all major media in Hong Kong. The two young actors, in particular, gained much kudos for their respective portrayal of Liu Zhiyuan and Li Sanniang in the first half of the play. In addition to being interviewed by the press, they were invited on a TVB entertainment program. In contrast Xie Yingge and Qin Yulou, the two older actors, received much less publicity.

The original plan was for five performances of the new "White Rabbit", which were sold out long in advance. But the Hong Kong Yueju opera fans' thirst remained unquenchable. The sponsor of the tour, after discussing the matter with the leadership of the Yueju Opera Theater, announced the addition of three more performances. It was at this crucial juncture that Xie Yingge, who played Li Sanniang in the second half, suddenly developed a heart ailment due to stress and fatigue and was incapable of taking the stage. As the crew and cast were thrown into turmoil by the unforeseen turn of events, Yu Qing'e, who played Li Sanniang in the first half, came to the rescue. She said that as a child she had learned from Master Xie to perform Li Sanniang through the entire play! The entire crew and cast worked all night to go over the lines and review blocking with Yu Qing'e. The success of the three additional performances exceeded all expectations. Yu Qing'e gave a performance that was just right and full of passion, winning over the entire audience. Even the habitually supercilious, proud Director He Shuye now looked at her with new eyes and said privately to Qin Yulou: "Manager Qin, you do have an eye for talent. Yu Qing'e has injected new life into Li Sanniang, giving a poetic and philosophic burnish to this character that was becoming stale." The Hong Kong media couldn't get enough of Yu Qing'e; her stage photos were plastered over newspapers big and small and she was hailed by public opinion as "more like the Xie Yingge of her youthful days than Xie Yingge herself".

After the triumphant return from Hong Kong of the troupe of the Yueju Opera Theater, Junior Miss pleaded illness and stopped coming to work. She did not even come to the "report card" performance of the new production of the "White Rabbit"; as a result Yu Qing'e played Li Sanniang through the entire play. Leaders at various levels of the cultural affairs department of the provincial government sent representatives to look in on her and wish her good rest and convalescence. The leadership's words were weighty and far-sighted: "Xie Yingge, you are the leading light of the art of Yueju opera in the province, a standard hoisted high in the cultural circles of the province, so you must take good care of your health. A weighty task falls on your shoulders, for you need to nurture more actors like Yu Qing'e so that Yueju opera will enjoy brighter prospects!"

The moment the visitors left, Junior Miss angrily swept all the gift packages brought by the official emissaries off the table to the floor and said bitterly: "It took only one Yu Qing'e to muscle me off the stage. If there were more like her, I'd be packed off to hell!"

It was only after she stomped off to her room upstairs that Sister Ten dared to collect the gifts off the floor. On account of Yu Qing'e, Sister Ten had received numerous chidings from Junior Miss, who had also vented her wrath on Senior Miss's head.

When Yu Qing'e had first stepped into the rehearsal room at the Provincial Yueju Opera Theater, put on that *qingyi* costume and started singing Li Sanniang in her mellifluous voice, it didn't take this Xie Yingge long to recognize who she was.

During the rehearsals, Yu Qing'e addressed her reverentially as "Master Xie", and it was with great effort that she had checked the seething fury and a tinge of fear within and went through the motions of working with her, always keeping her at arm's length.

When she came home from the rehearsals, this Xie Yingge emptied the vials of her wrath on Sister Ten, pointing her index finger at her: "So, Shi Mei, you had the nerve to put one over on me! Tell me now! Who really was that darned relative of yours? What was your purpose for letting her into the house? You'll not get away with it if you don't give me chapter and verse of this thing!" With that she picked up a teacup form the table, clenching it tightly in her hand. Sister Ten had never before seen Junior Miss in such a towering rage: all her usual elegance and poise gone, she now had the look of a leering, ferocious beast. Fearing an act of violence from Junior Miss, Sister Ten quickly crossed to where Senior Miss sat in her wheelchair to shield her with her roly-poly body. Junior Miss flung the cup on the floor; it landed with a racket, breaking instantly into pieces. Shoving Sister Ten aside, she stamped her feet: "Jieh! What did you do that for? Did you admit Yu Qing'e into the house with the intention of making her realize I am not the real Xie Yingge? Did you intend to have her expose the hoax the two of us had sprung on the world? You must regret your decision to let me take the name of Xie Yingge. You are wrong if you think you have been able to hide your twisted tortuous thoughts with that rictus on your face. I've seen through you. You hate me for stealing your man, am I right?"

Sister Ten gave a sharp cry: "Er Guniang, you, you are not human to say something like that!"

Contemptuous of the reprimand from a mere servant, Junior Miss continued relentlessly her tirade: "You found Yu Qing'e, you gave her your *qingyi* costume and personally coached her in performing the long sleeve dance. Did you think you could make her take my place? It won't happen because I am the only publicly acknowledged Xie Yingge. Jieh, quit your useless machinations … H'm h'm h'm! Ha ha ha!" The laughter was that of someone gone mad.

Senior Miss sat there stock still like a stone sculpture, seemingly deaf to the hysterical screaming of that woman calling herself "Xie Yingge", until that woman had exhausted herself with screaming and laughing. Then with her left hand she wheeled the chair to where Junior Miss was and said serenely: "Er Mei, I decided to be Yu Qing'e's teacher because she is fascinated by the Xie School of Yueju opera art and expresses a commitment to perpetuate it. She was performing Xishi in her home town in a small Yueju opera troupe. There was no way I could have foreseen Mi Jingyao's withdrawal from the new production of the 'White Rabbit' or the decision of the Provincial Yueju Opera Theater to second her to play Li Sanniang. You are the celebrated Xie Yingge. You have no reason to fear appearing on stage together with a young, beginning actor. If she turned out to have the capability to take your place, it could only mean you no longer live up to the name of Xie Yingge."

Privately Sister Ten rooted Senior Miss on. Senior Miss had got class and talked sense. Junior Miss fell silent, turned about and went up to her room. Wheeling herself to the French door, Senior Miss gazed out at the autumn-speckled yard and began to sing:

> As heavy flakes of snow flurry down,
> I look up in the sky and think of days of yore.
> Zhiyuan,
> I turn the millstone around and around,
> And I, Li Sanniang, could think of nothing that I
>   regret …

Sister Ten wheeled Senior Miss into the shade under the sweet osmanthus. With the sun directly above their heads, the shade, though only as large as a round table, was enough to cover them both. Sister Ten unfolded the woolen shawl and draped it over Senior Miss but with a flick of her left hand Senior Miss threw it off and said in stage speech: "You really think I am as frail as that Lin Daiyu character in the *Dream of the Red Chamber*? I am Li Sanniang, that even a thousand-jin millstone cannot crush ..." There was nothing for it but for Sister Ten to humor her. It was already late autumn, but the sweet osmanthus showed not the least sign of having lost its cheeriness. When a breeze sprang up, little pink and silvery white flowers would be blown off and fall to the ground, sending up whiffs of fragrance. As Li Qingzhao, the Song dynasty poetess wrote of the sweet osmanthus: What need for light green or deep crimson, You choicest of flowers!

In the balmy, perfumed breeze Senior Miss fell asleep. Sister Ten put the woolen shawl back over her; she knew that Senior Miss was strong of will but frail of body. Her doctor had left strict instructions that she mustn't catch a cold. Sitting cross-legged on the ground and leaning her head against the knees of Senior Miss, Sister Ten dozed off. Although she had worked her head off all her adult life, Sister Ten ate and slept well, spoke her mind and used her head sparingly. Soon she began to dream. She was transported back to the night of the wedding of Senior Miss and Wang Houcheng. Under the starry sky and in the moonlight the newlyweds planted in the southwest corner of this courtyard a sapling of sweet osmanthus about two feet high. In that period Wang Houcheng's devotion to Senior Miss was exemplary. Senior Miss made her name on the Yueju opera stage by performing the "White Rabbit". In that play Liu Zhiyuan and Li Sanniang also made their vow of eternal love under a sweet osmanthus tree ...

Sister Ten was roused out of her dream by the vigorous pushing of Senior Miss. Then she realized the doorbell was ringing stridently and she leapt to her feet to open the door. The doorbell had been installed by the electrician brought by Qin Yulou from the props team of the Yueju Opera Theater because the latter knew that Sister Ten was a bit hard of hearing and would often miss the knocking at the door when she worked in the kitchen.

Qin Yulou had said that Xie Yingge, being a celebrity in the cultural circles of the province, would of a certainty be visited in her illness by people in leadership positions in the cultural departments of the provincial government, and the installation of the doorbell would make sure that these people of high position would not, God forbid! be kept out.

Sister Ten was wondering what the ranking of the visiting dignitary would be this time and started to say as she opened the door: "You must be here to see Xie Yingge. She is not home—" only to see Qin Yulou, and, behind her, two young girls who seemed to have just emerged from a painting, one holding a big bouquet and the other carrying in her hands two bags containing beautifully packaged gift boxes. Sister Ten recognized in the handsome girl wearing a long braid the one that came some time before to learn the long sleeve dance from Senior Miss; the other equally handsome girl, whose hair was bobbed to a length normally appropriate for boys, looked familiar, but was visiting here for the first time. She quickly stood back to let them in.

A cloud appeared on the brow of Qin Yulou. "Shi Mei, did you just say Xie Yingge went out? So that means she's not too ill to go out then."

Qin Yulou being an intimate of the family, Sister Ten said with a sardonic tilt of her mouth: "There's nothing wrong with her physically. Da Guniang says she suffers from emotional trauma."

Given the presence of Feng Jianyue, who was not in on the secret, Qin Yulou said with a sharp look at her: "Oh! This is truly unfortunate timing! Here we have two outstanding young actors of our Theater to pay Master Xie a visit and she isn't home." Then she added: "Shi Mei, would you then kindly convey to her our good wishes? And also these gifts?"

With some reluctance Sister Ten said: "Now that Da Guniang has waked up from her nap, Master Qin, are you leaving without looking in on her?"

Yu Qing'e, the girl with the bouquet, took a step forward. "Manager Qin, why don't we pay a call on the elder sister of

Master Xie since we are already here? It was she who gave me that *qingyi* costume on our last visit ..."

Qin Yulou was quick to take the cue. "Right, right, right! The elder sister of Master Xie was in her days a Yueju opera actor in her own right, and an outstanding actor in the *qingyi* and the tragic female role at that!"

Sister Ten led the party into the courtyard, where in the shade and against a backdrop of clusters of tiny, silvery white flowers sat a woman in a wheelchair, clad in a black blouse and gray slacks, her complexion white and her features fine and regular but expressionless, giving the impression of a subject in a portrait painting.

Feng Jianyue, a stranger to the household, was the first to pause; Yu Qing'e on the other hand had an urge to rush forward but checked her impulse due to the presence of others. Qin Yulou, smiling, advanced toward her and bent down to her eye level: "Xiao Xie, you look great." Then dropping her voice she said: "Yu Qing'e, who had your blessing, really shined. You don't need to worry anymore." Then straightening up she drew Feng Jianyue toward her: "Xiao Xie, look! This is my pupil. She played the young Liu Zhiyuan in the new production of the 'White Rabbit'. She looks better than I do, don't you think?"

With her rictus of an expression, Senior Miss said: "She does have what you possessed when you were young. M'm, Yulou, you have an eye for talent too."

It was only then that Yu Qing'e stepped forward abashedly and called out in a low, quiet voice: "Master Xie!" and thrust the bouquet into Master Xie's lap.

Sister Ten hurried toward them: "Oh yo! Master Qin, I'm sorry there are no chairs in the garden. Come inside; tea is ready."

Yu Qing'e insisted on pushing the wheelchair. The party filed into the living room and took their seats. Sister Ten had, during the time of the exchange of civilities between the host and visitors, brewed a pot of top-grade Kaihua Longjing tea and set out four platters of pastries and sweets on the table. In fact much of the inventory of teas, wines and sweets consisted of visitors' gifts to Xie Yingge. Junior Miss, for whom too much of the goodies killed the appetite and novelty, stuffed them in the closet and forgot about them. Sister Ten saw nothing wrong in treating visitors to the neglected delicacies.

Depositing a handful of sweets in front of each of the girls, Qin Yulou said with a smile: "Since Master Xie is not home, you can treat her elder sister as Master Xie too. Don't stand on ceremony." Then to Senior Miss: "Xiao Xie, you must have read about the praise heaped on these two girls in the papers. We recently put on a 'report card' performance of the new 'White Rabbit' for the Yueju opera lovers of the provincial capital, with a cast made up exclusively of young actors. It proved very popular with the Yueju-opera-loving public."

Sister Ten interjected: "Oh yo! Master Qin, you are generous! Ceding the stage already at your young age? Septuagenarian and octogenarian actors gamboling on the stage of Beijing opera and Kunqu opera are a common sight!"

Qin Yulou said: "Yueju opera is different from Beijing opera and Kunqu opera whose actors have recourse to all kinds of head ornaments—'top ornaments', 'face ornaments', 'three kinds of back-of-head ornaments', you name it, enough to give any and every actor in the female role a pretty oval face. And once they don their loose gowns and long capes, any imperfections of their figure would be covered up. Whilst in Yueju opera, we go for 'simplified headdresses', with no elaborate ornaments to pretty up our faces; and our dress style features form-fitting long skirts and short jackets that show up the actor's figure. I've always known my strengths and limitations. I am after all no longer young. Even with all the makeup in the world I will never be able to compete with the beauty of youth. The comparison has been sobering! Well, as folks say, the Yangtze flows on, each new wave chasing the old. The old wave, I am sure, acts beneficially on the new in some small way."

Feng Jianyue hastened to say: "Master Qin, when Master Xie

recovers from her indisposition, she and you are going back to playing Li Sanniang and Liu Zhiyuan in the second half. We will only feel our feet on solid ground with our two masters bringing the play to a fine finish. Don't you agree, Qing'e?"

Yu Qing'e nodded, although privately her heart's desire was to play Li Sanniang from beginning to end. That was the only way she could feel fulfilled.

Suddenly remembering something, Qin Yulou said: "Xiao Xie, tonight's *Operatic Kaleidoscope* will air a taping of the entirety of our new production of the 'White Rabbit', starring these two girls. If your health permits, you might want to watch it and maybe diagnose their problems. There is always room for improvement."

Almost of one voice Yu Qing'e and Feng Jianyue said: "Master Xie, you must give us your valuable opinions!"

Senior Miss said with deliberation: "Shi Mei, we will have an earlier supper this evening so that we can watch the 'White Rabbit'." Though her face remained expressionless, her voice was tinged with excitement.

Sister Ten promptly responded: "Yes, Miss. Oh yo! I am no less eager to watch it! It was thirty years ago that I last saw the 'White Rabbit' performed by the two of you. I have missed it so much for so long!"

Feng Jianyue was bewildered. "Master Qin, did you also perform the 'White Rabbit' with *this* Master Xie?"

Qin Yulou managed to say with composure: "It's true. I did play opposite both the elder and the younger Master Xie."

Realizing her slip of the tongue, Sister Ten lapsed into guilty silence and busied herself pouring another round of tea from the purple clay loop-handled teapot and urging the pastries and sweets on the visitors.

After some chitchat Qin Yulou drew near Senior Miss. "Xiao Xie, I have another piece of good news to share with you. The Department of Culture of the provincial government has initiated a project of rush restoration of cultural treasures consisting of adding video to audio recordings of opera classics sung by the older generation of artists. It has galvanized people working in all genres of opera. The list of artists to be thus restored decided by our Theater includes Master Cai Lianfen!" then she paused, waiting for a reaction from Senior Miss. But no discernible reaction came, except for the still mobile left hand clenching a bit tighter on the armrest of the wheelchair.

Feng Jianyue whispered to Yu Qing'e: "How's Cai Lianfen related to Master Xie?"

Yu Qing'e whispered back: "Cai Lianfen is the mother of Master Xie!"

With a long-drawn "Oh" Feng Jianyue fell silent.

Wiping off tears from her eyes with the hem of her apron, Sister Ten sighed: "Hao Ma must be so happy up there that she is singing an aria now! Who will be playing in the video to be dubbed with Hao Ma's original recordings, Master Qin?"

Qin Yulou replied with a sigh: "Who else? It's Xie Yingge naturally. There is nothing more fitting than for the daughter to play in the video for her mother's recordings. The project will begin shortly. What worries me … is whether she's up to it health-wise. Xiao Xie, your younger sister always listens to you. She wouldn't have come this far without your help! Can I count on you to bring her on board?"

Sister Ten laughed. "Master Qin, your worry is misplaced. Er Guniang would give anything to beat others to it!"

Qin Yulou said: "If it really turns out as you say, I'd light a big votive candle to the Buddha with a loud Amitabha!" Given the fact that Qin Yulou had been put in charge of the "video dubbed with recordings" project at the Provincial Yueju Opera Theater and the track record of *that* Xie Yingge who got into the habit of dropping out of performances at the slightest criticism of the press (a situation that never failed to plunge the Theater in a crisis, saved only by Yu Qing'e, who was always ready as the more than competent understudy), Qin Yulou was worried that the project might not move along smoothly if Xie Yingge continued to give herself airs and play hard to get.

That afternoon after Qin Yulou and two girls left, Sister Ten tried to prevail upon Senior Miss, who she thought might have been exhausted by the visit, to get some rest in bed, but Senior Miss refused. Instead she sat in front of the French door with her face toward the sweet osmanthus in the yard and began singing arias of the "White Rabbit", until she had exhausted all the Li Sanniang arias from beginning to end and even recited without a single slipup all the spoken lines. By then the sun had sunk to the height of the garden wall and the trees had fallen into shade. As the light in the house dimmed in the twilight, Senior Miss's silhouette resembled a papercut glued onto the French door, a papercut that sang, as in a leather puppet show.

Sister Ten came in with a bowl and chopsticks; switching on the light, she said smiling: "Da Guniang, you must be tired from singing the entire play. Supper is ready. You did say you wanted an earlier supper. I'll bring in the water for you to wash your face and freshen up. The 'White Rabbit' is starting soon!"

Senior Miss wheeled her chair around, like Li Sanniang emerging from the dark, cramped mill shed. She listened, putting her head on one side. Detecting no movement or sound above the ceiling, she asked: "Has Er Mei come home?"

Sister Ten said: "Didn't Er Guniang say before leaving she was not coming home for supper? The master is not home yet. Do you want to wait for him?" Sister Ten knew Senior Miss's inquiring about her younger sister was actually an oblique way of finding out if Wang Houcheng was home.

Without a word Senior Miss wheeled herself to the door, where she paused briefly before turning back to the middle of the room. Sister Ten's heart went out to her, thinking to herself: "You care so much about him, but he never has a thought for you. He doesn't even make a phone call to say he's not coming home for supper. You can't count on men to remain faithful for long. There was one thing to be said for Liu Zhiyuan: at least he did not disown his lawful wife." She knew she had to keep her resentment to herself. Bringing in a basin filled with water, she wetted a towel in it and wiped off the face of Senior Miss. Then she turned on the TV and started feeding Senior Miss her pearl barley-lily-goqi berry porridge. In the meantime they watched distractedly a string of commercials of Liushen Medicated Lotion for rashes and insect bites, Rainbow TV sets or Little Swan clothes washers as they waited for the "White Rabbit".

Senior Miss's mandibular power was no longer what it used to be and she swallowed her food slowly, so that by the time she finished her bowl of porridge the pre-curtain chorus had begun:

> A bloom has survived many a storm,
> Oh cruel have been the vagaries of fate.
> Liu Zhiyuan may be known in history,
> Li Sanniang lives on in popular song.

Sister Ten got a plate, heaped on it some rice and a few helpings of the dishes of the day and seated herself in front of the TV with it to watch while eating.

Senior Miss watched, her face showing neither grin nor grimace , neither satisfaction nor sadness, as if she were beyond feeling in the manner of Buddhist monks chanting sutra verses before gods of clay and wood. The fact was that Senior Miss's soul had fled from her body into the play, leaving behind an empty shell.

In contrast Sister Ten was a noisy opera-goer given to non-stop commentary and analysis and humming familiar aria passages that sounded off-key. Fortunately they were not in an actual theater and Senior Miss, long used to this behavior, saw no need no spoil her fun.

As Liu Zhiyuan and Li Sanniang entered in the scene "Marriage of Liu Zhiyuan into the Li Family by the Melon Patch", instead of clapping her hands, which were encumbered by the plate of food, Sister Ten stamped her feet on the floor. "They look great! Da Guniang! And this Li Sanniang does bear some resemblance to you in your youth!"

When the scene "Liu Zhiyuan Taken in as Son-in-Law by His General" opened, Sister Ten jabbed a finger at the screen touching it: "This Yue Xiuying sings well but I can't compliment that face. Why did she apply so much black paint around the eyes? It looks as if she had been hit in the eyes by two fists. They look like bruises."

When the curtains parted for the scene "Giving Birth by the Millstone", Sister Ten quickly set down her empty plate and drew her stool closer to the TV, and said, patting her chest: "Oh yo! I'm so nervous! Can this girl really manage the long sleeves dance?" When Li Sanniang, in the throes of her labor pains and soaked in sweat, started doing "sparrow hawk pirouettes", the two long sleeves dancing like gyrating dragons in the air, Sister Ten burst into cheers and enthusiastic applause, then, suddenly remembering: "Da Guniang, she wouldn't have been able to perform this dance so brilliantly if you had not given her a few pointers and given her your *qingyi* costume to wear last time!"

It was then that Wang Houcheng opened the door and entered the house; he heaved the bulging professional photo bag off his shoulder and dropped it on the floor and sank into the sofa. Senior Miss, absorbed in the play, had her eyes glued to the TV screen, without even a sidelong glance at him. Only Sister Ten asked: "You're home, Master? Have you eaten?" Wang Houcheng replied with a terse "M'm", whereupon Sister Ten said: "Then please make yourself comfortable. We are watching the new production of the 'White Rabbit'. Oh yo! We haven't seen the play in a long time. Now we just can't pull ourselves away from it." With that she left him to his own devices and went back to watching the play.

Finally it was the scene of "Sanniang Rebukes Her Husband". Following a prelude played on the main Chinese fiddle at a slow tempo, Li Sanniang, prostrate on the ground, emitted from her mouth what sounded like a low sigh, a medley of plain speech, stage speech and opera singing: "In those sixteen years, the thousand-jin millstone be my witness, I have milled away many a morning and evening; In those sixteen years, the three-foot wide apron of the well be my witness, I've treaded upon it may a winter and spring …" Now craning her neck like a duck and holding her breath, Sister Ten stared fixedly at Li Sanniang, thinking: the last verse containing "sixteen years" was to be sung an octave above what went before. Would this girl make it? "In those sixteen years, the tear-stained sweet osmanthus be my witness, I have shed many a bloodshot tear …" Li Sanniang suddenly straightened her back, flung out her long sleeves and raising the pitch an octave higher let fly in spray-mouth fashion: "In those sixteen years, the bitter fish pond be my witness, I've confronted many a crisis of life and death …" Sister Ten shouted a "bravo", also an octave higher than normal. Then suddenly realizing she might have frightened Senior Miss, she glanced down—Senior Miss's face, forever fixed into a rictus, was now awash with tears, which continued to well out of her unblinking eyes.

Sister Ten knew Senior Miss's feeling was one of joy mixed with sad regret. Placing a hand on Senior Miss's thin shoulder, Sister Ten tried to steer her thoughts toward the joyful side of things: "Da Guniang, in appearance, singing and acting, this girl's style closely follows that of yours. She, more than Er Guniang, performs like you. You've found in her someone to take over the mantle of Xie Yingge. You can finally put your worries to rest." Dabbing the cheeks of Senior Miss with a paper napkin, she removed the tear stains from her face.

Inheriting the happy ending of the traditional versions, the new production of the "White Rabbit" showed Li Sanniang, at the earnest entreaty of her son Yaoqilang, finally forgave Liu Zhiyuan for neglecting his lawful wife and marrying another woman. The play ended with the grand reunion of husband and wife, of the entire family. As the curtains swished together, the closing credits scrolled up the TV screen. Sister Ten let out a long breath: "Thank goodness this Liu Zhiyuan still has some conscience left. That Yue Xiuying is also sensible. After all Li Sanniang is the lawful wife. Li Sanniang finds happiness again after so much suffering …"

A sudden irritation in her throat interrupted her and caused a fit of coughing. It was then that she became conscious of smoke filling the house. It turned out when they were watching the show, Wang Houcheng, huddled in a corner of the sofa, had been chain-smoking, with disastrous consequences.

Sister Ten sprang up, chiding: "Master, are you mad? Don't you know that Da Guniang has weak lungs and should not be exposed to cigarette smoke?" Rushing to the French door, she threw open the two sashes and grabbing a newspaper from the tea table began fanning the air to drive out the smoke.

Wang Houcheng, realizing he'd committed a blunder, hastened to grind out the cigarette and said falteringly: "S—sorry, Xiao Xie. I h—had some drinks ... w—with a friend ..."

Senior Miss asked, without looking at him: "Where's Er Mei?"

After a moment of silence Wang Houcheng said: "I—I don't know ... hasn't she come home yet?"

Senior Miss relapsed into silence. Still chasing the smoke, Sister Ten muttered: "You mean you don't know where she is? Funny you should ask us homebodies about her whereabouts!"

Ignoring her, Wang Houcheng picked up his photo bag and addressed himself to Senior Miss: "Xiao Xie, I'm tired from an evening of socializing. I feel light-headed. I'm going upstairs. You should also turn in early ..." With that the massive, slightly stooped frame of his swung out of the room.

Sister Ten gave a sarcastic grunt but checked herself, sparing Senior Miss the harsh words that were on the tip of her tongue. Nursing her resentment, she went back to sweeping the floor, mopping off the ashes and venting the residual smell of the smoke. It took a while before she was able to close the windows, help Senior Miss brush her teeth and give her a hot foot bath, and change her for bed. Then she laid herself down on her cot and sniffled the air before muttering to herself: "M'm, there's still a whiff of that smoky odor, but it's harmless ..." and presently she began to snore.

But sleep eluded Senior Miss, beneath whose serene exterior

contrary emotions clashed. When she saw Yu Qing'e interpret to perfection her Li Sanniang, she felt as if she were transported back to the stage of thirty years ago, as if she and Yu Qing'e had inhabited each other, as if it were she, Xie Yingge, playing Li Sanniang! Her mind flashed back to the thunderous applause of her audience, the flurry of press articles with glowing reviews of her performance and her fans' enthusiasm bordering on frenzy ... how many years now? It must be centuries since she last felt such joy! Wang Houcheng walking through the door woke her from her happy dream and yanked her back to grim reality—she could see that dejected, distraught look in Wang Houcheng's face and instinctively thought he must have had an argument with her younger sister. The thought occasioned both pity and contempt for him. How she regretted her flawed judgment in picking her man! He was supposed to have acquired wisdom with maturity. He was once a man with a clear head and vast ambitions. How had he metamorphosed into the vulgar, mediocre, weak-willed, timid, petty person he was now? Senior Miss stared at the darkened ceiling with her perpetually dry eyes as if Wang Houcheng's heart were somewhere up there and she wanted to penetrate to the depth of that heart to flush out and exorcise all the ghosts and demons lurking there!

She couldn't tell how much time had elapsed or if she had dozed off, or if it was only a brief moment and she had been awake all this time. In the dark stillness, a door opened with a soft creak, then closed with another creak, followed by the rustling of clothes against the wall and the tapping of high heels on the staircase ... all the way up.

"It's Er Mei. She's finally home." Senior Miss drew a breath and thought with bitter sadness: "That man must feel relieved now." Then her eyelids drooped and closed.

With an earth-shaking bang, a door was opened with a crash. Senior Miss reopened her eyelids.

"Are you crazy? What's this, so late in the night?" A woman's voice erupted, sharp as a knife.

"You, you are thick-skinned enough to come home! This late in the night, what have you been doing?" A man's voice boomed, muffled as thunderclaps behind dark clouds.

Slapping on the wooden slats on her bed with her left hand, Senior Miss cried out with all her force: "Shi Mei, Shi Mei!"

Sister Ten was finally roused out of her deep sleep and said in alarm: "Da Guniang, did you wet your bed?"

Supporting herself on her left hand, Senior Miss tried to sit up. She said breathlessly: "They are fighting, didn't you hear? Quick, my wheelchair, I need the wheelchair!"

Only then did Sister Ten notice the ongoing noisy drama playing out above the ceiling, a duel between a female and a male voice. She hastened to turn on the light and put a coat over Senior Miss. Then wheeling up the chair, she heaved Senior Miss into it. Without waiting for her to push the chair, Senior Miss started wheeling herself to the door of her room, urging Sister Ten all the while: "Open the door, the door!"

Sister Ten said: "It's drafty in the corridor outside. You can't go there, Da Guniang!"

A ruckus broke out above their heads, nothing less than the donnybrook created by the Monkey King in the celestial palace. In her haste and agitation Senior Miss rammed the door with her wheelchair: "Quick, open the door now!" No match for her strong will, Sister Ten reluctantly pulled the door open, whereupon Senior Miss wheeled herself all the way to the foot of the staircase, where she halted. Sister Ten quickly draped her in a woolen shawl.

The argument upstairs became more distinct:

. . .

"You think I don't know? You have kept in touch with him all these years. And why did you stay so long in the hotel he is staying at? Is it a case of Pan Jinlian seducing Ximen Qing, or Yan Poxi seducing Zhang Wenyuan?"

"You despicable jerk! You've been tailing me! Yes, I enjoy being with him and it's none of your business! What are you?

You are more shameless than Ximen Qing or Zhang Wenyuan, sleeping with the sister-in-law right under the nose of your wife …"

"Pop!" There was a crisp, sharp sound. Sister Ten got excited. "Somebody got slapped! Question is who slapped whom."

Senior Miss struggled to get up out of her wheelchair. Sister Ten pressed down on her shoulder and said in a quiet voice: "Let them fight! It'll open his eyes. That Xie Yingge is no this Xie Yingge!"

Senior Miss was on the point of chiding Sister Ten when the door upstairs was opened with a "pong" and promptly they heard footsteps coming down the staircase. Sister Ten started toward the living room pushing the wheelchair but it was too late for them to get out of the way. They saw a sallow-faced, disheveled Junior Miss coming down the stairs at a fast speed, with a suitcase in one hand and a windbreaker in the other, and at her heels a Wang Houcheng in pyjamas and leather slippers. Senior Miss called out in a husky voice: "Er Mei, where are you going at this late hour?"

Junior Miss snapped: "I'm going to the country to convalesce!" then stormed out of the door without once looking back.

Wang Houcheng started after her but Senior Miss maneuvered her wheelchair into his path, cutting Wang Houcheng off. Senior Miss said sharply: "Don't you think you've degraded yourself enough? Do you want to alert the entire block to the scandal?"

Dropping down on his heels, Wang Houcheng sank his face into his hands and moaned: "Er Mei—she, she has left me!"

Sister Ten interrupted him. "She's just trying to scare you! She'd never go down to the countryside. She can't tear herself away from the amenities of the provincial capital."

The vigorously shaking head of Wang Houcheng reminded one of a rattle drum being twirled. "You don't know. This time she's made up her mind. She's leaving for real."

Senior Miss considered for a moment before saying: "What really happened between you? Let's go inside to talk." She turned back, maneuvering the chair, and Sister Ten stepped quickly forward to push her inside. Wang Houcheng, taking leaden steps and shuffling his feet, followed in and sank into the sofa with a sigh.

Sister Ten poured a glass of water and set it down on the tea table in front of Wang Houcheng: "Master, drink some of this to clear up your head!"

Once back in the house, Senior Sister had kept silent and still, a fixed rictus in her face, eyelids drooping, looking like a millennial fossil.

In the glare of the sickly white light of the florescent lamp in the middle of the ceiling every detail of the room stood in relief, including the accumulated dust in inconspicuous corners. Taking a furtive glance at Senior Miss, Sister Ten gave a start: Senior Miss's eyes were not closed but opened a crack. Through the squinted eyes, her piercing gaze fell directly on the old newspaper under the glass cover of the "Eight Immortals" table! Sister Ten thought to herself: "Oops! Looks like Senior Miss is going to settle scores with Wang Houcheng!" then she thought in a vengeful vein: "It's time the scores are settled! Since Da Guniang found out he'd been sneaking into Er Guniang's room after midnight, she had never demanded an account from him nor had she said anything uncivil about it. Her tolerance only emboldened them into brazen openness!"

Sister Ten had waited on Senior Miss all these years, never leaving her side and had watched her grow up from a little girl into adulthood and decline in old age. This intimacy had enabled Sister Ten to correctly guess her thoughts eight or nine times out of ten. At this moment the eyes of Senior Miss fell on the old newspaper under the glass top of the "Eight Immortals" table, or more accurately, her eyes were locked on the stage photo in the upper right corner of the page—in the photo she was vibrant with youth and resplendent with beauty and that orchid-shaped dimple added immeasurably to her charm. After Wang Houcheng snapped that picture, he developed it the same night and printed an enlargement of twelve inches. And he used the subterfuge of personally delivering that photo to come to her home and propose marriage to her. He was then an urbane gentleman, with love in his eyes and a bashful air. Presenting the photo to her, he said: "Xiao Xie, it is my wish to be your lifelong photographer. Do you care to be the one in my picture forever?" Senior Miss snapped shut her eyelids, keeping her lifelong pain locked away inside her, letting loose the pain to course through her veins to all parts of her body. Such pain she had savored for more than a dozen years and such savoring had become part of her routine.

Wang Houcheng, who was sure that this time he was in for some serious dressing-down from Xiao Xie, braced himself for the impending storm. When nothing happened, he stole a glance at her and wondered if she had fallen asleep. With a discreet cough and a clearing of his throat, Wang Houcheng asked gingerly: "Xiao Xie, you must be tired. Why don't we talk about it tomorrow morning?"

Senior Miss snapped her eyelids open. "I'm still waiting for an explanation from you!"

Wang Houcheng, his mind seemingly made up, heaved a sigh. "Xiao Xie, you remember that Lu Mingjiu?"

Senior Miss slowly turned her face about: "Lu—Ming—Jiu? You mean that owner of the singing-only traditional opera troupe?"

With a slap on his thigh, Wang Houcheng said: "That's him! Can you imagine? A dirty old man like him … and Er Mei and he would …"

Senior Miss shot an icy retort at him: "So you consider yourself still young?"

After a moment of silence, Wang Houcheng thrust his hands into his thinning hair and sank his head between his knees, then groaned: "Xiao Xie, I've been a jerk, a despicable jerk. I've let you down …" then jerking his head up: "But are you totally blameless in this? You decided to pass her off as you and sent her to my side. You wanted me to present myself to the world as her husband and cautioned me against any slipup that could arouse suspicion.

Think in my shoes! Is it realistic to expect me to resist for long the temptations? I—I am a man, for goodness sake!"

Senior Miss wheeled her chair to the French door; it was pitch dark outside and her rigid form, stiffened by pain, blended into the darkness of night. Sister Ten said sharply: "Master, why are you saying this? Haven't you made her suffer enough?"

There was another moment of silence before Wang Houcheng found his voice again: "Lu Mingjiu has prospered. He now runs some kind of media company. He came often to the provincial capital to promote primitive folk songs and field songs and every time he came, Er Mei …"

Sister Ten sharply cut him off: "They used to be lovers. What right do you have to be jealous?"

Wang Houcheng passed a hand across his face. "Indeed I have no right to interfere with her freedom, but—but this Lu Mingjiu is trying to recruit Er Mei to his company …"

With a push on the wheel, Senior Miss whirled around to face Wang Houcheng; another turn of the wheel brought her within inches of him.

It was only then that Wang Houcheng mustered the courage to lift up his eyes to her and his voice was less timid. "Lu Mingjiu has built in his home town a stage for the performance of field songs, which is actually a night club. He has promised Er Mei the title of general stage manager, thinking her celebrity would lend respectability to his classless theater!" A brief pause, then he went on: "Xiao Xie! What he is after is not Er Mei but the Xie Yingge name. He is shrewd enough to recognize the value of that famous brand!"

Sister Ten stamped her foot. "Er Mei is out of her head!"

Senior Miss again wheeled herself to the French door and gazed out at the darkness, which had turned from ink black to the lighter shade of ink wash. Presently she said slowly: "It will be day soon. Go get some sleep. Shi Mei, you go with the Master tomorrow morning to the hotel where Lu Mingjiu is staying and get Er Mei to come home. Tell her that I will raise no objection if she decides to leave but at least she owes me an account!"

Sister Ten replied with a terse "M'm" and gazed through the window. Indeed the contours of the garden wall and the sweet osmanthus had begun to detach themselves from the pitch darkness.

After Wang Houcheng retired upstairs, Sister Ten started to change Senior Miss for bed when the latter began singing:

> ...
> I still recall our wedding night, the star following
>   the moon,
> And the jade rabbit-inhabited moon shining its love
>   on the star.
> I still recall us pouring our hearts to each other
>   under the sweet osmanthus,
> Sharing a wish for the early arrival of our child.
> I still recall the sudden turn of events that sent you
>   afar,
> How I've pined for you, teary eyes gazing at the
>   horizon, and dreamt of you.
> I've yearned for your return day and night,
> And waited for you year after year,
> Until the millstone handles broke and the mill shed
>   collapsed,
> Until black hair turned white,
> And dripping teardrops wore through my heart ...

Finally Sister Ten could stand it no more and interrupted her, with tears in her eyes and her nose sniveling: "Da Guniang, I beg you not to sing anymore! It's breaking my heart! Let's get some sleep. We have two more hours for a sweet dream!"

After putting Senior Miss to bed, Sister Ten, too tired to change, lay down in her clothes. Naturally unable to fall asleep, they had their fifty winks and rose when day broke.

As soon as breakfast was over, Senior Miss prodded Sister

Ten and Wang Houcheng to fetch Junior Miss from the hotel at which Lu Mingjiu was staying. But Wang Houcheng hesitated. "Xiao Xie, why don't I give the address to Sister Ten and leave it to her to fetch Younger Sister? She is still sore at me so my presence may make matters worse. Moreover I have a rush order from the Theater to print out the stage photos of the young actors …"

Sister Ten snatched the slip of paper with the address on it from his hand: "Fine! I'd much prefer to go alone, without any unnecessary interference. The Master can go ahead and do whatever he needs to do. Da Guniang, you just leave it to me. I'll drag her home if I have to."

And Sister Ten delivered on her promise. An hour later Junior Miss on her high heels entered the yard of the Xie household accompanied by Sister Ten, although without the suitcase she had previously taken with her.

Once in the living room Junior Miss burst out a "Jieh!" and started sobbing into her hands.

Senior Miss heaved a long sigh. "Why are you crying? I haven't even uttered a word of reproach!"

Junior Miss said through her sobs: "Jieh! I've been disloyal to you. We are despicable! We have been ungrateful … I had long wanted to end this ambiguous relationship, but Jieh Fu …" and she resumed crying aloud, with a vengeance.

Senior Miss wheeled herself to the French door, leaving her to cry to her heart's content. Slamming her cleaning rag down on the "Eight Immortals" table, Sister Ten said: "Er Guniang, are these tears of remorse or tears faked for a funeral? If you really feel you've done Da Guniang wrong, then you should continue to do your best as Xie Yingge and continue playing Li Sanniang. Stop wavering and feigning illness or thinking about becoming a general manager in some rural town. Wouldn't you be betraying the trust of Senior Miss if you did that?"

With the wheels scraping against the floor, Senior Miss struggled back to Junior Miss and said bitterly: "Er Mei, betraying my trust is the least of my worries. Beware the tricks up the sleeve of that Lu Mingjiu! You mustn't be duped by him!"

A gleam sprang into Junior Miss's eyes as she wiped off her tears with a facial tissue. "Jieh! That won't happen. I've known Lu Mingjiu for so many years. I know he is not a swindler. He wouldn't dare swindle me at any rate." Drawing nearer Senior Miss and squatting down by her wheelchair, she stroked her knees and said confidingly: "This is a once-in-a-lifetime opportunity for me! Lu Mingjiu has built a palatial theater to showcase field songs in my home town. The chief executives of the county and the town governments attended the ribbon-cutting ceremony. So how could it have been a swindle? His offer to make me general manager was known to the county and town chiefs, who welcomed it. Can you still believe it was a hoax? Jieh! Think about this. Xie Yingge rates as the foremost actor in the female role on the Yueju opera stage in the provincial capital, right? I am in addition a grade one actor in the national ranking. But how much do I make a month? How much do I get paid for each performance? Yet Lu Mingjiu has promised me half of his company's shares! That theater boasts not only a stage but also a KTV, a ballroom, a mahjong parlor, a pool hall, a cafe, a restaurant and a bar ... Imagine the nightly takes! The share of Xie Yingge in that profit will be enormous! Jieh! Didn't Deng Xiaoping say we should not be against a small number of people getting rich before the rest of us in the initial stages? Well, we will soon be among those that get rich ahead of the rest of the crowd!"

Senior Miss, a rictus on her face, gazed into the eyes of Junior Miss, whose eye shadows were smudged by tears, and said with distinctness: "I do not agree. Xie Yingge was, is and will always be a Yueju opera actor. I have no intention to ruin the image of Xie Yingge in the hearts and minds of her fans!"

Arching sharply her eyebrows Junior Miss said with a sneering "tch!": "Jieh! You are too naïve! Take a good look around you! Can you find one single person who does not get bored with dated stuff and seek the thrill of novelty? Xie Yingge is history on the Yueju opera stage—'fallen flowers borne away by the river when spring fades away'! Nowadays the Yueju opera fans are flocking to their new idol Yu Qing'e, the same Yu Qing'e who had been personally groomed by you, Xie Yingge, and who has now callously muscled Xie Yingge off the stage. Jieh! I had no choice. I was compelled by the new circumstanced to seek an alternative career on a broader stage."

Senior Miss shook her head. "The fans did not abandon Xie Yingge because they sought the thrill of novelty. It was you who have been so spoiled by the adulation of the fans that you have rejected all criticisms and bristled at the praise given Yu Qing'e and the others."

With another "tch!", Junior Miss said: "Jieh! You are wrong. I don't give a hoot about those boring articles written by those boring critics, who fall all over themselves to hail, herald and carry on their shoulders any young actress with some looks ..."

Ignoring those plaints, Senior Miss maintained her deliberate speech. "Er Mei! You have now recovered as far as I can see. There is now a rare opportunity for our Xie Yingge. I was told by Qin Yulou that the provincial government has started a project to rescue and salvage the works of old icons of local operas and you have been designated as the actor to play in the video to go with the audio of Cai Lianfen's arias. Er Mei, for my mother's sake and for the sake of our Xie Yingge, as well as for your own sake, you must give your all to this work! Go now and tell Lu Mingjiu you are declining his offer and rededicate yourself to performing as Xie Yingge!"

Junior Miss rose to her feet and fell back two steps. "No, Jieh, no way! I've crossed the Rubicon. I just handed in my retirement request to Qin Dajieh. Besides, Lu Mingjiu has used the name of Xie Yingge to register the theater for field songs." With a wrinkling of her nose she mumbled: "Besides, this so-called video-matching-audio rescue or preservation project is nothing but a solace prize, a sop. I have no stomach for joining the ranks of the nostalgics for the old glory days."

Senior Miss fell silent, and with her silence all life went out of the house, much as a boat that had sunk to the bottom of the sea.

Junior Miss could stand the hush for but a moment; she said, drawing a sharp breath: "Jieh! Let go of me. I will forever remember how indebted I am to you. When I roll in money, you will share in my prosperity and fortune."

At length Senior Miss spoke: "Er Mei, go tell Lu Mingjiu to change one character in the name he used to register the theater."

Junior Miss started: "What character?"

Senior Miss said with serenity: "Change Xie Yingge to Xie Jin'ge. I am reclaiming my name."

Junior Miss choked for a moment before recovering, then she burst into a peal of hysterical laughter and said, with a finger jabbing at Senior Miss and all the while shaking her head and laughing: "Jieh! I was right to say you are too naïve. Do you really think you can get your name back? Go and ask anyone in a theater. Who'd believe you when you told them you were Xie Yingge? Try it in the street and see if anyone would believe that. It's too late. The name of Xie Yingge now belongs to me. I've become the real Xie Yingge." Pausing for thought, she continued: "I can let you have your husband back, but you can't fault me for not being able to let you have your name back. Jieh, my advice to you is quit dreaming big dreams. You have found your arcadia away from worldly worries, so why bother your head about gain and loss?" then turning to Sister Ten: "Shi Mei, take good care of Jieh for me. When I get rich, I will not forget rewarding you. I got to go now. I have to go this afternoon to my home town to complete the registration of the theater." Then she crossed to the side of Senior Miss, her heels tattooing on the floor, bent at her waist to plant a kiss on the grizzled, thinned out hair and said in a tender tone: "Jieh, I will come back to visit you when I have the time. Just wait to hear the good news from us!"

With her heels tapping out a light and firm tattoo on the floor, Junior Miss walked out of this house as if she had walked out of a dream.

It was only after the gate in the garden wall was closed with a bang that Sister Ten let out a breath of suppressed indignation. "As they say, you can find red-blooded sincerity in stage make-believe, and make-believe among flesh and blood. Da Guniang, you have a truly ruthless sister. She can turn into your enemy from one moment to the next! You've been too kind to her, too trusting of flesh and blood. Don't feel too bad about it. Just treat it as a case of being robbed by a burglar. As folks say you may get the short end of the stick but you also get a longer life. Well, the important thing is you are here. Let's go out to the yard to get some air!"

No response came from Senior Miss. Thinking she was still too absorbed in her anger to pay her heed, Sister Ten lightly tapped her on her shoulder: "Da Guniang, why don't I call up Master Qin and ask her …" Before she had a chance to finish her sentence, she saw Senior Miss go limp and slip out of her chair to the floor.

"Da Guniang! Da Guniang! What's the matter?" Sister Ten rushed at a frantic pace to her side and found her face having turned gray, her eyes tightly closed and a dark red fluid oozing out of her mouth!

For the second time in sixteen years, Senior Miss was admitted to the provincial hospital's emergency room for cerebral hemorrhage.

Scene XIII   Success and Failure of the *Legend of the White Rabbit*

After her secondment to the Provincial Yueju Opera Theater, Yu Qing'e never swerved from her routine of going at first streak of dawn to the practice room to train her voice, walk her stage walk, stretch her legs, and do backbends and somersaults, even when she had worked late the previous night. No other young actors of the Theater, be they lead actors, support actors or walk-ons, had a similar tenacity in keeping up the basic training. After all, they were young and pretty and were frequent guests on TV entertainment shows, in opening ceremonies at corporate headquarters and galas celebrating traditional festivals, where they were invited to be present and to perform. These activities took so much of their time and energy that they necessarily had little left of either to be devoted to basic training. Qin Yulou, the deputy general manager of the Theater, realizing the problem, had raised the matter at several staff assemblies: "In traditional opera, it is important for the actors to keep their martial and singing skills constantly honed. It takes ten years of ongoing training to assure ten minutes of flawless performance on the stage. We can all look to Yu Qing'e for an example. Many of you were school friends of hers in the School of the Arts, but she has stood out in singing, acting, reciting and stage acrobatics and her portrayal of Li Sanniang has great popular appeal, all because of her persistence in daily practice and training. It is my hope that young actors will follow Yu Qing'e's example instead of gravitating toward outside activities that bring fame and material gain at the expense of basic training."

Deputy General Manager Qin's view received mixed responses, some positive, others less so. Feng Jianyue was the first to answer the call of her master and joined the very next day in Yu Qing'e's early morning training. With Mi Jingyao away for the shooting of a TV serial drama, Yu Qing'e took temporary possession of her bed in the room Mi Jingyao shared with Feng Jianyue. The latter gave Yu Qing'e this instruction: "When you get up in the morning, be sure to wake me up too. If I fail to be revived from sleep, you can go ahead and pinch me without mercy."

Shi Xiaotong was second to none among the younger actors as far as singing and martial skills were concerned but her plain looks meant much fewer opportunities to get invited to outside events and activities and consequently she derived scant extra income from outside sources. So when the fancy struck her, she was normally not averse to going to the practice room to loosen up her vocal cords and stretch her legs. But following the public praise of Yu Qing'e by Deputy General Manager Qin at the staff assembly, she assiduously kept herself away from the practice room. Qian Xiaoxiao urged her on: "Xiaotong, why don't you go to the practice room to show Yu Qing'e how you do consecutive back flips? I'm sure she can't do it as well as you." Shi Xiaotong said dismissively: "She is performing to the gallery of the brass so that she can impress the brass enough to want to keep her in the provincial capital. I wish her all the luck. I'm not going to show her up." In order to increase her odds to be chosen as the substitute for Mi Jingyao in the role of Li Sanniang, Shi Xiaotong had at her own cost and in great secrecy undergone a nose job and double eyelid surgery in a hospital in a small town. With the unexpected injection of the Yu Qing'e factor, her much-awaited opportunity evaporated. She understandably nursed a grudge against Yu Qing'e, who was now anathema to her. It turned out that Shi Xiaotong's portrayal of Yue Xiuying received good notices from the critics but Yue Xiuying's stage time was such a minuscule part of the new production of the "White Rabbit"—all of two arias—that she had no chance to become a "star" occupying center stage.

Never one to take defeat lying down, Shi Xiaotong would normally have been keen to face down her rival. But something had lately so disturbed her that her normally competitive nature was temporarily forced into the background. After the troupe's return from the Hong Kong tour, she had begun to feel pain around her rebuilt, lifted nose, which was unrelieved by pain killers. The swelling around her eyes, a legacy of her double eyelid surgery, instead of going down, had lately grown in size. When Shi Xiaotong called up the small town plastic surgeon who performed the procedures and demanded an explanation, the surgeon replied: "You've been instructed to rest at least for three months after the surgery before you can apply makeup or face paint. You however went on the Hong Kong tour less than a month after surgery. Face paint is toxic, you understand? So you must be having an infection." The doctor prescribed some oral antibiotics and topical ointment, which Shi Xiaotong took and applied as instructed by the doctor. After a course of treatment, those prescriptions failed to effect any improvement. The pain around the nose had by now spread to the entire face and the swelling around the eyes gave the impression that she was crying all the time.

These days Shi Xiaotong would first thing in the morning linger for a long moment before her mirror, looking at herself now close up now at a distance, and getting the impression that something was awry about her face. She was at first unsure what exactly caused the impression, but it came to her at length. She found to her dismay that the lifted nose had imperceptibly flattened into a low mound that became one with the bloated eyelids to form a loess plateau dominating her face. Even Qian Xiaoxiao realized there was a problem. "Xiaotong, your face is all blown up. You must not apply face paint any longer." But the new production of the "White Rabbit" was simply too popular with the viewing public and the performances were scheduled through to the year's end. There was nothing for Shi Xiaotong but to bite the bullet and stay the course, vowing to demand an account from the small town plastic surgeon once the performances came to a close.

For Yu Qing'e, on the other hand, these months of playing Li Sanniang were the best time of her life, her halcyon days. To her the things and the people of her home town were now as distant as the puffs of clouds painted on the backdrop of the stage. Li Sanniang had crowded all other thoughts from her mind. When she was interviewed by journalists during the day the talk revolved around Li Sanniang. In the evening she played Li Sanniang on stage. At night her dreams were inhabited by Li Sanniang. Yu Qing'e wished she were Li Sanniang herself. She'd much rather suffer the miseries of Li Sanniang, who was as good as imprisoned for sixteen years in a mill shed and had to bite through the umbilical cord to give birth to her child, than come back to reality to face an uncertain future. The suffering Li Sanniang was rewarded with a happy ending when she was reunited with her long lost son. Yu Qing'e, on the other hand, had to nip her child in the embryo in order to be able to play Li Sanniang! She knew she could expect no forgiveness from her husband and there was no likelihood of her ever returning to that home and therefore no happy ending was in the cards for her. Although her portrayal of Li Sanniang had proved a great success and the Yueju opera character Li Sanniang had nearly become her proprietary brand, her personnel file remained with the productions company in her home town. If her company desired her return she'd have no choice but to give up her Li Sanniang and the glory she'd worked so hard to achieve in the provincial capital. She recalled the promise of Qin Yulou at the time of her secondment to the cast of the new production of the "White Rabbit" that if the "White Rabbit" proved a big hit, the Provincial Yueju Opera Theater could induct her into its midst on account of her talent and arrange to have her household registration and her personnel file transferred to it. Now that the "White Rabbit" had gone from a red-hot smash hit into an incandescent one, Qin Yulou had remained silent on the matter of inducting her as a new talent as if she had forgotten all about it. Yu Qing'e had on several occasions wanted to bring up the matter with Qin Yulou but had hesitated for fear that Qin Yulou would fault her for being overly concerned about her self-interest and also that she might hear bad news from Qin Yulou that would definitely shatter her expectations.

One morning Yu Qing'e was running stage circles in the practice room. To make her practice more strenuous, she was doing a "mountain arms", a conventional Chinese opera posture, with her arms fully extended to the sides, with the left hand closed into a fist and the right hand opened into a palm, and a newspaper squeezed between her knees, and was moving in minced steps like a breeze rippling across a lake. After a few circles around the room she was already sweating profusely on her forehead and feeling sore in her calves, but Yu Qing'e soldiered on, because her daily schedule called for at least ten such circles. Suddenly the door was flung open by a panting Qin Yulou. "Xiao Yu! Quick, quick, quick…"

Yu Qing'e immediately stood down from her routine, her heart pounding wildly, wondering if there was movement in the matter of transferring her personnel file to the Theater.

Qin Yulou was finally able to speak, after recovering her breath. "Xiao Yu, come with me to the hospital now. Master Xie had a relapse and the medics are trying to resuscitate her!"

Yu Qing'e's heart gave a lurch. Misfortunes never seem to come singly! Time was too pressing for any questions or a change of clothes and she rushed with Qin Yulou to the hospital still wearing her practice suit.

In the corridor outside the ICU of the hospital they found a teary Sister Ten who kept dabbing at her eyes and a dejected Wang Houcheng, and immediately started pounding them with questions. Blinking her swollen eyes Sister Ten said with a catch in her voice: "With Buddha's blessing, her life is no longer in danger. But unfortunately she had lost her ability to speak. Da Guniang, who loves so much to sing Yueju opera, can no longer sing now ..."

Patting Sister Ten on the shoulder, Wang Houcheng said: "This is not the time for lamentations. We should present the details of Xiao Xie's treatment to Manager Qin to find out how the authorities could help."

This had the effect of inflaming Sister Ten. Even Yu Qing'e's presence did not temper her outburst: "All the benefits Da Guniang is entitled to have been usurped by Er Guniang. According to Xie Yingge's ranking, she should be moved to the high officials' ward after coming out of the ICU and given imported medicines which are more expensive and better. But the hospital is nowadays so profit-oriented. It says there are not enough beds and therefore as soon as Da Guniang is out of ICU she is to go home to convalesce. The hospital is wittingly putting her life at risk!"

Wang Houcheng added: "Manager Qin, please understand Shi Mei's angry outburst. I share her indignation. Da Guniang is so ill and her life is hanging by a thread. How can she be discharged now? Manager Qin, could you ..."

Qin Yulou was thoughtful for a moment before she said: "All right, I'll go talk to someone I know who works in the medical department of the hospital. You wait here for me." Then she turned and headed toward the bank of elevators.

Quietly Yu Qing'e walked up to the tightly closed frosted glass door of the ICU and leaned her forehead against the door frame, suddenly overcome by sadness. She had long understood that the patient lying in that room was the real Xie Yingge, her mentor and moral support. Her beloved teacher was fighting for her life in there, and yet she was powerless to help her. She let out a wail in her heart: "Master Xie——" as tears leapt to her eyes.

It was not long before Qin Yulou, somewhat cheered up, returned. "It's been settled, settled. The medical department has agreed to scrounge a bed for Xiao Xie. As for imported medicines, they unfortunately will have to be paid for privately. The Yueju Opera Theater cannot absorb the cost ..."

Wang Houcheng said with celerity: "Manager Qin, you've already been of great help. We are so grateful to you. Money is no object; we will be able to bear the cost. Thank you! Thank you so much!"

With a sharp glance in his direction, Sister Ten thought to herself: "Money is no object? How are you going to get it? By stealing or robbing?" But she kept herself in check out of deference to Qin Yulou.

Then Qin Yulou said, suddenly remembering: "Lao Wang, have you notified the other Xie Yingge? With her elder sister gravely ill, she couldn't very well turn a blind eye, could she?"

Wang Houcheng was suddenly afflicted with a stutter. "M'm, m'm, I—I just called but couldn't get through to her. I kept getting a message saying the phone had been turned off or a busy signal ..."

"Keep calling until she picks up!" said Qin Yulou with an edge in her voice. If that Xie Yingge had been there in front of her, she would have given her a good talking-to. Qin Yulou did not tell Wang Houcheng and Sister Ten that she had enclosed two thousand yuan in a red envelope to facilitate matters with the medical department. She was glad to have done this for Xiao Xie. She knew that Xie Yingge couldn't afford the high cost of the imported medicines. The other Xie Yingge had put in a retirement request, saying she was going to be general manager at some night club and would be making big money. Since Junior Miss had profited so much from taking the place of her elder sister, it was high time she repaid the latter.

As Wang Houcheng walked to the telephone by the staircase exit door to call the other Xie Yingge, Sister Ten cursed with a slap on her thigh: "For sixteen years Da Guniang has kept in her household a white-eyed wolf that devours men without spitting out the bones. It was she who upset Da Guniang so much that she collapsed..."

Qin Yulou was mystified: "What could she have said that upset Xiao Xie so much?"

Sister Ten rolled up her eyes as she recalled what happened: "She refused to do a video-over for Hao Ma's old audio recordings, dismissing the job as a sop for nostalgics addicted to a bygone age. She and her old lover have used the Xie Yingge name to register their so-called folk song theater. Da Guniang would have none of it, saying they were ruining the good name of Xie Yingge and wanted to reclaim the name for herself. Er Guniang taunted Da Guniang for her naiveté and said nobody would believe Da Guniang was the real Xie Yingge and Da Guniang should stop dreaming her pipe dreams ... After she left, Da Guniang collapsed. Master Qin, can't we sue her for attempted murder?"

Qin Yulou slowly shook her head and heaved a deep sigh.

Coming back from the public phone by the exit door, Wang Houcheng dared not look Qin Yulou in the eye and said with shifty eyes: "Er Mei—I finally got through to her ... she is going to immediately wire fifty thousand yuan over ... she said she couldn't tear herself away given the many things she had to attend to ..." Sister Ten said: "Thank heavens she's not coming. It might just mean the death of Da Guniang if she came!"

As family was barred from visiting patients in the ICU, Qin Yulou gave Sister Ten a few instructions before turning to Wang Houcheng: "You don't need to come in to shoot photos of the cast these days. Call me if there's any problem." The Theater had issued a cell phone to Qin Yulou to facilitate her official work.

She scribbled down the phone number and handed it to Wang Houcheng before leaving the hospital accompanied by Yu Qing'e.

While in the hospital Yu Qing'e had remained quiet, but emotions churned inside her. Now that she was alone with Qin Yulou, she reasoned that if she did not speak to Qin Yulou now, she wouldn't have another opportunity to do so once they were back in the Theater. She therefore summoned her courage: "Manager Qin …"

There was no inner peace and quiet for Qin Yulou either. She had kept the secret for the two Xie sisters for well over a decade and now one of them was barely clinging to life and what the other was doing was dishonoring the name of Xie Yingge. Could she really allow this Xie Yingge to die a lonely, anonymous death? How would she right the wrong by stripping them of their masks and restore to them their true identities? Once the secret was unveiled, how much of a shock would it be to the public? How much blame would be ascribed to her as Xie Yingge's co-star for over thirty years and as a leader of the Provincial Yueju Opera Theater? It was during this struggle to untangle this mare's nest that she heard Yu Qing'e calling out to her and she answered with an absent-minded "eh".

Yu Qing'e's mind was made up. Qin Yulou, accustomed to the easy and assured stage gait characteristic of the young male role type she had played for decades, took long strides, swinging her legs from the hips, offstage too. Yu Qing'e adapted her tripping gait to Qin Yulou's long strides and caught up with her. "Manager Qin, I … my mother has been asking me if my transfer is still under consideration." With that she waited in suspense.

As Qin Yulou kept plowing ahead in silence, Yu Qing'e's heart sank: it's over. It must mean the transfer is doomed. Presently they arrived at the bus stop and Qin Yulou finally came to a halt. The courage to pursue the question deserted Yu Qing'e, who restrained herself, trying to fight off tears. It was Qin Yulou who broke the silence with a sigh: "Xiao Yu, I know you are anxious to get the transfer. I've set the process in motion soon after the troupe returned from the Hong Kong tour. I had expected it to sail through, given the huge pile of newspapers carrying rave reviews of your performance—a matter of public record. But unexpected obstacles have slowed down the process. As they say, you trip even on level ground and run afoul of reefs even in calm waters."

Yu Qing'e's feeling was akin to that of Dou E when she heard the roar of the yamen runner announcing the execution hour: "Three quarters past noon—" followed by a quickening crescendo of drum, gong and cymbals that suggested the Grim Reaper's impatience to collect her life and that set one's innards aquiver. As persistent as the Dou E she often played on stage, who refused to die under a false charge, Yu Qing'e asked with a strained voice: "Manager Qin ... which high officials in the Theater objected to the transfer?"

Qin Yulou replied: "The Provincial Yueju Opera Theater has had no problem with the request, its artistic committee having approved it by an absolute majority. I thought you knew. It was your productions company that refused to let you go!"

Yu Qing'e choked, like someone held down at the bottom of a body of water with hands and feet tied, then, struggling and managing to get her head above water, she asked with an effort: "Manager Qin, did you not try to facilitate the matter with Party Secretary Zhang?"

Qin Yulou said with distaste: "Oh, that Party Secretary Zhang of yours! She seemed a changed person. It was she who held up the whole thing. Said something about the Provincial Yueju Opera Theater grabbing all the talent and taking the livelihood from the smaller troupes! She accused me of every evil! I've kept it from you for fear it would affect your performance."

Yu Qing'e now understood the Song dynasty poet Yan Jidao, who lamented the futility of dreams and even more the unbearable absence of dreams. She was tormented by the one thought: "Party Secretary Zhang? How could that be? How could the party secretary who had taken me under her wings and tried in every way to help me have put a spoke in the wheel of my transfer?"

Seeing her face white as a sheet, her blank stare and her distracted air, Qin Yulou hastened to comfort her: "Xiao Yu, don't worry too much. Too much worry might hurt your health and your ability to continue your performance. That would not be worthwhile. Besides I have not given up on this thing … Yes there is a new opportunity for you. Since the other Xie Yingge is unwilling to do the video-over for Cai Lianfen's old audio recordings, I might as well propose to the artistic committee of the Theater to put you on the job. Since the Department of Culture of the provincial government has direct charge of this cultural preservation project, your productions company will not dare keep you from taking the job. That would give you a few more months in the provincial capital."

Yu Qing'e gave a sickly smile, knowing Qin Yulou was sincerely trying to help her but also knowing that even if she were approved for undertaking the video-over of Cai Lianfen's old audio, it would only be a temporary job and she would have to return to her small town productions company in the end.

Remembering something else, Qin Yulou said: "Xiao Yu, aren't you on good terms with Party Secretary Zhang? There are still three or four performances of the 'White Rabbit' left for this season, followed by a hiatus for rest and reorganization of the production team. Why don't you take advantage of this slack period to go back to your home town and have a good talk with Party Secretary Zhang? My guess is she is also under some kind of pressure. Try to put your case before her and win her sympathy. Who knows but that things might turn out for the better?"

Yu Qing'e sensed a wave of warmth returning to the tips of her fingers, her heels, her cheeks and her breast. Her eyes regained their focus and she was seeing the surroundings with greater clarity. At all events, Party Secretary Zhang remained a hope, not much of one but better than none.

A quick calculation told her she had been performing Li Sanniang in the provincial capital since leaving her home town for almost half a year now. She had left her home town in an early autumn day when foliage had started turning red and yellow and streaks of green were still visible on the brows of the hills; now she was returning in hoary, windy freezing winter. On that trip from her home town to the provincial capital she had taken the first bus in early morning. As the bus progressed, the scenery outside became sharper in its outlines and brighter as the sky lightened. By the time it arrived in the provincial capital, the sun was a golden blaze. For the present trip back to her home town, out of concern about running into too many acquaintances who might spread the news about her return which did not necessarily serve her purpose, she decided to take a bus that left the provincial capital in the late afternoon when the sun was low. As the bus progressed, the scenery outside became increasingly blurred and indistinct. By the time it reached the small town, the west was streaked with afterglow, the clouds had sunk behind the darkening hills and twilight had descended on the town's streets, which teemed with pedestrians fluttering about like characters in a continuously running leather shadow show.

Yu Qing'e turned up the collar of her windbreaker to cover half of her face and keeping her head low she quickly melted into the twilight.

When Yu Qing'e arrived at the provincial capital six months before, she had written a long affectionate letter to her husband, hoping for forgiveness and understanding from him. But the letter went unanswered, gone, "like a clay cow wading into the sea". After returning from the Hong Kong tour, she collected the Hong Kong newspapers carrying glowing articles in praise of her performance and sent them to her husband. Again it went unanswered, "like a rock dropped into the sea", with nary a ripple. The stubborn silence of her husband was proof enough of his attitude toward her, so she decided not to disturb her husband's family's harmony this time and headed straight to her parents' home. Her parents were naturally very forgiving and tolerant, all the more so since their daughter had shot to fame as one of the top-tier young stars on the Yueju opera stage in the provincial capital. Her mother, a Yueju opera fan herself, was delighted beyond words and said not an unkind word about her running away from home after the abortion. In her mother's eyes, the return of her daughter was a triumphant one that deserved to be celebrated. But Yu Qing'e insisted that her mother not disturb the neighbors or friends and relatives about her visit. There was only one person on Yu Qing'e's list of people to see, and that was Party Secretary Zhang.

Yu Qing'e weighed different ways of approaching Party Secretary Zhang: if she went directly to the office of the productions company, necessarily carrying bags full of gifts, in the presence of so many eyes, rumors would start flying. She decided it would be counterproductive. What if she visited Party Secretary Zhang under cover of night at her home? She deemed it problematic too. There was a fair chance someone would see her; besides, she wouldn't be able to freely speak in a household with a large family such as that of Party Secretary Zhang. After carefully considering the various options, Yu Qing'e finally decided to send her mother to the home of Party Secretary Zhang to respectfully invite her to a home dinner. Her mother would act as a feeler. If the invitation was accepted, she would be able to consider how to broach the matter. If Party Secretary Zhang declined the invitation on some excuse, it would mean she was denying Yu Qing'e even that chance.

After her mother left for the home of Party Secretary Zhang, Yu Qing'e worked with her father in the kitchen to make preparations for the dinner, washing, slicing, peeling, scalding, so that the moment Party Secretary Zhang arrived the ingredients would go straight into the wok.

In the time it took for eating a meal, her mother was back. She came home empty-handed, meaning all the gift had been accepted, but no one came with her! Yu Qing'e felt a chill in her heart. "Party Secretary Zhang, she, she refused to come?" she asked in a tremulous voice.

Pouring herself a glass of lukewarm water, her mother took two sips of it before replying: "Party Secretary Zhang has an engagement tonight. She said she would come over to see you later when the function ended. I got there just in time, just as she was getting ready to leave."

Recovering from her initial dismay, Yu Qing'e said to her mother that she only needed to make two or three simple dishes. The three of them quickly finished eating their supper, cleared away the table and waited for the arrival of Party Secretary Zhang.

Yu Qing'e kept looking at the clock and mumbling why Party Secretary Zhang had still not come. Her mother chided pleasantly: "I thought you had seen the world in the provincial capital. It looks more like you'd just come out of some kind of Shangri-La cut off from the world, where you had been kept ignorant of the dramatic changes in civilization! No dinner party is a short affair. So don't expect her any time soon."

Yu Qing'e's father, overcome by drowsiness, went to bed, leaving the mother and the daughter to wait, yawn after yawn after yawn in front of the TV. They waited until the moon was low on the western horizon and the stars paled when Yu Qing'e decided Party Secretary Zhang was not coming, her casual promise to visit merely a subterfuge to make mother leave her alone. Just as she dejectedly told her mother to go to bed, Party Secretary Zhang let herself in.

The mother immediately perked up and hastened to brew tea and bring in a platter of fruit.

With her usual affectionate and good-natured manner, Party Secretary Zhang took Yu Qing'e's hands and looked her up and down, left and right, with a smile that rivaled that of a chrysanthemum in full bloom. "Xiao Yu, you've grown thinner. You must have worked too hard. It's no small feat to have achieved so much in the provincial capital. I've read the newspaper articles reporting on the success of your performances. I'm so glad for you, so proud of you. When you come back to work, our company will file an application to have you rated as Grade One National Actor, to which you are more than entitled! The other good news is the productions company has hired a fine playwright from Shanghai at high pay to write a script for *Story of the Kingdoms of Wu and Yue* based on the play *Xishi Returns Home.* Rehearsal will start as soon as you are back!"

Staring at her toes and licking her lips, Yu Qing'e said barely above a whisper: "Party Secretary Zhang, I thank the leadership for conferring such honor on me ... only ... Party Secretary Zhang, has, has Manager Qin of the Provincial Yueju Opera Theater called you on the phone?"

Party Secretary Zhang drew back, let go of her hands and took a sip of tea before saying slowly, with a sober mien: "Yes, she did call. Xiao Yu, what's your thinking on this matter?"

Yu Qing'e figured if ever there was a chance to say what she wanted, this was it! She owed it to herself to at least try: "Party Secretary Zhang, I've worked well with the crew and cast of the 'White Rabbit' at the Provincial Yueju Opera Theater and they hope I could stay there. I, I also think that the Provincial Yueju Opera Theater, being a major theater, will greatly help my career. So, so ..."

"So you desire to leave the productions company to go to the Provincial Yueju Opera Theater, am I right?" All traces of a smile left the face of Party Secretary Zhang, who now assumed a stern, awe-inspiring look. "Xiao Yu, let me be frank with you. It's not that I, party secretary, try to block your advancement. The leaders dealing with such matters in the county party committee have issued instructions to us. You, being an actor trained by the productions company of the county government, cannot just up and leave when the county badly needs you to help with its cultural promotion projects. The brass of the county party committee asked the productions company to try to persuade you to come back as soon as possible and the chairman of the board of the company already came to me several times demanding that you be called back. It was I who interceded for you, telling them that you should be allowed to fulfill your obligation to the 'White Rabbit' and not to drop out in midstream. Xiao Yu, you must understand that given the instructions of the leadership of the county party committee, it is not within the power of the productions company to let you go. Don't you agree?"

The mother added more tea to the cup of Party Secretary Zhang and deposited a fistful of sweets in front of her and hastened to agree: "You are right, Party Secretary Zhang. Your hands are tied. Only, Qing'e has no one to turn to but you."

The sternness in Party Secretary Zhang's face softened and she said with a faint smile: "Xiao Yu, as I see it, your career prospects with the productions company will not be inferior to what you'd have in the provincial capital. The provincial capital teems with young actors playing vivacious young female roles. True, you get the lead role in the 'White Rabbit' this time, but there's no telling if you'll have similar luck with future plays. In our company however you'll always be number one. Auntie Yu, what do you think? When Xiao Yu comes back to the company, she'll be close to home and you'll be able to take better care of each other, correct?"

There was nothing for the mother but to signal prompt agreement. In the wake of the tirade of the party secretary Yu Qing'e did not speak a word again but sat there like an audience member waiting quietly for the opening of a show.

The party secretary observed that Yu Qing'e had her emotions under control. She understood her: on the stage she radiated drama, but offstage she was sparing of words. Having said all she came to say, she rose to take her leave. The mother offered to see her out the door but she said: "Auntie Yu, please remain seated. Xiao Yu will see me out!"

Since the party secretary had specifically requested her company, there was nothing for Yu Qing'e but to rise to her feet and see the visitor out. Once outside the door, the party secretary fished a folded piece of paper out of a coat pocket and pressed it into her hand with a sigh. "The Zhao family asked me to deliver this divorce agreement to you. I didn't want to show it to you just now because I didn't want to hurt your mother's feelings. Take a look!"

Yu Qing'e took the thin piece of paper with a trembling hand.

Stroking her thin shoulder, the party secretary said: "Xiao Yu, before you put your signature to it, be sure to read carefully through the terms of the agreement. You must assert whatever rights that are due you. If you do not want to sign it, then I'll try to talk to the Zhao family once you come back to town. I know Xiao Zhao is still fond of you."

Yu Qing'e was silent as a shadow.

With another light pat on her back, the party secretary turned and walked away. After only a few steps she walked back to her. "Xiao Yu, there's something I've hesitated to tell you, but here it is. You know that the county leader I referred to once worked as your father-in-law's assistant, do you understand what I mean? If your mind is set on a transfer to the provincial capital, the only way to achieve it is to ask Manager Qin to get a high-level friend in the provincial Department of Culture to issue a transfer order, do you understand?" After the twice-repeated "do you understand?" the party secretary strode off with a light step down the dappled, moonlit lane.

Yu Qing'e, distraught and dejected, came back into the house, the twice-repeated "do you understand?" still ringing in her ears. She couldn't figure out the real message behind the rhetorical question. She found her mother waiting for her. "Qing'e," she said nervously, "I forgot to warn you to watch what you say to the party secretary. Her son has recently been recruited into a trading company upon the recommendation of your father-in-law. As they say, the mountain creek swells and recedes at whim and the petty-minded flip and flop!"

Yu Qing'e stared blankly at her mother; she was no longer able to tell which words uttered by the party secretary were sincere and to be believed. In this small town, a person could always, through some intricate, circuitous channels, be linked to someone else by a relationship of mutual gain. This intricate, tangled network of interrelationships in fact constituted the vast machinery that made the town tick.

Following the huge success of the Hong Kong tour of the "White Rabbit" of the Provincial Yueju Opera Theater, the public performances on home ground also proved so popular that additional shows had to be added and they lasted for over a month before closing. The provincial Department of Culture instructed the Yueju Opera Theater to carefully sum up the successful experience and richly reward those members of the cast and crew that gave outstanding performance and sterling service.

One day Feng Jianyue overslept and by the time she woke up the sun was already high in the sky. Roused by a chattering noise outside her window, she opened her eyelids and found bands of sunlight had stolen across her bed. She sat bolt upright in bed with a bewildered look: why did Yu Qing'e not wake me up to go with her to the practice room? Then it dawned on her: the new production of the "White Rabbit" has finished its run and a gathering to celebrate the event has been scheduled for ten in the morning. Her nerves thus calmed, she flopped back onto her bed. Turning her eyes toward the bed next to hers, she found the bed already made up, with the quilt neatly folded. So Yu Qing'e must have got up very early, as usual.

Glancing at her watch, Feng Jianyue decided it was time she got out of bed. After getting ready to go out, she figured by now the cafeteria's breakfast offerings would of necessity be meager and no longer piping hot; she might as well get Yu Qing'e to go with her to enjoy a bowl of soup noodles with preserved vegetable and shredded pork at the Grandma's Homemade Noodles across the street from the Theater. The only place where Yu Qing'e was likely to be found, outside of the dorm and the rehearsal room, was the practice room. Feng Jianyue knew it was past practice time, but since she was going there to look for Yu Qing'e, she decided to put on her practice suit. On second thought, since they might have no time to come back to the dorm to change after breakfast and might have to go directly to the celebration, she took off the practice suit and changed into a pair of silver gray slacks with flare bottoms and a purple gray light-weight, light fleece, narrow-waisted, popped-collar sweater. After examining herself at various angles in front of the full-length mirror and satisfying herself of the classical elegance of the dress and the grace of her bearing, she went out. Although Feng Jianyue had ended her one-sided infatuation with Brother Ah Ye, she was no longer able to revert to her previous state of a sloppily dressed, unsophisticated tomboy. In the bitterness of being jilted, she had molded herself successfully into a more feminine being.

As she had expected, Feng Jianyue found Yu Qing'e in the practice room, in the vast space of which a lone Yu Qing'e was executing one butterfly kick after another—pat-tat-tat, pat-tat-tat—like the fabled bird Jingwei flying stubborn, lonely missions, with rocks in its bill, to fill up the ocean.

Crooking a finger, Feng Jianyue gave two knocks on the door. At the sound Yu Qing'e stood down and looked at her, panting. Her hair was damp with perspiration, her eyes, despite the dark shadows under them, gleamed brightly. Feng Jianyue was pained by that desperate look of one fighting an uphill battle against formidable odds.

Feng Jianyue was aware that her transfer had not been proceeding smoothly and the closing of the present run of the "White Rabbit" meant her imminent departure for her rural home town. Feng Jianyue felt sorry for her and guilt-laden for compromising on her principles on that occasion in the distant past. The contrition smouldered like embers in her heart, threatening to reignite at any moment to prick her conscience.

"Eh, Yu Qing'e, why didn't you wake me up to practice with you?" Feng Jianyue feigned an ungracious tone.

"You should have seen how sound asleep you were. I, your wife, didn't have the heart to wake you up!" Instantly Yu Qing'e went into the mode of Li Sanniang in the "White Rabbit" and did a curtsy with great affection.

Whenever they entered the "White Rabbit" mode, the two of them would become intimate partners and a loving couple. As Liu Zhiyuan and Li Sanniang, they had successfully put the unfortunate incident in the past behind them and had revived their friendship.

Months before, Yu Qing'e was drafted into the "White Rabbit" team of the Yueju Opera Theater to rescue the imperiled play by replacing Mi Jingyao, who had deserted the production at short notice. Throughout the intensive rehearsals, they had no time or energy to think about the old grudge. Shortly after, Xie Yingge suddenly dropped out on a plea of illness, leaving the two of them to play Liu Zhiyuan and Li Sanniang through the entire play instead of only in the first half. In the scene of "Sanniang Rebukes Her Husband", Yu Qing'e, through the mouth of Li Sanniang, who chided Liu Zhiyuan for breaking his marital vow and taking another wife, vented her long suppressed resentment against Feng Jianyue. Feng Jianyue also, through the mouth of Liu Zhiyuan, poured her heart out to Yu Qing'e, begging her for forgiveness and understanding. The moment Liu Zhiyuan and Li Sanniang were reunited and fell into each other's arms, the ice in the hearts of Feng Jianyue and Yu Qing'e also thawed. There was wide praise among newspaper critics for their perfect chemistry and timing on the stage as well as the vivid portrayal of the emotions of the characters: "It's not uncommon to find false good-fellowship in everyday life; only once in a while does one witness true emotions so poignantly displayed on the stage." There could be no higher praise than this for the two.

After having their bowl of soup noodles at Grandma's Homemade Noodles, it was almost time for the celebratory event. Feng Jianyue asked Yu Qing'e if she wanted to go back to the dorm to change. Yu Qing'e said with a shadow of a smile: "We will not be on stage today, so what's the point of changing?" Together the two made their way toward the event.

The venue of the gathering was the largest rehearsal room in the Theater. As Feng Jianyue and Yu Qing'e stepped into the room, the first thing that struck their eyes was an eye-catching banner announcing in big, bold characters: "General Meeting to Sum up the Experience of the 'White Rabbit' Creative Team and to Launch the Shooting of the TV Serial Drama Based on the 'White Rabbit'".

Feng Jianyue was elated. Grabbing hold of Yu Qing'e's hand, she said: "Qing'e, they are really going to make a TV series of it! That means you can now stay in the provincial capital!"

Yu Qing'e stared at the banner for a long while, unable to believe her own eyes. Her heart swelled with the sudden appearance of a ray of hope. She suppressed her joy, keeping her eyes low and her lips tightly pressed together, and the gaiety of her heart from showing.

"Feng Jianyue, you are late!" A voice, high-pitched and affectionate to a fault, rose from among a knot of girls in the back of rehearsal room, "Eh—you and Yu Qing'e are thick as thieves offstage and onstage. You are an inseparable pair!" Laughter rang out from the girls.

Taking a closer look, Feng Jianyue saw, surrounded by the girls, a beauty "bright as the rising sun and white as moonlight". For a moment Feng Jianyue was dazzled and speechless with wide-eyed and open-mouthed astonishment. The beauty parted the dainty lips of her cherry-like mouth, to show a set of gleaming white teeth. "Feng Jianyue, you are not in a play! How come your 'spirit is floating in mid-air'?" she quoted Zhang Sheng upon meeting Cui Yingying for the first time in *The Story of the Western Wing*.

Recovering from her shock, Feng Jianyue said with some embarrassment: "Oh, it's Mi Jingyao! I thought it was some big star! I didn't recognize you. What good wind brings you here? How is your TV drama?"

The girls, all talking at once, couldn't wait to supply the answer: "Her TV drama will start airing on New Year's Day. Mi Jingyao is going to be a big star."

Detaching herself from the girls surrounding her, "like a swimming dragon scaring the geese into flight", Mi Jingyao laid an affectionate hand on Feng Jianyue's shoulder and chuckled into her other hand. "Why! How could you have forgotten me? We were the original couple!"

Feng Jianyue thought to herself: "What are you talking about? It was you who forced me to play your husband and you who muscled out my original wife." When she looked over her shoulder for Yu Qing'e, she was nowhere to be found.

Deputy General Manager Qin Yulou walked up to the makeshift podium and spoke into the microphone: "Girls, the meeting is starting, the meeting is starting. Take your seats. Please sit forward if you can."

The other members of the Theater leadership filed into the room and took their seats on the podium. Two strangers, one male and one female, of unknown affiliation, were seated in the honored middle. The girls discussed among themselves and hazarded guesses, pointing their fingers. Journalists from influential newspapers of the province occupied an entire row in the back of the room.

Deputy General Manager Qin, who presided over the meeting, introduced the invited guests. The middle-aged female stranger turned out to be the director of the center for TV drama productions newly established in the Provincial TV Station; the male stranger was the board chairman of a well-known private company of the province. Once the two strangers were identified, members seated on the podium started whispering to each other.

In the report delivered by the branch party secretary of the Yueju Opera Theater summing up the successful Hong Kong tour of the new production of the "White Rabbit", special mention was made of the proposition of the rising-star director He Shuye to elevate the aesthetic consciousness in tradition-bound Yueju opera, which proved not only eminently practicable but yielded remarkable results. At this mention, the girls exploded into enthusiastic applause and many turned, with both hands extended, toward He Shuye. It was then that Feng Jianyue discovered Brother Ah Ye had slipped into the meeting a while ago and had insinuated himself into the row of journalists. Seeing Brother Ah Ye for the first time since the return from the Hong Kong tour well over a month ago, Feng Jianyue felt a sharp burning sensation in her eyes. Brother Ah Ye appeared to have gained some weight; his facial complexion appeared fairer and he gave an overall impression of heightened spirits. No wonder Mi Jingyu had graced the meeting with her presence—they were inseparable! The thought lasting barely a second, she quickly moved her eyes away and banished He Shuye from her consciousness.

Following the report of the party secretary, Deputy General Manager Qin announced the award winners. The Theater had created the "Award for Artistic Performance", the "Award for Creativity and Innovation" and the "Award for Professionalism" to give due credit to members of the cast and crew of the new production of the "White Rabbit", who received, in addition to a certificate of excellence, varying amounts of cash remuneration.

On Director He Shuye and the designer of the melodic passages was conferred the "Award for Creativity and Innovation". After Director He Shuye received the certificate of excellence, Deputy General Manager Qin drew him down on a seat on the podium.

The "Award for Artistic Performance" was naturally given to Feng Jianyue and Yu Qing'e. When Feng Jianyue came up to the podium to receive the award, Qin Yulou asked her in a whisper: "Where is Yu Qing'e?" Feng Jianyue shook her head: "I don't know. She came with me into the room but soon disappeared." There was nothing for it but to have Feng Jianyue receive the award on Yu Qing'e's behalf.

Then Deputy General Manager Qin read out the names of the recipients of the "Award for Professionalism": "Shi Xiaotong, Qian Xiaoxiao." Only Qian Xiaoxiao stepped forward to go on the podium. Qin Yulou was not amused. "Where is Xiaotong? Why is she not attending this meeting?"

Scratching her head, Qian Xiaoxiao said haltingly: "She—she has been hospitalized. Her nose job was done with a substandard material, which had caused an infection and inflammation, so it had to be removed ..."

A buzz went up among the audience. Qin Yulou asked sharply: "Why hasn't she requested leave for her hospitalization?"

Qian Xiaoxiao mumbled: "She asked me to keep it a secret ..."

The explanation was greeted by giggles. Again Qin Yulou

had to ask Qian Xiaoxiao to pick up Shi Xiaotong's certificate of excellence on her behalf. As soon as all the awards were given out, Deputy General Manager Qin moved to the second item on the agenda and the general manager of the Yueju Opera Theater announced that the Provincial TV Network and the Provincial Yueju Opera Theater would jointly produce ten episodes of TV serial drama adapted from the White Rabbit, following which announcement the board chairman of a well-known private corporation, the bankroller of the project, made a rousing speech. Then the director of the TV network's center for TV drama production read out the names of the core members of the creative team. Although the outcome was almost a foregone conclusion, there was a glimmer of hope and wishful thinking in the minds of those concerned and a hush descended on the audience. Craning her neck, Feng Jianyue watched the doorway for signs of Yu Qing'e: where is she hiding herself? She had convinced herself that she and Yu Qing'e were the natural choice to play Liu Zhiyuan and Li Sanniang in the TV version of the "White Rabbit". If Yu Qing'e could hear the good news for herself, the cloud in her face would instantly lift and be replaced by a broad smile!

"The director will be—He Shuye." Amid the applause, Director He stood up, with his usual serious mien, and made a grave, dignified bow.

"The artistic directors will be—Qin Yulou and Xie Yingge." This was followed by a more enthusiastic round of applause. A smiling Deputy General Manager Qin nodded acknowledgment in a sweeping manner.

"Now we come to the main characters in the play! Liu Zhiyuan will be played by the excellent young actor Feng Jianyue." The applause was accompanied by cheers; the girls sitting front, back, left and right of Feng Jianyue extended their clapping hands toward her. When the General Manager beckoned Feng Jianyue to a chair on the podium the girls urged her on. As Feng Jianyue rose to her feet she once again looked in the direction of the door, hoping Yu Qing'e would make her appearance. The reading of the list resumed: "The female lead character Li Sanniang will be played by the excellent young actor Mi Jingyao ..." After a two-second hesitation and silence, the room resounded again with applause. As if petrified by a crash of the gong in the orchestra pit, Feng Jianyue froze. In the meantime, Mi Jingyao, with a smile in her pretty eyes sweeping the room, was walking up the aisle and when she saw Feng Jianyue struck dumb with shock, she clasped Feng Jianyue's arm and dragged her with her onto the podium, where they settled in their seats.

Feng Jianyue was oblivious to what happened or what was said for the rest of the meeting. All she knew was that she was again Liu Zhiyuan on the stage, who had just been taken in by Generalissimo Yue as son-in-law and made a general by him. It was only when his son Yaoqilang brought back his lawful wife's letter written in her blood that he realized the full extent of her suffering all these years and her precarious existence against tremendous odds. He could hear the desolate sobbing of Sanniang in the dark mill shed. He was unbearably guilt-ridden and castigated himself for abandoning his wife for another woman in his pursuit of fame and profit. He got on his horse and raced to the mill shed to beg forgiveness from Sanniang ...

At the close of the meeting, the room was abuzz with chatter as people started up to leave.

Waking from her reverie with a start, Feng Jianyue saw the general manager, the party secretary of the Theater and the distinguished guests leaving the room, talking and laughing, and she also saw Brother Ah Ye—Director He Shuye, rather, and Mi Jingyao in lively discussion as they made their exit. Feng Jianyue thought to herself that this time around she mustn't behave in a self-serving manner as she did at the time of graduation from the School of the Arts to the detriment of Yu Qing'e's career prospects, and that she owed it to Yu Qing'e to fight for her. Springing to her feet and taking long strides, she caught up with He Shuye and Mi Jingyao and planted herself before them.

The two started. He Shuye was embarrassed. "Xiao Yue,

what's the matter? We will be working together in this new project and we have plenty of time to exchange views in the future."

Mi Jingyao taunted, after a spell of laughter: "Liu Zhiyuan must be jealous at the sight of Li Sanniang in the company of the director."

Ignoring Mi Jingyao, Feng Jianyue looked He Shuye in the eyes and said sharply: "Director He, the part of Li Sanniang should go to Yu Qing'e. This is the consensus of all. You can't use the privilege of your office to reassign the part at your pleasure. If you persist in this course, then I am sorry, I will bow out too!"

His face a crimson red, He Shuye said in a suppressed voice: "Xiao Yue, you are talking without any basis. Listen, let me explain …" and as he said this he took Feng Jianyue's hand but Feng Jianyue wrested her hand free and said petulantly: "I don't want to hear your explanation. I don't want to know about the things you people have been up to outside of the public eye …"

"Feng Jianyue, calm down!" When Mi Jingyao stopped smiling, her heavily made-up face took on an unreal look, as if it were a pretty mask. She looked at Feng Jianyue in a supercilious manner and said with ice in her voice: "I see that if you are not told the truth, you will not back down! The TV version of the 'White Rabbit' has been tailor made for me at the request of the investors in the production. The part of Li Sanniang in it has been written with me, Mi Jingyao, in mind. Let me be frank with you, you owe the part of Liu Zhiyuan to my strong recommendation to my boss. And naturally, it was also I who recommended Director He to the producer of the show!"

Feng Jianyue stared in astonishment at He Shuye, who gave a self-deprecating shrug. "Xiao Yue, art can be noble but sometimes it has to climb down its high horse. In our society art without financial backing gets nowhere! So quit acting like a petulant child! We both truly should be grateful to Mi Jingyao for this opportunity to participate in the new creative endeavor!"

The charming smile returned to the face of Mi Jingyao, who said, with a nudge at He Shuye: "Director He, there is something that you should have clarified to Feng Jianyue a long time ago. I am not your girlfriend, right? Ma Hui, the host of *Operatic Kaleidoscope*, is. As long as there remains any doubt on this score, Feng Jianyue will always be hostile toward me. That would not be good for the stage chemistry between Liu Zhiyuan and Li Sanniang!"

He Shuye shot an angry glance at Mi Jingyao and was casting about for a way to explain the matter to Feng Jianyue, when the latter turned about and ran off. With her long legs, she bounded away like a deer.

Feng Jianyue didn't know where she was heading. All she knew was she didn't want ever to see Mi Jingyao and He Shuye again or hear their voice. Without realizing it, she had run back to her dormitory. It dawned on her as she came to the entrance of the dormitory that the person she most desired to see at this moment was Yu Qing'e and that desire had directed her steps toward the dorm.

The door to her dorm room was ajar. Feng Jianyue pushed it open to find Qin Yulou and Yu Qing'e sitting side by side on the edge of the bed in conversation. "Qing'e!" she called out in an emotional tone. Then she stopped short: the bedding of Yu Qing'e had been rolled up and tied down and at the foot of the bed stood a bulging suitcase.

"Qing'e, are you really leaving?" Feng Jianyue asked timidly.

Yu Qing'e stood up but she swayed on her feet and had to steady herself on the bed frame. Her lips cracked in an attempted smile but the result was worse than a grimace. "M'm, since I've accomplished the job I was given to do, it's time I go home."

Qin Yulou gave a soft sigh. "Jianyue, I understand how you feel. I tried my best to keep Yu Qing'e in our Theater, but … her work unit has refused to release her and has accused the Provincial Yueju Opera Theater of trying to muscle in on a local troupe and grab its star. Their complaint has gone straight to the Department of Culture of the provincial government …"

Yu Qing'e pulled Feng Jianyue's hand off Qin Yulou's shoulder. "Jianyue, don't give Manager Qin a hard time. She has done a lot for me already. I want to congratulate you on getting the part of Liu Zhiyuan in the TV version of the 'White Rabbit'. I know you will do a good job of it."

With a petulant twist of her body, Feng Jianyue said: "If you don't get to play Li Sanniang, I will refuse to play Liu Zhiyuan. I am not thrilled at the prospect of playing opposite Mi Jingyao. The way she puts it, it's as if the entire Theater depended on her favors. I can't stand her arrogance!"

Qin Yulou drew her favorite student to her and sat her down. Smoothing a few stray strands of hair toward the back of her ears, she said: "Jianyue, don't mind too much the attitude of Mi Jingyao. She has done our Theater a big favor after all. I've been told that many Yueju opera troupes had their eyes on this TV production and it was Mi Jingyao who succeeded in persuading the bankroller to put his money on our Theater."

Unappeased, Feng Jianyue said: "Mi Jingyao's singing is not up to par and her martial skills are poor. All she has going for her is a pretty face. It's no fun working with her."

Qin Yulou said: "There is one thing to be said for TV drama: the actor can lip sync and the long sleeve dance sequence can be performed by a dance double. Jianyue, even Yu Qing'e will not approve of your withdrawal from the part of Liu Zhiyuan for personal grudges. Right, Qing'e?"

Yu Qing'e nodded drily. "Jianyue, the Liu Zhiyuan character in Director He's version of the play has more creative interest and depth than any other parts you've ever played. So if you give up the chance to play him just for my sake, I will carry the guilt for the rest of my life and you will regret it for the rest of your life. Let's not create any more stress for each other, all right?" Her calmness of expression and evenness of tone belied the cold sweat drenching the woolen sweater she was wearing under her outer garment.

By appearing to take the matter in stride, Yu Qing'e released Feng Jianyue from her qualms. There are fair weather friends galore, but a kindred spirit is hard to find, and no one understood Feng Jianyue better than Yu Qing'e! Unable to contain her overflowing gratitude, Feng Jianyue rushed forward and put her arms around Yu Qing'e, her tears falling on the latter's shoulder.

"Toc, toc, toc toc toc toc …" someone tapped out on the half-closed door a drum rhythm signaling the opening of a play. The three in the room turned their heads and were astonished to find an elegant and svelte Mi Jingyao coming through the door. Feng Jianyue quickly wiped off her tears; Yu Qing'e turned around to look at her luggage. Only Qin Yulou took a step forward and said with a smile: "Mi Jingyao, you look sharp! Since we last saw each other you've matured a lot. You look more like a star now. I haven't had time to thank you on behalf of the Theater!"

Mi Jingyao said with a chuckle: "Manager Qin, it's so kind and gracious of you. After all it's the Theater that nurtured my talent!" She did a pirouette in the middle of the room, causing her skirt of light wool to spread out like a water lily. Then she said with emotion: "I shared this room with Feng Jianyue since we came to the Theater upon our graduation from the School of the Arts. We were very young then and did not want to get up early in the morning to exercise our voice. It was you, Manager Qin, who coaxed us out of bed one by one. We owe what accomplishment we have now to you, Manager Qin!"

As Mi Jingyao gave her speech, Yu Qing'e had heaved her backpack onto her shoulders and the moment the speech ended, she said: "Manager Qin, please continue your conversation. It's time I catch the bus at the bus terminal."

Qin Yulou hastened to say: "Xiao Yu, stay for lunch! I will ask the Theater to dispatch a car to take you …"

Yu Qing'e said: "That's not necessary, Manager Qin. There are so many distinguished guests at the Theater. You mustn't mind me!"

Picking up Yu Qing'e's suitcase, Feng Jianyue said: "Master, I will see Yu Qing'e off."

Mi Jingyao said with a smile: "Not so fast! I am the bearer of good tidings for Yu Qing'e. After hearing me out, Yu Qing'e will no longer need to leave."

Feng Jianyue blurted: "What good tidings? You mean you'll cede the part of Li Sanniang to Yu Qing'e?"

The smile on Mi Jingyao's face became somewhat strained. "You are one greedy Liu Zhiyuan! So you want two Li Sanniangs for yourself! There's no chance for that! But I can still get Yu Qing'e to be your wife, i.e. Yue Xiuying, the daughter of Generalissimo Yue. How's that? Does that satisfy you?"

Qin Yulou said: "What happened? Does Shi Xiaotong no longer wish to play Yue Xiuying?"

Mi Jingyao shook her head. "She certainly desires to be on TV, but how can she? The bad stuff used to lift her nose had been removed, but the damage done by the bungled double eyelid job couldn't be reversed and her face now looks worse than before the 'improvement'. On a stage, the disfigurement could, with makeup, be hidden from the audience, who sit at a distance. But no facial flaw has a chance to escape the lens of the TV camera, which magnifies it. For that reason I had a talk with the producer and the director to persuade them to use Shi Xiaotong as my background singer. The part of Yue Xiuying will go to Yu Qing'e. That way the cast will be a dream team!" Then she stopped and looked from one to the other of the three, with a smug expression, relishing her role of savior.

Qin Yulou and Feng Jianyue turned their eyes on Yu Qing'e. If Yu Qing'e could settle for less than she had wanted, this proposal at least had the merit of killing two birds with one stone and Yu Qing'e would get a chance to stay in the provincial capital for a time at least.

Only now was Yu Qing'e shifting her eyes to Mi Jingyao as she said in a *sigong* tune at a moderate, steady tempo: "Thanks for your helpful proposal, but I must go back. The rehearsal for the big production of my troupe *Story of the Kingdoms of Wu and Yue* will start soon and the other members of the cast have been waiting anxiously for the return of Xishi to the stage. I can't put off my return any longer."

Mi Jingyao was a little startled; she had expected tearful

gratitude from Yu Qing'e. With a shrug and a spread of her hands at Qin Yulou, she indicated she had done all she could.

Qin Yulou cried in resignation: "Yu Qing'e ..." Her voice trailed off even though she had so much to say.

Yu Qing'e drew near to Qin Yulou, gave her a hug and whispered into her ear: "I will not go to the hospital to say goodbye to Master Xie because my visit could unsettle her. When she gets better, Master Qin, will you please tell her for me that I will not let her down?"

Qin Yulou gave her a few pats on the back and let her go.

Feng Jianyue accompanied Yu Qing'e to the bus terminal. They did not act as Liu Zhiyuan and Li Sanniang in "Liu Zhiyuan Parts from His Wife and Goes off to the Army", parting in sobs and heartbreak. Instead they held each other's eyes and penetrated through them to the depths of their hearts.

Feng Jianyue hesitated before saying: "Qing'e, just now I was really worried that you might agree to Mi Jingyao's proposal. Thankfully you didn't."

A shadow of a smile flitted across Yu Qing'e's face. "You knew I wouldn't have consented." With that she turned about and boarded the bus; sticking her head out of the bus window, she called out to Feng Jianyue: "See you next month on the stage of the 'Contest of Young Traditional Chinese Opera Actors from the East China Region'!"

Feng Jianyue waved her hand at her.

The winter sky, pale and quiet, was crossed by an occasional V-formation of wild geese, whose shrill cries carried very far on the wind.

With the approach of the lunar New Year's Day, stores had been burnishing their signs and sprucing up shop windows, with colorful pennants of all descriptions and sizes flying and neon lights blinking riotously, adding welcome warmth to this city in the grips of a deep freeze. People crowded the stores for merchandise put on sale at steep discounts and snatching up foodstuffs required for the New Year festival, their tired faces now gladdened by a festive mood. Little did they know that the flame of the life of the once-famous Yueju opera actor Xie Yingge was flickering low and dying.

For a fortnight already Sister Ten had stayed by the bed of the comatose Senior Miss, not leaving her for a moment even when Wang Houcheng offered to relieve her so that she could go home and catch some sleep. Most of the time she had her eyes riveted to the vital signs monitor by the sick bed, watching the fluctuations of the green and red curves and chanting Amitabha under her breath. For her the only hope of Senior Miss's recovery was now in the hands of Bodhisattva.

A few days before, Senior Miss had sunk into a coma and her situation was dire. It was thanks to someone working in the Health Department, who was a fan of Qin Yulou, Senior Miss's stage partner of yore, that a few bags of blood serum were made available for Senior Miss, who, after the transfusion, did not come out of her coma but did see her vital signs gradually stabilize. One morning no nurse came to give Senior Miss her blood transfusion. Sister Ten got worried and hurried to the nurse station to remind them. After flipping through the pages of the patient's charts, the young nurse on duty said: "Oh, the blood serum you obtained has been used up."

Sister Ten became agitated at this information; she planted herself in front of the young nurse and said sharply: "Aren't you supposed to heal and cure? How can you stand by when a patient is in mortal danger? I don't believe you can't find blood serum in a large hospital like this!"

The young nurse was evasive. "The serum supply is very tight. It can't be lightly dispensed just to anybody. Without doctors' orders, we can't give blood transfusions to her."

This had the effect of further angering Sister Ten. "I know who gets the blood serum here. It's the people with money and power, am I right? Don't you belittle this patient! Do you have any idea who she is? She is the famous Yueju opera actor Xie Yingge!"

A laugh escaped the lips of the young nurse. "I know. Only you omitted a few words! She is the elder sister of the famous Yueju opera actor Xie Yingge!" With that she stepped around Sister Ten to continue her round.

Sister Ten gasped at the blow; her heart bled for Senior Miss. She returned to Senior Miss's room with gloom in her face and found Wang Houcheng and Qin Yulou already seated by the bed. She rushed over and caught Qin Yulou's arm as if she were grasping at a life-saving straw. "Master Qin, please try to get some more blood serum for Senior Miss! Senior Miss's condition always improves after a blood transfusion!"

Qin Yulou said falteringly, embarrassment evident in her tone: "Shi Mei, listen … that fan of mine … has done her best … you know, there's a limit to what she could do …"

Wang Houcheng said hesitatingly: "I overheard a patient's family saying that blood serum could be bought through blood scalpers. Should we not give it a try?"

Qin Yulou waved her hand. "No! Firstly we have no way of knowing if the illegal blood supply is healthy and clean. Secondly, I will be frank with you, I talked to the doctor in charge of Xiao Xie's care and was told her prognosis is not good. Blood transfusions only put off the inevitable end, at best …"

Sister Ten covered her mouth with a hand as her grief broke from her.

It was then that the patient in the neighboring bed cried out: "Eh, look! Your patient has just opened her eyes!"

The three hastened to the bed and indeed found Senior Miss with her eyes open. Those lifeless, dim eyeballs were moving sluggishly!

"Xiao Xie, Xiao Xie …" Qin Yulou and Wang Houcheng called out repeatedly and Sister Ten, with her palms put together, was chanting Amitabha in a low voice.

Senior Miss's left hand slipped out of the cover and was making back-and-forth motions across the sheet. Neither Qin Yulou nor Wang Houcheng could make head or tail of her intention and queried Sister Ten, who leaned over Senior Miss and took a long look at her eyeballs before the penny dropped: "Senior Miss wants to say something, but she is unable to voice it! Paper and pen! She needs paper and pen to write down what she wants to say."

They hurriedly whisked out pen and paper from their bags and pressed the pen into Senior Miss's left hand and put the sheet of paper under it. And lo and behold, Senior Miss began to slowly move the hand with the pen across the paper, stroke after slow stroke, producing wiggly, sprawling characters that eventually filled the sheet.

Finally Senior Miss's hand stopped moving; with the loosening of her fingers, the pen fell aside.

Pulling the sheet of paper from under her hand, Qin Yulou couldn't make sense of the lines crisscrossing the paper.

Taking the paper from her, Wang Houcheng looked at it, holding it first at close range and then at a distance, and thought about it. "I think I detected the three characters Xie Ying Ge ..."

Grabbing the paper from him, Sister Ten put it right before her eyes and cried: "Yes, I can make out the characters Xie Ying Ge. I may not know other words, but I recognize these three characters, even if they were shredded into eighteen pieces! She couldn't be clearer in her intention! She has been denied the name of Xie Ying Ge in her life; she's determined that in death she will have the name restored to her!" With that she started wailing again.

Leaning down over Senior Miss, Qin Yulou found her eyes closed once more; only, now two large tears perched at the corner of her closed eyes.

After a spell of crying Sister Ten looked up and said: "Master, and Master Qin, I don't know what you two think. I am determined to make her wish come true, if it means the death of me! If you will not say it, I will. I will talk to newspaper reporters and the Yueju opera fans. As long as I have a breath left in me, I will speak about this."

After a long consideration, Qin Yulou said: "The household registry and ID card are required to file for the death certificate.

Shi Mei, where are these two documents kept?"

Sister Ten said with dejection: "The household registry is kept in the chest of drawers. The ID card was given to Junior Miss when it was decided to ask her to pass off as Xie Yingge. What will we do if she refuses to give it back?"

Wang Houcheng passed a tense hand over his face and said in stifled anger: "I'll figure out a way to get Xiao Xie's ID card back!"

Qin Yulou gave a light nod. "It's so decided then. I will undertake to explain to the Theater what has gone on for the past sixteen years."

Senior Miss passed away three days before New Year's Day. She went to her last repose with a serene look on her face and handsome features. Sister Ten vowed that Senior Miss had her youthful look restored to her and appeared exactly as she did in the days when she rocketed to stardom in the 1960s while performing in the "White Rabbit".

The memorial service for Senior Miss was held in the afternoon of the lunar eighth of January, which coincided with her birthday. On a banner strung across the back of the hall was the inscription: "In memory of Xie Yingge, famous actor of Yueju opera." In the center sat a garlanded portrait of her, the same stage photo of her splashed across newspapers thirty years before, showing her half-turned face, noble and beautiful, with a deep, charming orchid-shaped dimple. Yueju opera fans came in droves to bow deeply before the portrait.

In a quiet voice Qin Yulou asked Sister Ten: "How did Wang Houcheng get Xiao Xie's ID card back from Xie Jin'ge?"

Sister Ten acknowledged ignorance with a shake of her head. "My master did not say and I did not ask. The night before Da Guniang passed on, Er Guniang came back to the provincial capital to visit her sister, and she returned to the house with my master that night."

As the memorial service drew to a close and friends and family members clustered about the casket were throwing petals into it,

Yu Qing'e arrived. The performance of the huge production *Story of the Kingdoms of Wu and Yue* of her company had run until the night of the seventh of January and the morning bus to the provincial capital had been canceled for the duration of the year-end festival, forcing Yu Qing'e to take the bus leaving at noon. She had taken a taxi from the terminal to the funeral home.

As Yu Qing'e looked up at the portrait of Master Xie, tears fell down her cheeks. That was the image of Xie Yingge that had been etched into her memory like a carving! She flopped down to her knees and touched the floor three times with her forehead in the direction of Master Xie. Getting to her feet, she whisked out that *qingyi* costume from her backpack. She tried to push her way to the front of the crowd surrounding the casket, but the crowd was already six deep and almost impenetrable. It was only with the help of Qin Yulou who parted the thick throng that Yu Qing'e was able to come near Master Xie and carefully drape the *qingyi* costume onto her body.

For the duration of the memorial service the PA played over and over that aria sung by Xie Yingge in the *Legend of the White Rabbit*:

> ...
>
> In those sixteen years, the thousand-jin millstone
>   be my witness,
> I have milled away many a morning and evening;
> In those sixteen years, the three-foot wide apron of
>   the well be my witness,
> I've treaded upon it may a winter and spring;
> In those sixteen years, the tear-stained sweet
>   osmanthus be my witness,
> I have shed many a bloodshot tear;
> In those sixteen years, the bitter fish pond be my
>   witness,
> I've confronted many a crisis of life and death.